Dust And Empty Dreams

Wayne Orr

Library of Congress Control Number: 2002093449

ISBN: 0-9708833-1-5

EAN-13: 9780970883315

First Printing: September 2002

Second Printing: May 2010

This book is dedicated to

Adam

Who did so much to promote

My first book

LONELY TEXAS ROAD

Special thanks to

Kim Orr

Who was always only a phone call

away with sound advice

And

to my beautiful wife,

Esther

who always made time to

help me with this project.

Esther's picture appears on the

front cover

CHAPTER I

Caleb Lovett was ready to get his butt out of Memphis. He had done pretty well there. Better than pretty well, actually. He had done better there than at any other place he'd ever been. Now he was ready to wave his magic wand and vanish. He knew from experience that as soon as you feel like you're on top of the world there's a ninety-nine percent chance that the sky is going to come crashing down any minute. It was just a matter of time before some of his investors would come charging into his office with cops and lawyers screaming for their money. Well he wanted to be long gone when that happened.

Lovett was already dressed and ready to get to his office for one last time. He was wearing a custom-made charcoal gray suit which looked good and fit perfectly. It was supposed to look good, considering what he'd paid for it. The shirt looked good, too, and that pleased him. He hadn't known what color he should wear but had settled on a white one. He had been afraid it might be too dull. But with a red and blue tie, it looked damned good. He glanced down at his black shoes; they were shined to perfection. "Not bad, Caleb Lovett," he told himself. "Not bad at all."

He'd already packed the rest of his clothes except for his suits into two suitcases and laid them on the back seats of his Malibu. He'd put his suits into plastic suit bags and placed them on top of the suitcases. The only other item he was taking with him was his CD player. He would pick up all new stuff when he got to Dallas. Now he was ready to drive the few blocks to his business office, Jones Financial Counseling and Investments, and close it down. With any kind of luck at all, he'd be on his way to Dallas by three o'clock.

He hadn't decided yet what he was going to do about the car. He was several months behind on his payments, and the finance company was threatening to repossess it. He'd told them something was wrong with the engine, and he wasn't going to make any more payments until they fixed it. He'd taken it in to the shop four times, and they couldn't find anything wrong. To hell with them. He didn't need a Malibu, anyway. He was thinking of getting something a hell of a lot better than that. He hadn't decided what it would be yet, but it would be something that would be hot enough to blow most cars off the road.

He had plenty of money to make the payments on the Malibu. That wasn't the problem. If they wouldn't fix the engine, he wouldn't make the payments. It was that simple. He'd probably drive the damned thing to Dallas or wherever he decided to go and then give them a call and tell them to pick it up. So they'd have to drive a thousand miles to get it. That was their problem. If they weren't going to satisfy their customers, what else could they expect?

When he was at work, he didn't go by his real name, Caleb Lovett. He used the name William Jones. He even had a bogus driver's license and birth certificate in that name. That made it easy for him to disappear without a trace when he decided it was time to close down his operation and go somewhere else. That was exactly what he was getting ready to do.

He left his room and went into the living room to see if he could find Mrs. Calloway, the landlady, to tell her he was leaving and wouldn't be back. She wasn't anywhere around so he wrote her a short note. He took it into the kitchen, laid it on the kitchen table and put the room key on top of it. Then he went outside, got into his automobile and drove away.

A young couple was waiting by the entry door of his storefront office. He recognized them as Sara and Jason Stafford. If he remembered correctly, they were in their early twenties. They had been at his place the previous afternoon and had left a check for five thousand dollars for him to invest for them. Probably they had talked it over after they got back home and decided they had made a mistake and wanted the check returned. That happened pretty often. When it did, he'd give them his standard spiel hoping they would change their minds and leave the investment with him. Sometimes it worked, and sometimes it didn't.

As he got closer, he could see Jason shifting about as though he was a bit nervous. He was probably rehearsing in his mind exactly what he wanted to say.

Lovett walked up to the young man and held out his hand. "Jason, Sara. Good to see you again so soon." He shook Jason's hand and then Sara's. "Hey come on in. I'll brew us a pot of coffee."

He unlocked the door and led them inside. Then, while he was removing his coat and hanging it up, he continued, "What can I do for you good people this morning?"

"Well, we've kinda been thinking it over and—" Jason was able to get out.

"Yeah, we were wondering. You told us we could change our mind. You know, if we decided—" Sara stammered until Lovett interrupted her.

"Sure. No problem. A better opportunity has come up, and you need your money back, right? Just have a seat while I put on the coffee to brew. I'm not worth a darn in the morning until I've had my coffee." He pointed to a couch, and the two of them sat down.

As soon as they were seated, Lovett went to the other end of the office and into a storage room near the back wall, put coffee and water into the coffee machine and turned it on. Then he came back to where the Staffords were sitting.

"The coffee will be ready in just a minute if you folks would care for some. Now, maybe I was jumping the gun. You're back for your money, right?"

"Yes, sir," Sara said in a small voice. "We just decided we're not quite ready yet. We should've thought about it a little more before—"

"What it is," Jason said, trying to help her, "there were some obligations we just hadn't taken into consideration. But later, when we feel we're ready, we'll come straight to you."

"I appreciate that, Jason. I really do. But hey, you don't have to make any promises like that. When the time comes, you invest that money where it'll be safe and provide you with the best return. But first and foremost, make sure it's safe. I'll forego a couple of percentage points any day to get rock solid security."

"Then you're not angry that we came back?" Sara asked him, her voice a little stronger, now.

"Of course not," he said looking at both of them. "I'll tell you what would have made me angry. If you'd changed your mind and had *not* come in to tell me. Because we agreed yesterday afternoon on what the terms were. When you left here, I had your word, and you had mine. I'm not about to make a one hundred and eighty degree turn less than twenty-four hours later."

"We appreciate that, Mr. Jones. Frankly, we were afraid you might get upset when we told you."

He laughed. "Well, I'm glad I laid that concern to rest. Now, it's going to take me just a minute. I have a form I need you to fill out. It's no big deal, just an FDIC requirement. That's the Federal Deposit Insurance Corporation. Old Uncle Sam has got to get involved in everything when it comes to managing the public's money. And actually, that's not bad. It's really another layer of protection for the consumer."

Jason's face turned suspicious. "What kind of form are you talking about?"

"Nothing really. Just a 517. It has to be on file with the FDIC when a customer withdraws his or her money before the thirty-day grace period. You remember, I promised you what they call a ten percent surety bonus if you keep your money on deposit between thirty and sixty days. And of course, it accelerates to fifteen percent between sixty and ninety days and so on and so on. Well, this 517 is merely your acknowledgment that you understand you're not entitled to the surety bonus. It keeps you from coming back later and demanding that ten percent. Now, I know you wouldn't do that. I doubt if one in a million would. But it's a government requirement, and frankly, it's no big deal."

"Well, let me see it," Jason said. "I want to read it first. What if I don't want to sign it? You'd still have to give us our money."

"Sure, I would. Hell, it's yours. It's not mine, and it's not the government's. It's yours. But I would have to put a twenty-four hour hold on it while I filed a 518. A 518 basically tells the FDIC that the customer has exercised his right to circumvent the 517 filing requirement. I don't do that in this office. I call my home office, and they do it electronically. That way, the hold release will be effective within twenty-four hours."

"But," Sara hazarded, "what if the government doesn't get back to you?"

"Again, no problem. You're still protected. Twenty-four hours after I file the 518, I'm authorized to release frozen assets whether or not I've received a response. I'm not just *authorized*, I'm *required* to release them. Shoot, they can't do anything else. After all, it's *your* money. Now there's one more thing a 517 does I forgot to tell you about. It flags your name and social security number. Then you'll be forbidden from investing your money in a financial institution like this one for one year. That's because of what they characterize as your premature withdrawal."

He stood up. "No use talking about it all morning. I'll get you that 517, and you can look it over while we have a cup of coffee."

He went into his corner office, rummaged through a desk drawer for ten or fifteen seconds and returned with a form.

"Why don't you both review it and see if you want to fill it out? Believe me, there's not a doggoned thing they can do about it if you don't." He went to the storage room and returned in a couple of minutes carrying coffee, creamer and sweetener on a tray.

"I've got everything here," he told them. "Fix it however you like it. There's sugar and Sweet'N Low, whichever you prefer."

The three of them fixed their coffee, and then Jason said, "Are you sure our money would be safe here?"

"There's no doubt about that. Up to two hundred and fifty thousand dollars, that is. That's as high as the FDIC protection goes. There are ways, though, to get around that. That two hundred and fifty thousand applies to an *account.* And you two, as a married couple, are entitled to at least three accounts. You can have one in Jason's name, one in Sara's name and a joint account in both names. That would protect you up to seven hundred and fifty thousand dollars. And look at it this way: if you lose any money that's protected by the FDIC, it's because the government has gone broke. If that ever happens, we're all going to be in trouble no matter where we have our money unless we have it in gold bars buried in the back yard."

"We've been talking it over and—" Sara told him.

"Maybe with a little belt tightening, we could get by without withdrawing our check," Jason said. "What do you think? We want your honest opinion."

"Let me put it this way, Jason. And Sara. I won't tell you to leave it here as long as you don't feel comfortable doing that. But I'll tell you this. I have every penny of my own personal funds invested here, and I have had for a long time. And I've done very well. I know a lot of other people who could tell you the same thing. But in the final analysis, nobody can make that decision except the two of you. So if you have any doubt at all, draw it out. Think about what kind of a future you want. Check us out. Then, if *you* decide this is the way to go, we'll be here."

"But if we take it out, we can't reinvest it for a year. Is that right?"

"Unfortunately, that's right. I wish there was some way to get around that, a waiver or something, but unfortunately there isn't."

"Maybe we'll go ahead and leave it for a while. At least thirty days. If we draw it out after that can we still turn around and put it right back in?"

"Sure, you can. And the beauty of that approach is you would get your ten percent surety bonus. But you couldn't get another ten percent in thirty more days. You could still withdraw it with no penalty, but you would have to wait sixty days before getting another surety bonus. And it would be reduced to five percent instead of ten. But shoot, that's only fair. You would already have your ten percent."

Sara looked at her husband. "I don't know, honey. What do *you* think?"

He grinned. "Hell, let's go for it. It's only money."

Then he said to Lovett. "Hey, is it all right if we just go ahead and leave it for a while?"

"Personally, I think it would be a sound business decision. And if that's what you want to do, I'll certainly support you."

"That's what we're going to do, then. Forgive us if we took up too much of your time."

"Not at all. Not at all. That's what I'm here for."

"Well, I suppose we'd better scoot," Sara said. "Thank you so much for your help. We feel so much better now. Both of us do."

Lovett shook their hands again and said, "If you change your mind, come right straight back. I'll be here."

"Oh, I don't think we'll do that," Sara said. Hand in hand she and Jason went out the door.

Lovett poured himself another cup of coffee and went into his office and began reading a newspaper. He'd decided to wait until noon. Then he'd hang the *Out To Lunch* sign on his door and leave. It was going to be one hell of a long lunch.

He'd like to get a few more investments before twelve o'clock. It would be nice if they were in cash. He had to peddle the checks through a middle man named Johnny Igloo for fifty cents on the dollar. The five thousand dollar check he'd just salvaged was only worth twenty-five hundred. He didn't know how Igloo was able to cash them without getting caught. But Lovett knew he was managing somehow. Otherwise, the man wouldn't still be in business.

The door opened, and a woman walked in. Lovett recognized her as one of his customers, but he couldn't remember her name. She was looking all around to see if she could locate anybody. Lovett laid the newspaper on his desk and went to greet her.

"Yes, ma'am. Can I help you?"

"Oh. Hello, Mr. Jones. I'm Carla Peabody. Remember me?"

"Of course, Mrs. Peabody. Why don't you sit down?" He pointed to the couch where the Staffords had been sitting. She sat where he indicated, and he sat down beside her.

"Now. What can I do for you, today?"

"I hate to do this Mr. Jones, but it can't be helped. Joey, that's my youngest son, has just been arrested. They say he ran over somebody with his automobile and then left the scene. They've charged him with hit and run. Now, I know my Joey wouldn't do that. That's what I told the officers. But there was nothing they could do. Anyway, I have to take out ten thousand dollars for a down payment to a lawyer." She was clutching a wad of dirty tissues in her right hand and rubbing them against her face as she talked.

"Certainly, Mrs. Peabody. I understand." He knew what the time was, but he looked at his watch. "Darn, it's eleven o'clock. It's a shame you didn't come in just twenty minutes ago. The truck just picked up all our money and delivered it to the bank. The FDIC is in the process of auditing our books, Mrs. Peabody, and you know what that means. All our assets have to be in place by twelve noon."

"But Mr. Jones. I *have* to have it today. What am I going to do?"

"Okay. Let's see what we can work out. Exactly when do you need it?"

"I must have it by three. No. Before three because I have to be at the courthouse by three."

"Oh. Why didn't you tell me? I thought you needed it right this second. Three. That's no problem at all." He paused for a moment and then continued, "Look, Mrs. Peabody. "I'll tell you what we can do." He took out his wallet and handed her a twenty dollar bill. "You go somewhere and have yourself something to eat. I'm sorry, but that's all I have on me right at this moment. Then come back at one forty-five, and I'll have you a certified check for ten thousand dollars. It'll take me a few minutes because I'll have to go to the bank and explain to the FDIC people why I need it. How does that sound?"

"Are you *sure* you can get it? I really do have to have it."

"Sure, I can get it. Don't worry about that. The money doesn't belong to them. It belongs to us. I'll get it, all right, Mrs. Peabody. Now you go to a nice restaurant and relax. And be here at one forty-five sharp; I'll have you that check."

Her face lit up. "Oh thank you, Mr. Jones. I'm sorry to be so much trouble. But as soon as I get little Joey out of this mess, I promise I'll bring it back. Of course, I may need to draw out a bit more before I can do that, to satisfy that greedy lawyer. But I'm not going to touch a cent more than I have to."

"Don't you worry, Mrs. Peabody. You don't need my permission or anyone else's for that matter. That money belongs to you. I'll see you right back here at one forty-five."

As soon as she walked out the door, Caleb Lovett began closing down. Before she was back for her money, he'd be long gone. He'd already stayed in Memphis longer than he'd intended to stay when he first set up his business. One thing he'd learned over the years: Don't push your luck. When it's time to move on, pack up and go. And never look back.

Maybe he should have listened to Sammy Norton. Sammy had already been gone a month. Sammy had tried to talk Lovett into going with him, but Lovett had declined.

"Jesus, Sammy. This is the best thing we've ever had going. Leaving here is like walking away from a goldmine."

"That's why we've got to go. The goddamned sky falls in just when it looks like everything's perfect. Take my word for it, partner. I know."

Well, old Sammy had been wrong. In the four weeks he'd been gone, Lovett had raked in almost more money than he could count. But now things were about to start getting messy. So he'd grab his winnings and get while the getting was good. He wasn't worried about being located after he left. William Jones would just drop off the face of the earth.

Lovett went into the storage room at the back of the office where he brewed his coffee. Several mops and brooms were hanging on one wall. A deep sink was in one corner. The coffee pot was sitting on a cabinet top in another corner. Lovett opened the doors to the cabinet and removed the paneling from its back wall. That was where his safe was. It would be impossible for anyone to find it unless he knew precisely where to look.

There were two bags in the safe. His cash was in one, and his checks were in the other. He was tempted to count the cash but decided he better not. He didn't need to waste a goddamned minute. Besides, he knew how much was there. Twenty-seven thousand, five hundred and change. He loved to count it, though, just to feel it in his hands.

He opened the bag with the cash in it and took out ten fifties and one twenty. He needed the twenty because some places didn't like to take fifties. He'd given Mrs. Peabody his last twenty and had to have something in his wallet for spending money. He didn't really need as much as he'd taken, but it was always a whole lot better to be safe than sorry.

He wasn't sure how much the checks were worth. Except for the Staffords', not very much. Whatever the amount, he'd take them by Igloo's place, cash them and get out of town.

Lovett put the bags into a briefcase and set it on the floor by the front door. Then he put on his coat and stuck his revolver into its pocket. He looked around to see if he'd forgotten anything and decided he hadn't. He turned around the sign hanging on the front door. Now, instead of saying *OPEN*, it said *CLOSED*. Right under *CLOSED*, in smaller letters, was *OUT TO LUNCH.*

Lovett locked the door and threw the keys onto the floor in the middle of the room. The door could still be opened from the inside but not from the outside. As he turned off the lights, he wondered what Old Lady Peabody was going to do when she came back to get her money. Probably have a goddamned heart attack.

Before opening the door to leave, he took one last look around. Then he picked up his briefcase and walked outside. As soon as the door closed behind him, that chapter of his life was over. He felt a little twinge of regret. That place had really treated him well. But it was a goddamned cinch that pretty soon a lot of the idiots who had invested with him would be coming back after their money. Then the shit would really start hitting the fan. He wished he could be there to see the expressions on their stupid faces when that happened. But he wouldn't be able to. He'd be long gone.

He'd probably go to Dallas, now, but it didn't really matter. He had enough money to last him while he was making up his mind. As soon as he could, he'd get in touch with Sammy. Old Sammy was a lot of fun. He was the luckiest son of a bitch Lovett had ever seen. He really had a knack for finding hot pussy, and he could always come up with an idea or two for picking up some easy cash.

Lovett looked where the Malibu should be parked, and the goddamned thing wasn't there. For a moment he couldn't believe his eyes. He remembered exactly where he'd left it, and the goddamned thing was gone. His suits and other belongings were lying on the dirty asphalt pavement. Then he realized what had happened. The fucking finance company had repossessed his goddamned car.

He needed a taxi. He went to his pile of belongings and looked for his cell phone. He breathed a sigh of relief when he saw it was still there. He started to dial information, but at that moment he saw a taxi entering the parking lot. He ran toward it waving his arms. The driver saw him and drove over to where he was.

"You need a taxi, mister?"

"Yeah. I sure do. Right over here." He went over to where his belongings were lying.

"They repossessed your car, right man?" The driver chuckled when he asked his question. He looked like he was from somewhere in the Middle East.

"No. They didn't repossess my fucking car. Some goddamned kids stole it."

"It looks to me like they repossessed it, man."

Lovett began picking up his things, and the driver got out and helped him. They put everything in the backseat, and Lovett got into the front seat with the driver.

"Where to, my man?"

Lovett didn't know Igloo's address, but he knew how to get there.

"Get out of the lot right where you came in and take a left. Then I'll direct you."

Lovett hoped to hell Igloo would be home when he got there. He dialed the man's number. Igloo answered right away.

"This is Jones," Lovett told him. "I'm on my way to your place right now. Will you be there?"

"Yeah. I can wait a few minutes. I was on my way out when the phone rang. It's a good thing you didn't call two seconds later."

"Thank you, Mr. Igloo. I'm on my way, now. I'll be there in two minutes."

As they pulled out of the parking lot they met another car coming in. Lovett got a clear view of the driver's face. It belonged to Mrs. Carla Peabody. She must be awful anxious to get her goddamned money, he thought. He'd told her not to be back until one forty-five. It wasn't even twelve yet.

It had been less than twenty minutes since she left his place. She hadn't even taken the time to eat lunch. But that was her goddamned problem. He didn't have time to be worrying about Mrs. Carla Peabody anymore. She owed him twenty dollars since she hadn't bought lunch with the twenty dollar bill he'd given her, but he wasn't going to worry about that.

Maria Alicia was tired. It had been a hard day at *Señora* Montemayor's laundry. It seemed like everyone in Loma Linda had brought in their dirty clothes to be washed and ironed. Maria was glad to be home where she could fix herself something to eat and then relax.

She had bought a *True Love* magazine at *Señor* Montemayor's supermarket. It would be nice to read it for a while before she went to bed. The people in the stories were so worldly and sophisticated. Perhaps someday Maria would be like they were.

Now that her father had died, Maria had nothing to keep her in Loma Linda. She was considering selling the house her father had left her and leaving the little village. She could go away and take some courses at a business college. She might even decide to go to Mexico City. Some of her friends had told her there were many good jobs in the larger cities for girls with business skills.

At any rate, there was no future for her in Loma Linda. Most of the young people had moved away. She felt that if she didn't leave, too, the rest of her life would be drab and boring. No doubt, she would end up as an old maid. She certainly knew of no man in Loma Linda she would want to marry. All of them who had remained there were dull and colorless.

But she had another reason for wanting to get away. Her *Tío* Juan was beginning to make her feel uncomfortable. He'd come by her house several times in the past month looking for a place to sleep. Every time he came, he was so drunk that he had trouble talking. Usually, he could hardly even stand up.

Maria didn't like the idea of letting him come inside, but because he was her father's brother, she couldn't bring herself to refuse him. Once, he'd fallen onto the floor and passed out almost as soon as he walked through the front door. Maria had tried to wake him up so he could sleep in a bed, but she couldn't rouse him. She covered him with blankets, and he slept where he'd fallen.

Maria took some beans and rice from the refrigerator. They were already cooked and stored in small plastic containers. She took a pan from a cabinet under the counter and placed it on the stove. She put the beans and rice into the pan making sure they didn't mix together.

While that food was heating up, she shredded some lettuce and tomatoes and cut up some onions. Then she made herself a *taco* and a *burrito*. When her dinner was ready, she put some ice cubes into a glass and filled it with Coke.

Maria was lonely as she ate. She felt like she was about the only young person left in Loma Linda. She could hardly wait until she sold her house and moved away.

She finished eating her dinner and put everything away. Then she cleaned the table and washed the dishes and put them in the cabinet. With those chores accomplished, she was ready to sit on the couch and read. She had a television set but very seldom watched it. Most of the programs were American shows, and they either had subtitles in Spanish or had Spanish dubbed in.

She sat down and opened her *True Love* magazine. She hadn't even begun to read it when she heard a knock at the door. It had to be *Tío* Juan. There was nobody else who would be visiting at that time of the evening. She stayed where she was hoping he'd go away. But that didn't work. The pounding on the door resumed louder than before. Maria sighed, laid down her magazine and went to answer the door. *Tío* Juan was standing there just as she had expected him to be.

Maria was shocked by his appearance. He was dirty and disheveled, and the front of his shirt was covered with vomit. His face was flushed, and his eyes were bloodshot and teary. He pushed his way inside without waiting for her invitation.

"Ah, my beautiful *sobrina*," he said as he staggered through the door. He tried to embrace her, but she stepped away.

"You look awful," she said. "And you smell even worse."

"I'm ill," he told her. "I need a place to sleep." He went to her couch and lay down.

Maria went to her bedroom closet where her father's clothes were still stored. She got some briefs, socks, a pair of trousers and a shirt, all of which had belonged to her father, and took them into the living room. She hoped she could coax *Tío* Juan into taking a bath and changing into the clean clothes. It looked as though that wasn't going to happen. The old man was fast asleep and snoring loudly.

Maria shook him, and he came half awake and opened his eyes.

"Get up," she said, vigorously shaking his shoulder and arm.

"I'm sick. I need to sleep," he mumbled.

"You need a bath. You're going to ruin my beautiful couch," she told him.

Tío Juan didn't respond. He closed his eyes and began snoring again. Maria kept shaking him hoping he'd wake up and get off her couch. He was too filthy to be lying there.

It soon became apparent he wasn't going to get up. She knew that by morning the couch would be as filthy as he was if he spent the night on it. She decided she would do her best to make sure that didn't happen.

She went back into her bedroom closet where she had several extra blankets and quilts folded up and stacked on the floor. After getting two blankets and two quilts, she brought them into the living room. She laid one of the blankets aside. She folded the other one and the two quilts and placed them on the floor by the couch forming a pallet. She knelt down on the folded covers facing the couch, reached her arms over *Tío* Juan and got a good grip on his shoulder and waist. Then, by pulling with all her strength, she rolled him off of the couch and onto the pallet.

He emitted a surprised grunt when he landed on the makeshift bed but didn't wake up. He shifted his position slightly as if to get more comfortable and then resumed his snoring. Maria stood looking at him in disgust for a few moments shaking her head. Then she got her *True Love* Magazine and sat down in a chair and began reading. From time to time she glanced at *Tío* Juan, but he didn't stir. It looked like he'd be sleeping soundly for the remainder of the night.

At ten o'clock, Maria decided to go to bed. *Tío* Juan hadn't moved, but he was still snoring quite loudly. She was afraid he might get too cold if she left him uncovered so she picked up the blanket she had left lying on the floor and covered him with it. Then she got ready for bed, said her prayers and lay down.

At about two o'clock, Maria woke up. *Tío* Juan was standing naked by her bed looking down at her. Just as she opened her eyes, he pulled back the covers and began getting into the bed. Maria screamed at him to leave, but he lay down beside her, looking at her through bleary eyes. She got up, grabbed a robe and put it on and went to another room. *Tío* Juan got up and followed her.

"Get away," she screamed.

"Come here, my sweet *sobrina*," he said, staggering toward her. He almost had his hands on her when she stepped forward and gave him a hard shove in the chest. He stumbled backwards and sat down on the floor.

"Get out," she shouted. His filthy clothes were lying in a heap on the floor. She picked them up and threw them onto his lap.

"Get dressed, and get out of here," she told him. He continued to sit without moving.

"Get out of here before I call the police," she said loudly.

He laboriously maneuvered his way onto his hands and knees and slowly stood up leaving his clothes lying on the floor. She picked them up and thrust them at him.

"Put these on," she said firmly.

He took them and stood studying them as though he was trying to figure out what they were. Then he carried them to the back door, opened it and walked outside.

"You can't go out like that," she told him. "Put on your clothes."

He paid her no mind and began to wander off in the darkness.

"Wait," she said.

He stopped and turned toward her. Maria went back to the couch and picked up his shoes. She looked for his socks but didn't see any. She carried the shoes to the open back door and threw them outside.

"Get dressed," she shouted and closed the door. She stood there for about ten minutes and then opened the door and looked outside. *Tío* Juan was gone. So were his clothes and shoes. Maria breathed a sigh of relief. She locked the door, made sure the front one was also locked and checked all the windows. Finally she went back to bed but wasn't able to sleep. Even though she was tired, Maria was glad when the sun began to light up the eastern sky.

Lovett felt like he had it made. His briefcase was stuffed full of money. More money than he'd ever seen before in his life. Johnny Igloo had cashed his checks, and from Igloo's place, Lovett had gone straight to the bus station and boarded a bus for Dallas. He'd put his gun into one of the suitcases because he didn't feel comfortable carrying it. If the cops ever found it on him, he'd certainly be in trouble. They had no reason to search him, but sometimes those sons of bitches didn't need a reason. Anyway, he felt more comfortable with it in the suitcase.

He'd put his wallet there, too. It had his phony identification in it, and he didn't like the idea of carrying both sets. After he'd traveled a little way, he realized he'd left his spending cash in the wallet. He hadn't even thought about taking it out and sticking it in his coat pocket. But it was too late to worry about that now. He'd just have to hope the luggage didn't get lost.

He was a little pissed off at the finance company for picking up the Malibu, but it really wasn't that much of a loss. He'd planned to let it go back, anyway, as soon as he got to Dallas. He'd buy something a hell of a lot better than a Malibu when he got there. Besides, it was more fun riding a bus.

He dozed off a couple of times. The noise from the bus's engines and the hum of its tires on the road were almost like a lullaby. He didn't really need to sleep because it was still too early. But it would be kind of nice if he could drift off. It would sure make the time pass a whole lot faster.

Normally, he didn't have any trouble going to sleep. But a bunch of half-drunk rednecks were having a party three rows in front of him. He gathered from their conversation they were on their way to Dallas to work on some big construction project. He hated the idea of listening to them the entire trip and was glad when they got off at Little Rock and didn't get back on. He figured they were planning to raise a little hell there before continuing their journey. As far as he was concerned, it was Little Rock's loss and his gain; he leaned back in his seat and thanked the Lord for small favors.

He was able to get a few minutes of sleep after that. But at the next stop, a little lady about ninety years old got on the bus and sat down in the seat right across the aisle from him. After a few miles she dozed off and kept moaning and making all kinds of snoring noises. Every once in a while, she would jump like somebody had goosed her, holler something like, "Oh, oh, oh," and wake up. A couple of times she looked at Lovett sheepishly and apologized. One time he'd drifted off and was sleeping quite soundly when she whimpered loudly and jerked awake. The sound woke him up, too, and for a moment he didn't know where he was. He looked her way, and she was crying.

"I'm sorry," she told him so softly he was just barely able to hear her words. Her face was wet with tears, and Lovett wondered what kind of a dream had woke her up. Then she leaned back and in a few minutes seemed to be asleep again. He figured he might be able to get back to sleep as well, but he was wrong. His traveling companion kept snoring and moaning and fidgeting around in her seat, and Lovett quickly came to the conclusion he might as well get used to the idea of staying awake for the rest of his journey or at least until she got off. But here they were halfway to Texarkana, and she was still on the bus.

He glanced her way, and she happened to be looking his direction. She smiled a wan smile and said, "My, I didn't realize this trip would be so tiring." He could see she was exhausted. Her face was lined with tiny wrinkles and looked like dry parchment, and she had dark rings under her eyes.

"How far are you going?" he asked her, more just to be saying something than out of any genuine interest.

"Oh. I'm going all the way to Dallas," she said. "My baby brother just died. He and I were the only two left. Now it's just me."

Dallas was about two hundred and fifty miles further down the road as far as Lovett could remember. He figured that with all the stops, it would be five or six more hours before they got there. Most of the towns weren't very big. The only one of any size he could remember was Texarkana. He figured there might be a few more, but he couldn't think of any.

"I'm sorry," Lovett told her just to make conversation. If her brother was anywhere near as old as she was, it wasn't anything to get excited about. When people get that age they're supposed to die.

"Thank you," she told him. "I am, too. I always thought I'd be the first to go. But one never knows the Lord's will."

"No. One never knows."

It seemed sad to Lovett that a ninety-year-old lady had to ride a bus to her brother's funeral. As far as he was concerned, somebody should have gotten her an airplane ticket. He hoped someone would be waiting for her when she got off the bus. He didn't want to ask her, though, if anybody would be. If she told him no, it would make him feel even sorrier for her than he was feeling already, and it still wouldn't help her get to her brother's house or wherever she planned to stay while she was there. There wasn't anything he could do about it, anyway, and besides it wasn't any of his concern.

He was eager to get to Dallas even though he didn't know yet exactly what he was going to do when he got there. He knew, of course, he was going to try to get in touch with Sammy. Sammy would certainly have a few ideas. But in the meantime Lovett would have to get a job. He didn't want to sit around doing nothing and fritter away his money. It had been too hard to accumulate for him to do that. Furthermore, he doubted he'd ever get his hands on that kind of cash again. He'd put it in a savings account where it could draw a little interest while he decided what his next venture was going to be.

He'd probably get a job selling. That was what he was good at. It didn't make a goddamned bit of difference what he was selling, either. Just give him something to sell, and he'd sell it.

His legs were cramped from the long ride, and he was ready get off the bus and walk around at the next stop if they had a few minutes. If not, that would be okay, too. If a ninety-year-old woman could ride the bus all the way to Dallas, it certainly wouldn't hurt him.

His little traveling companion interrupted his thoughts. "Excuse me, sir. Do you know how much further it is to Dallas?"

"I was just thinking about that," he informed her. "I think it's about two hundred and fifty miles, maybe a little less. It's still quite a ways."

"Oh, goodness. That far? I didn't realize it was that much further. How much longer do you think it'll take?"

"Probably five or six hours if we stop in every little town."

"Oh goodness," she said.

"Is anybody going to meet you when you get there?"

"Yes. I've already made arrangements. Some lawyer's supposed to pick me up. He'll be at the station. I have his name here somewhere." She rummaged through her purse and found a business card. "Yes, here it is." She handed the card across the aisle to Lovett. "I can't read it without my spectacles." The card read: Jerome H. Spencer, Attorney at law. Lovett read the name out loud and handed the card back to her.

"Yes, I remember now. Mr. Jerome Spencer. That's quite a distinguished name, don't you think? I went to school with a boy named Jerome. He was a very bright lad. Anyway, Mr. Spencer has a key to the house. I suppose I'll spend the night there."

"How'll you get to the funeral?"

"Mr. Spencer promised he'd take me. I really don't know anything about him. I think he plans to buy Jimmy's house. To tell you the truth, I'm not very well prepared to talk to him. I didn't expect Jimmy to die. I always thought I would go before he did." She paused for a moment and then said, "Young man, I don't even know your name. I'm Carrie Clawson." She offered Lovett her hand. He took it carefully because he didn't want to hurt it. It felt as fragile as an eggshell.

"Pleased to meet you, Mrs. Clawson. My name's Cal. Cal Lovett.

"Oh, look," she said. "I think we're stopping."

Sure enough, she was right. The bus pulled off the interstate, and in about five minutes it was at a service station which also served as the bus station for the little town. Lovett asked the bus driver how long they would be there and was informed they would be leaving as soon as the bus discharged and picked up passengers.

"We'll be in Texarkana in about an hour, and we're scheduled to be there for twenty minutes. You'll have time to get off and walk around there for a little while if you want to," the driver told him. Four passengers got off the bus and seven got on. The bus pulled out of the station and was on its way again.

Mrs. Clawson's eyes were bright and wide open. Lovett hoped everything would work out for her when she got to Dallas. Although it wasn't any of his business, he couldn't help being concerned. He wished she had stayed in Little Rock or whatever that place was here she got on. It just wasn't right for her to be making such a sad journey all by herself.

"I hope Mr. Spencer doesn't forget," she told him. "I suppose I could get a taxi, but I wouldn't be able to get into the house without a key."

"He'll be there," Lovett assured her. "Maybe you can call him from Texarkana just to remind him. But I don't think that'll be necessary. I'm sure he hasn't forgotten."

"I'm sure you're right. He has the bus schedule and has assured me he'll be there."

She leaned back and closed her eyes again, looking tiny and defenseless. He wished there were something he could do. He didn't know why he felt that way. He hadn't told her brother to die, and he certainly hadn't told her to ride a bus all the way from Little Rock to Dallas. She should've stayed home where she belonged. But still, he knew it would be hard to stay away from your little brother's funeral even if you were ninety years old. Especially if you were the only relative he had left. In about five minutes, she was fast asleep, and her face was a bit more relaxed. He grinned at the sight because she was breathing very softly without the hint of a snore.

Lovett was able to get a little sleep, too; he woke up when the bus stopped at Texarkana. He got off taking his briefcase with him. He wanted to be damned sure nobody but him got their hands on it. He got a bar of candy and a Pepsi and walked around for a few minutes. When he got back on the bus and took his seat, Carrie Clawson was still fast asleep.

Her purse was sitting on the floor by her feet. It was so large it almost looked like a small suitcase. He figured as small as she was, she probably had trouble carrying it. He wondered what was in it. It was open, but it was leaning away from him at such an angle he wasn't able to see inside.

She shifted in her seat, and one of her feet hit the purse and tipped it in his direction. At the same time, the top opened wider so he could see inside. Lovett was surprised at what he saw. Her handbag seemed to be almost full of cash. All the bills he could see were fifties and hundreds.

She woke up and looked around for a moment as though she was trying to get her bearings. Then she leaned over and got her purse, placed it in her lap and put her frail little arms around it holding it tightly. She looked around again as though to see if anyone had seen the money. Lovett averted his eyes and pretended to be looking elsewhere.

He figured there ought to be some way he could get his hands on that cash. He sure as hell needed it a lot more than a little ninety-year-old woman. Somebody her age didn't need that much money. In the first place, she was too old to enjoy it. She would just spend it on doctors and prescription drugs and shit like that. If she couldn't pay for those things, it didn't make any difference, anyway. She would still get what she needed. Medicare or Medicaid or some other government program was always around to pick up the tab.

In the second place, she wasn't about to live long enough to spend it all. How much longer could a ninety-year-old woman live? As far as Lovett was concerned, she was already living on borrowed time. Her brother was already dead. She would probably die any time, now, herself. What good would all that money do for her after she was dead? Not a bit, that's what. Her goddamned lawyer, Jerome Spencer, would stick it in his pocket. Lovett was sure he needed it a hell of a lot more than any lawyer.

His best bet was to figure out some way to get the purse and get off the bus before it got to Dallas. Mrs. Clawson would have to be sound asleep, though. Right now, she was gripping it with all her strength. But she would doze off again after a while, and her arms would relax. If that happened while they were at a station loading or unloading passengers, he'd take it and disappear.

Then he realized he couldn't do that. He'd checked his luggage all the way to Dallas and had made the mistake of checking it in his own name. When Mrs. Clawson discovered that her purse was missing and Lovett had vanished, she would report it to the cops and give them a good description of him. They would know who he was as soon as they checked his luggage. If he couldn't devise a fool proof plan, he'd just have to forget it. He had plenty of money in the briefcase, anyway.

He leaned back in his seat and went soundly to sleep. When he woke up, the bus was entering Dallas. He was glad. His legs were tired and stiff. He had to go to the bathroom, and he was hungry. He looked at Mrs. Carrie Clawson. She was fast asleep, but her arms were still wrapped tightly around her purse. There wasn't any way he could get it without waking her up.

It seemed like it took forever to get from the city limits to the bus depot. But finally they got there, and the bus stopped. Lovett wasn't sure what he was going to do in the morning, but right then he was going to get a taxi and go to a nice hotel. There would be plenty of time later to start making plans.

It seemed like everyone was getting off the bus. Lovett wasn't in any hurry so he waited for the aisle to clear before he started to get up from his seat. The little old lady was still asleep. He wondered what would happen if someone didn't wake her up and the bus went on to Waco. He doubted that would happen. The driver probably had some kind of a manifest and would make sure that all the passengers got off at their proper destination.

Lovett decided he'd save the driver some trouble and wake her up himself. He leaned over and said, "Mrs. Clawson." She didn't move so he said it louder. When that didn't wake her up, he reached over and grasped her shoulder. As soon as his hand touched her, she fell sideways away from his grip. He realized instantly that she was dead.

Lovett couldn't believe his luck. He picked up her handbag, and carrying it and his briefcase, walked to the front of the bus. The driver was standing outside by the door helping people down the stairs.

"You had better check on the lady near the back of the bus," Lovett told the driver. "I think she's dead."

"What? Who's dead?"

"The little lady near the back."

The driver quickly got onto the bus followed by several other people who had overheard what Lovett had told him. Lovett went into a restroom and opened the stolen purse to see how much money was in it. He was disappointed. All it had was two hundreds, three fifties and seven ones. Shit, he thought, it was hardly worth the goddamned trouble.

He put the money in his briefcase, threw the purse into a trash can and went to wait for his luggage. It didn't take long for it to arrive. In a few minutes, he had it loaded onto a cart and started outside to find a taxi.

Three men came into the depot through the door he was approaching walking straight toward him. He recognized them as three of the passengers who had been on the bus. Two of them had been in the seats behind him, and the other one had been sitting behind Mrs. Clawson.

As they approached the cart, the men split up to let him through. One went to his left and the other two to his right. Just as he was even with them, one of the men suddenly turned toward him and grabbed him in a bear hug around his chest. Lovett was pushing the cart with both hands. He'd placed the briefcase on the cart so he didn't have to bear its weight but was holding its handle tightly in his right hand. He almost lost his grip on the briefcase when the man embraced him, but he barely managed to hold on.

Almost at the same instant the first man grabbed him, the other two men seized him also and shoved him sideways through a door not two feet away. He hadn't realized it, but he was walking by a restroom door when the attack began.

A man was standing at a urinal peeing when the four men came crashing through the door. The fellow turned away and ran into one of the stalls. The men slammed Lovett against a wall and began pounding him with their fists. One grabbed the briefcase but couldn't wrest it from Lovett's grasp. Lovett felt a fist crash against his jaw and almost lost consciousness, but still he didn't release his grip. They kept pummeling away, and he knew he couldn't hold out.

He worked himself into a corner, and with all the strength he could marshal, Lovett wrenched the briefcase away from the man who was holding it and dropped it behind his back. Then, instead of merely trying to ward off their blows and protect himself, he went on the attack.

He brought up his knee catching one of his assailants solidly in the testicles. The man screamed loudly and collapsed to the floor. Then Lovett brought around a hard right hook catching another attacker flush on the temple. The man staggered backward but didn't fall. Lovett found himself with a little room to maneuver. He lifted up his right leg, spinning around as he did so. The karate kick caught one of the men in the side, and the fellow fell to the floor. Lovett thought it was the same man he'd punched in the temple.

He turned and grabbed the briefcase hoping he could escape. But it was no use. The uninjured man tackled him and knocked him to the floor. In an instant, the other two were all over him as well. He felt their kicks striking him all over: head, chest, arms, legs. Blackness began to settle in, and someone said, "We've got it. Let's go."

But one of the men paid his partner no attention.

"Take this," the man screamed. "And this, and this, and this." He was relentlessly kicking Lovett's prone form as he shouted. Lovett could feel the impact of the blows but felt no pain. Then the pounding against his body ceased. He heard the men running away and tried to get up but could not.

Someone came out of a stall, stared at him for a moment and then went to the door, opened it and began shouting for help. In a moment, the restroom was full of people. One of them knelt beside him.

"Can you hear me?"

Lovett could hear the man and see him, too, but he didn't feel like answering. He just wanted to get up and leave.

"Don't move. Just try to relax."

Lovett tried again to get up, but he still was unable to move. The attempt exhausted him, and he felt like he was going to pass out.

"Relax," the man told him. "Take it easy. Help will be here in just a minute."

The man was right. All Lovett had to do was relax until he regained his strength, and then everything would be all right. He closed his eyes and felt himself dozing off. Several people lifted him up slightly and moved him onto a stretcher. If they would just leave him alone for a while, he'd be okay. But if they wanted to put him on a stretcher, that was all right, too.

He was very thirsty. Maybe one of the people would bring him a drink of water. At least ten or fifteen people had come into the restroom, and he knew that no more than three or four had put him on the stretcher. The others were just standing around, staring.

Maybe he'd get up, drink some water and leave. All he had to do was pick up his luggage and go. There wasn't any law that said he had to stay on the stretcher until an ambulance arrived.

Lovett opened his eyes and was very confused by what he saw. He wasn't in the restroom anymore. He was lying on a bed in a hospital room. A nurse was standing by his side reading something from a clipboard. She looked at him and smiled.

"Well, good morning, Mr. Lovett," she told him cheerfully. "How are we this morning?"

"Where am I?" he asked, totally disoriented.

"You're in the hospital in beautiful downtown Dallas."

"How did you know my name?"

"We found your driver's license in your coat pocket. They got everything else. That *is* your name, isn't it?"

His wallet with his phony identification was still in his luggage, and hopefully no one had gone through that. His gun was there, too. With any kind of luck no one would look into his luggage. He hoped not. He didn't want the cops to ask him why he was carrying a gun and an additional set of identification.

"Yes. I'm sorry. I was just confused for a minute. I don't even remember being brought here."

"You were in pretty bad shape. You've been beaten up quite badly. How do you feel now?"

"Not too bad. I'm ready to leave."

"Are you strong enough to talk to the police?"

"The police? Not really. I'd rather they not get involved. There's not much they could do, anyway."

"There's a Sergeant Bernard waiting outside. He insists on talking to you when you're strong enough." The last thing on earth Lovett wanted to do was to talk to a cop. But it looked like there was no way around it. He might as well let the son of a bitch in and get it over with.

"Sure," he told her. "Send him in."

The interview didn't last long. There were three assailants. He didn't know who they were. He'd seen them on the bus, but he'd never seen them before that. He wasn't sure where they had gotten on. He had no idea why they had attacked him. Maybe they thought he had money because he was dressed in a suit. He'd been carrying about five hundred dollars and they had gotten it all. He planned to stay in Dallas for a while, but he didn't know how long, maybe for a long time if things worked out. He didn't know where he'd be staying.

When the policeman asked for his permanent address, he gave the one on his driver's license. It was the address of a rooming house where hardly anybody ever stayed more than a month. But he said he was planning on staying in Dallas and would get a Texas drivers license as soon as he got settled. The officer thanked him and left.

Lovett knew what had happened and why it had happened. But he wasn't about to tell the police or anyone else for that matter. Evidently, the men had seen the money in Mrs. Clawson's purse and had been scheming to get their hands on it. They had seen him take the purse and had devised a plan to relieve him of the money. Unfortunately for Lovett, in addition to getting the old lady's cash, they had taken his as well.

When Sergeant Bernard left, the nurse came back into the room. "By the way, Mr. Lovett, my name is Vicki Carver."

"Pleased to meet you, Miss Carver," he said.

"They beat you up pretty badly. It looks like you won't be able to work for several days."

"Well, I'm between jobs anyway. I'll find something when I get out of here. I guess I'll have to. Those thieves took every cent I had. So I *do* have to find something right away, even if it's only temporary."

"What kind of work do you do?"

"Well, just about anything. But mainly selling. I can sell anything. You heard about the fellow that could sell refrigerators to the Eskimos? Well, that's me."

Another nurse stuck her head into the room and said, "Miss Carver. There's an emergency in Mrs. Cider's room." Vicki rushed outside, and she and the other nurse hurried away.

Lovett wondered what he was going to do, now. He didn't have a job, and he didn't have a cent. Just a few hours before, he was practically on Easy Street. And now he was destitute. He'd have to get a job somewhere, at least until he could figure out his next move. It didn't matter what kind of work it was, either. If he had to flip hamburgers for a while that's what he'd do. He wouldn't be broke for long, though. He'd be back on his feet, both physically and financially, in no time.

He wouldn't have a cent when he got out of this place, but he wasn't afraid. He was angry as hell that he'd been mugged, but he wasn't afraid. He'd find some way to get to a rooming house and tell the owner his problem. He was sure that he could convince somebody to let him stay there on credit until he got a job. The problem would be getting around from place to place with no money and no car. It would be impossible to haul his luggage around without a car. Maybe he could sweet talk Vicki into letting him leave his stuff at the hospital for a few days until he got situated. Not the gun, of course, but everything else.

Then he remembered something that had completely slipped his mind until that moment. Not everything had been taken, after all. His goddamned wallet was in one of his suitcases. And now he remembered that he'd put a little over five hundred dollars in it just before he left Memphis. Five hundred dollars wasn't very much compared to what he'd lost, but it was a hell of a lot more than nothing. He'd have to find his suitcases before somebody began snooping around in them.

About an hour later, Vicki Carver came back into the room. "That poor woman," she said, shaking her head.

"Is she okay?" Lovett wondered.

"No. She's is very bad shape. Now, if I'm being too presumptuous, please tell me. But my father needs somebody who knows something about bookkeeping. He's had a lot of trouble finding anybody willing to work. He says nobody wants to work anymore. Would you be interested in something like that?"

"Maybe. But listen, Ms. Carver. Did they bring my suitcases? Are they around here somewhere?"

"Yes, they did. In fact, they're in the corner on the other side of that bed. And your suits and CD player, too." He breathed a sigh of relief. He'd check them out as soon as she left and make sure that his gun and wallet were still there.

"I could talk to your dad. We could see. What I would really like is a job selling. But I'll take anything right now."

"Okay," she said, "I've got to go. I'll see you later. You just try to get well."

Yeah, I'll get well all right, he thought, but right now I've got to check out my suitcases.

CHAPTER II

Maria Alicia left the little *tienda* and walked down the dusty road toward her house carrying a bag of groceries. She was slender and graceful. She had full breasts, a tiny waist, firm round hips and buttocks and long slim legs. Her dark eyes shone with happiness. She had just seen Jorge Rojas. He'd driven by in a shiny red car as she was entering the store. She thought her heart would stop when he looked her way and smiled.

He was so beautiful, so *guapo*. He was far too sophisticated for the girls in Loma Linda and never paid them any attention. Maria had been told that he had *nóvias* all over Mexico. Many were older than Jorge, and some were married. All were rich and fashionable and lived in big cities. Maria had heard that some of them gave him money or bought him elegant clothes.

Jorge had grown up in the largest *hacienda* in Loma Linda. It sat high on a hill about a kilometer outside of town. His parents were very rich. They owned a silver mine which employed many of the town's residents. As soon as Jorge graduated from high school he went away to Mexico City to college. Maria had been told that he was now a lawyer and was working for a large law firm in Mexico City. She had heard that he spent much of his time in New York and Europe. She couldn't imagine what he was doing in Loma Linda.

The road was dusty and unpaved. Maria walked carefully to avoid tripping or turning an ankle on the large rocks that protruded above its surface. Now, she was walking even more slowly than she usually did hoping she might see Jorge's car again before she reached her house. She arrived at her front gate and breathed a sigh of disappointment. The red automobile was nowhere in sight.

She had to set the bag of groceries on the ground to unlatch the gate. While she was opening it, Jorge's car came into view and headed down the road in her direction. She moved the groceries through the gate, set them down again, closed the gate and began to lock it. Maria didn't look at the approaching automobile. Instead, she pretended not to notice it.

Jorge stopped his car and got out. Maria glanced toward him as though she had just that moment seen him. He walked over to where she was standing.

"Yes?" she said, her voice a question. "Can I help you, *señor?*"

"Hello, Maria," he answered. "Do you know who I am?"

"Of course, I know who you are, *Señor* Rojas. Everyone in Loma Linda knows who you are. But how do *you* know *my* name?"

He smiled. "How could I *not* know you?" The sound of his voice made her tremble. "How could I *not* know the most beautiful girl in Loma Linda? How could I *not* know the most delicate flower in this part of Mexico?" He was looking into her eyes. She was still working with the latch.

"So what they tell me is true." Her heart was pounding. She hoped her voice didn't give her away.

"And what is it they tell you?"

"That you're a terrible flirt with a golden tongue."

"Oh. Is that what they say?" Before she could answer, he said, "Let me help you with those groceries."

She had just finished securing the gate. He reached down, unlatched and opened it and came inside.

She picked up the bag and said, "That's all right. They aren't heavy." She walked toward the front door, and Jorge walked by her side. She stopped and turned toward him.

"Is there something I can do for you, *Señor* Rojas?"

He smiled again. "You asked me that earlier, didn't you? Yes. There *is* something. Let me introduce myself. I'm Jorge Rojas." He extended his hand. She couldn't take it because she had her arms wrapped around the bag of groceries. He took her small right hand in his and said, "You don't need to call me *Señor* Rojas. Please call me Jorge. And I hope I may call you Maria."

She smiled. "Yes, Jorge." They both stood for a few moments, and Maria said, "It was very nice meeting you, Jorge. Now if you'll excuse me, I have to put away the groceries."

"Of course. I didn't mean to disrupt your schedule. But now that we've been properly introduced, I'd like to ask you something."

"Yes?"

"I'm giving a party at my parents' house next week. Do you know where that is?"

"Yes. I know."

"I would like for you to be my guest."

"But why? You know so many people." She almost said girls instead of people. "We just met. We hardly know each other."

"That's precisely why I hope you'll come. Because we're neighbors. We both grew up in Loma Linda. This is our home. Will you at least think about it?"

"But it's so sudden. We've lived here forever, you in your huge *hacienda* on the hill and I in my little casa here in town. This is the first time we've even spoken."

"I know. And that's sad. But there's no sooner time to change that than now."

"But we're so different."

"Sure, we're different. You're a *muchacha* and I a *muchacho*. But don't the French say *'viva la difference'?*"

She blushed. "You know that's not what I meant."

"How are we so different, then?"

"You're educated and sophisticated. You live in Mexico City and travel all over the world. I'm poor and uneducated. I've never been but a few miles from Loma Linda. We both were born here, but we grew up and live in different worlds."

"I hope you don't hate me because of my parents' wealth," he said.

"I don't hate you nor do I hate them. I'm who *I* am, and you're who *you* are. Neither of us chose our position in this life. God made that decision for us. Who am I to question Him?"

"You're a very beautiful woman, Maria," he said. Her face was burning. She set the bag on the ground and turned to open the door but had trouble getting the key into the lock.

"Let me do that," he said and took the ring of keys from her hand. His fingers touched hers and it felt to Maria as though a current of electricity flowed through her fingertips along her arm and to her heart.

He opened the door and turned to face her. His lips were very close to hers. She could just barely resist the urge to kiss him. His large gray eyes looked into hers. Maria hoped he'd kiss her. If he did, she wouldn't resist. His face moved closer, and she closed her eyes.

"Think about it," he said. She opened her eyes, and he'd stepped away. For a moment, she didn't know what he meant. Then she realized he was talking about the party.

"I work," she said. "Besides. You haven't even told me what day it's going to be."

"Why don't you give me your telephone number? I'll call you when arrangements have been made. Don't worry about your work schedule. It'll be in the evening after work." He went to his car and returned with a pen and notepad. She gave him her telephone number without waiting for him to ask again.

It had been a week since Maria had talked to Jorge. She had seen his car the next day, but then it seemed to have disappeared. Every evening after work she had waited for him to call, but the telephone hadn't rung. He'd probably gone back to Mexico City and forgotten about her. If he had, it was just as well. He was too rich and handsome to waste his time on a simple village girl when the women he usually associated with were so cultivated and elegant.

The telephone rang, and Maria answered it. "Do you know who this is?" a voice asked her.

Of course, she knew. It was Jorge.

"Certainly, *Señor* Rojas." she said.

"*Señor* Rojas?" he said. "I'm not *Señor* Rojas. I'm his son."

"I'm sorry, Jorge. It just slipped out."

"My beautiful Maria. Did you think I'd forgotten you?"

"I didn't think anything. I know that you're busy and hold a very important position."

"I'm never too busy to talk to you, Maria. You've been in my mind constantly since the last time we talked. How are you doing, my beautiful flower?"

"Quite well, thank you. And you?"

"Ah. Very well. Especially now. I'm calling from Mexico City. I'll be in Loma Linda this coming Saturday. I plan to have a small party at my parents' house at about seven o'clock in the evening. If you recall, I mentioned it the other day. Do you think you could find the time to come as my guest?"

Maria could think of nothing she had rather do. But she was frightened. Everyone there would be so sophisticated and would be dressed in the latest fashions. She was afraid she wouldn't fit in. Probably the other women would look at her simple dress and laugh.

"I don't know, Jorge. I've never been to such a nice place before. I'm not sure I would know how to act. I don't want to embarrass you in front of your friends."

"You could never embarrass me, Maria. Everyone there will be green with jealously and envy."

"All right. If you really want me to, I'll go."

"I really do. I'll pick you up at your house at six thirty."

"Thank you, Jorge." Her heart was singing.

"*De nada*," he said. "Don't forget." She held the telephone for a long time after he hung up, and then she hung up, too.

"How could I?" she said.

Caleb Lovett had been staring at the Benson project folder for the better part of the afternoon and didn't have a clue what he was looking at. It was Vicki's fault. She had promised him that her father, Walter Carver, would give him something easy. Well the old son of a bitch sure hadn't. The folder had seventy-three pages in it, and there were rows and columns of numbers on almost every page. It was Lovett's responsibility to write the numbers onto a form and then key them into the computer.

He didn't know why they had to be in the computer. It sounded like so much busy work to him. Hell, they were already in the folder. If anybody wanted to see them, all he had to do was take out the goddamned folder and they were right there in black and white. That made a lot more sense than trying to get them out of the computer as far as Lovett was concerned.

He'd asked his boss, Robert Presser, a pasty faced little fellow who looked like a goddamned fag, why it was necessary to have the information in both places.

"Well, we've just bought a new computer system. As you've no doubt noticed, we're not creating any new paper files. Everything is in the system. What we're doing now is converting the old files. We'll keep the paper files for backup for three years and then destroy them. But the redundancy you were concerned about is really a nonissue."

Lovett felt like saying, Fuck you, asshole, but didn't. Instead, he said, "I see."

Okay, maybe they did need the numbers. But even so, they shouldn't be giving that kind of idiot work to him. They ought to give him a secretary to do shit like that. Copying numbers from a list onto a piece of paper wasn't exactly the kind of work he ought to be doing.

He'd told Vicki he wasn't happy with the job. What he wanted was a selling position. He'd told her about a thousand times he was a lot better at selling than he was at setting at a desk and looking at numbers. She ought to know you can ruin your eyes doing that.

She had talked to old man Carver, and he told her Lovett had to be patient. As soon as he had the information from all of the project files input to the computer, Lovett would be assigned somewhere else.

"And where in hell," Lovett asked her, "is that going to be? Out in one of the warehouses stacking boxes?"

"No honey. It'll be something else. Something better than that."

"I hope so, because I'm just this close to walking away from this goddamned place." He held his thumb and forefinger about an inch apart to show her just how close that was.

"Baby, it'll be different when we get married. He promised me that as soon as we get married, he'll give you a big office all to yourself. He doesn't expect you to make a career doing what you're doing right now. He just wants you to learn some of the details of the business from the bottom up before he promotes you to a management position."

That was another thing bothering Lovett. He wasn't sure he wanted to get married. But she went with the job. Lovett wasn't about to fool himself on that score. She was part of the package.

Vicki wasn't bad-looking in a plain sort of way. She was a little too short and heavy, but he'd seen a whole lot worse. She had a freckled face, a cute little pug nose, big green eyes and red brown hair which hung just below her shoulders. What he liked most, though, were her really big tits.

She was also a great piece of ass. When they were in the sack, she went crazy. She would moan, bite and thrash about, her arms and legs wrapped tightly around him. And when she came, her eyes would glaze over, and she would scream so loudly you could hear her a block away. The first few times he thought she was faking, but he soon came to realize that she wasn't.

He'd have been happier, though, if she were taller and slimmer. It would also be great if she had blonde hair. But he reckoned you can't have everything in this life. At least, when Lovett and Vicki got married, he'd have a soft job and plenty of money. He was sure of that. Old man Carver was so rich it would take a year just to count his petty cash. And, hell, if Lovett wanted a little extra pussy on the side now and then, that wouldn't pose a problem.

Lovett didn't like Robert Presser even a little bit. Just because the fellow had a goddamned college degree, he thought he was real hot shit,

Well Lovett had news for that little son of a bitch. He wasn't going to spend the rest of his life watching Presser strut around giving orders. In fact, he'd already made up his mind what he was going to do as soon as he married and got his promotion. He'd fire that conceited bastard in no time flat. But in the meantime, he'd do what he was told. If they wanted him to punch a bunch of stupid numbers into the computer, that's exactly what he'd do.

He turned his attention back to the pages in front of him and made pretty good progress for a few minutes. Then his mind began drifting, and it was difficult to keep it focused on what he was trying to do. He decided he needed a cup of coffee. Maybe that would give him a caffeine boost and perk him up enough to finish the job. Anyway, it was worth a shot.

He closed the folder, shoved it to the middle of his desk and stood up. He picked up his coffee cup, left his desk and walked slowly to the snack area. When he got there, one of the clerks had already cleaned up the area and put the coffee pot away. Lovett glanced at his watch and was surprised to see it was already four fifteen. He hadn't realized it was so late. Hell, it was almost time to go home.

He rinsed out his cup and placed it, upside down, on a couple of paper towels lying on the counter top where the coffee pot normally sat and then returned to his desk. It was clear he wouldn't be able to do much in the ten or so minutes left in the day so he figured he might as well go home and start out fresh the next morning.

He turned off his computer, picked up the folder from his desk and put it into the safe. Then he grabbed his coat from the hanger behind the desk but didn't bother to put it on. He rode down the elevator carrying his coat folded over his arm, left the Carver Building and walked across the parking lot to his old Taurus and got inside.

Mr. Carver had given him an advance on his salary for the down payment on the car and had cosigned for the loan. But that was no big deal. As far as Lovett was concerned the car wasn't much more than a piece of junk. It didn't make any sense for him to have an old Taurus while Robert Presser was driving around in a Lexus. He guessed he had to be patient, though. After he and Vickie were married awhile he would get something better.

He'd see Vickie in a couple of hours at her parents' house. He'd been invited there for dinner and was expected at seven o'clock. He wasn't all that excited about going, but both her father and mother had insisted. He didn't think it would make sense to piss them off. At least not until he and Vicki were married and he had his promotion.

He had a couple of hours to kill so he decided to go to *Orlando's* for a martini or two. Nobody made better martinis than *Orlando's*. When he got there, the parking lot was almost full. He pulled up near the front door and stopped the car and got out leaving the engine running. A parking attendant said, "Good afternoon, Mr. Lovett" and gave him a little salute.

"Good afternoon, Jerry," Lovett responded. He walked toward the door as the valet got into the Taurus and drove it away. That kind of attention made him feel like a big shot. He liked it. Everyone at *Orlando's* knew who he was. They'd seen him often enough with Vicki and her parents. Apparently, someone had told Orlando that someday Lovett would be the old man's son-in-law.

The place was jammed. Lovett went to the bar and ordered a double martini. It was dry and cold on his tongue. He finished it quickly and ordered another. Just as the bartender delivered it to him, Orlando came into the room and stood beside him.

"Mr. Lovett. Welcome to my establishment. Come with me. We have a beautiful table ready for you."

"Hi, Orlando. Good to see you." They shook hands. "But I'm not going to be eating here this evening. Just a couple of martinis, and then I have to leave. I'm having dinner at the Carvers'."

"Thanks for coming by. Please extend my regards to Mr. and Mrs. Carver. And to Miss Vicki. Oh, yes. Especially the beautiful Miss Vicki."

As Orlando walked away, Lovett stood sipping his drink and feeling important.

Maria showered, put on her makeup and applied just a bit of perfume. She looked at the clock. It was only five thirty. Still an hour before Jorge was due to arrive. That was all right, though. She didn't mind being ready early. It was much better than having to rush around at the last minute.

She left the bathroom and went into the bedroom where her clothes were lying on the bed. Maria hadn't had any trouble deciding what she was going to wear. She had only one nice dress. It was black and sleeveless and had a built-in bra. The dress dipped low in the back, but its neckline was quite modest and cut just low enough to reveal the beginning swell of her breasts. The hemline was slightly above her knees.

She put on a pair of black pantyhose and a black half-slip. Then she pulled the dress over her head and looked into the mirror. Maria was pleased at what she saw. She decided she looked all right. Actually better than all right. She looked good.

She was also going to wear her beautiful wrap. Not that the weather was cold, but Maria thought it would make her look more stylish. She picked it up from the bed and put it around her shoulders. Then she looked into the mirror again.

"Hello, you woman of the world," she said. Her reflection smiled a beautiful smile.

She wished she had a string of pearls to wear with the dress. In many of the stories she read and in the shows she saw on TV, the women almost always wore pearls with their black dresses. Of course, those women didn't live in dusty little villages in Mexico. They lived in large glittering cities like Paris or New York and were usually rich and worldly.

She decided she didn't need pearls, anyway. She would wear the gold chain with a gold cross that she wore every day. Her mother had left it to her. It was much more beautiful than pearls.

She checked her little black handbag to make sure she had her lipstick, blush and a makeup case with a mirror. They were all there as were a few *pesos* which she didn't think she would need. She looked at the clock again. It was five forty-one. It had taken her only eleven minutes to get dressed.

She decided she would read while she waited for Jorge to arrive. She took her *True Love* magazine to the couch and sat down. But even though she did her best, she was unable to get interested in the story she was trying to read.

Maria turned on her TV set but paid no attention to what was showing on the screen. She was thirsty so she went to the refrigerator and got a cold soda. Then she came back to watch the program. It was an adventure show set in Los Angeles. It had originally been filmed in English, but Spanish had been dubbed in. It was disconcerting to watch the actors' mouths as they talked because their lips were not synchronized with the words they were saying.

She watched the program for a while and then began flipping through the other channels. When she couldn't find anything she liked any better, she turned the TV off and picked up her magazine again. It took her a minute or two to find her place. Then, after finishing a page, she had to read it again because she couldn't remember what she had read.

She checked the time, and it was four minutes after six. She turned the TV back on but didn't try to understand what was happening. She just sat watching the action on the screen.

In a few minutes she heard a car drive up. She looked out the window and saw it was Jorge's car. Jorge got out of the vehicle, came to the front door and knocked. Maria waited about fifteen seconds and then went to the door and opened it.

"Ah. My beautiful flower," Jorge said as soon as he saw her. "I hope I'm not too early."

"Good evening, Jorge," she responded. "Of course not. You're exactly on time."

Lovett woke up and looked at the clock. It was already time to get up, but he didn't want to get out of bed. He wanted to go back to sleep. It wasn't because he was tired, though. He just didn't feel like going to the Carver Building and copying a bunch of stupid numbers from a goddamned file.

He knew they made optical readers that would allow the computer to read and input the numbers automatically. He didn't know why the company big shots didn't have sense enough to buy one. If they did, they could get the whole job done in about ten minutes. He'd suggested that to Presser. That little bastard had told Lovett he'd considered that approach and decided it wouldn't be appropriate for that particular application.

That only told Lovett one thing. They didn't want him to use anything that would let him finish his job faster and easier. They just wanted to keep him busy doing grunt work until they could figure out what his permanent assignment was going to be.

Lovett climbed reluctantly out of bed and went to the bathroom. He shaved and showered quickly and went into the kitchen. He couldn't find anything he wanted to eat. There were corn flakes and Cheerios, but he was out of milk. He started to make some coffee but decided against it. It would be a lot easier to go out somewhere for breakfast.

He went to a *Burger King* and ordered an egg and sausage sandwich. A pretty little blonde number took his order. She was tall and slim with a firm round ass and nice big tits. Her hair was sort of tousled, and she had full pink lips and smoky blue eyes; she looked like she was still half asleep. She'd probably been awake all night screwing. Lovett knew if he had something like that in bed with him, she wouldn't get a hell of a lot of sleep. He'd make damned sure of that.

He felt his dick began to stir as he looked at her and decided he wouldn't mind having a piece of that right then. Last night after he'd eaten dinner at the Carvers, he'd tried to get Vicki to go somewhere with him so they could be alone. But for some reason, she hadn't wanted to go. She wanted to stay and visit with her parents. He didn't mind that. Hell, he liked to visit with his parents, too. Christ, everybody does. But it wouldn't have hurt her to have gone with him for a few minutes. How goddamned long does it take to go somewhere and knock off a piece of ass? But that hadn't happened, and he was still a little pissed off about it.

After a couple of minutes, one of the servers set a tray in front of him with his food on it, and he carried it to a table. He took a bite of his sandwich and a sip of the hot coffee. Here he was getting ready to go to a goddamned job he hated so a doughy-faced fag he also hated could be telling him what to do. And while he was hating everything else, there was one more thing he could add to the list. He hated the idea of getting married to a big-titted bitch just because she knew how to screw like a champion and her father was rich. What would old Sammy Norton think if he knew what kind of a predicament Lovett had gotten himself into? He'd probably bust a gut laughing.

Lovett wondered why old Sammy hadn't looked him up. He'd written the son of a bitch a letter and given Sammy his address. He'd called Sammy at his old number, but it was disconnected. He'd even looked for Sammy on the Internet but hadn't been able to locate him. Lovett was quite sure, though, that Sammy had received the letter. It probably had to be forwarded a dozen times, but surely, he'd gotten it. Otherwise, it would have been returned.

Lovett looked at his watch, and it was seven thirty. He was supposed to be to the office by eight. He had time for another cup of coffee. If he was a few minutes late the world wasn't going to come to an end. The numbers would still be in the project folders waiting for him. They weren't about to go anywhere. He refilled his cup and went back to the table.

Why in hell hadn't Vicki been a little warmer toward him after dinner last night? She had acted like she had a chip on her shoulder or something. She was probably trying to act all prim and proper around her parents. She wanted them to think their little girl was still a virgin. Well, Lovett had news for them. She wasn't a virgin, and she hadn't been one when he met her. She knew more about sex than any other woman he'd ever met. And she sure hadn't learned it from reading magazines and going to the movies.

He ought to give her a call and ask her why she hadn't treated him a little nicer. But he'd left his cell phone in his car and didn't feel like getting it. It wasn't worth wasting his time just to ask her why she had been such a goddamned indifferent pain in the ass.

Somebody had left a newspaper lying on a table across the room from where he was sitting. Or maybe the *Burger King* people had put it there. *McDonald's* always seemed to have newspapers for their customers so perhaps *Burger King* was trying to keep up with them. He decided he'd check it out real fast and see if it had anything worth reading. He still had a little time to kill before he had to get to work.

He got the paper and brought it to his table. Then he noticed it was yesterday's paper. He wasn't going to waste his time reading a day-old newspaper. But it really burned his ass that they would leave it out when they knew that no one in his right mind would want to read the damned thing.

Burger King made pretty good coffee. It was only a fast food place and a lot of people liked to made fun of it and pretend they were too good to eat there. Even if the food wasn't of gourmet quality, it was pretty good. A hell of a lot better than some of the food you had to pay five times as much for at more expensive restaurants. And their coffee was a whole lot better than the coffee they served at most places. He decided he'd get one more cup. Anyway, the refills were free.

When he got to the Carver Building, it was a little after eight thirty. He went straight to the file cabinet and took out the Benson folder. Presser saw him come in but didn't say anything about his being late. It was a good thing he didn't. Lovett had had just about all he could take of Mr. Robert Presser.

Lovett saw Presser walking toward his desk and knew that the man was coming to talk to him. Lovett didn't really feel like talking right then. He'd finally figured out what he was supposed to be doing and was making a little headway. Of course, he shouldn't be surprised that Presser had chosen that exact second to come to his desk and interrupt him. His boss was the kind of person who always chose exactly the wrong time to do anything he ever decided to do.

Lovett pretended he didn't see Presser coming. Even when the man sat down by his desk, Lovett ignored him. Presser waited a few seconds for Lovett to acknowledge his presence and then cleared his throat. Lovett looked at him as though he had just that moment seen him and said, "Oh hi, Mr. Presser."

"Hello, Cal. Since today's payday, I thought I'd save you the trouble of picking up your check." He laid an envelope on Lovett's desk.

"Thanks. I had almost forgotten it was payday." He really hadn't. But what else was he supposed to say?

"And by the way. How are you doing on your file conversion project?"

"Fine. I've finally got the hang of it, and I'm converting like crazy."

"Good. Good. Because we really need to finish right away. There are a number of other projects we can't move forward on until we finish this particular phase of the conversion project."

"Well, like I say. I'm converting like crazy."

"Have you had the opportunity to input any of the data, or are you still transcribing?"

"Well, right now I'm still transcribing. It was a pretty slow process at first, but now things are going a lot smoother."

"Okay, we have sixty-seven folders that haven't been processed yet. How many of them have you got transcribed?"

"Actually, not too many because it took me quite a while to get up on the learning curve. But it's going pretty fast now. I think I can get all the data copied in a few more days."

"Okay. Just so we're on the same wavelength, all the data should be on the transfer forms and ready for input by close of business Thursday. That gives us two more days. Actually a bit more because we still have a couple of hours left today. Do you think we can do it?"

"I don't know. Like I say, I just got the hang of it. But now it's moving pretty fast. Yeah, I think so."

"Thanks, Cal. Sounds good. But if it looks like we're going to hit any snags that'll adversely impact that projection, I'll need to know before we go home tonight. The bosses wouldn't be happy, but at least it would give us the opportunity to reevaluate our options. We don't want to give them any last minute surprises."

If the little son of a bitch could set around all afternoon interrupting Lovett's work and calling him Cal, then the least Lovett could do was to call Presser by *his* first name.

"Sure, Robert. I'll keep you up to speed. We don't want to lose the opportunity to reevaluate our options should that become necessary, and we certainly don't want to give our bosses any nasty surprises."

"Good boy," Presser told him and stood up and left. As soon as Presser was gone, Lovett muttered under his breath, "How many goddamned folders have you got transcribed, *Cal*? Well, to tell you the truth, *Robert,* I haven't transcribed a goddamned one."

At four twenty, Lovett finished copying the numbers from the Benson folder onto the data input sheets; he got up and put the folder into the file cabinet. There were sixty-six more to go. There was no way in hell he could finish in two more days. It would take him a lot longer than that just to get the numbers transcribed. He had no idea how long it would take to key them into the computer. In the first place, he wasn't a very good typist. And in the second place, he didn't know the exact procedures to follow or how long it would take him to learn them.

But then he remembered what Presser had told him. He had until Thursday to get the goddamned data written onto the forms. Presser hadn't mentioned any deadline for punching it into the computer. They would have to give him at least another week for that. If he really made an effort, maybe he could get the job done after all.

There wasn't any use in worrying about that shit right then, though. He wanted to get his ass out of there and back home. He wasn't about to start on a new project folder so late in the afternoon. It was only ten minutes until quitting time so he ought to go ahead and split. But if Presser saw him leaving early, he'd probably get all upset. Lovett decided he'd grab a cup of coffee. By the time he finished drinking it, it would be time to go home.

He picked up his cup and started to go back to the snack area, but then he remembered they shut the place down around four or four fifteen. Somebody ought to put a stop to that. What if he wanted work late some night to make sure he got all the files converted by COB Thursday? He wouldn't be able to have any coffee while he was doing it. He figured he ought to go into Presser's office and complain. How in the fuck could he put in any extra hours if there wasn't any coffee?

If that was the way they wanted to operate, it was all right with Lovett. As far as he was concerned, that was their way of telling him they didn't want him to do any extra work. That suited him just fine. They were in charge of the business, and he was nothing but a goddamned peon. When it was time to go home, he wouldn't argue. He'd just wash out his cup and get his ass out of there and go home.

He went into the snack area, and sure enough, everything was cleaned up and ready for the next day. He washed out his cup, put in upside down on the table like he always did, and went back to his desk. The time was four twenty-seven.

He pulled up the games menu on his computer and played a couple of games of solitaire. He lost them and then played one more which he won. By the time he finished the third game, it was four forty-one. He shut down his computer and headed for the door. He hoped Presser saw him. That way he couldn't accuse Lovett of leaving early.

Lovett went by a grocery store and picked up a TV dinner and a six pack of beer and headed for home. He thought he might go out somewhere and see what was going on. Probably not very much on a Tuesday night. Week nights were generally pretty slow. And Tuesday nights were usually the slowest of all. Maybe he could watch some television, but he didn't know what was on.

While he was trying to decide what to do, he saw a Blockbuster store. His problem was solved. He'd just go inside and pick up a movie. He hadn't seen a good movie in quite a while. He pulled into the parking lot, parked his car and went into the store. Right away, he saw *Spider-Man 3*. He picked it up and took it to the checkout counter. He'd seen the two original movies and liked them both. He hoped this one would be as good. He got into his Taurus and headed for home.

When he got there, he had two messages on his answering machine. He laid the TV dinner and DVD on the kitchen table, put the beer in the refrigerator and turned on the answering machine. The first message was from Vicki. She said she was sorry she had neglected him last night, but if he'd give her a call, she would make it up to him. Well, at least she realized what a pain in the ass she had been. As far as Lovett was concerned, that was her way of apologizing. Maybe she could come over to his place, and they could watch the movie together. Or hell, they could even go out for a while, and he could see it another time.

Lovett couldn't believe the next message. It was from Sammy Norton. Lovett had been thinking about old Sammy just that morning.

And now the big son of a bitch had called him. If that wasn't a coincidence, Lovett didn't know what else to call it.

Sammy was on his way to Dallas and was going to be there sometime during the night. He left a cell phone number where he could be reached.

"I'm on my way you mangy son of a bitch," Sammy's voice told Lovett. "Call me if I've got the right number. If I'm talking to somebody else, excuse me, partner. Now, Cal, if you can't get me, keep trying. I doubt if I can find your goddamned place in the middle of the night. I sure as hell don't want to sleep in the car, and I'm too goddamned broke to get a hotel room."

Lovett called the number Sammy had given him, but the telephone was turned off. Well, he'd keep calling. Sammy wasn't going to keep it turned off all night. Hell, he'd be waiting for Lovett to return his call.

Lovett read the cooking directions on his TV dinner and stuck it into the microwave oven. He couldn't get over Sammy's call. He wondered what his old buddy was up to. Sammy probably was working on some kind of a scam. Every time Lovett saw him, Sammy was involved in some kind of a con game. His schemes always seemed like sure fire winners that couldn't fail. A few of them actually made money. Usually, though, something would go wrong, and Sammy had come very close to being thrown into jail on several occasions.

Lovett got a beer from the refrigerator and took a couple of swallows while he waited for the microwave oven to turn off. Then he picked up the telephone and called Sammy's number again. The damned telephone was still turned off. Well, to hell with old Sammy. If he was too dumb to turn on his telephone, that was his problem. Lovett was going to finish dinner before he tried to call Sammy again.

He finished his beer, grabbed another from the refrigerator and got his dinner from the microwave. He started to put the movie into the DVD player but decided not to. He'd wait until he finished eating. Then he'd give Sammy one more call. If Sammy's telephone was still turned off, Lovett would start watching the movie. Anyway, Sammy had Lovett's number. There was no use in wasting the entire night trying to call a telephone that wasn't turned on.

Lovett sat down at the table and began eating his dinner. It wasn't bad. It had turkey covered with some pretty good gravy, corn, potatoes and cherry cobbler. Not the greatest meal in the world, but not the worst, either. He finished his beer and started toward the refrigerator to get another. He'd just stood up when somebody began banging on his door.

Whoever it was, it sounded like the son of a bitch was about to knock the damned thing down.

Lovett went to the door and opened it to see what was going on. Sammy was standing there with a stupid grin on his face. A couple of girls were standing right behind him.

"Surprise!" Sammy said.

"Come in, you dumb son of a bitch," Lovett told him. He held the door open, and Sammy and the girls came inside.

"Come on in. I was just eating something. Sit over there on the couch." One of the girls sat down, but Sammy and the other one remained standing.

"Look here," Sammy said, pointing to the girls. "Have you ever seen any better looking pussy in your life? Of course, you haven't. They're identical twins. This one's April and that one over there's May." Then he said to the girls, "This is Cal, the guy I've been telling you about."

"Hi, girls," Lovett said.

"What you got to eat?" Sammy asked him. "We're hungry as bears."

"To tell you the truth, I don't have much. I had just heated up a TV dinner when you started trying to knock down the door."

"Hell. Let's go somewhere and eat something," Sammy said. Then he asked the girls, "You all want to go out and get something to eat?"

"Sure," April responded.

"Yeah, sure," May echoed.

Sammy went to the table and looked at the dinner Lovett had just begun to eat.

"Throw that garbage in the trash," he suggested. "Hell, let's find a real place that serves real food."

"I know a place that serves really good food," Lovett said. "We can go there. It's pretty goddamned expensive, but that doesn't matter. I have a company credit card."

"Okay. Hell, I was going to treat, but if you want to, that's even better."

Lovett picked up his beer can and drained it. Then he picked up his dinner and threw it into the trash can.

"You got any more of them?" Sammy asked, indicating Lovett's beer.

"Yeah. I have a couple in the refrigerator. Help yourself."

"I've got to use the little girls' room before we go anywhere," one of the girls said. Lovett didn't know whether it was April or May because he already had forgotten which was which.

"Me, too," said the other one. Lovett pointed to the bathroom and said, "Over there," and both girls went inside.

"Hell," Lovett told Sammy. "I've been trying to get in touch with you forever. The last time I heard, you were in Austin. Are you still there?"

"Yep, I still am. And I've got something really good lined up. I'll tell you about it later."

The girls came out of the bathroom, and Sammy said, "I guess I'd better go, too."

"Yeah. Me, too," Lovett told him.

When everyone was ready to leave, Sammy asked Lovett, "What you driving, Cal?"

"Right now, this beat up old Taurus. But I have a good job and plan to buy something better real soon."

"Well, I've got an Expedition. It has plenty of room. Why don't we all go in it?"

"Suits the shit out of me," Lovett said.

When they got in the vehicle, Sammy said, "Okay, you navigate."

"Turn left when you leave the parking lot," Lovett told him. "Then at the first stop sign, you turn left again. I'll tell you where to go from there."

CHAPTER III

Lovett hoped Orlando wouldn't be there that night. He didn't want the word to get back to Mr. Carver that he was seen at *Orlando's* with a couple of girls. It wasn't any of the old man's business what Lovett did on his own time, but it would still be better for him not to know. Lovett led the others inside and gave his name to the hostess. Then he asked her if Orlando was there. He was relieved when she told him Orlando had already gone home and wouldn't be back until the next day.

While they were waiting for their names to be called, the night manager, Mr. Gabriel, recognized Lovett. He came over and said, "Ah, Mr. Lovett. Thank you for coming in tonight. I happen to have a very good table for you and your guests. Please follow me." As they followed him, one of the girls, her eyes wide open in amazement, said, "Wow! Isn't that something?"

Sammy said, "Jesus. Why didn't you tell me you were a VIP?" Lovett just winked at him but didn't answer."

Mr. Gabriel was right about the table. It was beautiful. Of course, all the tables in *Orlando's* were beautiful with white linen tablecloths and centerpieces of fresh cut flowers. The one Gabriel led them to was adjacent to a large window which overlooked a magnificent garden with leafy shade trees, emerald grass and brilliant flowers of every color and hue. A dancing fountain displayed every color of the rainbow. The garden was brightly illuminated by a hundred lights. As Lovett and his visitors watched, two squirrels played tag on a gnarled tree.

"Is this satisfactory, Mr. Lovett?" Mr. Gabriel asked him.

"Yes, thanks. It's great."

"Enjoy your dinner," the man told them and walked away.

They picked up their menus, and Lovett said, "Don't be bashful. Remember, I've got a company credit card."

He'd planned to order a salad, a filet mignon, a baked potato and of course, a martini. But after the royal treatment he was getting, he wondered if he shouldn't order something a bit more exotic. What the hell, he thought, a filet mignon is what I want, and at the risk of being gauche, that's what I'm going to have.

"I'd like the New York strip with a baked potato, and a salad," Sammy said. "I guess I'll drink a Manhattan."

"We're going to take the baked flounder. But we don't want two orders. We'll just ask for two plates and split it. And we want Manhattans, too, just like Sammy," one of the girls said.

"Hell. No need in splitting the flounder. You can each get one," Lovett told her.

"No that's okay. We always do this."

A waiter came to their table and said, "My name is Andrew. I'll be your server tonight. Would you care to order drinks while you're perusing the menu?"

"Sure, why not? And while you're at it, would you bring all of us a large glass of ice water with a slice of lemon?" Lovett said.

"No problem." Andrew waited for them to order their drinks and walked away. A few minutes later he returned with their water and the drinks they had selected.

"Are you ready to order now, or do you need a little more time?"

"Yeah. We're ready," Lovett said.

After they had ordered and Andrew had left, one of the girls said. "Wow, this place is really something."

"I feel foolish asking you this," Lovett said, "but give me some kind of a clue. One of you is April and the other one's May. How do I tell you apart?"

"Well, I'm April. But before we explain that, I would like to tell you something that I think's funny. It's not really a joke. Somebody told me once that it was more of an anecdote than a joke. Of course, it isn't funny to everyone. You've got to have a certain sense of humor to really get it," April said.

"Yeah. I know what she's getting ready to tell you," May told him. "In a way, it's not funny at all, but in another way, it's kind of cute. It's more like an inside thing for me and April. You'll see what I mean when you hear it."

"You can come up with a lot of cute names for twins," April continued. "That's what most people try to do. Well, what about triplets? See, our mom thought we were going to be triplets so she had to come up with three names. That's a little harder than coming up with two names for twins. Of course, it turned out we weren't triplets, after all. So we ended up named April and May. But what other name do you think our mom had decided on? That's the cute part I was telling you about." She paused, and Lovett waited for her to finish her story.

Finally, when he realized she was waiting for him to say something, Lovett said, "Hell, that's easy. If it was a girl, she would have named it June. I don't what she would have named it if it was a boy."

"You know, I don't think she ever considered it might be a boy. At least she never said anything about that. But you're wrong, anyway. She was going to name it March. You know, March, April, and May."

"That doesn't make any sense. March isn't even a name. June is, but March isn't," Lovett said.

"I know. That's what makes it so cute."

"Hell," Sammy said. "It's not cute. It's dumb."

"Mom used to tell us that story when we were little kids," May said. "I think she was just teasing and didn't want us to take it seriously. I guess we still think it's funny because we grew up hearing it from the time we were little kids."

"Okay," Lovett said. "When you put it that way, I can sort of understand what you're saying. There's a lot of things that happened when we were kids that we still like to think about, but they wouldn't mean a thing to somebody else."

"Yes. That's exactly what I was trying to say," April said, "but it's so cute because everybody picks June and nobody picks March."

"Okay," May said, "I'm May. Let me try to tell you how you can tell us apart. A lot of people have trouble with that. But we're really not that much alike when you get to know us. You can tell right away from this beauty mark on the side of my chin. April doesn't have one. But there are other differences, too. Look at my eyes for example, and then look at April's. See, mine are almost the color of the sky, and hers have a little green in them like the ocean. And hers are rounder than mine."

"Bigger, you mean," April interrupted.

"Yeah. I guess they're bigger, too, but not much. Anyway, my hair's longer, but I suppose that doesn't really count because I could get it cut, or she could let hers grow out. My hair's naturally a little lighter, but that doesn't make any difference, either, because you can make your hair any color you want to. Her cheekbones are a little higher, but it's hard to see the difference when we're both wearing makeup. Her mouth is bigger, and her lips are fuller. I don't know. What else, April?"

"I'm taller. Quite a bit taller, in fact. Stand up and he can see." They stood up, and April was about an inch taller.

"Of course, that's not too noticeable, if I'm wearing higher heels than she is," May told him.

"I'm slimmer than she is, but my boobs and butt are about the same as hers," April said.

"Not really. You just look slimmer because you're taller. I think we're about the same."

"Well, I suppose I'll just remember the beauty mark," Lovett said.

"That's the easiest way. But after you get to know us a while, you'll see we're really not all that much alike. Superficially, sure, but basically we're a whole lot different."

"Okay, but in the meantime, I'll remember the beauty mark."

"You're funny," May told him. The waiter returned with their food, and they began eating.

"So, what have you got up your sleeve?" Lovett asked Sammy.

"Right now I'm working the same scam we ran in Memphis. But I'm shutting it down as soon as I get back. Then I have something that sounds real promising, something I've never done before. Hell, Cal, you'd never in a million years guess what it is."

"Probably not. So lay it on me, partner."

"It's a cancer cure machine."

"A cancer cure machine? Shit, Sammy. Nobody's going to fall for a scam like that."

"A lot of people do. They all claim they won't until it happens to them. But when they see themselves wasting away and dying and the doctors not able to help them, hell, Cal, they'll try anything."

"Isn't it awful easy to get your butt in real bad trouble doing something like that?"

"It's just like anything else. You've got to know when to stop. Don't push your luck. Get what you can, and then disappear."

"Oh, that's awful," April said. "Building up those poor people's hope and taking their money when you know you can't help them."

"Hell, the cancer doctors do the same thing. They can't cure them any more than that machine. And they know they can't. But they keep poisoning them with chemo and burning them with radiation and charging them ten times as much as we're going to charge," Sammy said.

"You really think it'll work? You think it's better than our investment business?"

"Yes, I do. Right now, anyway. The SEC is busting its butt trying to stamp out investment schemes like ours. Of course, they'll never catch even ten percent of the people involved. Hell, not even one percent. But the ones they do catch are going to be in big trouble. They'll make an example of those people and throw their asses in jail for fifty years. I plan to steer clear of it as soon as I shut down the one I'm working now. Now, here's what I want to ask you. How would you like to come down and be my partner? You know how well we work together."

"You know, I think that'd be a good idea. I'm getting pretty tired of this goddamned place to tell you the truth. When you going back, anyway?"

"Real soon. A couple of days at the most. I've got to talk to the guy that owns the machine. He told me he'd be ready to let me have it in two or three weeks. He still has one patient he's working on. So I plan to keep my investment business open for two more weeks, maybe a couple of days more than that, and then close it down."

"Are you ready for me now, or do you want to wait until you get the cancer cure contraption?"

"Hell. I'm ready right now if you are"

"You can count me in, partner. My goddamned job sucks. And the boss's daughter thinks she owns me just because I work for her old man. I'm about ready to tell a few people to kiss my ruby red ass."

"All you men do is talk about business," April said.

"You're right," Sammy agreed. "Hell, let's forget about business for a while. I think we should find someplace to party. You know a few places, don't you, Cal?"

"Yeah, I reckon I do at that."

The telephone was ringing, but Lovett didn't feel like getting up to answer it. He and May were sprawled naked across his bed. April was lying on the couch wrapped up in a blanket, and Sammy was asleep in Lovett's recliner. Lovett decided to let the phone keep ringing. The answering machine was set to answer it after five rings.

"Aren't you going to answer that goddamned thing?" Sammy yelled across the room at him.

"I'm going to jerk it out of the goddamned wall. That's what I'm going to do," Lovett answered.

He climbed out of bed and went across the floor. Just as he was ready to pick up the telephone, the answering machine took the call. It was Presser. He sounded mad as hell. He wanted Lovett to call him right away.

Lovett turned around without picking it up and started back toward the bed. "Fuck you, Robert Presser," he said.

Before he got back into bed, the telephone started ringing again.

"I thought you'd unplugged that goddamned thing," Sammy told him.

"Shit. I forgot." He went to the ringing phone and picked it up.

"Hello," he said. It was Vicki. She sounded worried.

"Sweetheart. Mr. Presser has been trying to locate you. Is anything the matter?"

"Is your father there?"

"Yes, why?"

"Would you give him a message for me?"

"Of course, baby. What do you want me to tell him?"

"Tell him that Caleb Lovett said 'fuck you, you dumb son of a bitch.' And I've got one for you, too, sweetheart. Fuck you, you ugly pig." He hung up the phone.

"While I'm on a roll, I might as well make it three for three," he muttered to himself. He picked up the telephone again and rang Presser's number. As soon as Presser answered it, Lovett said. "Hi, *Robert*. This is *Cal.* Go fuck yourself, you goddamned queer."

He unplugged the phone from the wall without bothering to hang it up, pitched it into a corner and went back to bed.

He didn't know how long he'd been asleep when somebody started pounding on the door and woke him up.

"Jesus," May said. "This place is worse than Grand Central Station." The banging continued.

"Whoever it is, run their asses off," Sammy suggested.

April woke up and said, "What's going on? What's all that racket?" She unwrapped herself from the blankets she had been bundled up in and stood up groggily. She was just as naked as May and Lovett were.

"Jesus. Somebody tell them to stop; they're giving me a headache." She headed for the bathroom.

Lovett looked through the peephole, and Vicki and Walter Carver were standing by the door.

Lovett hurried to the bathroom and opened the door. April was sitting on the toilet peeing.

"Hey," she said. "Get out of here. Doesn't anybody have any privacy around this place?"

"Hurry up and finish. We need you out here."

He went back to the door and shouted, "Who is it?" He wanted them to know he was there so they wouldn't leave.

"Goddamn it, Lovett. Open this door."

"Just a minute, sir."

Sammy was looking at Lovett like he was crazy, and May was putting on a pair of panties as fast as she could. Lovett ran over to her. "No. Stay just like you are."

"I'm naked as a jaybird."

"I know. That's the way I want you." He went near the door and yelled, "I'll be right there." Then he went into the bathroom, and April was sitting on the side of the tub, getting ready to put on her panties. He took them out of her hands, and she looked at him like he was out of his mind.

"Come out here a minute," he told her. She shrugged her shoulders and followed him out of the bathroom. Sammy was still sitting in the recliner watching the show.

Lovett walked to the door and motioned for the girls to come to where he was standing. "Come over here," he whispered.

"But there's somebody out there," April protested.

"Yeah. I know. That's what's going to make it so goddamned funny."

The pounding started again. "I don't know what's taking you so long," Carver shouted.

"Open the door," Lovett told the girls.

April giggled and swung the door open wide enough to reveal the three of them. The old man's eyes got big, and he started opening and closing his mouth over and over. No words came out, but he was making *"oh, oh, oh"* sounds.

Vicki just stared for a moment and then turned and ran away.

"Didn't Vicki give you my message?" Lovett asked.

"You. You. You're fired," the old man sputtered. He turned away and followed his daughter out of the building.

Lovett closed the door and the girls burst out laughing. "That old man was really mad," May said. "He's going to have a stroke."

"Was that your girlfriend? She's sort of fat," April said.

Sammy, who had gotten up from the chair while all the excitement was going on, came over to join them. "Shit," he said, "I'm hungry."

"Yeah. Me, too," Lovett told him. "But it's got to be your treat. I imagine my company credit card has just been canceled."

"No sweat. It's my turn anyway. Let's find something to eat and get out of this goddamned town."

"Sounds like a plan to me," Lovett said.

When Jorge and Maria drove up to the Rojas *hacienda*, it looked even more imposing than it did from the village. A dozen cars or more were parked at the edge of the circular driveway in front of the house. Maria knew nothing about automobiles, but all of them were clean and shiny and looked expensive.

"It looks like the guests are already arriving," Jorge laughed. Maria didn't answer him. She was too overwhelmed.

Jorge pressed a button on a garage door opener remote control unit mounted on his automobile's sun visor. One of the garage doors opened, and Jorge drove his car into the garage. He pressed the button again and the door closed behind them. Maria was fascinated. It seemed almost like magic. Of course, the first time she saw a TV set operated by a remote control unit she had felt the same way.

Jorge got out of the car, walked around to the passengers' side and opened Maria's door for her.

"Thank you, *señor*," she said as she got out.

He led her across the garage floor and into the house. As soon as he opened the door to go inside, Maria could hear rock and roll music playing loudly. She sometimes heard the same kind of music on the radio or TV. When she did, she always changed the radio station or TV channel. She preferred to listen to the Mexican music she had grown up with.

They went through the kitchen and into the family room. It was crowded with people laughing and talking. A table on one side of the room was covered with bottles of wine, liquor and mixes. Two big bowls of punch were sitting on the table, one near each end. There were two more tables in the middle of the room loaded with food.

Maria had never seen a place so large and magnificent. For a moment she felt insecure and out of place. What was she doing there? she wondered. What was a poor little peasant girl doing in a place like this?

Jorge looked at her and grinned. "How do you like it?" he asked.

"It's wonderful. It's— It's— It's beyond description."

Before he had a chance to respond, a pretty blonde girl saw him and shouted, "Look. It's Jorge."

It seemed like all the people in the room stopped what they were doing and rushed over to greet him. The girl who had seen Jorge and alerted the others of his arrival was the first to reach him. She threw her arms around his neck and moved her body shamelessly against him. As she kissed him, Maria could see that she was using her tongue as well as her lips.

Jorge was kissing her just as intensely as she was kissing him. The sight embarrassed Maria, and she looked away. In a few moments another girl with large breasts and long legs playfully took the blonde's arm and pulled her away.

"It's my turn now, Eva."

Eva said, "All right, Rosa. But keep it short."

Then she said to Jorge, "Later, Jorge" and walked away.

Rosa grabbed Jorge and kissed him the same way Eva had, and Jorge responded in the same way he'd responded to Eva's kiss. Maria stood watching, feeling foolish. Jorge hadn't yet introduced her to anybody.

A tall handsome man who appeared to be about forty-five came over to where Maria was standing.

"Hello," he said, "I'm Gustavo Villa. I'm a friend of *Señor* Rojas. I don't think we've met."

"My name is Maria," she said. "So you're a friend of Jorge?"

"Yes. And you're the beautiful Maria he's told me so much about."

Jorge disengaged himself from Rosa, saw Gustavo and said, "Oh. There you are. I see that you and Maria have already met."

"Yes," Gustavo answered. "And she's is even more beautiful than you told me she was."

"Maria. *Señor* Villa is my superior. He's done me a great honor by coming here today."

"You must be a very important man," Maria told Gustavo.

"I try to make people believe that," he answered with a smile.

Maria saw Eva watching from across the room. The girl glared at Maria. Her green eyes were cold. Jorge looked toward Eva, and her face lit up with a smile. Still, it seemed to Maria that Eva's eyes didn't change.

Jorge said, "If the two of you'll excuse me for a moment—" and walked away without finishing his sentence. Maria felt a pang of jealously as he went to where Eva was standing.

"Come," Gustavo told her. "Let me fix you something to drink. And let's partake of this marvelous food." He led Maria to the table where the drinks were sitting.

"What'll you have?" he asked her. "They have everything here. Wine, rum, tequila. Everything."

"I think I'll just take a soda."

"Look. They have a blender. I can mix you something cold and mushy."

"Okay. But please don't make it very strong."

"Let me see if I can find something in the refrigerator," Gustavo said. He went to the refrigerator and opened the freezer compartment.

"Ah, ha. Look what I found." He reached into the freezer and took out a can of frozen lemonade.

Maria was looking at him with a puzzled expression on her face. She had no idea what he was doing.

Gustavo laughed. "I'm going to make us some frozen rum daiquiris. You'll like them. I can assure you of that."

He opened the can and dumped its contents into the blender and then filled the empty can with rum which he poured on top of the frozen lemonade. Then he filled the blender with ice cubes from the freezer compartment of the refrigerator, put the top on the blender and pressed a button on its side. Maria watched in fascination as the blender began mixing the concoction.

Gustavo stopped the blender, added some more ice and then started it again. He let it run for a few seconds and then stopped it.

"There's not enough rum," he told her. It's not mixing properly."

"Please don't make it too strong," she said.

"All right. I should add more rum. But since I'm such a nice fellow, I'll use water instead." He filled the lemonade can one quarter full of water, poured it into the mix and turned on the blender again. In less than a minute, the mixture looked smooth and creamy.

Gustavo poured some of it into a wineglass and handed the glass to Maria.

"Taste it," he told her.

She took a tiny sip and liked it. "This is good," she said.

"Of course, it's good. Didn't I promise you that you would like it?"

He filled another glass with the mixture for himself. Then he said to Maria, "Now let's see what they have to eat."

He picked up a plate and handed it to Maria. She looked around for Jorge, but he was nowhere in sight. She was holding her plate in one hand and the drink in the other.

"Let me have that," Gustavo said and took the glass from her hand. The room was so crowded that there was no place in it for him to put their drinks while they served themselves. A set of French doors at the rear of the room opened onto a sundeck. Gustavo took the drinks through the doors and set them on the deck's railing.

He came back to where Maria was standing and picked up a plate. "We can eat on the deck," he told her.

"I don't see Jorge," she said. "Do you know where he is?"

"Oh. You know Jorge. He's around somewhere."

"Maybe with Eva," Maria said.

"Yes, maybe. Or perhaps with Rosa. Perhaps with someone else. You know Jorge. I'm sure he'll show up sooner or later. He always does. Anyway, let's not worry about our host. He's a big boy and can take care of himself. Let's partake of the fabulous food."

Maria wasn't hungry. Her heart ached.

Gustavo began putting food on his plate. Maria did the same, not paying any attention to what she was getting.

When their plates were loaded, they went outside onto the deck. All the chairs were taken so they set their plates on the railing next to where Gustavo had placed the drinks.

A man and woman were sitting at a table a few feet from where Gustavo and Maria were standing. They were leaning forward and looked as though they were intensely inspecting the table's top. Maria watched them idly as she took a bite of her food. The man was putting some white powder on the table's smooth glass top. Maria was shocked. She had seen enough TV shows to know what they were doing.

Maria tugged at Gustavo's sleeve to get his attention. As he turned toward her, the woman she had been watching put something that looked like a short straw into her nose and inhaled, drawing the powder into her nostril.

"Look," Maria said. "They're using cocaine."

"That's stupid." Gustavo said. "Right in plain sight of the whole world."

"I must leave. I can't stay here." She began walking toward the door.

"It'll be all right. I'll tell them to go inside and find a place where they won't be seen."

"No. It *won't* be all right. I must find Jorge. I must go home. I should not have come, Gustavo. I should not be here."

She ran back into the house and hurried through each room but couldn't see Jorge. Gustavo was following her as she searched. He caught her arm.

"Relax, Maria," he said. "I'll take you home if that's what you wish."

"Thank you, Gustavo. But I want to tell Jorge I'm leaving. I don't see him."

A young man who was standing near said, "Oh, *señorita*. Jorge is upstairs."

"Come on, Maria. I'll take you home. I'll come back later and tell him you've gone."

Maria didn't listen. She ran upstairs. She heard Gustavo's footsteps following her, but she paid them no attention. When she got to the top of the stairs, she was standing in a hallway. There were doors the length of the hallway, but they were all closed except one. The open door led into a bathroom. Jorge was behind one of the closed doors, but she had no idea which one.

Maria stood feeling stupid. Her heart was filled with disappointment. Jorge was probably in one of the bedrooms with Eva. She decided she wouldn't bother to tell him she was leaving. She would just ask Gustavo to take her to her house.

The bedroom door closest to her opened. She had a clear view of the bed. Jorge was lying on it naked entangled with a girl who was also naked. Maria couldn't tell who the girl was, but she looked like Eva. Rosa had opened the door. She was standing looking outside as naked as the other two.

Rosa looked at Maria and Gustavo and smiled.

"I knew I heard some little mice creeping around outside the door," she said. "The two of you are welcome to join us."

Maria didn't answer. She turned and fled. The sound of Rosa's laugh followed her.

Gustavo caught up with her at the bottom of the stairs.

"I'll take you home," he told her. "I'll take you anywhere you wish to go."

"Thank you, Gustavo. Please. I would like to go home."

She followed him to his car. When they were inside and driving toward Maria's house, Gustavo said, "We should not let the night go to waste, Maria. It's too young, and you're too beautiful. Let's go somewhere and get better acquainted."

"Thank you, Gustavo, but I'd really like to go home."

"Home it is," he said.

They drove a few minutes, and he said, "I'm so thankful I came tonight. When Jorge told me he was going to introduce me to the most beautiful girl in northern Mexico, I didn't believe him. You know Jorge. You know how he exaggerates."

"He told you I was coming?"

"Of course. He wanted me to meet you. He said you were perfect for me. I think he was right, Maria."

Maria was filled with anger at his words. Jorge had lied to her. He'd never intended for her to go to his house as his *nóvia*. She realized how simple she had been. Jorge had brought her as a present for his superior. She felt like asking Gustavo to take her back to Jorge's house so she could tell Jorge how angry she was. But it wasn't worth the effort.

She directed Gustavo to her house. When they got there, he got out of the car and walked around it and opened her door.

"Could I see you again?" he asked her.

"You're very kind, Gustavo. But I think I'm too young for you. You need someone much more worldly and sophisticated than I."

"Perhaps I can call you?"

"Thank you, Gustavo. I'll let you know."

"I'm sorry Jorge misled you."

"I've always been told that lawyers don't tell the truth. I should've known not to believe him."

"Did he tell you he's a lawyer? He's not a lawyer. He's merely a clerk in my office. Our firm had to hire him because his father is so rich and influential. But even his father's wealth wasn't enough to get him into law school. He does nothing but deliver papers from office to office. As I said before, Maria, I'm sorry he deceived you."

She laughed. "Don't be sorry. I was a very naive girl with stars in my eyes. I'm not sorry he deceived me. I'm glad I found out. I was ready to do something very foolish. Something I'm not yet ready to do."

Maria smiled at him. Then she turned and ran up the sidewalk to her front door. She opened it, turned and waved to Gustavo and went inside her house. Her mother had always told her that experience is the best teacher. Well, she thought, she had certainly learned something tonight. Jorge would never fill a woman's life with love and midnight kisses. He'd bring her nothing but dust and empty dreams.

Sammy turned the sign around and hung it on the door. He and Lovett were closing their business for the last time. Lovett had the bag of checks and was ready to cash them. He'd cashed the checks the last time, five days before, and didn't like the man he'd dealt with, a fellow named Marvin Mercer. Mercer had scrutinized each check very carefully and had refused to take two of them.

"Everyone's trying to run funny checks on me," he complained. "I shouldn't even give you thirty cents anymore. I'm about ready to change it to ten cents, take it or leave it. I might even get out of the goddamned business entirely."

When Lovett asked him why he didn't want the two checks he'd rejected, Mercer told him they didn't look right to him. As Lovett was leaving, Mercer warned him. "Don't ever try to run any funny checks by me, mister. Because, if you do I'll cut your goddamned balls off."

Lovett had started to answer him but didn't know how to respond. He felt like walking over to where Mercer was sitting and kicking his ass across the goddamned room. But he decided not to. He and Sammy needed Mercer to cash one more batch. Besides, the son of a bitch probably had a gun and knew how to use it.

"I don't like your goddamned check casher," Lovett told Sammy. "He only pays thirty percent, and besides that, he has a real shitty attitude. He told me he was about to go to ten percent or maybe get out of the business altogether. How were you able to put up with the son of a bitch all this time?"

"It wasn't the easiest thing in the world. Hell, he was the only one I could find. But, hey. Chill out. As soon as we get rid of the paper you've got in that bag, we won't have to deal with him anymore."

"You know what I've been thinking? If we ever get into this racket again, we should stop accepting checks. Make them bring in cash. Hell, they can cash them easier than we can, and they get one hundred cents on the dollar. That way we'd get to keep all the profit for ourselves."

"Yeah, that's true. But I don't think it would work. People are afraid to just walk up to you and give you a bag full of money. When they give you a check, they feel like they have a little more protection. Anyway, as far as I'm concerned, it's a moot point. Like I said before, I don't plan to get back into it once we close up here."

"When do we see the cancer machine guy?"

"Next week. He wants to use it for a little while longer. Hell, I don't mind having a week with nothing to do." Sammy reached into his pocket and pulled out a card. "Anyway, here's the guy's card." He handed it to Lovett.

Lovett took it and looked at it. The card said *LARRY DANIELS* on the first line. Below that legend was written: *Only Jesus Heals.*

Lovett shook his head and said, "What in hell does that mean, 'Only Jesus Heals'?"

Sammy chuckled. "I asked him the same thing. He said that's for protection. He thinks if he ever gets caught, that'll help him. They won't be able to throw him in jail for practicing medicine illegally."

"He must be pretty stupid. If the cops find him treating somebody with cancer, they'll throw his ass in jail no matter what his card says."

"Yeah, I know. But he thinks it'll help. He'll claim he's a faith healer or some bullshit like that, and he thinks if he ever gets arrested, they might go easier on him," Sammy said.

"Well, I'm afraid he's in for a rude awakening," Lovett chuckled.

"I'm afraid you're right."

"If we're done here, I'll take these checks on over to our friend's place. Once I get the money in my hands, I may kick a little butt just for fun."

"You'd better be careful. He runs around with a real mean crowd. They'd just as soon shoot you as look at you."

"In that case, I'll just leave the dumb son of a bitch alone. Where you going to be when I get back?"

"Come on over to my place. Maybe we'll go out somewhere and celebrate."

"Why don't you try to locate April and May while I'm gone. If we're going to celebrate, we might as well celebrate."

"They're gone. They went to Houston to work in some strip joint."

"Well shit. Okay, I'll see you at your place in an hour or so." Lovett grabbed the bag of checks and went outside and headed toward his car. Just as he got inside, two police cars came into the parking lot and pulled up in front of their business. Two men got out of each car, trotted up to the door and tried to open it. When they discovered it was locked, they began pounding on it.

Lovett got out of his Taurus, locked the doors behind him and went back to the building to see what was going on. When he got there, one of the cops asked him, "What do you want?"

"I have an appointment in a few minutes. They plan to review my portfolio."

"Forget about your portfolio, and go on back home," the cop told him. "This place is closed."

"I don't understand. What's going on?"

"Go home. This is police business," the cop told Lovett.

Lovett figured he might as well leave. He certainly couldn't do anything for Sammy. And besides, if they realized he was Sammy's partner, they would arrest him, too. Damn it, he thought. One minute more, two at the most, and they would've been home free.

He wondered how much longer Sammy would ignore them before he decided to open the door and let them come in. Maybe he figured if he stayed quiet and out of sight, they would go away. Lovett doubted if they would, though. If they had a warrant they would probably give him a few more minutes and then force their way in.

The cops were standing around like they weren't sure what action they should take next. If Sammy thought about it, he could go out the back door and leave while they were making up their minds. He realized that if he'd thought of that, Sammy had, too. Sammy had probably already gone out the back door and left. Lovett wondered why the cops hadn't thought of that probability and gone around to the back themselves. As if they were reading his mind, two of them left the group and hurried around the building.

The back door of Sammy's business opened into an alley. Across the alley, not fifty yards from the door, was the back of a small shopping center. In front of the shopping center, adjacent to the main road, was a taxi stand. That was where Sammy would most likely go.

Lovett drove out of the lot, onto a side road and around to the front of the shopping center. Sure enough, he saw Sammy standing near the taxi stand looking frustrated. Unfortunately for Sammy, there were no taxis in sight. But on the other hand, there were no cops either.

Lovett drove to where Sammy was standing, stopped his car and rolled down his window.

"Need a lift?" he asked.

Sammy got inside. As soon as he was seated, he asked Lovett, "How'd you know I'd be here?"

"Hell, you had to be here or still inside. There wasn't any way I could help you if you were there. So there wasn't any place else to go but here."

As Lovett drove away, Sammy said, "Let's get our asses to your place. They probably don't know where I live, but I don't want to take any chances."

They drove to Lovett's place and went inside.

"Wait for me here," Lovett suggested. "We'll figure out what to do when I get back."

"Man, that was close," Sammy told him.

"I'm not sure we're out of the woods yet."

"Yeah. I think so. Why don't you go ahead and cash those checks. Then come on back here and we'll decide what we ought to do, now."

Lovett drove to Mercer's place. A sign on the door said the business was closed on Wednesdays and Mercer would be back the next day. That didn't bother Lovett. He wondered why somebody would close on Wednesday, the middle of the week. Mercer was probably out robbing widows and orphans on that day. Whatever the reason, it was Mercer's business. Lovett reckoned that the man could close up his place any time he wanted to. He figured he'd go back to his apartment and visit with Sammy for a while. Maybe they could even find someplace to raise some hell before they got started in the cancer curing business.

When Lovett got home, Sammy was on the phone. He finished his call and told Lovett something had come up that could mess up their schedule a bit. A buddy of Sammy's needed him right away. He had to go to Laredo and haul a load of pot to Dallas. He'd be gone for at least a week.

"When you gonna leave?" Lovett wanted to know.

"In the next couple of days. He'll let me know."

"So what do I do? Sit on my butt waiting for you to come back?"

"That would be my recommendation," Sammy said. "Shoot, a short vacation never hurt anybody to my knowledge. Or if you get bored you can always start running the cancer curing business on your own 'til I get back. I've got things lined up so there shouldn't be any problem with you doing that. Right now, though, I think we ought to go out and find a little pussy."

The washing machine stopped, and Maria began removing the clothes from it and putting them in the dryer. It was the last load of the morning. She was glad. It had been a busy morning, and she was tired and hungry. She would take a few minutes to eat her lunch while the load was drying and use the remainder of her break for reading. Then she would spend the afternoon pressing the clothes she had washed that morning, putting them into their plastic coverings, and hanging them, in alphabetical order by the customers' names, on the display hangers.

Maria loved to read. She often fantasized about visiting some of the exciting places she read about and experiencing the adventures of the characters in the story. Sometimes when she went to sleep at night her dreams were a continuation of the stories she had read.

The villagers laughed and shook their heads in amusement. "Ah, that Maria," one of the old women laughed. "What enjoyment can she possibly get from staring at black letters on a white page? How can she see anything of interest or beauty there? What she needs is a hot-blooded young man to get her mind off such foolishness."

"She's just showing off," her companion replied. He was a wizened little fellow with dark wrinkled skin and tobacco stained teeth. "By the time she has a houseful of dirty-faced kids and a husband to cook for, she'll forget all about that silliness. If I were a few years younger, I would be happy to teach her a few things."

"You would have to be at least a hundred years younger, you mangy old goat, to show that girl anything. Just look at the way she's built and how her body moves. She was born knowing more than you'll ever learn."

"You may be right," the old man cackled, "but if I couldn't teach her anything, I would be more than willing to let her teach me."

"Shut up. You're a dirty old man and should not be thinking such thoughts."

Maria started the dryer. Then she picked up her lunch and a *True Love* magazine and took them to a little cubbyhole in the back of the shop. She laid them on a table and went to the coffee pot which she always kept ready and drew out a half cup of coffee. She added three heaping teaspoons of sugar and filled the cup the rest of the way to the top with milk and carried the mixture to the table. She opened a bag and retrieved her lunch, a bean *burrito*, a *tamale* and a little plastic container of crisp lettuce and fresh sliced tomatoes. She placed the food in front of her and opened the magazine to a page marked by a small piece of folded paper. Having accomplished those rituals, she began to eat slowly and to read.

The story took place in the United States. The main character was a young woman named Brenda; her husband's name was Tom. They both were well educated and made large amounts of money. Tom was a surgeon and Brenda was an architect. They had three children, two boys and a girl, all of whom went to private schools. They lived in a large elegant house and both drove expensive cars. They frequently ate out at fine restaurants and had vacations at some of the most exotic places in the world. Yet they were not happy.

Tom was having an affair with one of the nurses at the hospital where he worked, and Brenda had found out. Now she was eyeing a handsome young assistant, twelve years younger than she was, and Maria was afraid Brenda would soon have an affair with him. He was breathtakingly handsome, and Maria could certainly understand how Brenda felt. But that still didn't make it right. She hoped Brenda would wake up and come to her senses. Then maybe she could talk to Tom, and they could work things out. But it didn't look like that was going to happen. Brenda was angry and hurt and was determined to get even.

Maria sighed. She wished Brenda and Tom could realize how lucky they were to have all the wonderful things they had. But life is not like that. Her father had always told her that no matter how much money some people have, they're never happy. The more she read, the more she realized how wise her father had been.

Maria was just getting into her story again when *Señora* Montemayor came back to where she was sitting and said, "Ah, Maria. I see you're reading again."

"Yes, *señora*. I thought I would read for a few minutes before doing the ironing."

"Reading is very good, Maria. I'm not sure the magazine you're reading could be classified as great literature, but all reading exercises and strengthens the mind. I have some very good books at home I think you would like. Tomorrow I'll bring you one. As interesting as your *True Love* magazine is, I think you'll find the books I plan to lend you even more to your liking."

Maria liked the stories of love and passion that she was used to reading and doubted that the dusty old volumes *Señora* Montemayor was planning to bring her would be nearly as interesting. Nevertheless, she answered politely, "Oh, thank you, *señora*. That's so kind of you. I would love to read some of your books."

"I apologize for interrupting your lunch hour," *Señora* Montemayor continued, "but I have something important I would like to discuss with you. The orphanage over in Santa Rosa is getting five little *muchachos* from some of the surrounding villages. In fact, one of them is from right here in Loma Linda. The authorities would like for the boys to spend a few nights here until arrangements can be made to have them picked up. Father José has asked me if I know someone who could take care of them for a few days. Someone whom I could recommend. I immediately thought of you, Maria. Do you think you could do us that little favor?"

"But what about my work here at the laundry? And at *Señor* Montemayor's supermarket?"

"Oh, the *señor* and I have already discussed that. We've agreed that you can take time off from your work and dedicate your total energies toward taking care of the orphans for as long as you're needed. Of course, we would continue to pay you during your time off because you're such a sweet and hard-working girl and also as a favor to Father José. The orphanage would pay you, as well. So you see your act of kindness would not be without its rewards."

"I'm gratified that you have so much confidence in me, *señora*. How many days would the children be with me?"

"Oh, four or five. A week at the most. Then you'll do it, Maria? Can I tell Father José you'll do it?"

"Oh yes. I will. It will be an honor."

"Good. Then you must go straight to your place and make ready. The children will be here tomorrow morning."

"But what about the ironing? There's much ironing to be done this afternoon."

"Hang the ironing. I'll get *Señora* Velasquez to do that. She's as slow as a turtle, but I can make do with her for a week."

"I could finish the ironing and still get ready for the orphans."

"No, that won't be necessary. Now go, you silly girl. A van will deliver the boys to your house at eight o'clock tomorrow morning. You'll have to spend the rest of the afternoon getting ready for them. You'll also have to go shopping for food. Young children eat a lot, especially young boys. Here's some money." She handed Maria a large sheaf of bills. "This is from the church. If you should run out before the boys are gone, be sure to let me know, and I'll get you more."

It was a large amount of money. More than Maria earned in a week. She was sure it would be enough.

"Thank you, *señora*. I assure you I'll spend it very wisely. I'll return all of it I don't need and keep a careful record of everything I buy."

"That won't be necessary, Maria. Father José and I are putting our full trust in you and giving you full authority over handling the money. I'm sure you'll do an excellent job. And don't scrimp. We want the boys to be treated well and to have plenty of nourishing food while they're in Loma Linda. So go now, and get prepared."

"Yes, *señora*. I'll do that. I'll go straight to *Señor* Montemayor's supermarket and begin my shopping."

CHAPTER IV

Sammy and Lovett were sitting in a beer joint in Austin. They had closed their bank account. Lovett was keeping one hundred dollars for himself, and Sammy was taking the rest with him. Lovett didn't figure he *needed* any more than that because he still had the checks. Once he cashed them, he'd have plenty of money.

Sammy's friend had just called him and told him the deal to move the pot had been finalized, and Sammy was needed the next morning.

"Fine," Sammy had told him. "I'm ready to rock and roll."

"Give me a call as soon as you know how long you'll be gone," Lovett told Sammy. "I'll take care of the checks tomorrow and then see the cancer guy."

"Just hang onto the money," Sammy answered. "You'll need it until you get the cancer curing business generating a little revenue. And don't forget. I've already paid for the damned machine, so don't let them tell you any different. Just go ahead and pick it up. Anyway, I'll be back as soon as I can."

"What if he balks when he finds out you're gone? What if he tells me you haven't paid for the damned thing?"

"That won't happen. He's a strange dude. But he won't lie to you. You've heard about a man's word being his bond. Well, that's just not true anymore in most cases. But I know Daniels well enough to know that in his case it is. If he gives you his word, it's as good as gold."

"I hope so," Lovett said.

"Don't worry. I know so," Sammy assured him.

Sammy left Lovett's apartment at ten o'clock the next morning. As soon as he was gone, Lovett got into his car and drove to Mercer's place. He went inside, and Mercer was sitting behind a desk reading a magazine. He saw Lovett come in and motioned him over. Lovett walked over and laid the bag of checks on his desk.

"What you got?" Mercer asked.

"A few checks I need cashed."

"Okay. Let me take a look." He picked up the bag and stood up.

"There's sixty three hundred and thirty-five dollars in there. I've totaled them on a list inside the bag."

Mercer didn't answer or open the bag. He went into a room at the back of the office. In a few minutes, he returned with a different bag which he handed to Lovett. Then he sat down at his desk, picked up the magazine he'd been reading when Lovett came in and continued reading. Lovett opened the bag.

Mercer took his eyes from the magazine and looked at Lovett. "Don't worry," he said. "It's all there. Six hundred thirty-thee dollars and fifty cents."

"Bullshit. That's only ten percent. We agreed on thirty."

"Well, now I'm agreeing on ten, so get your ass out of here, and be thankful for what you've got." Mercer started reading again.

Lovett pitched the bag onto Mercer's desk without taking out any of the money. He'd rather take the checks all the way to Memphis and cash them there than to accept what Mercer was trying to give him. Johnny Igloo would give him fifty percent. It might not save him a hell of a lot because of the long drive, but it would be a hell of a lot better than letting this son of a bitch rob him blind. He'd tear them up into little pieces and flush them down the toilet before he'd give them to Mercer for ten percent.

"Here," he said. "Just give me back the goddamned checks. I'll take them somewhere else."

"You got the money. I got the checks. We already made our transaction. I'm telling you one more time, and I'm not going to tell you again. Take your goddamned money, and get the hell out of my shop."

"I'm telling *you* something one time, and *I'm* not going to say it again. I'm not leaving here without the goddamned checks. If I have to break your fucking neck to get them, that's all right. Because, I swear to God, that's what I'll do."

Mercer reached in front of him, grasped the middle desk drawer handle and began opening the drawer. Instantaneously, Lovett tackled him, driving him to the floor. He got up from on top of Mercer, opened the drawer the rest of the way and looked inside expecting to see a gun. There was nothing there, though, except odds and ends such as paper clips, ballpoint pens, an eraser, several pages from notepads with writing and numbers scribbled on them and other assorted office junk.

"What's wrong with you, you damned maniac?" Mercer asked him, rising slowly from the floor.

"You should know better than to make sudden moves like that. How was I supposed to know what you had in there?"

"This is my office and my desk, you crazy maniac." Mercer had fully regained his feet. He reached into the drawer and took out a roll of Tums. "It's none of your goddamned business what I was trying to get. But here it is. Some goddamned Tums. Now are you satisfied?"

"I'm sorry, but you brought it on yourself. I'm still waiting for the checks."

"Okay. I'll get you the checks. Hell, I've been doing you a favor by taking them at all. You can have the damned things, but forget about ever trying to do business here again."

"Hell. I've forgotten that already."

Mercer led Lovett into the room where he'd taken the checks. A safe was sitting against the back wall. Mercer motioned to a chair and said, "You might as well take a seat and make yourself comfortable. The lock's on a timer, and it takes seven minutes to open it once I dial in the combination. That's why I didn't want to get the damned things back out."

Lovett didn't believe him. It had taken Mercer no more than three minutes to get the money he'd given Lovett for the checks.

"That sounds like a bunch of shit to me. You opened it a while ago in a couple of minutes. How come it's going to take seven minutes, now?"

"Again, it's none of your business. But when you came in, the goddamned safe was open already. Now it's locked. Does that satisfy you? Because if it doesn't I don't give a shit." Mercer knelt down in front of the safe, blocking Lovett's view, and began turning the dial. Then he turned toward Lovett and said, "Come over here and look at the timer. You'll see what I mean."

Lovett went over to see what Mercer wanted to show him. He looked down but didn't see a thing except the dial.

"I don't see any timer," he said.

At that instant, he heard somebody behind him, but before he could turn to see what was happening, something hit the back of his head with such force that he almost collapsed. A second blow struck him. That time he wasn't able to remain on his feet but crumpled to the floor.

"What kept you? The son of a bitch almost killed me," he barely heard Mercer say.

"I'm sorry, boss. We got here as fast as we could."

"Okay. Joe, go over and lock the door. And put up the closed sign. Now, the rest of you grab the son of a bitch and hold him. I'm going to make him sorry he ever saw my face."

"You want us to take him somewhere and finish him off, boss?"

"No," Mercer said. "But we're going to make him *wish* he was dead."

Joe went to lock the door, and three men picked Lovett up and held him, preventing him from falling down. Mercer walked away, and in a few seconds he returned putting on a pair of gloves. Lovett was hanging limply in his captors' arms, unable to support any of his weight and just vaguely aware of what was going on.

"Keep him like that," Mercer told his men. "Keep him standing up."

Then he showed Lovett a wooden box about six inches long, four inches wide and three inches deep. He held it about six inches in front of Lovett's eyes. "Do you know what's in this box?" he asked, his voice almost a shout. "Well, I'll show you." He opened the box. Lovett was just barely aware of what the man was doing and saying. Mercer took out an item that looked like a piece of dried meat.

"It's a tongue. A goddamned human tongue. I cut it out of a son of a bitch ten times meaner than you. And I'm right on the verge of cutting yours out and feeding it to my dog."

Joe said, "You want me to get the knife and metal cutter, Mr. Mercer?"

"No. Not unless the son of a bitch is dumb enough to come back."

Then he brought his right fist around and landed a hard blow to Lovett's belly. It knocked all the air from his lungs, and blackness closed in on him, but he was still conscious. He felt another punch land on his temple and bright lights flashed in his head. Two more blows landed, and he almost lost all awareness of what was going on. He could vaguely hear the voices of the men around him but was unable to remember where he was or what was going on.

He barely saw a man walking toward him carrying a bucket. Lovett watched the fellow dumbly wondering who he was and what he was doing with the bucket. The man held it with one hand on its handle and the other on its bottom rim. When he got close, he brought it up and forward toward Lovett's face. Cold water splashed against his head and streamed down his body, flooding him. It filled his nose and mouth causing him to choke and gasp for air, but it also cleared his head somewhat.

Mercer laughed and said, "Feeling better now, tough guy?" and hit him in the solar plexus. Then he said to one of the men, "Go find a blanket or something. I don't want the son of a bitch bleeding all over the place."

Lovett could feel warm liquid running down his face and realized it was probably blood mingling with the water. In a few minutes, the man whom Mercer had sent away returned with a blanket. As groggy as Lovett was, he wondered how they had managed to find one so fast.

"Put it on the floor and lay him on it," Mercer told the man with the blanket and the ones supporting Lovett. In a few moments Lovett was lying on the floor. Mercer walked around him kicking him several times. Lovett didn't know how many times the man kicked him because he was unconscious after the second blow.

He woke up in a hospital room and looked around. For a while he was confused. He thought he was in Dallas and had just been robbed of the money he'd taken from Mrs. Clawson's purse. But the place looked different. Then he remembered what Mercer and his men had done to him. I'll make that son of a bitch pay for this, he thought groggily before drifting back off to sleep.

Lovett didn't know how long he'd slept, but when he woke up it was dark. He remembered being beat up, but he had no idea how he'd gotten to the hospital. His chest was wrapped tightly in an elastic strip, and the upper half of his head and one side of his face were covered with bandages. He had to pee and wanted to get up and go to the bathroom. When he swung his legs around and off the side of the bed and started to stand up, he discovered he had an IV connected to his arm.

He sat for a moment pondering what he should do. The tube was attached to a bottle hanging from a small portable stand. He turned sideways so he could place both hands on the mattress on the same side of his body and got out of the bed carefully, turning to face it as he did so. He stood for a moment, his hands resting on the mattress for support, while he regained his equilibrium. Then he grasped the stand he was tethered to and went into the restroom pulling the stand in with him.

Lovett looked at himself in the mirror. He could see only the right half of his face. His head and the other side of his face were swathed in bandages. He opened his hospital gown and saw he was wrapped in a tan elastic strip from his neck to his waist. From what he could see, Mercer had done a real good job on him. Well, Lovett had news for that son of a bitch. Marvin Mercer had picked the wrong person to mess around with.

He went slowly back to the bed, situated the IV stand properly and lay down. Just as he got positioned the way he wanted to be, a nurse came into the room.

"Mr. Jones," she said. "Are you awake?"

"Yes. What happened? What time is it?"

"It's twelve fifteen. Would you like to talk to the police?"

"No. Please. Can't it wait until morning?"

"Certainly, if that's what you prefer." She handed him three pills and a glass of water. "Take these," she told him. "They'll help you sleep."

"Thank you," he responded. He put them into his mouth and drank the water she handed him. But he held the pills against his cheek and didn't swallow them. He didn't want to sleep, and he didn't want to talk to the cops. He just wanted to figure out some way to get out of there and go home.

As soon as the nurse left the room, Lovett got out of bed again. He had no idea how he was going to leave without being seen. But he was going to try. He'd just take it one step at a time and hope for the best. The first step was to get the IV out of his arm. He removed the tape holding the needle in place and extracted the needle. Okay, Caleb Lovett, he told himself. That was step number one, and it went off without a hitch. Now it's time for step number two.

Lovett's pants and shirt were lying on a chair, and his shoes and socks were under it. Getting dressed was step number two. He picked up his shirt and trousers and sat down on the chair where they had been lying. Lovett was relieved that his wallet was still in one pocket, and his car keys and a handful of change were in the other.

If he needed to use a pay telephone and was able to locate one, the change would come in handy. He hoped his car was still parked in front of Mercer's place where he'd left it. If he could figure out a way to get there, he'd find out. At least, he wouldn't have to worry about trying to find the keys.

It didn't take him long to get dressed. Hell, if all the steps were going to be as easy as the first two, walking away undetected was going to be a piece of cake. But before he could make any more progress, he had to figure out exactly what his third step was going to be.

A box of surgical gloves was on a table next to the chair he was sitting on. He reached over and took out a handful. He figured they just might come in handy. And since they were free, it would be pretty hard to beat their price.

He hoped he was on the ground floor. If he was, he could just climb out a window, find a telephone somewhere and call a cab unless the windows were sealed shut and couldn't be opened. He went to the window and looked out. It looked like he was about six or seven stories above the ground.

Lovett looked out the door to see if he could figure out the layout of that part of the hospital. The door opened into a hall. To his right, maybe twenty-five feet from where he was standing, he could see one end of the nurses' station. The rest of it was blocked from his view because of the width of the hallway. There was no one in sight. But he knew there were people at the station just beyond his view because he could hear them talking.

To his left, the hall seemed to end at an outside window. But mounted on the ceiling, just before the window, was an exit sign with an arrow pointing to the left. He decided it was time for old Caleb Lovett to do a little exploring. He stepped through the door and shuffled to the end of the hallway.

Sure enough, there was a metal exit door to his left. A sign on the door said FIRE EXIT ONLY. For security purposes, the door could be opened only from the inside. That prevented anyone from gaining access to the floor without going past the nursing station. Lovett went through the door and closed it quietly behind him. In a few minutes he was downstairs in a well lighted parking garage.

If he could find a pay telephone, he could call a taxi. He looked in all directions and couldn't see one nor could he see any signs indicating that there was one in the garage. He began looking into the windows of some of the cars hoping somebody had left a door unlocked and an extra key where he could get it. He knew that people sometimes leave a set behind the sun visor or under the seat or maybe even in the ignition, but he was afraid to try to open any vehicle's doors to see what he could find. It was too easy to set off an alarm, and he didn't want to take any chances. Furthermore, the garage was so well lighted that anyone who happened to be in it could see him clearly.

After a few minutes of looking through windows, he decided he needed to come up with a better plan. He didn't want any security people to see him snooping around. They would just confront him and call the cops. He didn't feel like trying to explain what he was doing there.

A man and a woman came into the garage, got into an automobile, started it and drove away. As the car pulled out of the parking space, the lights swung around toward where Lovett was standing. He had to duck down quickly behind a van to keep from being seen. As soon as the car headed toward the exit and its lights were no longer pointed his way, Lovett stood up again. He decided to leave the garage and see what was outside.

There was an exit door near the stairway he'd come down. He opened it and looked outside. The door opened onto a sidewalk that lay in front of the hospital. He was only a few feet from the building's main entrance. The outdoors parking lot was about one hundred yards away. There were seven handicapped parking spaces against the sidewalk, and one had a vehicle parked in it. The other six were empty.

He decided his best bet was to walk to a main road. Once he did that, he might be able to find a service station or a 7-Eleven with a pay telephone outside, preferably in the shadows well away from the store. Then he could call a taxi and give the driver some cock and bull story. He knew the driver would expect him to explain what he was doing there and what had happened to him.

He'd tell the man he'd been in an automobile accident several days ago. Then, tonight, he and his wife were coming home from visiting his parents. She was driving the car because of his injuries. They had gotten into an argument about her driving. She told him to drive the goddamned car himself. When he got out and began walking around it to take her up on her offer, she drove off and left him there. He waited for about an hour expecting her to return, but she never did. So now he had to take a cab home.

That explanation sounded pretty plausible and would probably work. The driver wouldn't give a shit anyway as long as he got his money for the trip. Now that he had his story figured out, the rest was easy. All he had to do was walk God only knew how many miles without being seen by a nosey cop, find a telephone, make a call and hope a taxi would come and pick him up. He knew he wasn't about to get anything accomplished standing and gazing out of a parking garage door all night. The only way to get to where he was going was to start walking.

Just as he started to leave the garage, someone opened the front door of the hospital and came outside. Lovett stepped back inside and pulled the door almost closed leaving only a small opening to peer through. He decided he'd wait until whoever it was went on about his business and got out of sight. But the man was coming toward Lovett moving slowly and painfully on crutches. It occurred to Lovett he was probably the crippled guy who was parked in the handicapped parking space. It would probably take him a million years to get to his car and drive it away at the rate he was moving.

While he was watching the man's tortured progress, Lovett came up with an idea. He'd just borrow the man's car. The fellow looked so goddamned helpless that Lovett didn't think he'd be able to put up much of a fight. He was happy that he'd had the foresight to get the gloves. He put on a pair as he waited.

Finally the man got to the car. He leaned one crutch against the automobile's back door and used the other one to balance himself. Then, with his free hand, he fished through his pocket searching for his keys. When he retrieved them, he began trying to find the right one to unlock the door.

Lovett opened the parking garage door and began walking toward the crippled man's car at the same time the fellow leaned his crutch against its door. The man was so engrossed in what he was doing that he didn't even notice Lovett's approach. Lovett arrived at the front of the car before the man was able to locate the correct key.

The fellow heard Lovett's footsteps and turned his face toward Lovett and smiled. Lovett stepped off the sidewalk. He wanted to grab the crutch the crippled man was leaning on and snatch it away causing him to fall. But he was afraid that as beat up as he was, he wouldn't be able to do that. Instead, he kicked the lower end of the crutch knocking it out of the man's grip.

Lovett's action accomplished what he wanted it to accomplish. The handicapped man sprawled face down onto the pavement. He lay on the dirty asphalt, arms spreadeagled, grasping the set of keys in his right hand. Lovett put his foot on the man's wrist and leaned over and grabbed the keys away from him. He tried the door and it was still locked. The little fool must have been as dumb as he was crippled. He'd been fucking around with the damned door all night, and it was still locked.

Lovett unlocked the door and got into the car. The man didn't move or utter a sound. Lovett wasn't worried about that. The fellow was right outside the front door of the hospital, and somebody would find him. Actually, he didn't really need to be found. His crutches were right next to him. If he had any spunk at all, he'd grab them, get up and go back into the hospital. Surely, somebody in there could help him find a way to get home.

Lovett didn't take off the gloves. He didn't want to leave any fingerprints. He wasn't sure how to get to Mercer's place where he hoped his car was still parked, because he didn't know exactly where he was. Looking the way he did, he didn't want to stop at a service station and ask. In a few minutes, he saw highway 183 and breathed a sigh of relief. He knew exactly how to get to where he wanted to go.

He was starving when he got home. He couldn't remember the last time he'd eaten. A half loaf of bread was lying on the counter by the sink. He hadn't bothered to close its wrapper right the last time he opened it so it was probably dry and stale. He looked in his refrigerator to see what he could find. Not very much. Only a few slices of cheese and bologna.

He made himself a sandwich using two slices of cheese, two slices of bologna and lots of mustard. It wasn't the greatest feast in the world, but it would have to do until the morning. He usually had Pepsi and beer in the refrigerator, but he didn't have either one. He put some ice into a glass and filled it with water. He'd have to make do with that.

He finished the sandwich and was still hungry. While he was making himself another one, he remembered he had an unopened bag of potato chips in one of the cabinets. He finished fixing the sandwich and opened the chips. They were fresh and crisp and really improved the meal.

When he finished eating, he felt much better. He was tired and sore and ready to go to bed. But first he had to remove the elastic binding from around his chest and the bandages from his head and face. His ribs were tender to his touch, but he didn't think they were broken. His face was blotched and puffy and had several cuts that were crusted with dried blood. His left eye was swollen shut and there was a gash in the eyebrow that had been sewn shut. He figured he'd be as good as new in three or four days.

He stripped to his briefs and got into bed. He went to sleep instantly and didn't wake up until almost noon.

When Lovett got up, he looked into the bathroom mirror and saw a swollen face staring back at him. It wasn't as swollen as it had been when he went to bed. He'd slept like a rock and the rest had been good for him. He was supposed to have a meeting with Larry Daniels that afternoon to see when Daniels could deliver him the cancer cure machine. He didn't feel like he was in any kind of shape to have a meeting. He decided to call the man and see if they could postpone it.

Daniels' card that Sammy had given him was lying on the kitchen counter top against the wall just under the telephone. Lovett called the number on the card.

"God is love," Daniels answered. "Larry Daniels speaking."

"Mr. Daniels. This is Cal Lovett, Sammy's partner."

"Oh. Mr. Lovett. Thanks for returning my call. Something's come up. Would it be terribly inconvenient if I kept the machine for another week?"

Lovett didn't know what the man was talking about. Lovett certainly wasn't returning any call.

"I beg your pardon?" he said.

"I know you were supposed to pick it up today. But if I could keep it another week or so I'd certainly appreciate it. Of course, I'll reimburse you. I'd be happy to pay you a thousand dollars a week for as long as I keep it. It shouldn't be over two weeks, three at the most."

Lovett still didn't know what Daniels was talking about. But whatever it was, it sounded like a good deal, unless it was some kind of a scam. Maybe the son of a bitch planned to keep it three weeks and then not pay Lovett the three thousand dollars. Well, he was way too smart to fall for something like that. Besides, Sammy had assured him Daniels could be trusted. And Sammy wouldn't have told him that unless he was sure.

"Okay. But I'm a little short of cash right now. Do you think I could get the first week of that right away?"

"Sure. That's what I was going to suggest. You want to come on over and pick it up? It's real easy to get to my place. Or we can meet somewhere if that's more convenient."

"Why don't you come over here? I got mugged last night, and I don't feel like going anywhere."

"Oh my Lord," Daniels said. "I'll be right over."

Lovett gave Daniels the directions to his place. As soon as he hung up the telephone, he called a pizza place and ordered a large pepperoni pizza and two cans of Pepsi. He felt like he was about to starve to death.

While he was waiting for the pizza to be delivered, he checked his answering machine to see if he had any messages. He had one. It was from Larry Daniels asking Lovett to call. That was why Daniels had thought Lovett was returning his call. He was glad the man needed to keep the machine for a little longer. He wasn't in any shape to be treating cancer patients until he got a little better.

The pizza delivery man brought him his pizza, and Lovett had just sat down to eat it when he heard a knock at the door. He opened it, and a man was standing there.

"You must be Mr. Lovett. I'm Larry Daniels," the man told him, extending his hand. "Please call me Larry."

"Call me Cal." They shook hands.

"Your face looks terribly bruised. Did you see a doctor?"

"Yeah. He sewed up my eyebrow and sent me home. But he told me it's not as bad as it looks."

"I hope he was right because it looks awful." Daniels was a small man. He was about five foot six and weighed maybe one hundred and thirty-five pounds. He was dressed in a brown suit and brown shoes and was wearing a brown hat. His tie was brown and yellow. He had on black horn-rimmed glasses. Lovett thought he looked like an absent minded professor.

"Come on inside," Lovett said. Daniels came in and sat on the couch.

"We have a darned problem. We have this eighty-seven year old man that just won't die. The doctors gave up on him and gave him a month to live. That was six months ago. His grand kids found us and paid us forty thousand dollars to cure him. We said normally we can guarantee a cure but we couldn't in this case. His doctors had been giving him useless treatments too long, and his health had deteriorated to a point where it would be difficult to save his life. But we would do our best. It looked like the old geezer would die within a day or so, and we would have an easy forty thousand dollars.

"Instead of dying, though, he just keeps getting stronger. Right now, it looks like he might live forever. To make a long story short, I'd like to treat him three more weeks. If he isn't dead by then, I'll just deliver the machine to you and not show up when his next appointment is due."

"Why don't you stop, now? You already have your forty thousand dollars."

"Yeah. But they're still paying me two thousand a week, additional. I can't walk away from that."

"I suppose not. Anyway, three weeks sounds good to me. It's going to take a while for me to get back to one hundred percent."

"Look. I just brought the full amount. Three thousand dollars." He handed Lovett a certified check. "I went ahead and had it certified. It would've been good anyway, but I don't like to do business that way. I'd rather it be certified. You've never seen me before, and you don't know me from Adam."

"I would've taken a personal check. Sammy already told me I could trust you. And Sammy usually knows what he's talking about. I'd offer you a beer or something, but I'm totally out."

"That's okay. There was something else I wanted to talk to you about, but since those muggers got a hold of you, I guess I'll just have to forget it."

"Go ahead and tell me. I'll be as good as new in a few days."

"There's something going on in Old Mexico, but they need a white man that can speak Spanish to pull it off. A month or two ago, a fellow I know asked me if I knew anybody who could speak Spanish and might be interested in doing the job. Well, I didn't know anybody, but when I told Sammy about it, he told me about you. Anyway, I didn't mention it right away because you don't look like you're in any condition to get involved in something like that for a while."

Lovett wondered what could be happening in Mexico that he could help anyone with. His Spanish was passable because he'd grown up in San Antonio around a bunch of Mexican kids. Before he left Texas, he used it in some of his investment schemes when he was dealing with Mexicans. They were so dumb they would buy anything from a white man who could speak Spanish. He never had made much money, though, because they were so poor that if he'd gotten everything they had it wouldn't have been much. Still, he couldn't speak Spanish well enough to run some kind of a scam in Mexico where it was the native language. He wondered what Daniels had in mind.

"What's going on in Mexico?" he asked.

"From what I understand, it's a pretty good arrangement. There's a lot of rich Arabs looking for young *señoritas* to take home with them. They've found a way to get them in Mexico if they pay off the right people. There's an organization that finds them and delivers them to a distribution point. They need an American businessman to act as a go between."

"Does it pay enough to make it worthwhile?"

"I don't know exactly, but I understand it's quite lucrative. And one more thing. All the girls are young and pretty. I've been told you get as much nookie as you can handle. That's one of the perks that goes with the job."

"Lucrative. Now that's a word I like. Where could I find out more about it?"

"You think you might be interested?"

"I would sure like to look into it."

"I'll get back to you. And thanks for letting me hold on to that machine a while longer."

Lovett was feeling much better. Well enough, in fact, to pay a visit to Mr. Marvin Mercer. He'd made up his mind. No son of a bitch was going to treat him the way Mercer had treated him and live to tell about it. Not only had the man almost killed him, he'd robbed him of sixty three hundred and thirty-five dollars. Well, actually only nineteen hundred because they had agreed on thirty percent, but any way you sliced it, it was still a lot of money. But even more than the money, it was the goddamned principle of the thing.

At four o'clock in the afternoon, he drove to the shopping center where Mercer's office was located, parked nearby and went to the front door and peered inside. Mercer was sitting at his desk talking to a young couple. Lovett planned to hang around until the man left and then follow him home. There was a tavern in the same shopping center. He decided it would be the perfect place to wait while he kept Mercer's office under surveillance.

He went back to his car, drove it to the beer joint and parked directly in front. Then he went inside and ordered a beer. He carried it to a booth by a window which afforded him a clear view of Mercer's office. Then he leaned back and began slowly drinking the beer.

He finished that beer and went to the bar to order another. He needed something to munch on so he grabbed a package of peanuts and returned to his booth to continue his vigil. By the time he finished his second beer, it was four thirty-five, and Mercer hadn't yet left. But neither had the couple he'd been conversing with when Lovett looked inside. He figured that as soon as they left, Mercer would close up the place and leave.

He didn't want another beer so he decided to get into his car and wait. It shouldn't be very much longer. As Lovett walked out the door, the couple Mercer had been meeting with emerged from the front door of his office. Lovett watched as they walked to their car and got inside. Then he got into his own and started it. In three or four minutes, Mercer came out and got into a Cadillac DTS, and in a few moments he was driving out of the parking lot.

Lovett followed him for about five miles. Then the man drove into a residential subdivision of large, expensive houses. Lovett had thought Mercer made a lot of money, but he hadn't suspected he was making enough to live in a neighborhood as nice as that.

A construction crew was working behind one of the houses. They had dug a ditch five or six feet deep and three feet wide. It extended from the yard behind the house to a storm drain at the side of the adjoining road. Two men were placing black perforated drainage tile in the bottom of the ditch. Three more were loading wheelbarrows with crushed stone and dumping it over the tile, covering it with about a foot and a half of the material.

Mercer turned his Cadillac into the driveway of the house where the construction was in progress. Lovett pulled over to the curb and watched. The garage door opened, but Mercer didn't drive his automobile into the garage. Instead, he got out of the car and went around to the back where the work was going on. He chatted with one of the men who looked like he was probably the boss and then went through the garage and into the house leaving the garage door open.

Lovett had seen enough. He started his car, pulled away from the curb and drove back to his apartment. It was Tuesday afternoon, and Mercer would be closed the next day. If Mercer would only cooperate, Lovett would do what he planned to do then.

Maria woke with a start when someone yanked aside her covers. Before she could resist or even move, a man was on top of her, holding her in his muscular arms. In a moment, he had her slender body pinned to the bed and was tearing away her nightgown with rough and callused hands. She knew immediately it was *Tío* Juan. The disgusting old man, reeking of tequila and rancid sweat, quickly ripped away her clothing and held her completely naked in his strong arms; her own slim arms were immobile in his vice-like embrace.

In total panic, she realized he was naked, too. She could feel his rigid penis against her belly and knew she was about to be raped. She began screaming for someone to help her but knew it was no use. No one was within hearing distance except the five little *muchachos* in the next room she was taking care of.

She worked her right hand free and began clawing at his face and eyes. She saw a blur of motion and felt his fist strike the side of her face. Waves of darkness threatened to engulf her, but she tried to hold them off. The old man began working his knee between her legs forcing them apart. She resisted with all her strength but wasn't strong enough to stop him.

He covered her mouth with his, and she could hardly breathe. His slobber covered her face. Its stench choked her. Some of it seeped into her mouth tasting putrid and rank. As he was concentrating on trying to enter her, he relaxed his hold slightly. She was able to get both hands loose and frantically began clawing his face again.

All at once, she saw movement by the side of her bed and heard the sound of children crying. She realized that the little boys were standing there, crying loudly, watching what was going on. *Tío* Juan struck out in anger hitting one of the children and knocking him several feet away. The little tyke fell to the floor screaming loudly.

"Get away from me, you filthy little bastards," the old man raved at them. "Get away from me you stinking little devils."

The children didn't move. They just began wailing louder.

He got to his hands and knees relieving Maria of some of his weight and stared at the children balefully. "*Ándale*, scat. You evil little mischief makers."

Maria squirmed free, jumped to her feet and darted out the door. In an instant she was fleeing like a shadow down a dark street, her tiny feet scarcely stirring the dust as she ran. She looked back, but the night was so dark she could see nothing, nor could she hear any sound of pursuit. The rocks cut her feet, and she knew they were bleeding. One foot hit a large stone, and she was sure the force had broken a bone. She tried to keep running but could not. Her injured foot was unable to support her.

She slowed to a walk, barely moving, limping badly. Both feet were on fire. A sharp pain ran from her injured one up the length of her leg to the small of her back. She stopped, turned and listened carefully but could hear nothing and was sure no one was behind her. Suddenly she realized she was on a dark street, in the middle of the night, completely naked. She was overcome with shame. If anybody saw her, she would never be able to salvage her reputation.

It wouldn't do her any good to try to explain. Everyone in Loma Linda would have his or her version of what had happened.

"She always acts so much better than the rest of us," the girls would say, "and all the time she's nothing but a *puta*. Fornicating in the night with that dirty old uncle of hers for a handful of money to buy that cheap jewelry she always flaunts as though it were gold. Gold my *nalgas*. Nothing but cheap brass if you want *my* opinion."

"If she puts out for that old man, she'll put out for anybody," the men would proclaim nodding their heads wisely.

But fortunately, the night was so dark that no one could see her. Even a bat would have become lost in its inky blackness.

She had to get something to wear. She knew everyone on the street but was too embarrassed to knock on anyone's door. She saw a dim light ahead. It looked like it came from *Señora* Lopez's house. *Señora* Lopez was the old fortune teller who lived near the end of the block. Everybody said the old woman was a *bruja,* but Maria didn't believe that. Every time they met on the street, *Señora* Lopez greeted her with a smile; the twinkle in her eyes definitely wasn't witchlike.

Maria limped painfully to the old woman's door and knocked. "Who's there?" a voice demanded.

"It is I. Maria Alicia. Please help me; please let me in," she cried softly.

In a moment the porch light came on catching Maria in its glow.

"Please, turn off the light," she pleaded. "I don't want anybody to see me."

The light went off immediately, and the door opened.

"Come in, baby," *Señora* Lopez said, grabbing Maria by the hand and pulling her inside. "What happened to you, child?"

Inside the house, Maria lost her composure completely and began to cry. Her feet were hurting so badly she could no longer stand. She sat down on the floor and grasped them with her slender hands. Their soles were oozing blood.

"My *Tío* Juan tried to touch me," she was able to get out.

"*Touch* you? Are you telling me that mangy old goat tried to *rape* you? Is that what you're telling me, Maria Alicia?"

"He has crept into my room before, but I've always been able to shoo him away. This time I couldn't make him leave."

The old woman went to a closet, rummaged through it, and emerged in less than a minute holding a bright red robe. "Put this on, little one."

Maria did as she was told as *Señora* Lopez continued, "Stay just where you are while I run you a hot bath. While you're bathing, I'll minister to those graceful little *pies*. Then we'll find you something to wear."

She helped Maria to her feet and began helping her walk toward the bathroom, but the girl protested, "I fear for the safety of the *muchachos*. They aren't safe with him."

"What *muchachos*?"

"I'm taking care of five little orphans. Tomorrow the authorities will pick them up and take them to the orphanage in Santa Rosa. At this moment they're at his mercy."

"Don't worry, *mi hija*," *Señora* Lopez responded grimly. She darted quickly into an adjoining room and returned an instant later carrying a shotgun and a flashlight.

"What are you doing?" Maria asked in a trembling voice.

"You just wait here. I'll be back in a few moments to run that bath for you. But right now I'm going to bring those *muchachos* over here where they'll be safe. I can take care of Juan Guardia. If that old fool tries anything, I'll shoot his *cajones* off."

Then seeing the fear in Maria's face, she added, "Don't be afraid, little one. He has probably passed out by now. Even if he hasn't, he'll know better than to give *Señora* Lopez any trouble. He knows who I am, and he knows I won't put up with his foolishness." She opened the door, and carrying the flashlight and gripping the shotgun tightly, she left the house.

Maria sat on the floor not knowing what to do. She was worried about *Señora* Lopez. She didn't like the idea of her going into the night to face *Tío* Juan alone, but she was even more afraid for the children. There was no telling what her *tío* might do to them. She knew there was nothing for her to do but pray so she crossed herself, bowed her head and said, "Oh, blessed Mother. I beseech thee that no harm come to *Señora* Lopez on her mission to help me and the children. And please protect the *muchachos*. And I beg thee, blessed Virgin, to help *Tío* Juan find his way to a straighter pathway so he may salvage the remainder of his troubled life. Amen." She crossed herself again and felt a bit better.

She examined her feet. They were tender and bleeding. She carefully felt the right one, the one she thought she had broken, and decided it was only badly bruised. In a few days, both would be healed.

She knew now that she would have to leave the village. Actually she had known it for some time but hadn't been able to force herself to accept it. Ever since she was a little girl, *Tío* Juan had looked at her in a manner that made her feel uncomfortable. But she had never been worried because her father had always been around to protect her.

But after her father died, *Tío* Juan had begun hanging around and bothering her. For a while, she could handle his clumsy advances. But he kept getting more and more annoying and demanding, and even before the events of tonight, she was beginning to be just a little afraid. Now she knew she had to go away. Maybe the Virgin Maria would intercede, but Maria wouldn't depend on that. *Papá* had always told her to pray as though everything depended on God, and to work as though everything depended on her.

She hated the idea of walking away from her house before it was sold. She would have to talk to a real estate agent and have him put it on the market for her.

Papá had left her the house when he died, and it was the only thing in the world that she owned. She knew that if she left the village before she sold it, she would never get it back. *Tío* Juan would make sure of that. He knew exactly which local bureaucrats to approach to get the title changed from her name to his. A few *pesos* placed in the right hands would do the trick.

Tio Juan had been very angry when *Papá* had left the house to her. He'd told Maria many times that it should have been his. A woman, especially one so young and naive, had no business owning property. And besides, *Tío* Juan would have taken care of her. Wasn't it a *tío's* duty to take care of his *sobrina?* She knew exactly how he wanted to take care of her. Just the way he'd tried to take care of her tonight. She shuddered as she remembered the feel of his repulsive body against her.

I must get away from him, she thought. But how? Maria was faced with two major problems. She didn't have any money, and she didn't have any place to go. She had never been more than fifty miles from Loma Linda. She knew she couldn't just walk away across the seemingly endless wilderness. She would have to get someone to help her. She knew everyone in the little village. But there wasn't a soul whom she could turn to for help.

Then she had an idea. Tomorrow she would call a real estate agent and put her house on the market. Then maybe she could visit her *Tía* Carla who lived in Los Angeles, California, until the house sold.

Carla wasn't really Maria's *tía.* She had been a close friend of Maria's mother for as long as Maria could remember. She was a widow when Maria was growing up. Shortly after Maria's mother died, Carla married a *Norte Americano* named Bill Davenport and moved to the United States.

Carla and Bill visited Loma Linda once or twice a year. When they did, they always came to see Maria and her father. After Maria's father died, they still came to see her. The last time she had seen them was several months before. They had invited her to come visit them in the United States. Maria had just laughed at the time.

"Look," Carla had told Maria. "Since Alfredo died, you don't have any reason for staying here. There's nothing here for you." Alfredo was Maria's father.

"Loma Linda is my home. I have lived here all my life. But you're right, *Tía* Carla. All the young people are moving away. I don't know yet what I plan to do. I may sell my house and move to one of the large cities. Perhaps, I'll stay here. After I've made that decision, maybe I'll visit you and Bill."

Carla opened her purse and took out a card. "Okay, Maria. I know you need some time to think. This is my business card. It has both my home telephone number and my work number on it. If you would like to visit us sometime, give me a call. And call collect. No kidding. I think you would like it, and I know it would be good for you. We would even lend you money for an airplane ticket."

An airplane ticket wouldn't be of much use to Maria. Probably the nearest airport was in Monterrey. Monterrey was many miles away. What Maria would need was a bus ticket, not an airplane ticket. She wondered if Carla was just being nice or was really serious. Maybe Maria could call her and borrow enough money for a bus ticket to Los Angeles. She would promise to get a job and pay Carla back as soon as she could.

Even though she knew only a few words and phrases in English that she had learned in school, she was sure she could find a job in Los Angeles. Once she had asked Carla if there were any Spanish speaking people there.

"Sure," Carla had responded. "There are places where they don't speak anything else. In some areas of Los Angeles you don't see anybody but Spanish speaking people. There are thousands of people from Mexico, Puerto Rico and South America. But most of them were born in the United States. They spend their whole lives among people who share their language and customs. They have never had a need to learn English or the American ways."

Maria found it hard even to imagine traveling so far away. California wasn't only in another country; it was in another world! She wished she had Carla's card with her. She would like to hold it in her hand and look at the phone numbers. She would have to get it tomorrow when she went back home. She began to feel a touch of excitement. Just maybe she could call Carla and find out if it were really possible for her to leave Loma Linda.

She wondered what was happening up the street in her dwelling. She hoped *Tío* Juan wasn't giving *Señora* Lopez any trouble. Probably not, she decided. If the sight of the older woman's determined face wasn't enough to intimidate him, the shotgun she was carrying certainly was.

Maria got slowly to her feet, went to a window by the front door and peered outside. The night was so dark she could see nothing except a few lights shining through the windows of some of the houses. One of the places so illuminated was her little abode. As she watched, the door to her place opened, and *Señora* Lopez, holding the flashlight in front of her, came outside leading the five little boys. The six of them came marching up the street together.

Maria opened the door and waited for them to arrive. When they came inside, she noticed that the little boys' faces were smeared with tears.

"Come, boys," *Señora* Lopez told them. "Follow me." Then she said to Maria, "Wait right there. I'll put some quilts and blankets on the floor for them. They'll be fine." She herded the boys into an adjoining room.

She returned in about five minutes. "Don't worry about the *muchachos*. They're young and resilient. They'll sleep like babies tonight and will be in excellent condition tomorrow."

"Thank you, *señora*. I'm so grateful. Tell me. What happened at my *casa?*"

"Nothing. He was as gentle as a lamb. I started to run him off but decided it wasn't worth the trouble since you and the *muchachos* are spending the night here. But I warned him he'd better be gone by early tomorrow morning. That wasn't just an empty threat, and I made sure he knew that. I told him if he ever tries to touch you again, I'll shoot his balls off. If that doesn't stop him, I know people at the police station who would be happy to throw him in jail for me. But if he's not afraid of the police and doesn't mind spending some time in jail, I have friends who are much meaner than the police. Friends who would enjoy nothing more than cutting him into tiny little pieces and feeding him to the buzzards."

"*Señora*, you didn't tell him all that!"

"*Si, mi hija, a*nd he knows me. He knows that every word I told him is true. We'll take these *chicos* back to your house tomorrow. I'll go with you to make sure he's gone. I'll have a friend of mine put secure locks on your doors and windows so he can't get in. But after what I told him, I'm sure he won't even try. If he does, I'll have some of my friends talk to him. It'll take only one little conversation for them to make their point.

"But that's enough idle chatter. Now that the children are settled in for the night, we must get you into a nice hot bath."

CHAPTER V

Maria's feet were bruised and painful. It was difficult for her to walk or even stand. *Señora* Lopez went to Maria's house and picked up some clothes and shoes for her. The older woman put them into a paper bag so none of the curious neighbors would know what she was carrying, and took them back to her house where Maria and the children were waiting. Maria got dressed. Her feet felt a little better after she put on her shoes but not much. Then Maria, *Señora* Lopez and the *muchachos* began their promenade down the street to Maria's house. When they got there, some men were hard at work installing locks on Maria's windows and doors.

Señora Lopez called one of the men over. "Fausto," she said, "this is *Señorita* Guardia. She's the owner of the house. Maria, meet Fausto Garza. He's the best carpenter and handyman in Loma Linda."

"*Señorita*," Fausto told her, "we've fixed the windows and doors so the devil himself can't enter without your invitation. Before we did our work, a blind man with the brains of a donkey could have entered with no trouble at all. A house without secure locks on its windows and doors is an open invitation to any burglar or other assorted riff-raff who may happen to pass by. It's not safe for a young woman to be in a house which has unsatisfactory locks."

"I'm very pleased to meet you Fausto, and thank you so much. Tell me how much I owe you so I can pay you for your work."

Fausto told her the amount. "All right," she told him. "Be here at two o'clock, and I'll have your money. I have to get it from my employer because I never keep money in the house." Actually she did have a few *pesos* hidden away, more than enough for him. Further, the people from the orphanage would pay her for taking care of the *muchachos* when they picked them up, and that should happen well before two o'clock. Still, it didn't bother her to tell him that little white lie. Even though she was a truthful girl, she didn't think it was wise to let people know that she kept any money in the house or that she was expecting more. Word gets around quickly in a small village, and there are always people more than willing to relieve anyone of any money that he or she may have stashed away.

After *Señora* Lopez and Fausto left, Maria played games with the children. Their favorite was hide and seek. It was amazing how many tiny little nooks and crannies they were able to find to hide in. When they were tired of that game, she taught them blind man's bluff. She was having as much enjoyment as they were as they ran laughing and squealing through the house. She had never seen little boys have so much fun before. Finally they grew tired and hungry, and she knew it was time to fix them something to eat.

When lunch was over, Maria had them help her carry the dishes to the sink and wipe off the table top. Then she had them sit down and gave them pencils and drawing paper she had purchased at *Señor* Montemayor's store.

"What shall we draw, *señorita?*" one of the boys asked her.

"You may draw whatever you like."

"Can we keep our pictures?" another little tyke wanted to know.

"Of course, you can."

"Good," he said. "I want to keep mine because I like to have pretty things."

"What are you going to draw that's so pretty?"

"Why, you, *señorita.* I'm going to draw you. Because you're the prettiest thing I've ever seen, and I want to keep a picture of you forever."

"I want to draw you, too," the first boy said. "Is it all right if I draw you, too?" he asked her.

"Sure, if that's what you want to do," she said smiling.

So suddenly it was unanimous. All the children would draw *Señorita* Maria and would keep the pictures forever.

It was twelve thirty and time for the van from the orphanage to arrive. Maria called the boys into the living room and told them, "I've loved having you gentlemen here as my guests. But now it's time for you to go to your new home. I'm sure you'll like it there, and I'm sure everyone there will like you and take good care of you. Now, I have a little present for you."

She opened a box and took out five packages beautifully wrapped in red paper with a blue bow attached. Each package contained a coloring book and a box of crayons. Maria had asked *Señora* Montemayor if the boys would be allowed to keep them at the orphanage. The *señora*, in turn, had consulted with Father José who assured her they could indeed keep them.

The boys were very excited about their gifts and wanted to open them right away.

"Can we, please, *señorita?*" they begged.

"Sure," she laughed. But you won't have time to use them here. The van to take you to your new home will be here any minute."

She went to a window and looked outside, and sure enough, a minivan was coming up the road toward her house. She was certain it was the vehicle from the orphanage. There were no vehicles so new and shiny in the entire village. It pulled up in front of Maria's house and parked. A uniformed driver got out, came to the front door and knocked. Maria opened the door.

"*Señorita* Guardia?" he asked her.

"Yes. I am she. You must be from the orphanage."

"Yes, that's where I'm from. My name is *Señor* Montoya." He had an identification tag clipped to the lapel of his uniform jacket. He touched it importantly and continued, "This is my identification. I'm employed by the orphanage as this badge clearly indicates. I trust you have the five young men who have been entrusted to your care?"

Maria smiled. "They're here. But they're hardly young men. Just barely boys. I would almost classify them as babies."

"Whatever you say, *señorita*. Once I've verified that they're here and ready to travel, I'm authorized to present you with your compensation."

"Wait here for just a moment, *por favor*." She went into the kitchen where the boys were sitting, and in a moment she returned with them in tow.

"Very good," *Señor* Montoya said. "Very good, indeed. There are five, just as my documents say there should be. All right. Here is your fee." He handed her a sealed envelope with her name printed on it.

"Let's go, gentlemen," he told the boys.

Maria followed him as he led the orphans to the waiting minivan. She hugged and kissed each of the little fellows and watched them climb into the vehicle. When they were inside, the driver said "*Gracias, señorita*," got into the van and drove away. As she stood watching it go, the boys turned in their seats and began waving. She stood waving back until the van was out of sight. Then she went inside the house, opened the envelope and counted the money.

It was exactly what they had agreed on. She extracted enough money to pay Fausto and put it into her pocket so she would have it handy when he came to collect. Tomorrow morning she would go back to washing and ironing clothes in *Señora* Montemayor's laundry, and cleaning *Señor* Montemayor's supermarket three nights a week after it was closed. But the rest of the day belonged to her. She could do whatever she pleased.

First, of course, she would straighten up after the *muchachos.* That wouldn't take long because she had tried to keep the place in pretty good shape while they were there. After that, it would be nice to take a leisurely walk around the plaza, but her feet hurt too badly for that. Probably she would spend the day reading. *Señora* Montemayor had brought her a copy of *Little Women* which she had begun reading not expecting to like it. After a few pages, she had decided it was much better than her *True Love* Magazine.

She thought it would be a good idea to soak her feet in hot water while she read, so she got a galvanized tub from her back porch and placed it in front of the couch. She used a bucket to fill the tub with water from her hot water faucet.

When the tub was full, she decided she might as well indulge herself so she opened a package of Epsom salts and poured its contents into the steaming liquid. She tempered the mixture with cold water, but not too much. She wanted the solution to be as hot as her feet could stand without hurting them more. She put a snow-white towel on the couch to dry off her feet when she took them out of the water. In a few minutes, she was comfortably seated, soaking her feet and reading *Little Women.*

She was becoming immersed in the story when there was a knock at the door. She walked gingerly across the floor to answer it, and it was Fausto. She paid him the amount they had agreed on, and he thanked her profusely and left. She went back to the couch and began to read again.

The real estate office where *Señor* Pablo Soto worked was no more than two kilometers from Maria's house. Normally, Maria could have walked there easily. Now, she was afraid to attempt the journey on her injured feet. In fact, they had bothered her so much that *Señora* Montemayor had noticed Maria was limping that morning as she tried to do her work.

"What happened?" *Señora* Montemayor had asked her.

"I'm afraid I sprained my ankle," Maria had answered.

"Well, go home, Maria. On second thought, I will take you in my automobile. You must stay off your feet. It takes a bad sprain like that a long time to heal."

While they were on their way to Maria's house, Maria had told *Señora* Montemayor she was thinking of putting her house up for sale. After telling Maria how sorry she and her husband would be to see Maria leave the village, the *señora* had given Maria the telephone number of a real estate agent.

"His name is *Señor* Pablo Soto," *Señora* Montemayor had told her. "He's a very good agent. I'm sure he can sell your house for you. As much as we would hate to see you leave, we realize Loma Linda has nothing to offer a young person."

Maria dialed the number the *señora* had given her. After several rings, a woman's voice said, "*Bueno?*"

"My name is Maria Alicia Guardia," Maria told her. "Could I please speak to *Señor* Pablo Soto?"

"Certainly. I'll get *Señor* Soto immediately."

In a few moments, a man came onto the line. This is Pablo Soto," he said. "Can I be of help?"

"Yes, *señor*," I wish to sell my house."

"Tell me where it's located. I'll be right there."

"You don't need any more information before you come?"

"No, *señorita*. Just tell me how to get there."

She hung up the telephone and waited for Soto to come. In less than five minutes a car came down the road and stopped in front of her house. A short heavy-set man got out. Maria walked gingerly to the front door to let him in. He opened the gate, came to the door where Maria was waiting, and knocked. Maria opened the door.

"*Señorita* Guardia?" he asked.

"Yes. I'm Maria Guardia."

"I'm Pablo Soto." They shook hands. "Please call me Pablo," he said. "And may I call you Maria?"

"If you wish, *señor*."

"Pablo," he said. "Pablo, *por favor*. Now, Maria. Is this the house you wish to sell?"

"Yes, it is. Do you think you can help me?"

"Do you have a husband? A father, perhaps?"

"No, *señor*. My father is dead."

"I'm sorry, Maria. Of course, I can sell your house. Of course, I can. It's quite unusual to see a beautiful young girl with a house to sell. Unusual indeed. Has anyone told you how much we should ask for it?"

"No, *señor*. I thought perhaps you could help me establish a price."

"How did you acquire it?" Soto asked. Maria wondered why he needed to know that. What difference did it make how she had acquired it? Nevertheless, she answered him courteously, "My father left it to me, *señor*."

"Oh, I see. Well, Maria. Let's take a look at your house. You wait right here. First, I wish to walk around it and see how it looks from the outside." He opened the door. "I'll be right back," he told her.

Maria started to follow him so she could answer any questions he might have, but her feet were aching, and she didn't feel like walking. She decided that if he needed any information from her, he could ask when he got back inside.

Maria sat on the couch and waited. In a few minutes, Soto knocked on the door. Maria opened it, and he came back inside. He walked slowly from room to room. Every time he entered a room, he studied it carefully and said, "Hmm."

He opened the kitchen cabinet doors, looked inside and said, "Hmm." He turned on the faucet and said, "Hmm" again. He proceeded through the entire house saying, "Hmm" every time he observed something. After he'd finished inspecting the house, he said to Maria, "This is a very nice house. We'll have no trouble selling it."

"Oh, thank you," Maria responded. "I'm so happy to hear that."

"But first, you must get a copy of the official deed and have it certified. My company must be certain the house is registered in your name. It's not often a young girl owns a house like this. Generally, they have a father, a husband, perhaps even a brother or an uncle to give them guidance."

Maria had already told him that her father had left the house to her. She didn't think it was necessary to tell him again. Instead, she said, "I'll get the necessary papers as soon as I can and bring them to your office."

"Thank you, Maria. It's a very nice house. I should have no trouble selling it. Don't forget to ask for me when you bring the papers."

"Of course not, *Señor* Soto. I'll take the papers directly to you."

Pablo Soto went to his car and drove away.

It was exactly twelve o'clock noon when Lovett parked the stolen car he was driving and watched the construction crew working behind Mercer's house. They had finished laying the drainage tile in the ditch Lovett had seen the day before and had covered it with crushed stone. Two men were placing black plastic sheeting over the stone. A truck filled with dirt was waiting to dump the load into the ditch as soon as the men in it completed what they were doing and got out of the way.

Lovett was quite sure Mercer was home because the garage door was open and he could see the man's Cadillac parked inside. He looked around the neighborhood. The houses sat on large lots, probably an acre or so in size, and were surrounded by mature trees; the lawns were thick, green and well maintained. Most of the vehicles sitting beside the curbs and in the driveways were luxury cars and SUVs. Two Lincoln Navigators were parked in front of one of the houses. Most of the vehicles were probably parked inside. All of the houses had two or three car garages.

A couple of minutes after Lovett parked the car, the workers who were covering the crushed stone clambered out of the ditch and stood at its edge waiting for the rest of the crew to finish what they were doing. One by one, the other men stopped working, too, and came over to join their companions. At about five minutes after twelve, they all climbed into a couple of trucks and left, apparently for lunch.

Lovett got out of the car and walked across the back yard to the work site. He looked exactly like the men who had just left. He was dressed in dirty blue jeans, a large red and black cotton shirt and steel toed work boots and wore a yellow hard hat and yellow vinyl gloves. He'd smeared some black grease across his face and was wearing sunglasses and carrying a large wrench in his right hand.

He walked to the back door and knocked. Mercer opened it. Lovett hoped the man wouldn't recognize him because if he did it would make it more difficult for Lovett to execute his plan.

"Yes?" Mercer said.

Lovett said in a hoarse whisper which he hoped would disguise his voice, "We've cut a power line. We need to find your fuse box."

Mercer stared at Lovett as though he was trying to figure out what he was talking about.

"Hurry. It's about to burn out your wires," Lovett said, trying to keep his voice hoarse and raspy.

Mercer, still looking bewildered, turned to lead Lovett to the electric power box. The moment the man's back was turned, Lovett kicked the door shut with the back of his foot and swung the wrench he was holding with all his strength. It caught Mercer squarely on his temple, and the man collapsed to the floor. Lovett stuck the handle of the wrench through a loop on the side of his jeans and let it dangle there. Then he quickly bent down, grasped the unconscious man under his armpits, picked him up, dragged him a few feet to a recliner and placed him in it. He leaned the recliner back enough so Mercer lay still and was in no danger of falling out.

Having accomplished that chore, Lovett removed the work glove from his right hand. It would be too cumbersome to finish the rest of his work wearing it. He still had on a thin surgical glove to prevent him from leaving any fingerprints or getting powder burns on his hand. Then he extracted a large caliber pistol from beneath his shirt and placed it in Mercer's right hand carefully positioning the latter's fingers and thumb in a grip around the handle and his forefinger on the trigger. He brought Mercer's hand and the gun up to where the end of the barrel was against the man's temple. At that point, he was ready to put the final touches on his job.

But then he changed his mind. The sound of the shot would possibly be loud enough to be heard by neighbors. Lovett placed Mercer's hand, still limply holding the gun, in the man's lap. Then he went to the bathroom and found a bath towel. He returned to the chair and wrapped the towel around Mercer's hand and the gun. He worked his own hand inside the wrapping positioning his trigger finger so it could control his victim's. Then he brought the gun back up to Mercer's temple and fired.

The powerful explosion accomplished what he hoped it would. Blood, brain tissue, bone fragments and hair splattered the chair, the floor and a wall about seven feet away. It had certainly destroyed any evidence of the damage the wrench had inflicted to Mercer's temple. Lovett was happy with the results. The whole operation had taken about two minutes.

He'd like to search the house to see if he could find any money but knew it would be too dangerous to do that. He'd done what he'd come to do. He was ready to put his work glove back on and leave when he saw a plastic bag on the floor next to the chair where Mercer was lying.

He picked it up and looked inside. It contained a big white envelope and a small wooden box. Lovett took out the envelope and opened it; it was stuffed full of large bills. He stuck it into his rear pocket.

He recognized the box. It was the one that contained the object Mercer had claimed was a human tongue. He decided he might as well take it with him, too. The son of a bitch lying on the chair sure didn't need it anymore.

Lovett went through the back door and toward the stolen car. A rabbit was in the yard watching him. It hopped about twenty or thirty yards away and then stopped and looked around, whiskers twitching. Lovett crossed the street, got into the car and drove away. He was pleased with how smoothly the job had gone. Mercer's death would be listed as a suicide. There was no way on earth the cops could come to any other conclusion. They wouldn't even be suspicious. Lovett was a perfectionist and had made damned sure he hadn't left any loose ends. Loose ends have a tendency to unravel. The old saying that an ounce of prevention is worth a pound of cure certainly applied to the present situation.

He was hungry but didn't relish the idea of eating at a *McDonald's*. It didn't make sense to eat in a hamburger joint when he had enough money to go to the fanciest steak house in Austin and order the most expensive steak on the menu. There was a place called *Charlie's Steak House* that served excellent steaks. It was about five miles away, and he could get there in less than ten minutes. But it would be pretty stupid to go anywhere until he got rid of the car he was driving. He'd park it, get his own car and go to *Charlie's Steak House* in it. That would take ten minutes, fifteen at the most. He wasn't going to starve to death in ten or fifteen minutes.

He made a left turn and headed to where his automobile was parked. He'd driven maybe a half block when he heard a siren and saw flashing lights in his rearview mirror. He reached under his front seat, took out his pistol and laid it on the seat beside him. A dirty sweater was lying on the seat, and he pulled it over the pistol concealing it. He just wanted the gun handy; he wouldn't use it unless he had to. He moved to the left side of the road and slowed to a stop hoping the police car would go around him. It didn't pass him but pulled up right behind him and stopped. He gripped the steering wheel with sweaty hands and closed his eyes.

The cruiser's siren stopped wailing, and then its horn began sounding. Lovett put his hand under the sweater and grasped the gun's handle, his finger on the trigger. He sat that way waiting to see what the policeman was going to do. That son of a bitch didn't know how close he was from being blown away.

The officer got out of the car and ran to Lovett's window. Lovett watched the man approach in the rearview mirror. It seemed that he was seeing everything through a rosy haze. He was glad his window was down. He wouldn't have had the strength to press the button to open it.

"Move your car," the policeman shouted. "You're blocking the road!"

Lovett didn't know what the man was talking about and just stared at him dumbly. He was ready to bring out the gun and fire. But then he realized the cop was just telling him to move the car.

"Move. Get out of the way," the policeman shouted and turned and ran back toward his car.

Completely befuddled, Lovett pulled forward. The police car moved forward, too, siren screaming, and when it got to the spot where Lovett had been stopped, it made a left turn. Only then did Lovett realize what had happened. When he stopped, he'd blocked off the road that emergency vehicles use for crossing the median strips and making U-turns.

Lovett was glad he hadn't had to kill the son of a bitch. He breathed a deep sigh of relief and drove to where his car was parked. A few minutes later he was on his way to *Charlie's Steak House*.

Maria put some hot water into her tub. In a few minutes she was sitting on the couch soaking her feet and reading *Little Women*. She was glad *Señora* Montemayor had given her the book. It was very interesting. She had barely got seated when there was a knock at her door. She wondered who it could be. Perhaps *Señora* Montemayor needed her back at the laundry after all. Maybe *Señora* Velasquez wasn't able to work fast enough. After all, she was old and moved quite slowly.

Maria took her feet from the tub, dried them hastily and moved slowly to the door. Peering through the door's small window, she saw Andres Gonzalez, a young man who never worked as far as Maria could tell but always seemed to have plenty of money. She wasn't acquainted with him but had been told that he was a hoodlum who was always in trouble with the police and was just as well left alone. Parked in the street in front of her house was a dilapidated old automobile which she assumed was his.

She didn't know whether she should open the door, but it was broad daylight so she felt like no harm could come from finding what he was there for. She released the deadbolt and opened the door slightly.

"What is it? What do you want?" she demanded.

"*Señorita*," he said, "I'm afraid I'm the bearer of dreadful news. May I please enter for just a moment?"

"That won't be necessary, Andres. You can state your business from where you're standing," she responded.

"Very well, *señorita*. It's your *Tío* Juan. Something terrible has happened."

"What is it, Andres? What are you telling me?"

"I'm afraid he's dead, *señorita*. Someone murdered him, and the police think it's you. They're on their way here now to take you to the police station for questioning."

"Andres. That can't be. There must be a mistake!"

She felt weak; her legs trembled. She was upset and angry at her *tío* for what he'd tried to do to her, but she didn't want anyone to kill him. Perhaps *Señora* Lopez was responsible. But no, that couldn't be. Maybe, when Maria's *Tío* Juan had tried to rape her, the older woman could have done it in anger, but not now after so much time had passed.

"I wish it were a mistake, *señorita*. But unfortunately, it's true. Of that I'm certain."

"But why do they think it was I?" she was barely able to get the words out. "Everybody knows I couldn't do anything like that."

"*I'm* not accusing you, *señorita*. The accusers are the police. Please forgive me for what I'm about to tell you, but I'm only repeating what the police are saying. They say you fled totally naked from this house two nights ago, and you were fleeing from your *tío*. They say you killed him because of your anger and shame. If you'll forgive my observation, *señorita*, your feet are badly bruised. Such bruises could hardly be avoided by one running barefoot down a rocky road on a dark night."

"Why are you telling me this? If the police are on their way, what can I do? I certainly can't run away across the prairie. Besides, I'm innocent, and I'm sure the truth will be revealed."

"*Señorita*. Again I ask your forgiveness. Don't you see that the truth is irrelevant? You're young and alone. With both your father and your *tío* gone, there's no one to protect you. I heard the Chief of Police laughing that he'd get a good price for delivering you to the warden. That old man's personal *muchacha* has gotten too old to satisfy his wants. I find it my duty to inform you that a beautiful young woman in a remote and isolated prison is a great prize. But while the warden would enjoy a paradise on earth, your life would be hell."

"That can't be true. The law doesn't allow things like that to happen." But she had heard tales of such things. What Andres was telling her could very well be true.

"*Señorita.* I'm aware of a *tía* of yours who lives in the United States. I can get you to her place. But we must leave here this very minute. If the police arrive before we leave, it'll be too late."

"But I'm innocent."

"Perhaps you are. But as I told you before, that's irrelevant. The warden needs a new *muchacha* and has had all the police chiefs in the area searching for one. Whoever finds her will be rewarded handsomely. Fate has entered into the picture and has chosen you. The only way you can avoid the future that destiny has in store for you is to leave with me immediately. Now, I've done my duty. If you choose to wait here for the authorities to pick you up, I can leave with a clear conscience knowing I've done my best."

"Why do you care? Who'll pay you for your efforts?"

"I care for two reasons and for them only. First, I don't want to see you made the property of that dirty old man. And second, I've been told that your *tía* who lives in Los Angeles is very rich. I hope she'll reward me for my efforts when I deliver you to her."

This was crazy. She decided she should go up the road to *Señora* Lopez's house and talk to her before making any decisions. But then in the distance she heard the wail of sirens. It sounded like several police cars coming her way.

"Wait here," she said. She went to the couch and slipped on her shoes. Andres was certainly right in his observation about her feet. They seemed to her to be even more swollen than they had been right after they were injured. She went to the room where she kept her little hoard of money. She retrieved it quickly, put it into her purse and went slowly back to where Andres was waiting.

"Okay," she said, "let's go."

They got into the car and had gone only a short distance when three police cars, sirens blaring, pulled up in front of her house and stopped.

She supposed that she was fortunate indeed that Andres had warned her in time.

"Thank you, Andres," she told him, "but there's no need for us to try to go to the United States. The trip is too long and would be impossible for us to make. Just stop at Sandia Dulce. I have friends there who can help me. I'll talk to them before I decide what to do. But I do want to thank you. I don't have much money, but I want to give you this for your trouble." She handed him most of her money keeping just a small amount for herself.

"Oh, that won't be necessary, *señorita*," Andres said. Nonetheless, he took the money and put it into his pocket.

As the car carried them down the dusty road, Maria looked out the window at the arid land, sparsely covered only with small twisted trees and prickly pear cactus. She could imagine the lizards scurrying about and a few hardy jackrabbits. She knew that without help it would be impossible to escape from that harsh country. Earlier, she had been musing about running away from *Tío* Juan. Now she was actually fleeing from the police. In spite of what her *tío* had tried to do to her, she was sorry he was dead. Perhaps they would never find the real killer, and she would always be blamed.

Suddenly she realized the gravity of the situation she found herself in. She no longer had even the remotest idea of what the future held for her. Her entire life had changed in an instant with Andres's knock on her door. She felt numb and hopeless; her body began to tremble as she cried silently. Maybe she should have stayed. Perhaps *Señora* Lopez could have helped her. But what if the *señora* could not and Maria ended up as some foul old warden's plaything? She knew she would find some way to kill herself before she would let that happen.

Although she had told Andres that she had friends in Sandia Dulce, she wasn't sure she really did. Consuelo Hernandez, a woman Maria used to go to school with, had married a man from there shortly after graduating. His name was Carlos Vasquez. His father owned some kind of a business there. If she remembered correctly, it was a hardware store. Consuelo was the person whom Maria hoped to find.

Maria had never seen Consuelo after she moved away. She wondered if the woman still lived in Sandia Dulce. Maria prayed that she would be able to find her. If she couldn't, she didn't know what she would do. She was afraid to go back home and equally fearful of making a trip to an unknown world with a man she didn't know.

She began thinking about what Andres had told her and wondered how he'd known that she had fled naked from her house. Nobody knew that except *Tío* Juan and *Señora* Lopez. It would have been impossible for anyone to have seen her. Even if some of the neighbors had been looking out their windows or doors they could have seen nothing. It was too dark. She remembered that she couldn't even see the ground as she fled down the road.

There was also something else that puzzled her. Andres had mentioned her *tía*. She didn't know how he could have been aware of her *Tía* Carla's existence. Maybe he had heard about her from *Tío* Juan, but she doubted that. Even if he had, it was such a trivial bit of information that he surely wouldn't have remembered it.

Andres had lied to her, but she didn't know why. Perhaps the police *were* after her. She had seen the cars herself. But that didn't alter the fact that Andres was lying. She decided that leaving the village had been a mistake. She had to go back. She had no doubt that she could depend on *Señora* Lopez to hide her until she found out the truth.

"Andres," she said, "Thank you for what you've done for me, but I think we're making a terrible mistake. I would like to go back to Loma Linda. Would you please take me back?"

"But *señorita*. You face too much danger there. You can't go back."

"I have few *pesos* with me. Here, you can have them." She handed him the rest of her money. "And I have more at my house. Several thousand *pesos* *Tío* Juan keeps hidden there for safekeeping. I had forgotten about it because it doesn't belong to me. But now that he's gone, I'll show you where it is. You may keep it for your kindness to me and for the trouble you've gone to in my behalf."

"There's a road about a kilometer up ahead. We can turn around there and return to the village. But before we do that, I'll once again explain to you why it's imperative that you don't go back."

"Thank you, Andres. You're a very good man."

In less than a minute, Andres said, "There's the road I told you about. We can turn around there." Maria saw a rutted trail that led off into the scrawny trees. A green bus was parked on the trail about fifty yards from the road. *Los Hermanos Hernandez* was written on the side in bright red letters. Andres pulled off the roadway and stopped the car but didn't turn off the engine.

"Why are we waiting? I think we should go back. I'm sure *Tío* Juan's money is still where I last saw it. We must hurry and get it before it's found by somebody else."

Three men got out of the bus, and one of them motioned to Andres who began driving toward them. As they got closer to the men, she recognized one of them. He was *Tío* Juan. Her mind couldn't comprehend what her eyes were seeing. He was supposed to be dead. But what Maria was looking at wasn't a ghost. Something was wrong. Maria didn't know what was happening. But she knew something was wrong, and she was weak with fear.

Andres looked at her and laughed. "It seems like I was mistaken about your *tío's* demise. Unless perhaps he's like a *gato* and has many lives."

"What is this, Andres? What kind of an evil trick is this?"

His eyes were hard. "My name, *puta*, is *Señor* Gonzalez. Remember that when you speak to me. You were always *Señorita* Superior in Loma Linda. Well, you're not so wonderful any more. From now on, you're nothing but a common prostitute. *Señorita* Superior no longer exists. She has been replaced by Maria, the common whore."

Maria felt the blood drain from her face which had turned as white as plaster.

"Andres, please."

"So. You haven't yet learned your place. Don't worry. I plan to initiate you into your new role. I'll be your first client, and then I'll go back to Loma Linda. When the villagers begin to wonder where you've gone, I'll wring my hands and say 'poor *Señorita* Guardia. I hope nothing bad has happened to her.'"

When they reached the location where the men were standing, Andres stopped the car. *Tío* Juan went to the passenger side and opened the door.

"Well, *Sobrina*. Imagine meeting out here in the middle of nowhere. Life is full of little coincidences. Don't you agree, Maria?"

"What is this, you degenerate?"

"There have been rumors that I am dead. I merely wanted you to see my face so you would know those rumors are not true. It would be very sad if you should leave our village thinking your beloved *tío* is dead. I'm afraid it would burden your heart with more anguish than it can bear. And one more thing I need to tell you. Those policemen who came to your house just now were not there to question you. A friend of mine called them for me. I only had to pay him fifty pesos for the favor. He told them your house had been broken into. When they discover that there was no burglarly, they will scratch their heads and wonder who made the call. It will remain a little mystery that is never solved."

One of the men standing near *Tío* Juan interrupted. "We must leave. Here's the money." He handed the old man an envelope. "How you and the boy divide it is up to you. It's none of my concern. But move that car and go. You're blocking our way."

"Very well, *Señor* Hernandez," *Tío* Juan said and began walking toward the car.

"Come on, boy," he said to Andres. "Let's go."

Andres, who had been listening quietly, said, "I have a suggestion to make. I would be pleased to return half the money due me for the two of you to spend any way you choose. In exchange for that, I would be allowed to initiate this girl into her new profession. I could do it quickly right in the bus, and it wouldn't significantly delay your departure. As an added bonus, you're invited to watch the show. I'm certain you would find it both amusing and stimulating."

Maria listened, her body numb. Suddenly she found herself running. She couldn't even feel the pain in her battered feet. She dodged around a tree, and one of its low branches struck her face. Its thorns cut her skin, but she didn't slow down. She didn't know where her feet were taking her. It didn't matter. She had to keep going. She had to escape.

The telephone rang, and Lovett answered it. "Hello," he said. "This is Lovett." He was hoping it was Sammy. He hadn't heard from his old buddy for a while and had begun to get worried. It wasn't like Sammy to be gone so long without calling.

"Cal. Larry Daniels here. I've got the information about that Mexican job I was telling you about the other day. Are you still interested?"

"Sure. At least I'd like to check it out. By the way, have you heard anything from Sammy?"

"No. Nothing at all. The last thing I heard he was going to help a friend of his make a few deliveries. I'll let you know it I hear anything else. Anyway, if you're going to be around for a while, I'll be right over."

"Sure. Come on. By the way, how's your patient coming along? The old guy you were telling me about."

"It's looking better. He's beginning to get a lot weaker. I expect he'll be dead in a few days."

"Keep your fingers crossed. And sure, come on over. I can at least see what it's all about."

"Better yet, let me give you a name and phone number. I'm sure Mr. Teller would like to talk to you before either of you make a commitment."

"I hope you didn't tell him my real name," Lovett said.

"Nope. I remembered. I told him your name was William Jones just like you wanted me to do. That's the name Norton used when he talked to the fellow. He told me it's the name you like to go by."

Lovett drove to the address he had been given and rang the doorbell. The door was opened by a wizened little man of about seventy.

"You must be Mr. Jones," he said. "Come on inside." The man led him into a living room.

"Sit here," he told Lovett indicating a couch. Lovett sat down. "I suppose you're Mr. Teller," Lovett said.

"Yes. I'm Mr. Teller, all right. But not the Mr. Teller you want to see. I'm his granddaddy. Now you just make yourself comfortable, Mr. Jones, and young Arthur will be in directly."

In a few minutes a man who appeared to be about thirty years old entered the room. Lovett stood up, and they shook hands.

"William Jones," Lovett said. "Just call me Bill."

"Arthur Teller. Call me Art. Pleased to meet you, Bill. Would you care for something to drink?"

"Are you having anything?"

"Yeah. I've got some pretty good Scotch I like to sip on once in a while. You like Scotch?"

"Sure. Got any soda? I like it about half and half."

"What about ice?"

"Yeah. Lots of ice."

The little man who had greeted Lovett came into the room. "I'll get it, Arthur," he said.

"Thanks granddad," Teller told him. Then he said to Lovett, "Let's go out to the patio if you don't mind." He led Lovett to the back of the house and through a pair of French doors.

"Let's sit here," he said, pointing to a glass topped patio table. He placed his drink on the table and sat down. Lovett did the same. They were in a big back yard shaded by large live oaks, magnolias and other trees and bushes. There was a swimming pool, just off the patio, five feet or so from where they were sitting.

"Nice place," Lovett said.

"Yeah. We like it. I guess I'll just get right down to business. I'll tell you straight out we're in a bit of a bind. Our regular man is indisposed and can't be here. Now, normally, that wouldn't pose a problem. But we're in the middle of something we can't put on hold, or at least we don't want to. Sammy Norton told us you'd be able to do the job. That's why I'm talking to you right now."

Lovett didn't have any idea what kind of a job Teller was talking about. He took a sip of his Scotch. He knew a little bit about liquor and knew that what he was drinking was good. Probably expensive, too. He set the glass back down.

"I'm sorry, but you'll have to back up a bit. I'm completely in the dark."

"Sorry. I thought Daniels had given you a little background."

"No. Not really. Just that you wanted an American who could speak some Spanish. That's the sum of what I know."

"Okay, let's start from the beginning."

The men watched Maria for a moment, and then *Señor* Hernandez said to Andres, "Bring her back, but don't harm her. She's a spirited one, and I'm pleased about that."

Andres took off after her, running in long loping strides. In a few moments he caught her and wrapped his strong arms around her, pinning hers to her side. She struggled furiously but was hopelessly outmatched. Laughing, he half dragged and half carried her back to the other men.

As he took her back, he whispered into her ear. "Ah, Maria. Today's your lucky day. As soon as we get to that bus, I'm going to take you on a wonderful journey. I'll change you forever from a little girl to a woman. I'm sorry I won't allow you much time to savor your anticipation. Because that journey will begin in just a few moments from now."

When the two of them got back to the others, *Señor* Hernandez said, "Very good, young man. Now move that car and go. We've had enough delays already."

"But what about my offer?" Andres asked him.

"No. Not this one. She's for a very special client, and a lot of money's at stake. He demanded a virgin, and a virgin we must deliver."

"But he wouldn't have to know."

In an instant, Hernandez's face flushed red and angry. He took a handgun from his coat pocket, aimed it in Andres's direction and fired. The bullet missed Andres' head by less than a foot and struck a tree just behind him. Then Hernandez fired another shot which hit the ground inches from Andres' feet and ricocheted away with an angry whine.

"Mother of God!" the man screamed to *Tío* Juan. "Get that ignorant donkey out of here before I lose my temper." Then he thundered to Andres, "Go, you stupid ape, and keep your mouth closed. I don't want to see it open or hear it make another sound."

Andres stared dumbfounded for an instant, and Hernandez fired again. The shot went a few inches over Andres's head. Without another word, the frightened young man bolted toward his car. *Tío* Juan wasn't far behind. They got into the battered vehicle and drove back in the direction of Loma Linda.

Maria saw the action, but none of it seemed real. She didn't know where she was, nor did she understand why she was there. Her feet were hurting her so badly that she decided she had better sit down. Otherwise, they would refuse to support her and she would fall. That would make her look clumsy and embarrass her. She didn't want to lose her dignity in front of these two strangers who were watching her with expressionless eyes.

She sat on the ground, removed her shoes and gently began massaging her feet. They were hot in her soft hands.

Hernandez went to where she was sitting, took one look and demanded, "What happened? How did you get those injuries?" Without waiting for Maria to respond, he turned to the other man and said, "Pedro. Get to the bus and bring Blanca. She'll know how to minister to this poor girl." Pedro trotted quickly toward the bus. Maria didn't pay any attention to what was going on. She just kept massaging her feet.

In a few minutes, Pedro returned accompanied by a woman who appeared to be in her early to middle twenties. She was darker than Maria and very pretty. Her skin was smooth and flawless. Her hair was almost black, fluffed out with a natural curl; it didn't quite reach her shoulders. Her breasts were full and firm. She had a tiny waist and softly rounded hips and buttocks. Her legs were long and slim, as perfect as a showgirl's. The men walked away and left the women alone.

The girl knelt down beside Maria and said, "My name is Blanca. Let me look at those feet." She took the right one in both of her hands. It was the one that appeared to be the most badly bruised. Maria didn't resist or protest. She moved her hands away so she wouldn't interfere with what Blanca was doing.

While she was busy in her examination, Blanca repeated, "My name's Blanca. What do they call you?"

"Maria. Please tell me yours again."

"Blanca."

"That's a beautiful name."

"Perhaps. I'm used to it, though. To me it's just a name."

Then, as if waking up in an unfamiliar place, Maria cried out, "Blanca, why am I here? What'll they do with me?"

"You'll be all right."

"When can I go home?"

"You'll be all right. Please don't ask that question of Raul or Pedro. That'll only make them angry. As long as you don't make them angry, you'll be okay. But if they lose their tempers, they can do very bad things."

The answer frightened Maria. "I don't understand. Are you saying I can't go home?"

"Not for a while, but you'll be all right. I'll help you all I can. Please don't argue or disagree. Try to be pleasant. No harm will come to you as long as you heed the advice I'm giving you. That's all I can tell you. Please don't ask me anything else."

"Blanca. You're scaring me! Can't you tell me anything at all?"

"Quiet! The men are returning. I'm forbidden to discuss anything except your injuries. Don't let them know we talked about anything else. You must tell me now how you did this so I'll have something to tell them should they ask."

"My *tío* tried to rape me. I hurt them fleeing from him."

Raul and Pedro came strolling over to where the girls were sitting. "Well," Raul asked Blanca, "how bad are the injuries? Do we need a doctor?"

"No. Nothing's broken. Only badly bruised. She'll be fine in a week."

"Good. Make sure she is. Now we must get to the bus. We've already wasted too much time."

"I must wrap her feet in something before she walks any more. She can't put her shoes back on because her feet are too swollen." Blanca said.

"That won't be necessary. Pedro and I'll carry her," Raul responded. "Come Pedro. I'll get her shoulders and you get her feet." Maria cringed at the thought of their touching her, but she remembered Blanca's advice. She would do as she was told and not make them angry. Maybe, in time, they would grow complacent. She would wait until that happened, and then she would make her escape. She didn't know how she would do it, but she was sure that somehow she would. She would *have* to find a way.

The men picked her up and carried her to the bus. Blanca opened the door for them, and they lifted Maria inside. As soon as she entered, she saw three other girls sitting in the bus's seats. All were young and pretty. They were shackled in place by one chain around a wrist and another around an ankle. The face of one of the girls was covered with a large bruise as though it had been struck by a hard fist. The bitter taste of terror rose to Maria's throat, and she thought she was going to choke.

They put her in a seat, and Pedro went to the back of the bus, rummaged through a toolbox and retrieved a set of chains identical to the ones that were on the other girls. He brought them back to where she was sitting, and in less than a minute, she was chained securely to her seat in the same manner as the others.

CHAPTER VI

It seemed to Lovett that the project couldn't be very difficult to pull off. Teller's clients were from the Middle East. They were flying into Mexico to acquire some merchandise as Teller put it. Actually they were coming to pick up some Mexican girls and take them back to their country.

The men had already paid Teller and his associates. Teller didn't tell Lovett how much, but from some of the things he said, Lovett estimated it was about one hundred thousand American dollars for each girl. He gathered that one of the girls was costing them two hundred thousand or more. That seemed like a hell of a lot of money to Lovett. But at the same time, he knew that a lot of people would be getting their cut. The people who rounded up and delivered the girls, all the assorted middlemen and of course, the officials who would be bribed to look the other way.

Teller would take care of the middlemen and government officials. The funds would be deposited into their various accounts by electronic transfer. Lovett, however, would have to pay the men who actually abducted the girls and delivered them to their purchasers. He'd take enough American money with him for that purpose. The cash would be in dollars instead of *pesos* because the people he'd be dealing with preferred American dollars to their own money. Teller said it also made it easier for him to keep his accounts straight.

Lovett had to take the money to a place near Monterrey called *El Rancho Torres*. He didn't need to be concerned about security. A police escort would accompany him to the ranch. He'd wait there until the girls were delivered. Teller didn't know how long that would be. It could be anywhere from two days to more than a week.

While he was there, he'd go to the airport and pick up the guests. After that, he'd socialize with them and with *Señor* Torres, the owner of the ranch. When the girls arrived, he had to talk to them telling them what was going to happen and how they were expected to behave. He didn't have to worry about what he was going to say because the speech was already written. All he had to do was practice it some to make sure it sounded smooth when he delivered it. That didn't worry him. He figured he could give a speech about as good as anybody could, even if it happened to be in Spanish.

A couple of brothers, Raul and Pedro Hernandez, would bring the girls to the ranch. The brothers were presently traveling throughout northern Mexico rounding them up. There was hardly any risk involved because most of the girls were orphans. Those who were not were too poor to do anything about their plight. And of course, the right officials had been paid off so there was no danger of the ranch being raided.

All the girls would be very emotional and agitated when they got to the ranch. Some would probably try to run away, to fight or otherwise resist their captors, or to engage in other disruptive behavior. It wouldn't be surprising if some of them tried to commit suicide.

Lovett wouldn't be responsible for insuring that the girls didn't escape or harm themselves. But he'd be expected to help the others safeguard the merchandise. After all, the girls represented a large investment which had to be protected just as any other large investment is protected.

"I doubt if any of them can escape," Lovett had told Teller. "I don't see how they possibly could if the system's organized properly. But what if one gets sick or dies or manages to commit suicide? Won't that jeopardize the entire operation? Hell, they're already paid for."

"We've tried to hedge our bets for such a contingency as that. We generally try to pick up one or two extras. You know, it's a strange situation. The ones that are contracted for are worth thousands. The extras are almost worthless. I suppose that's just the way the law of supply and demand works. But at least, we're able to sell them to whorehouses in Nuevo Laredo or some of the other border towns. They don't pay a whole lot, but it covers expenses. The main thing, though, if one of them dies or gets damaged, we have insurance."

It sounded to Lovett like it was an easy way to make some money while he waited for the cancer cure machine to become available. Still, he didn't know why they needed him, and he told Teller that.

"Of course, you're bringing down the money for some of the people involved. But there's something else that's probably even more important. Somebody has to represent this office and keep things moving in the right direction. You'll be the one who picks up the clients at the airport, for example. If you left it to the people down there, they'd probably forget it entirely. If you weren't there, the customers and Torres could cheat us blind. They could take the merchandise and claim they never got it. Then we'd have to give our clients back their money. Believe me. We've thought about it, and someone has to be there."

"Okay. You've convinced me. But I sure wouldn't give them back the money. Not after I got my hands on it, I wouldn't. You shouldn't either."

Teller laughed. "It's not quite that easy. The money's held in escrow until you and the customers certify that the merchandise is serviceable and has been accepted."

Lovett could use some of the girls while they were at the ranch. But the ones that would actually be available would have to be negotiated between him and purchasers. That benefit was specified in the contract between the customers and Teller's organization.

He was advised that some were strictly off limits. In the group he'd be monitoring for example, there was a young virgin worth more than twice as much as any of the other girls.

"You can't fool around with her," Teller had told him. "She's prime stuff and will have to be medically certified as a virgin by the purchasers' private physician before any money can be released from escrow."

Maria gazed out a window as the bus rolled down the crumbling road. Seldom did she see another motorized vehicle. Quite often, though, she saw a goatherd tending a few goats or a wrinkled, sun darkened man sitting by a little shack made of mesquite branches, mud and grass watching a couple of burros. From time to time she saw small groups of people trudging slowly along the road carrying little bundles or pushing rickety carts full of ragged clothes, dented pots and pans and other pathetic odds and ends.

She supposed that they were families on the move. It was desolate country they were passing through, and she couldn't imagine where the people she saw were coming from or where they were going. As far as she could see on either side of the bus there were no houses. Only the miserable little shanties of the men who tended the goats, burros or other livestock. She pitied the families for the life they lived, nomadic and hopeless. But then she realized that their lives were probably better than hers. They plodded into a future which they knew and could understand, however bleak. Hers was shrouded in total mystery.

Raul Hernandez sat down by her interrupting her daydream. "What are you thinking, little one? Your face is sad and troubled."

"I'm afraid. I don't know why I'm here or where you are taking me." Her voice broke because she was almost crying. It took all her resolve to hold back her tears.

"Don't be afraid, Maria," he told her. "We've taken you to keep you safe from your *tío*. He's an evil man. He had already made arrangements to sell you to the warden of your district prison. Many authorities were involved. You were to be tried and found guilty of a crime. The particular offense didn't make any difference. We discovered what they had in mind and won't let it happen. We're risking our lives by helping you."

Maria didn't believe a word he was saying. She was sure that Raul and *Tío* Juan had planned and executed the entire scheme. There was no use in telling him that, though. It would only make him angry, and it certainly wouldn't help her escape.

"Why are you doing it then if it's so dangerous? You could take me to Sandia Dulce. I have friends there who can hide me."

Raul laughed a good-natured laugh. "*Muchacha*, you're so young and naive. How long could you remain hidden? There are no secrets in this world. Word quickly spreads. You would be found in very short order and taken back to Loma Linda to confront your fate. No. Sandia Dulce is out of the question."

"I don't wish to seem impertinent, but since I'm not to return to my village or to Sandia Dulce, can you please tell me where I *am* going?"

"I can't tell you that, Maria, but I can tell you this. No harm will come to you. You'll be taken very good care of and lavished with expensive gifts. You'll be blessed with luxuries you can't even imagine. That much I can tell you but no more."

"May I ask you one more question, *Señor* Hernandez?"

"Go ahead, Maria."

"I don't want to seem ungrateful, but what if I don't wish for the life you've described? What if I merely want to continue to live the simple life I've always lived?"

"You said you would ask one more question, but you asked two. That's all right; I will treat it as one. This is your answer. You can't go back to the life you lived in the past. You have no choice in that matter. Fate has chosen another pathway for you. I urge you to accept that pathway gracefully. Life will be very pleasant for you if you elect to do as I'm suggesting. It can be very unpleasant otherwise. Whether you choose to make it pleasant or unpleasant is up to you. But remember and be assured of this: Nothing you wish for nor nothing you do will alter the direction or the destination that fate had chosen for you. You must excuse me now." He got up and returned to the front of the bus.

As soon as he left, Blanca came back and joined her. "Are you feeling better? Are your feet okay?" She set Maria's shoes on the seat beside her. "Keep these. Perhaps you'll need them later."

"Thank you, Blanca," Maria told her. "Yes. My feet are much better. But I'm frightened. I don't know what is to happen to me. No one will tell me a word."

"I'll tell you what I know. But if Raul or Pedro finds out that I told you, they'll be very angry, and my life may even be in danger. Have you wondered what happened to the girl with the bruised face? How she got the bruises? Pedro did that to her. Do you know why? Because she didn't show him enough respect. She refused to look him in the eyes when he was talking to her. He demanded that she do so, and she still refused. In retaliation, he beat her. All you can see is the damaged face. That's nothing compared to the rest of her body. I thought he had broken her ribs. I examined her and don't think he did. He may have cracked some, but none were actually broken."

"But why didn't Raul stop him? He doesn't seem that bad."

Blanca laughed bitterly. "He's a thousand times worse that Pedro. Pedro is mean because he's slow-witted. Raul is brilliant. That allows him to invent ways to be cruel that Pedro can't even dream of. Now I'm going to tell you some things. Once I've done that, I'll be at your mercy because if you even hint to the men what I've said, I'll disappear and you'll never see me again. Do you understand how serious this is?"

"Then don't tell me. I don't want your life to be put in danger because of me."

"Tonight we'll pick up one more girl. From there we'll go to Monterrey. They'll park the bus on a ranch several kilometers outside of town, and that's where we'll dine and spend the night. Maids will dress us splendidly in the finest garments so we may show ourselves off to our best advantage. Some very wealthy men from across the ocean will be there. They have come to look at the girls to see if they come up to their expectations."

"Their expectations? I don't understand. What do they expect from us?" Maria asked softly.

"They won't be concerned with you and me tonight. Only the others. If they're pleased with what they find, they'll take them to their country to be mistresses, concubines or playthings for themselves, their sons or perhaps for their friends or business acquaintances."

"What are the girls' names? I have yet to meet them."

"The bruised one's name is Sandra. She claims to be an American. The little one with black hair is called Helena. The other's name is Susan."

"Will they want Sandra? Will the bruises perhaps make her less desirable in their eyes?"

"Who knows? She's a beautiful girl even though quite impertinent. Quite likely they'll accept her, perhaps at a reduced price, perhaps not. Otherwise there's a brothel in Nuevo Laredo that would be happy to take her."

Maria sat stunned, trying to absorb what she was hearing. It didn't seem possible. Perhaps Blanca was wrong.

"Are you sure? You couldn't be mistaken?"

"I'm sure, Maria. But it won't be so bad for them. They're orphans. None has ever had enough to eat or a decent place to sleep. Where they're going they'll live in luxury. Don't feel too sad for them."

"Will the same thing happen to me?" she cried out.

"Quiet, Maria. The men will come back to see what's troubling you. Let me massage your feet. If they come to see what's going on, they'll notice I'm trying to help you." She took Maria's feet in her hands; their condition seemed slightly improved. As Blanca stroked Maria's feet, she continued her narrative.

"Okay, here's what they plan for you. Tomorrow evening, a very rich man from across the ocean will come. He has more money than you can even imagine. He owns airplanes, pleasure ships and mansions all over the world. If you satisfy him, you'll become his number one mistress. You'll have children for him because his wife is barren. You'll live a life of leisure and prestige and be showered with gold and precious stones."

"And if he doesn't approve of me will I also end up in the Nuevo Laredo brothel? It doesn't really matter. In either case I would be nothing but a *puta*. Oh blessed Mother of Jesus. Why is this happening? Blanca. I must escape tonight. Please help me. I'll kill myself if I can't get away."

"There's nothing I can do. Nothing anyone can do. Please accept that, Maria, and make the best of it. It'll not really be so bad."

"Do you honestly believe that? We must leave. Both of us. We can go away together."

"Hush. Be quiet. Raul is coming," Blanca cautioned her. As the man approached, Blanca said, loudly enough for him to hear, "Yes, they're much better. In a day or two they'll be as good as new."

"So they're better, then?" Raul said as he approached. Then he asked, "Maria, has anyone told you about the festivities planned for tonight?"

"No. No one has told me about any festivities. I would love to hear about them if you would be so kind as to inform me."

"Tonight we are going to have an extravagant party. There'll be music, champagne and good food. Blanca has been to these affairs before, and she can confirm what I'm telling you. Don't worry about what you'll wear. That'll be taken care of. You'll have ladies in waiting to help you get dressed and ready for the occasion. Does that not sound like a pleasant way to end this long and dusty journey?"

"I've never been to a party before except for birthday parties. I'm sure I'll love it. Where will it be, *Señor* Hernandez? I'm lost and don't know where we are. Will it be in the ballroom of a grand hotel?"

"My, but you have an imagination, Maria. However, it'll not be held in a grand hotel. It'll be a much better party than that. It'll be held in the magnificent home of a friend of mine who owns a large ranch not far from here. If your feet are well enough, you may even wish to enjoy a few dances."

"If I may offer an opinion, I don't think she'll be able to dance, *Señor* Hernandez. Her feet are much better, but I don't think it would be advisable for her to overexert them yet. Perhaps in a day or two."

Raul's face turned dark at the interruption, "If I need an opinion from you, I'll ask. It's terribly impolite to interject unsolicited advice into a conversation. I would suggest that you go up front and talk with the girls there. I'm sure you can provide them with an abundance of free guidance they'll be eager to hear."

"I'm sorry. I was rude." Blanca got to her feet and walked quickly to where the other girls were sitting.

Pedro removed the chains from the girls allowing them to move about as they saw fit. All the girls began to walk around. Maria put on her shoes and gingerly went to where Sandra was standing and said, "Hello. My name's Maria. They tell me you're called Sandra."

"They're dirty bastards. All of them. Sons of whores." The hate in her voice made Maria cringe.

"Quiet. You'll make them angry."

"So. I make them angry. They weren't angry when they kidnapped and beat me. They weren't angry when they decided to sell me to a perverted Arab. So if I make them angry, can they do anything worse than what they've already done?"

"But they can beat you more. They can put you in a brothel."

"Look. I'm an American citizen. They can't do what they're doing. I have papers to prove it right in my purse. I've told them I'm an American, but they just laugh. 'How can one as dark as you are be an American?' they ask me. 'Americans have white skin, blonde hair and blue eyes.' They're too stupid to listen."

"Why don't you show them these papers? Then they'll have to release you."

"I can't do that. They would destroy them, and then I would have nothing." Suddenly her face clouded over with fear. "I should not have told you. If you breathe a word of this, they'll take the papers from me and destroy them. Then all hope will be gone."

"No. I won't tell."

"You must not. Please swear to me that you won't. Swear on your mother's grave." She looked at Maria with desperate eyes.

"I swear. On my mother's grave, I swear. But you should find some place to hide them besides your purse. You must put them somewhere safe."

"I know," she said, her voice filled with fear. "But there's no safe place for them. None at all."

Maria was about to ask Sandra to tell her more about her wonderful papers, but Raul came up and joined them. "It's nice to see you girls becoming acquainted. What have you been discussing? I've been watching you, and it seems as though you're having an intense and interesting conversation."

"It was girl talk. Something you would neither enjoy nor understand," Sandra said and quickly walked away.

Raul's face flushed an angry red. "Someday, she'll go too far. I should take her for a walk and teach her some civility. But fortunately, that'll not be necessary. I'll be free of her soon enough."

"Perhaps she's just frightened."

"You're a very sweet girl. However, you're very naive and don't know the ways of this world. Maybe I'll reconsider and keep you for myself. One of the others will be adequate for your Arab prince."

He waited for her response, but she could think of nothing to say. "Well," he said, "That's something to contemplate. For both of us. Consider my words, Maria."

"Yes, *Señor* Hernandez," she responded, her eyes downcast. She wasn't trying to be enticing or coy. She knew that if she looked at him, she couldn't keep the contempt she felt for him from showing in her eyes.

Raul touched her face with his fingertips and said softly, "You're in my soul, Maria." Then he went to the front of the bus. "Stop the bus, *Hermano*," he told Pedro. "The girls need a break."

Pedro pulled the vehicle to the side of the road and stopped. Raul walked back to where the women were sitting and said, "Ladies. I know some of you need to use the restroom. Unfortunately, we don't have the proper facilities on the bus, and I apologize for that. Each of you will have to go into the trees to do your business."

While Raul was talking to the women, Pedro went to the back of the vehicle and got a rope about thirty feet long and carried it to where Raul was standing. The girls looked at it with fear and confusion in their eyes.

"Only one of you at a time will be allowed to go," Raul continued. "We want to insure your privacy so no one will accompany you. But while we respect your privacy, we'll not do anything to jeopardize your safety. We don't want you to wander away and get lost so we've devised a plan to minimize the possibility of that happening. We'll secure one end of the rope around your waist, and Pedro will hold the other. When you're ready to return, you'll have no trouble finding your way back. I think that explains everything."

He handed Susan a roll of toilet paper and told her, "Okay. You'll go first." She took the paper and waited for Pedro to tie the rope around her waist. When Pedro had it securely fastened, he said, "Let's go" and led her through the door of the bus. The same procedure was repeated until all of the girls had had the opportunity to relieve themselves.

Maria was the last to go. As soon as Pedro attached the rope to her, Raul told him, "I'll escort her." He took the rope from his brother's hand and followed Maria outside. Knowing Raul was holding the rope that was tied around her waist made Maria feel unclean. But she had to urinate so she closed her eyes and did it very quickly hoping that Raul was unable to see her. When she finished, she walked back to the bus, and Raul untied the rope. As soon as both got back on board, Raul told her, "Wait here. I have a surprise for you." She had no idea what he had in mind.

Pedro started the engine and was ready to drive away when Raul and Maria boarded the bus. Raul said, "Wait a minute, Pedro. We're going to teach Maria how to drive."

Pedro looked at Raul as though his big brother had lost his mind. "It's a skill that will be of no use where she's going," Pedro said.

"Perhaps she's going nowhere. Perhaps we'll make other arrangements."

"What arrangements might that be?" Pedro said.

"As of this moment there are no arrangements. I said perhaps. And perhaps is perhaps is perhaps. Only that and nothing more."

"You confuse me when you talk in riddles, big brother. Very well. We'll teach Maria to drive." He got out of the driver's seat.

Raul told Maria, "Okay, my lady. Sit behind the wheel where Pedro was sitting, and we'll show you how to drive." The engine was still running, and Raul reached over and turned it off.

"I want you to learn everything. How to start the bus as well as how to drive it. When you've finished the Hernandez brothers' training course, you'll be an expert. You'll be able to get a job as a chauffeur for some rich old lady to drive to and from her beauty appointments."

Maria noticed that all the other girls were watching her and felt a blush creep to her face. They must surely wonder what favors she was doing for Raul to rate such special treatment.

"Sit down," Pedro told her.

"Yes," said Raul. "Just sit and relax, and above all, don't be afraid."

She sat as directed. "Okay, Pedro," Raul said. "You be the instructor. It'll only confuse the poor girl if she has to listen to both of us at the same time."

"Okay. First you have to make sure that the shift lever is in park. Otherwise, the bus will not start. Then you turn the key. No wait a minute." He took the key from the ignition and handed it to her. She looked at it a moment as though she wasn't sure what she was supposed to do. "Take it. Take it and put it back into the ignition." She did as she was told.

"That's right. Okay. Now turn it." He reached down and turned the key, starting the engine. Then he turned it back off.

"Now, you do it." Maria started the engine.

"Very good!" the brothers exclaimed excitedly.

"Now," said Pedro, "it's time to start the bus moving. We have to move the shift lever to drive. Now, put your foot on the brake and press on this button. We can't move the shift lever until you're holding down the brake pedal and holding in this button. Look. See where I'm putting my foot? Put yours there."

He removed his foot from the pedal, and she put hers on it. "Now move the lever to drive." He guided her hand to the shift lever and helped her place it in drive. "Now, let's go. But before we begin moving, we have to be certain that no other vehicles are coming. Look in the rearview mirror there and see if anyone's behind us. All right, it's clear. Let's go. Just hold onto the wheel, and look at the road." Maria was trying to obey his directions but was sitting rigidly, her face white.

"It's okay. Relax. Hold onto the wheel, and I'll help you." She gripped the steering wheel tightly with both hands, and Pedro also placed his hand on it.

"Okay. Slowly push down on the gas pedal." He put a foot on the pedal and applied some pressure. "Look. Right here where my foot is. Put your foot there." He took his foot away from the gas pedal, and the bus, which had begun to inch forward, slowed to a stop. Maria put her foot on the pedal and gave the bus a little gas but nothing happened.

"That's it. That's it. Just press a little more."

She applied more pressure, and the bus began to move.

"Perfect. Perfect. Now use the wheel to make the bus go where you want it to go." Pedro turned the steering wheel slightly to the left. Maria, concentrating on guiding the bus, released the pressure on the gas pedal, and the bus began slowing.

"The gas. Push down more." She pushed it almost to the floor, and the bus lurched forward.

"Great," Pedro said. He was steering the vehicle because Maria was concentrating on the gas pedal.

"Relax, *muchacha*. You're doing great. Just slow down a little bit." In a few minutes, she was controlling the vehicle's speed as well as steering it.

They let her drive about five miles, and Raul said, "Okay, let's stop." She took her foot from the gas, but wasn't sure what else she was supposed to do.

"Okay, don't look down. Don't take your eyes off the road. Now, put your foot on the brake pedal. But don't look down. I'll guide your foot." He reached down and guided her foot to the pedal.

"Press down, but not too hard. That's good. A little more." Maria brought the vehicle to a stop right in the middle of her lane.

"That's good. Now drive to the shoulder of the road, and park there."

She pulled the bus to the side of the road without mishap.

"Okay," Pedro told her, "keep your foot on the brake until you put the shift lever in park." When she did that, the brothers began to applaud. She got shakily from the seat, went to the back of the bus and sat down. Her knees were weak. Her entire body was trembling.

Pedro got behind the wheel again, and in a few moments, the bus was on its way. Maria saw Raul look back to where she had sat down and was afraid he'd come and join her. Instead, he turned away and sat in the seat just behind Pedro.

Sandra came and sat beside her but didn't say anything right away. After a while, she said, "He has his eye on you, and that's good. If he decides to keep you for himself, don't do anything that will discourage it. As long as you're still in this country, you have a chance to get free. If they send you across the ocean, all hope is gone. As loathsome as he is, it's much better to stay here with him than to be sent away."

"I get sick just thinking about him or seeing his face. When he brushes against me or even comes close to me, I feel unclean. I would die of revulsion if he ever touched me the way he wants to touch me."

"I know. But when we are faced with nothing but unthinkable choices, we must take the one that's the least repugnant. If he likes you, that gives you one more option. I urge you to seriously consider what I'm saying. You're fortunate, Maria."

"We must not give up hope. We may yet be able to escape."

"Yes. I'm still considering that. But if we can't, I've already made up my mind what I'll do. I'll kill myself before I allow them to sell me as if I were a chicken or a goat to be transported to a far away land."

It scared Maria to hear Sandra talk that way. It made everything seem so hopeless.

"We must pray, Sandra. I'm sure our blessed Savior will hear our prayers and liberate us from these evil men."

"Yes we must pray. But it may be too late to ask Him to save our earthly bodies. We must pray that He will accept our impure souls into His merciful hands."

Pedro pulled the bus off the road, drove about fifty yards up a rutted lane and parked near a tree. It wasn't a large tree, but it was one of the larger ones that Maria had seen. It wasn't tall enough to cast any shade to the top of the bus. But at least, it shielded its side from the sun.

Pedro and Raul got the shackles from the tool box and soon had all the girls except Blanca chained to their seats.

"We apologize for the delay, ladies, but you'll not have to wait here long," Raul told them. "In a few minutes we'll have another guest. As soon as we have made her comfortable, we'll go to *Señor* Torres's ranch where there'll be a party in your honor. You'll be served the most delectable food and the finest wine. So please bear with us for just a bit longer."

In about ten minutes, a battered old truck, its bed covered by a dirty canvas tarpaulin, came rattling up and stopped about twenty yards away. Two men got out, went to the back and opened the tailgate. One of them, a big unshaven fellow with a large belly, crawled under the canvas covering while the other stood by the back of the truck and waited. In a few moments, the big man came backing out dragging a young, frightened girl by one arm. He got her out of the truck and onto the ground where she stood frantically looking around holding her right hand in front of her eyes trying to block out the harsh sunlight.

The big man was still grasping her left arm; the fellow who had been waiting seized the right one, the one she had been using to shade her eyes, and the two of them dragged her unceremoniously toward the waiting bus. Pedro met them at the door and helped them get her inside. They quickly shoved her into a seat and applied a set of chains. She sat bewildered, looking around her, not making any noise except the sound of her panicked breathing.

Raul and the two who had delivered the girl went outside, and Raul gave the large man an envelope stuffed with money. The man extracted the bills, counted them and shook Raul's hand. The other man then shook hands with Raul, and the two of them got into the truck and left. The entire operation, from the time the truck arrived until it drove away, had taken less than ten minutes.

The new girl looked around at the others as though she was trying to figure out what was happening, then closed her eyes, bowed her head and began crying softly. Maria watched her and felt a lump of hopelessness rise to her throat. Her chest was heaving uncontrollably, and she realized she was crying, too.

Raul came back to where Maria was sitting and said, "Don't be sad, Maria. I have plans for you that will lift your spirits. Come up and drive for us." She was ready to refuse, to tell him to leave her alone and go to hell. But from the corner of her eye she saw Sandra looking at her as though the girl was trying to send her a signal.

"Do as he says. *Por favor,*" Sandra mouthed noiselessly. Maria nodded almost imperceptibly. "I would be honored, *Señor* Hernandez, if you're not afraid of the danger these unskilled hands may put us into. But I beg you to stay nearby to make sure that I do everything correctly."

She followed him to the front, and he motioned for her to get into the driver's seat. When she was situated under the wheel, he told her. "All right, Maria. Our destiny is in your hands. Show me that you can drive the bus with no help from me. Don't be afraid. I have complete confidence in your ability."

"I'll try. But please stay close in case I encounter any problems."

"Sure, I'll stay close. But not so close as to distract you the way you distract me. Okay. Start the engine. Then stay on this road. In about two hours, we'll turn off onto another road. At that point you will stop, and Pedro will take over. Don't worry. I'll let you know when we're almost there."

Maria started the bus, carefully checked the rearview mirrors and pulled the vehicle smoothly onto the road. Driving didn't seem nearly as difficult or complicated as it had the first time, and in a few minutes she was beginning to feel quite confident and proud of herself. But she knew she couldn't become complacent. She had to find a way to escape. Otherwise, in just a few hours, she would be aboard an airplane headed for a faraway land to begin a new life, a life that she couldn't even begin to imagine.

She had seen pictures of people crossing the desert on camels, the white sun beating down on them creating shimmering heat waves above the hot sands. She wondered if that was the life she was going to. She couldn't do it. The blessed Maria wouldn't allow it to happen. She prayed a silent prayer, "Oh, blessed Mother of Jesus. I beg of Thee to deliver me from this danger I find myself in and back to my humble home in Loma Linda. Give me a sign, blessed Virgin, pointing out what I need to do."

Perhaps the blessed Mother responded because Maria suddenly remembered what Sandra had told her: *"He has his eye on you, and that's good. If he decides to keep you for himself, don't do anything that will discourage it. As long as you're still in this country, you have a chance to get free. If they send you across the ocean, all hope is gone. As loathsome as he is, it's much better to stay here with him than to be sent away."*

Maria was pleased. Certainly that was the sign that she had requested. "Thank you blessed Maria," she said silently. "I'll do as you have instructed me to do. I know that no harm will come to me as long as I do your will and the will of the Lord Jesus."

Lost in her reverie, she had neglected to pay attention to the road and suddenly realized she had crossed the center line and was in the wrong lane. She turned the wheel back a bit too sharply, causing the bus to sway, but was able to get back into the proper lane and moving straight down the highway again.

"Be careful," Raul admonished her. "You must not cross the center line. You must concentrate on what you're doing."

"I'm sorry, *Señor* Hernandez. It will not happen again." She knew now what course of action she would take. She would encourage Raul not to sell her to the rich Arab but to keep her for himself. That's what the Virgin had told her to do, and she would obey. She didn't know what God had in mind for her because He works in mysterious ways. But she knew that as long as she followed His will, no harm would come to her. God and the Virgin Maria would protect her from this evil man.

"Okay, ladies," Raul said. "We're approaching *El Rancho Torres.* In a few minutes, you'll be able to enjoy all the luxuries you have ever dreamed about and more. Luxuries you can't even imagine."

Up ahead was a gate with a huge sign arched over it that said *EL RANCHO TORRES.* Pedro stopped the bus, and Raul got out and went to a speaker mounted on a post by the side of the gate. He pressed a button and spoke to someone, and the gate swung open. Pedro drove the vehicle through the open gate and stopped. Raul got back on board, and the gate closed behind them. They were now on a road with large, lush palm trees bordering each side.

About a half mile down the road, they came to a huge mansion constructed of large blocks of pink granite. It was surrounded by a ten-foot high fence made of stone pillars about twenty feet apart and steel pickets which looked like spears with very sharp points spaced between them at intervals of approximately eight inches. The lower ends of the pickets were imbedded in a concrete foundation a foot wide. They were held rigidly in place by two horizontal steel braces. One of the braces ran between the pillars and was welded to each of the pickets six or seven inches from their tip. The other, which was also welded to the pickets, ran parallel to the upper brace, halfway between it and the foundation. A gate constructed in the same manner as the rest of the fence blocked their way. The gate opened as they approached, and Pedro drove the bus through.

They proceeded around the house and continued down a gravel road for two hundred yards or so where there were two cabins. Pedro parked the bus, went back to where the girls were sitting and unlocked their chains.

When the women were free, Raul said, "Okay, ladies, we're here. Follow me, and I'll show you your accommodations." The girls followed him from the bus with Pedro walking behind the procession. Raul led the little band into the cabin nearer to where the bus was parked.

The cabin had two rooms, both of which were quite large. One was a combination living room and kitchen. It had a butane stove and a small refrigerator in one corner. There was a large table, surrounded by eight chairs, in the middle of the room. A sofa and a love seat were sitting against one wall, and a television set was on the opposite side of the room.

The other room was a bedroom. It contained a twin bed and two full sized beds with a night stand between them. A bathroom was in one corner. There was a door in the back wall that opened outside to the back of the cottage.

"I'm sure that all of you are tired and hungry," Raul told them. "There's a bathroom over there. Go in and freshen up, and they'll bring you some food shortly. Later tonight, after the party I've told you about, you'll sleep here."

Raul finished speaking, but nobody moved; they kept looking at him as though they were waiting for him to tell them more.

"That's all. The food will be here momentarily. After you eat, you'll get ready for the big fiesta. As you'll see when you enter the bathroom, there's a large bathtub where you may soak in hot perfumed water.

There's also a shower. You may choose to enjoy either. But that'll be later. Right now, just prepare yourselves for lunch."

Having said that, he left the cabin. Pedro had already gone, and the girls found themselves alone for the first time since they had been seized and forced onto the bus.

Blanca said, "Follow me, and I'll show you how to use the bathtub. There's also a shower, but I don't think you'll want to use it once you've seen the tub."

She went into the bathroom, and the other girls followed her. When they were all situated so they could get a good view of the tub, Blanca said, "Okay. This lever controls the drain. When it's up, in this position, it keeps the water in the tub." She pulled up the lever and turned on the water. The girls watched as water slowly began to fill the tub.

"This faucet controls the hot water, and this one controls the cold water. As you can see, right now I'm allowing only hot water to flow into the tub. Now watch." She turned on the cold water faucet. "If the water begins to get too hot, you can turn on the cold water and cool it off." She left both faucets running for a while and then turned them off.

"They have many good things here you'll enjoy." She opened a bottle and poured some liquid from it into the tub. "This is bubble bath. Now watch." She turned on the hot water faucet full force. Immediately, the tub began to fill with bubbles.

"In addition to that, there's sweet smelling soap for you to bathe with, shampoo for your hair and perfumed body oil that you may rub onto yourselves when you're finished."

The girls watched her, their eyes wide open in fascination.

"But you'll do all that later, after you eat. Someone will be here to help you get dressed for the party and to help you fix your hair. Right now, though, you'll just use the bathroom and wash up a bit. Okay, girls, I have to leave. I'll be back in a few minutes to make sure you're beautiful for tonight's festivities." She left the bathroom, and the girls followed her. They watched as she went through the living room, opened the door and was gone.

Helena said, "Do any of you need to use the bathroom right now? I really have to go."

"Go ahead," Sandra said.

Helena immediately went back inside. The others remained standing where they were, waiting for Helena to emerge. While they were waiting, Sandra went to the door at the back of the room and tried to open it. It didn't budge. Then she went into the living room and tried to open the door through which they had entered the cabin. It was just as securely locked.

Helena came out of the bathroom, and Susan went in. Sandra began inspecting the windows. They were small, and all were covered with steel bars. She shrugged her shoulders, looked in Maria's direction and said, "*Así es la vida.*"

"Yes," said Maria. "Such is life."

Just when they had all finished using the bathroom, the front door opened, and Pedro came in carrying a large aluminum pot. He was followed by two heavyset women who appeared to be in their sixties. Both were carrying food. Blanca, also carrying a pot, completed the procession. Pedro went to the range, set his container on it, and without saying a word, turned around and left. The two women who had helped him deliver the food went with him.

Blanca said, "Okay. This is our lunch. It'll be ready in a few minutes. There are dishes in the cupboards and knives and forks in the drawers. If some of you will help set the table, we can eat soon."

Sandra looked at her and said, "I thought we were going to a big fiesta at the main house. Have they changed their minds?"

"Yes. There's been a change. You'll eat here. We'll go to the party later."

All the girls were used to working and immediately pitched in. Some began helping with the food; others began putting the dishes and eating utensils onto the table. Sandra found some napkins and put one by each plate. Maria took two ice cube trays from the refrigerator, emptied their contents into a plastic bowl and began filling glasses with the ice. After she had accomplished that, she refilled the trays with water and placed them back in the freezer section of the refrigerator.

"Look at these knives," Sandra said to Maria. "They're completely useless. I was hoping they would be made of sharp steel, but look. Nothing but worthless plastic."

"Be careful, Sandra. Don't try anything foolish tonight."

"It's too late to be choosy. I'll try anything that offers any hope at all, no matter how foolish it may be."

In about twenty minutes, the food was ready. A large platter with slices of both white and yellow cheese, sliced fresh tomatoes and shredded lettuce sat in the middle of the table. Next to it was a pan containing strips of chicken, beef and goat meat resting in a thin, spicy sauce. There were also bowls of *tamales*, probably made of pork; Mexican style rice; pinto beans; and flour and corn *tortillas*. In the pantry, they found various flavors of sodas which they poured into their ice filled glasses.

As soon as the other girls began eating, Blanca said, "I'm sorry I have to leave." She went to the front door and knocked. Someone who had been waiting outside, probably Pedro or Raul, opened it, and Blanca left.

Maria wasn't hungry. She knew, however, that she needed nourishment so she forced herself to eat. She had hoped that by now she would have come up with a plan to escape, but she had thought of nothing. As she slowly ate her food, she watched the other girls. They ate as though they hadn't had an adequate meal in years. Probably they hadn't. All of them except Sandra seemed to be enjoying themselves as though they had forgotten the predicament they were in. Sandra was eating slowly just as Maria was, and it looked as though she also was forcing herself to eat.

They had barely finished eating when the door opened, and Blanca came back into the cabin. "Girls," she said. "There's been a change of plans. There'll be no party tonight. The gentlemen who were expected have been delayed. You'll have two or three days to enjoy yourselves as you wish."

"What'll we do?" Helena asked.

"There's a large swimming pool behind the main *hacienda*. We'll be able to swim as much as we want. Bathing suits will be provided. If you don't care to swim or want to do something else, you may watch television or listen to music. We have videos of the latest movies and music by the most popular artists. I'm sure you'll enjoy yourselves."

"When can we go swimming?" Susan asked.

"Tomorrow. The pool will be available all day tomorrow. Tonight you may watch TV or listen to music. You can stay up as long as you like. Those who want to listen to music can come with me to the other cabin. Pedro will accompany us. Those who want to watch a movie on television can stay here."

Everyone decided they wanted to watch a movie. Blanca turned on the television set. "I'll be back soon with a movie," she told them and left the room.

When Blanca was gone, Sandra told Maria. "This is good. This will give us three more days to plan our escape."

"Yes," Maria said. "And three more days to pray."

CHAPTER VII

Two days passed, and Maria's feet were feeling better. She was sure that if she had the opportunity to escape they would be well enough and strong enough to carry her to freedom. In another day, they would be almost healed.

The girls had been swimming all day and had just returned to the cabin and eaten their dinner when the front door opened, and Blanca and the two women who had been bringing them food entered the cottage. One of the women was carrying two blow dryers which she laid on the table. None of the girls except Sandra knew what they were, but they didn't seem to care.

"Help us clean up," one of the women told the girls. Everyone began clearing off the table and stove and putting the dishes into the sink.

"It's time to get ready," Blanca said. "Sandra, you go first. *Señora* Salguero will help you.

"But it has only been two days," Sandra said. "They told us it would be three."

"No," one of the women said. "They're ready for you tonight."

She went to Sandra and took her by the hand. She was a dark little woman about sixty-five years old with black flashing eyes. "I'm *Señora* Salguero. Come with me," she said. "I'll make you beautiful." She led Sandra into the bathroom.

They emerged about twenty minutes later, and *Señora* Salguero motioned to Helena and said, "Come with me." Helena followed the older woman into the bathroom.

Sandra was wearing only a robe. Her hair was wet, and she smelled of delicate perfume. The woman who had brought the blow dryer, *Señora* Salazar, said, "Come with me, *muchacha*" and led her to one of the chairs by the table. "Sit here," she told her. Sandra did as she was told.

Señora Salazar began drying Sandra's hair using a brush and the blow dryer, but before she was finished, Helena had finished with her bath, and *Señora* Salguero led Susan into the bathroom.

Señora Salazar told Helena, "Sit right here," motioning to another chair. "I'll be ready for you in just a minute." Then she said to Sandra, "Could you just continue to do what I've been doing? It's not really very difficult."

"Certainly," Sandra responded. She had used blow dryers for years. She took the dryer from *Señora* Salazar and continued drying her hair. The older woman picked up the other dryer and began to work on Helena.

When Sandra's hair was ready, she said to *Señora* Salazar, "Okay. I'm ready. What do you want me to wear?"

"Come with me," Blanca told her. "Everything you'll need is right next door." The two of them left the cabin. As they walked outside, Maria saw Pedro waiting for them by the door.

When Maria was bathed and her hair done up by *Señora* Salazar, Blanca led her outside. Pedro, who had accompanied all of the other girls, wasn't there. Instead, Raul was waiting to escort her to the other cabin. She was dressed in nothing but a thin robe and a pair of cloth shoes one of the women had scrounged up to protect her bruised feet. Maria discovered she could walk comfortably with hardly any pain.

"Go to the cabin, and help the others," Raul told Blanca. "They need you there. I'll bring Maria." When Blanca disappeared inside the cabin, Raul put his arm around Maria's waist. His touch made her feel naked. His hand moved downward and cupped her buttocks. Her body went rigid. He moved his hand back to her waist and said, "Relax, *muchacha bonita*. I don't wish to frighten or harm you."

"Please. May I just get dressed?"

"Yes. But don't be afraid. There's something I want you to know. I won't let you leave with that foreign donkey. You'll stay right here with me, Maria. I've made up my mind."

She didn't reply. She had always assumed that Blanca was his woman. If that were true, did Raul plan to keep them both? She doubted that. But she decided she wouldn't try to guess what he had in mind. That would be nothing but a useless exercise.

Raul had told the girls they would be dressed by maids. It turned out that wasn't quite true. Blanca, *Señora* Salazar and *Señora* Salguero were in charge of that. They took Maria into a room which looked like a fine women's clothing store. Scores of beautiful gowns were hanging there. Maria had never seen such finery.

"I'll help you pick out something," Blanca told her. "But it must be close fitting and white. I told them you'd look beautiful in pink, but they refused to listen." She took a long white dress from one of the hangers and said, "Try this on."

"But I need some underwear."

"Tonight, we wear none. I'm sorry, but that has been decided."

"I can't be seen dressed only in that."

"I'm sorry, Maria. I don't make the rules."

"Then can I wear something less revealing?"

"No. This has been selected for you. If it fits, it's what you'll wear."

"It would do no good for me to talk to *Señor* Hernandez?" She almost said Raul but caught herself just in time. She had a strange feeling that Blanca wouldn't be happy to hear her call him by his given name.

"No. It would probably upset him. I already suggested something else, and he got quite angry. I'm sure he wouldn't want it to be brought up again."

Maria tried on the dress, and it was a perfect fit. She was embarrassed, though, when she saw herself in a mirror. No part of her body was concealed. Her large breasts, which were usually constrained by a bra, and her shapely rear end, moved naturally as she walked about as though she were wearing nothing. There was hardly anything left to the imagination. It was almost as if she were naked.

"Look at me, Blanca," she pleaded. "I look like a *puta*. Do I really have to go like this?"

"Yes. I'm sorry. Please, just make the best of it, and don't make a scene. Raul can be very cruel when anyone disagrees with him. More cruel than you can begin to imagine."

Blanca left her to help one of the other girls, and Sandra came over to where Maria was standing.

"I saw a pair of scissors on the big closet's shelf. They're against the back wall on the right side as you open the door. They're long and sharp. I'm going to try to get them without being seen. Maybe I'll be able to use them." A look of dismay crossed Maria's face.

"I'm not telling you this to alarm you, Maria. I just wanted you to know where they are in case I should fail to get them and you decide that you need them."

"Please don't touch them, Sandra. They'll bring you nothing but trouble."

"Don't ask me that. Just pray for me. Pray to the blessed Virgin that I may succeed in this effort. Ask our blessed Savior to take my soul to heaven if I should fail."

Raul and Pedro escorted the women to the *hacienda*, and Pedro rang the bell. In a moment the door opened, and they were met by a tall, slim man dressed in a tuxedo.

"Welcome to *El Rancho Torres*," he greeted them in a deep voice. "*Señor* Torres is expecting you. He's right inside. Please do come in." Maria could hear loud *mariachi* music coming from the room just beyond the entryway.

The foyer opened into a large room with a smooth shiny floor and a stage at one end. Maria expected to see the *mariachis*, but there were none. The music she heard was blasting from two large speakers, one at each end of the stage. A big table was sitting to one side of the room rather close to the stage. It was set with plastic champagne glasses and paper napkins. Several bottles of champagne in buckets of ice were on the table. Four chairs were on each side, and a chair was at each end. The rest of the floor was empty.

A formally dressed man, rather heavyset and with a pockmarked face, was standing in a far corner of the room. He was holding a large brown envelope in his right hand. Maria thought that he was probably *Señor* Torres, and the envelope contained the Hernandez brothers' fee for the delivery of her and the other girls.

Raul went across the floor to greet him. "*Señor* Torres," Maria heard him say. The man handed the envelope to Raul who accepted it. It was so thick and bulky that it took him a while to work it into his inside coat pocket. It looked to Maria like it contained a great deal of money. Raul and *Señor* Torres shook hands and disappeared into another room where Maria could no longer see them.

Pedro led the girls to the table and had them sit along its sides, but he remained standing. He took a bottle from one of the ice buckets and opened it with a loud pop. Some of its contents flowed out of the top and down its side, spilling onto the table.

"All right, ladies. It's time for champagne," he told them.

He served each of them a drink and then sat down at one end of the table and poured himself one. He held his plastic glass in front of him and said, "To happiness and riches beyond your imagination" and quickly drained the glass.

The girls, taking their cue from him, began taking little sips from their glasses. Maria tasted her wine wondering if this was the magnificent party she had been promised.

Pedro opened another bottle and said, "Drink up, ladies. Don't be shy." He got up and began moving around the table refilling glasses. While he was doing that, *Señora* Salazar and *Señora* Salguero brought bowls of salsa and tortilla chips and placed them on the table.

Maria wondered what was going to happen now. She didn't have to wait long to find out. Raul and a man they hadn't seen before came to the table. The newcomer was wearing a dark blue suit with a white shirt and a blue and white tie. His black shoes were a shiny as a pool of oil. He was holding a small wooden box in his right hand.

Raul said, "Please excuse the interruption, ladies, but there's someone very important I want you to meet. He has traveled from America for this occasion, and we're honored to have him here. You don't need to know his name because you'll never be expected to address him. However, he has been gracious enough to reveal it. His name is Mr. Jones. Now that you've heard it, don't take advantage of his generosity and say things that are inappropriate or embarrassing. Any question you may have or any comment you may wish to make will be directed to me, and if it's pertinent, I, in turn, will pass it on to him. Do any of you have any questions?"

The girls looked at him as though they hadn't understood a word of what he had told them. Nobody made a sound.

"All right. I'm glad you understand. Mr. Jones is in our country to select some girls to travel to a far away country where they'll enjoy great wealth and prestige. For those who are so chosen, it will indeed be a great honor. You will live in a beautiful house, dress in the most elegant clothing and eat the finest food. Your life will be a life of ease and luxury. But Mr. Jones can enlighten you much better than I. Mr. Jones."

"Ladies," the man said in a thick American accent, "I represent a very wealthy man from across the sea. Some of you will be chosen tonight to go to his country. Now, I'm going to be very blunt. Those of you who pass my inspection will go. So listen closely to my words. If you are agreeable and do as you're told, you and I'll get along just fine. If you don't cooperate, it will do you no good. I'll make you unhappier than you can even begin to imagine, and you'll still do what we've decided for you to do."

"I'm an American citizen," Sandra interrupted. "I'll not be sold like an animal. You have no right—"

As soon as she began speaking Pedro jumped to his feet and rushed to her chair. He wrapped his right arm around her throat and dragged her backward across the floor. One of her shoes came off and stayed under the table. She wasn't able to utter a sound because his arm was choking off all air flow making speech impossible.

"Wait," Jones told him. "Bring her back, but make certain that she remains in her chair." Pedro turned and retraced his steps still dragging the helpless girl. Maria and the others watched in shock. Pedro set her down roughly and loosened his arm slightly. She began breathing again making hoarse gasping sounds. Then she began struggling and rose halfway to a standing position. Pedro tightened his hold again, grabbed her hair with his left hand and very roughly wrestled her back into the chair.

"Very good," Jones told Pedro. "Now keep her there. I have something I want to show her. And it's just as well that the others see it, too."

He opened the box he was holding, walked slowly to where Sandra was sitting and placed the box on the table in front of her. All the girls were trying to see what was in the box but were unable to. Jones put his right hand into his coat pocket and took out a handkerchief. He reached down and extracted something from the box, using the handkerchief to prevent his hand from coming in contact with the object. He held the item up so everyone could see it. To Maria, it looked like a small piece of leather or a dried up piece of meat. Everyone was staring at it intently trying to discern what it was.

"I won't leave you in suspense," Jones told them. "This is the tongue of a beautiful young girl. A girl very much like any of you. She talked too much. She didn't know how to show respect." He paused and waited for the effect of his words to sink in. "But she doesn't talk too much anymore. She listens respectfully and knows her place." He was holding up the object as he talked so that all the girls could clearly see it.

"I know you're eager to hear how this story ends. Well, the girl is living happily in a large mansion. She's in charge of all the female housekeeping staff. She's well fed and content. But it could have had a happier ending. The young son of a fabulously rich family desired her greatly. He wanted to make her his number one concubine. But of course, that was impossible. It would have been a disgrace to both him and his family to consort openly with someone who had been so disrespectful that she had lost her tongue. So, now, she can enjoy his company only when he sneaks away occasionally to see her. His number one concubine spends her days shopping and riding around in beautiful cars.

"I wish to pose a question to you lovely women. Do any of you want to lose your tongue tonight? Because if you do, we have a table set up in the other room and a gentleman waiting there to perform the operation. And remember this. If you do choose to go in there and have him work on you, it won't exempt you from taking the journey we've been discussing. But it *will* make that journey much more unpleasant."

He continued to talk, but Maria could no longer understand what he was saying. Her mind was numb. She seemed to be watching him and the others in the room from a long distance away. His voice was a humming monotone. The words were garbled and ran together and no longer had any meaning. She was lightheaded and was afraid she was going to faint. In a few minutes, her mind began to clear again, but her legs were so weak that she knew that they wouldn't be able to support her if she should attempt to stand up.

Maria looked across the table to see how Sandra was faring. She was sitting with her eyes half closed and a far away expression on her face. Pedro had one hand resting heavily on her right shoulder and the other gripping her hair. She gave the impression that she hardly knew where she was and was totally unaware of Pedro's presence.

Sandra began shifting around in her chair as though she were trying to get herself into a more comfortable position. Without taking his eyes from Jones, Pedro relaxed his hands a bit to let her get better situated. She moved her right hand as though she was trying to pick up her purse from the empty chair next to her.

Maria listened intently to Mr. Jones trying to understand what he was saying. Her head was becoming clearer, and his words were beginning to have meaning. She glanced back at Sandra just in time to see the girl's hand come out of her purse gripping a long pair of scissors. Sandra brought them up with all the strength and speed her small body could muster. Their point entered Pedro's mouth and exited through the side of his cheek. Her hand reversed its direction and snapped back as quickly as a rubber band bringing the scissors with it.

Pedro grunted, released her shoulders and hair and brought his hands to his punctured face. Blood ran through his fingers and onto Sandra, the table and the floor. Sandra was up in an instant, stabbing at his face and chest. The scissors made a gash across his temple and another on his upper arm before he was able to react.

He struck out with his large right fist catching her squarely in the face. Her nose collapsed, and blood spurted from the shattered area where it had been. His other fist caught her jaw, fracturing it. She fell to the floor, and he grabbed a chair and began beating her.

"Enough," shouted Raul. "Enough, little brother."

But Pedro was so enraged that he couldn't hear anything except a loud roaring in his ears. He continued to pound her until the chair was so badly splintered that he could no longer use it effectively.

"Stop," Raul said. "They can use her in Nuevo Laredo." He grabbed Pedro around the waist, trying to hold him. But Pedro wouldn't be restrained. He lashed out with his foot, catching the helpless girl flush in the temple. Only then was Raul able to drag him away a few steps.

"Did you not see what that whore did to me?" Pedro screamed.

"Yes, brother. And we'll take care of your injuries. But now she's dead and worth nothing. We could have gotten a good price for her in Nuevo Laredo."

Pedro held both hands to his injured cheek as the blood continued to flow.

"Look, brother. Look at my face. Can you not see what she did to me?"

Raul had released his hold on Pedro. "Yes, I see. Blanca will take care of you. Tomorrow you'll see a doctor."

Pedro stepped forward to where Sandra lay and kicked her head viciously again.

"Take that, *puta*. That's your payment for what you've done to me."

The man who had greeted them when they arrived came rushing into the room to see what was going on, paused a moment and then left. A few seconds later he returned with *Señor* Torres.

"How could this have happened?" Torres demanded angrily. "There was no need for this kind of stupidity."

Pedro face flushed a dark red, and he started to reply, but Raul stopped him.

"Get the girls back to the cabins," Torres told Raul.

Raul grasped Pedro by the arm and said, "Take the girls back. I'll join you in a few minutes."

Maria noticed that Sandra's purse was still on the table. She stood up, walked by where it was sitting, and picked it up. She was terrified that someone would challenge her action, but nobody did. Then she joined the other girls who had also risen to their feet. In a few moments Pedro was directing Maria and the other girls out of the main house toward the cabin they had been in earlier that evening.

As soon as Pedro and the girls exited, Raul turned to *Señor* Torres and Mr. Jones and said apologetically, "I'm sorry for what happened. We'll get everything straightened up quickly and still be able to conclude our business tonight. Is that not correct, Mr. Jones?"

"I don't see any problem," Jones responded. "As far as I'm concerned, all the girls are acceptable. I'll still have to examine them a bit more closely, but from what I've seen, I don't anticipate any difficulty at all."

"I want to make one thing very clear," Torres said to Raul. "I'm extremely unhappy about what transpired here tonight. Such actions can't be tolerated. The risk is too great. I'm telling you this as a friend. If it should happen again, your brother will be severely punished. There won't be a second chance. For his own safety, I urge you to dissuade him from participating with you in any future transactions."

"I'll talk to him. It won't happen again," Raul assured him.

"Please listen very closely, my friend. Talk is not enough. Convince him that he's not to come here again. I beg you to hear what I'm telling you because it's said with the utmost urgency."

"All right. I'll heed your advice."

"We have to get someone to replace that one," Jones said, pointing to Sandra's body.

"We can do that," Raul assured him. "We'll send Blanca in her place."

"Very well. She'll be more than satisfactory." Blanca's fate was sealed with that casual exchange.

"We have to get her out of here and get this place straightened up," Torres said, touching Sandra's body with the toe of his shoe.

He turned and called out, "Miguel, come in here."

The slim man who had summoned him earlier immediately appeared.

"Get somebody to clean up this place. We'll be back in an hour," Torres told him.

"Yes, sir," Miguel said.

Pedro sat on a chair, a bandage covering one side of his face. He was holding a pistol by the handle, letting its weight rest on his knee. The exposed part of his face was pale and bloodless. Blanca, who had placed the bandage on his face, was in the other room out of sight. Maria sat on the couch with the other girls. They were holding each other. Tears flowed down their cheeks and fell to the floor. Helena was crying softly, but no one else was making a sound.

The door opened, and Raul entered followed by *Señora* Salguero. The *señora* stopped near the entryway and waited. Maria watched Raul as he approached the couch where she and the other girls were sitting. He stood there for a few moments looking at them as though waiting for them to acknowledge his presence. None of the others even seemed to know he had come in.

"All right, ladies," he said, "It's time to return to the *hacienda*." Not a one of them reacted to what he said. It seemed they didn't even know he was there and were just barely aware of where they were and what was going on.

He waited a few moments and then said, "Come on, ladies. Everything's going to be all right."

Pedro, touching the tips of his fingers gingerly to his bandage, rose to his feet and began walking toward Raul as though he was going to help him. Raul saw Pedro approaching and held up his hand.

"Just relax, brother," he told him. "Sit back down and relax. I want you to wait for me here. *Señora* Salguero will help me." Pedro hesitated for a moment but then sat back down.

"You're needed here," Raul told him. "I'm leaving Maria in your charge. I want you to look after her while I'm gone. I'll return as soon as I conclude my work in the *hacienda*. It shouldn't take very long."

He paused a moment as though he was mulling something over in his mind and then said in such a quiet voice that Maria could only barely hear the words, "Be sure that she's restrained. We don't want her to endanger herself by walking away."

While Raul was talking to his brother, *Señora* Salguero approached the girls and gently urged them to their feet. Maria stood up with the rest of the girls. "Sit down, *mi hija*," *Señora* Salguero told her. "You'll wait here."

Maria sat down and looked around uncertainly.

"Don't be afraid, *muchacha*. I'll be back in a little while." Maria knew the older woman meant well and was trying to comfort her. She was certain, however, that there was nothing the little lady could do. Her fate was solely in Raul and Pedro's hands.

Maria sat and watched as *Señora* Salguero herded the girls slowly toward the door. Raul caught up with them, and in an instant, he, the girls and the *señora* were gone.

Pedro got to his feet as soon as he and Maria were alone. "Come," he told Maria. "We must go to the other room." She didn't even think of trying to defy him. The vision of Sandra's crumpled body was too vivid in her mind.

Pedro, holding his pistol carelessly, ushered her into the bedroom and pointed to a chair near the bed. "Sit there," he commanded. She did as he directed, but as soon as she was seated, he changed his mind. He pitched the gun onto the bed, grasped her wrist in a strong hand and led her to the closet. Then, still holding her firmly, he opened a trunk which was on the closet's floor and began to rummage through it. He pulled out a set of shackles, released her arm just long enough to close the trunk and then, carrying the chains in one hand, led her back to the chair.

For the first time since she had been captured, only one person was guarding her. She realized that if she was ever going to have a chance to escape, that time was now. She could no longer wait for a miracle to intervene in a dim, uncertain future. As soon as Raul and the others returned, all hope would be gone.

She had to get her hands on Pedro's gun. She was quite certain she would know how to use it. She had seen Pedro fire it several times. All he had done was point it and pull the trigger.

Maria had made a firm decision and suddenly found herself feeling a shred of hope mixed with her fear. She did appreciate the risks involved. She had seen how quickly Sandra's life had been extinguished when she tried to resist. But Maria refused to dwell on that thought. She had decided what she was going to do and was ready to proceed with her plan.

Pedro began placing the restraints on her wrists. "We must do this for your own good," he told her. "If a beautiful girl like you should wander outside into the night, her life and virtue would be in jeopardy."

"How could that be? There's no one here except the people who belong here and the girls. I don't think any of them would want to harm me, not even Mr. Jones. After all, he'll make a great deal of money when I'm sold. He'll probably get more money than you and your brother, and for what? You two are the ones who are taking the risks. Then a rich *gringo* comes to our country and reaps all the profits."

Pedro's face turned angry. "You're right. He's nothing but a pig."

"Yes. He's nothing but a pig. But that makes no difference. He's still the one who'll get most of the money."

"Shut up," Pedro shouted angrily. "I'll get my share. Raul will get his, too. Why am I even talking to a woman? They're all stupid and like to get involved in things they don't understand. Now, no more arguing." He started to put on the chains.

"I'm sorry. I didn't intend to be disrespectful. Please don't do that. There's nowhere I can go. Besides, I may not want to leave as long as the two of us are alone."

He studied her closely as though trying to decide what she meant by that remark and how he should respond. Finally he asked her, "Do you find me attractive, *señorita*?"

"Am I at liberty to find you attractive? Am I at liberty to do any thinking at all? I understand that your brother plans to sell me to a rich Arab. What I wish for and what I think do not matter."

Pedro, who had been standing in front of her, sat down on the bed. When he did, she turned her chair to face him.

"*Señorita* Maria, I'll forget the chains, at least for now. Perhaps we can talk for a while. There's no harm in talking. We can become better acquainted while we wait for the others."

"You asked me if I find you attractive, and I'm afraid I was rude. I was rude because I'm frightened. I can't bear the thought of being sent to a strange land with no hope of ever seeing my friends or family again. But now I'll answer your question. Yes. I think you're attractive. If things were different, perhaps I could stay here with you."

A pleased expression came over his face. "Would you like some wine, Maria? We have some very good white wine. I think I'll get each of us a glass." Without waiting for her to respond, he got up.

She waited until he was in the other room before she picked up the gun. She positioned the chair so she could rest her hands on its back supporting the pistol's weight. She stood there, the gun pointed at the door, waiting for Pedro to return. She heard him moving around in the kitchen, and after an interval that seemed to be a long time, he appeared in the doorway.

He took two or three steps before he realized that Maria had his gun. He stopped and demanded angrily, "Put the gun down, *puta*, before I break your neck."

Her body was trembling violently, and she was so frightened that she almost obeyed. Her legs were so weak that they felt as though they were about to collapse and let her fall.

"Get out of my way," she whispered weakly. "*Por favor, señor*. I must leave."

"I'll show you, you treacherous whore," he screamed. He dropped the wine glasses and rushed toward her. She braced, waiting to feel the crushing blows of his fists. He was almost upon her when she heard the gun firing again and again and felt it bucking in her hands. Pedro fell backward onto the floor. Blood was splattered on the wall behind him and flowed from beneath his body in scarlet streams.

She laid the gun on the chair, grabbed Sandra's purse and started for the door. Then she remembered that Pedro always kept the keys to the bus in his coat. She set the purse down and searched Pedro's pockets. The keys were there. She retrieved them, picked up the purse once more, went into the front room and headed for the door leading outside. Before she could open it, she saw Raul through the window. He was approaching the house and was about ten feet from the front steps.

For a moment she was so petrified that she couldn't move. But then she remembered Sandra's broken little body lying on the floor. Raul was one of the men responsible for that. He was also the one who was planning to sell her like an animal. Suddenly, all her fear evaporated, and her mind was clear and focused. She felt no remorse for what she had done to Pedro and what she was about to do to his brother. They had brought it upon themselves.

She dropped the purse and keys on the floor, rushed to the chair where she had left the gun and picked it up. She came back into the front room and aimed the pistol at the door, waiting. When it opened, she didn't say a word. She began pulling the trigger again and again. Raul slumped to the floor almost blocking the exit. She picked up Sandra's purse and the keys and started to step over Raul's body and leave the cottage, but then she changed her mind once more.

She realized that she had no clothes other than the dress and the shoes and stockings she was wearing. She didn't even have any underwear. She went into the bedroom and into a closet where she had seen a trunk. She opened it quickly and began taking things out and throwing them aside. She didn't see anything that looked like it would fit her or seemed appropriate for her to wear on the journey which she hoped was about to begin. Finally, near the bottom of the trunk were a pair of boys' trousers, two red and black plaid cotton shirts and a pair of boys' white knitted briefs.

Her feet were throbbing some, but they were much better than they had been when she first arrived at *El Rancho Torres*. In the corner of the closet, she spied a pair of shabby worn out shoes; she removed the ones she was wearing and put the others on. She hoped they would protect her feet better than the ones she had discarded.

She wasn't particularly happy with what she had found but was afraid to spend any more time in the cottage. She had to leave before the others found her. She grabbed a man's coat which was hanging in the closet and wrapped it around the trousers, shirts and briefs making a small bundle which she could easily carry. Then she went back into the front room and picked up Sandra's purse and the keys to the bus.

She was about to leave when she remembered the packet that *Señor* Torres had given Raul earlier in the main *hacienda*. With a pounding heart, she knelt down, opened his coat and removed the envelope. It was thick and heavy. Then she stood up, grabbed the items she was taking with her, stepped over Raul's body and stepped through the open door into the brightly moonlit night.

She threw her bundle, the envelope and the purse onto the floor of the bus, climbed inside, closed the door and got into the driver's seat. Her hands were shaking, and she dropped the keys when she tried to find the one she needed to start the vehicle. "Help me, blessed Virgin," she beseeched as she retrieved them from the floorboard.

It took her a while to get the right key into the ignition, but once she got it inserted, she had no trouble starting the bus and getting it moving. She was worried that the gate in front of the house might be closed but decided that if it was it wouldn't stop her. She would drive the bus through it, knocking it down if necessary. But when she got to the gate, she was relieved that it was open.

The gate near the main road was open too. She wasn't surprised. She knew that the blessed Virgin had opened it for her. As she left El Rancho Torres and came to the main roadway, she saw a sign indicating the way to Monterrey. She turned the bus in that direction hoping that her nightmare was over.

As soon as she left the ranch, a firm decision formed in her mind. Now that she had Sandra's magic papers, she would leave Mexico and go to Texas. She was no longer safe here. If the authorities found her, she would be charged with two murders, stealing the bus and only the good Lord knew what else and would certainly spend the remainder of her life in jail.

She didn't know English and didn't know how she would make a living in the United States, but she knew that the blessed Virgin would take care of her as long as she did her part. Her *Tía* Carla, had told her there were places in Los Angeles where the people speak nothing but Spanish. Undoubtedly there were places like that in Texas, too, especially in the large cities like Houston, Dallas and San Antonio. She had decided she would go to Texas instead of California because Texas was so much closer.

Maria was a fast learner and not afraid of work and was sure she could find a job in one of the big cities. Perhaps someday she could learn English and find herself a better job. She was still young enough to do that. But enough daydreaming. First she had to get away.

Every instinct urged her to hurry. She wanted to press the gas pedal hard against the floor and drive at the vehicle's top speed until she got to Monterrey. But she knew that to do so would invite disaster. The first policeman who saw the speeding bus would stop her, and she would be unable to explain what she was doing in a bus that didn't belong to her. She imagined herself being held in jail while they investigated. It would be only a matter of time until they found Pedro and Raul's bodies. Then any hope of freedom would be lost forever.

It took all the resolve her heart could command to keep the vehicle moving at a reasonable speed, but knowing the risks she would be facing if she did otherwise, she was able to do it.

The bus seemed to creep down the road, and she wondered if she would ever reach Monterrey. But still, she wouldn't go any faster. She focused her eyes on the deteriorating asphalt in front of her and continued to drive. From time to time she glanced down at the speedometer to make sure she was still within the speed limit. Then, reassured, she would cast her eyes ahead hoping to see the skyline of the city in the distance. But nothing was in front of her except the same monotonous view.

She saw a side road that was hardly more than an animal trail and pulled off the highway to change her clothes. Maybe if she put on the garments she had taken, she could pass for a boy. She knew that her hair could easily give her away. But fortunately for her, one of the brothers had left a big felt hat in the bus. She was able to pile her hair up on the top of her head and hide it under the hat.

She threw away the clothes she had been wearing and quickly changed. The trousers fit her well enough. Both shirts were too large so she chose the smaller of the two. When she finished changing, it was apparent that she would never be mistaken for a boy. Her breasts were much too large and her hips and buttocks were too softly rounded and feminine. She remembered the coat and put it on to see if it would help. It was large and shapeless and hung to her knees. She hoped it would provide her the camouflage she needed. The envelope she had taken from Raul's pocket was still lying on the floor of the bus so she put it in the coat's pocket.

Lovett was very angry. What Pedro had done was beyond stupidity. There was no excuse for destroying expensive merchandise the way he had done. Teller had told Lovett that they generally had several extra girls in case something happened to one of them. But they had only one. Lovett wasn't sure that Raul had intended for her to be a spare. He probably had wanted to keep her for himself. But when his stupid brother threw a tantrum and killed one of them, Raul had no alternative but to throw her in as a replacement.

Lovett couldn't understand why they didn't bring in three or four extras or even more. It was a hell of a lot better to be safe than sorry. It seemed to him that it couldn't be very difficult for them to find a dozen extras if they wanted to. There had to be a thousand girls running around all over Mexico that they could pick up.

What would happen if something else went wrong? Well, he'd just hope to hell it didn't. He knew one thing that he was going to report to Arthur Teller. He had better send somebody down to get things better organized. It was a Mickey Mouse organization they had going if Lovett had ever seen one.

He figured he and Sammy could straighten it out in no time if they wanted to, but he certainly didn't want to. He was sure that Sammy would share those sentiments. Once he got out of Monterrey and back in the good old USA, he was ready to stay there for a while. He didn't care how much money Teller offered him to go back.

He wasn't about to return home, though, until he took advantage of one of the fringe benefits that went with the job. Teller had told him that he could select some of the girls for his own pleasure for as long as they were at the ranch. All he had to do was to check with *Señor* Torres to find out which ones were available. He knew that Maria was strictly off limits.

He had found that out when he told *Señor* Torres that she was his first choice. Torres had told him she was the one who couldn't be touched. Lovett's second choice was the spirited one named Sandra. But Pedro had ruined that choice. So then he selected Helena. She was small and dark with black hair and black flashing eyes. He figured that she might fight like a wildcat, but that would make the experience more exciting. When he told *Señor* Torres whom he had chosen, the man had laughed and told Lovett that he'd be exhausted but content the next morning.

"I hope you're right, my friend," Lovett had responded. "And I'm confident that you are."

"Just remember to be finished with her by eleven o'clock tomorrow. They have to be bathed and perfumed and ready to be transported to the airport by three o'clock."

"That'll give me exactly enough time, my friend. Not so little as to leave me unsatisfied and not so much as to leave me bored."

Señor Torres laughed and slapped him on his back, "Well put, my friend," he said. Then he looked at his watch and told Lovett, "I have to leave for a while. If I don't see you tonight, I will tomorrow. May you have a spectacular night."

"Thank you, my friend. I'm certain of that."

"Miguel will let you know when the lady is available and will take you to your room."

As soon as Torres left, Miguel appeared. "Could I fix you a drink, sir?" he asked.

"Thanks. Scotch and soda."

Miguel left, and in a few minutes he returned with the drink.

"If that'll be all, sir, I have some things I must attend to now, but I'll see you soon and show you where you'll spend the night. Please feel free to make yourself at home until I return. In the meantime the house is at your disposal. There's a bottle of Scotch and plenty of soda on the kitchen counter near the sink should you care for more."

"Thank you, Miguel." The man left the room.

Lovett sat sipping his drink and anticipating the pleasure awaiting him. He could visualize Helena's dark skin and flashing eyes. He could almost feel her warm body in his arms.

He saw a television set in the corner of the room and decided he might as well watch it for a while. He found a remote control unit lying on a table near the TV, took it to the couch and turned on the set. At least half the programs were American shows. Some had Spanish subtitles and others had Spanish dubbed in.

When he finished his drink, he went to the kitchen and mixed another. By the time he started on his third, he was wondering when he'd be shown to his room. He was ready to partake of the treat which was waiting for him. Someone must have been reading his mind because Miguel appeared and said, "Your room is prepared if you're ready to retire for the night."

"Thank you. Yes, I think I'm ready."

Miguel led him down a hallway to a closed door.

"Before you go inside, *señor*, there is something I wish to explain. Your lady is secured to the bed for her well being and yours. If she were free to move about, she could very well damage herself trying to resist. We don't want that to happen because we've already lost one of the girls tonight and don't have any extras." He opened the door to the room.

Helena was naked, lying spreadeagled on her back, her arms and legs securely fastened. A gag covered her mouth.

"She's already prepared. We've inserted cream so you'll have no trouble entering her. That'll make it more pleasurable for you and reduce the chance of damage to her. There are condoms on the dresser which you're requested to use."

"I'd rather not use them," Lovett said. "That takes away from the enjoyment."

"We insist that you do so. They'll prevent her from getting pregnant and protect you from any disease that she may be carrying. She'll remain constrained just as you see her for as long as you wish. When you're finished, press the button by the lamp, and someone will come and take her away."

"*Señor* Torres told me I could have her all night. Couldn't we untie her and just lock the door or something? I don't think she'd put up much of a fight. She knows it would be useless."

"I'm afraid that's impossible. Those dull-witted Hernandez brothers didn't bring us enough girls. If something should happen to even one more, it would result in great inconvenience for everyone. Perhaps things will be better organized the next time, and you won't have to face such an annoying situation." He left the room.

Lovett was somewhat irritated, but he had to agree that Miguel was right. There was a great deal of money involved, and it wouldn't make sense to risk damaging any more of the girls. He wondered why they were even allowing him to use her at all. If he were running the show, nobody would touch any of the girls. He'd put them under lock and key and guard them like gold.

It wasn't going to be at all like he had imagined. He had thought they would spend the night together in each other's arms. He knew that she very well could have put up a fight. But finally she would have given up because she would quickly find out that struggling was useless.

To hell with the rubbers, Lovett thought. There wasn't any way he was going to use one of them damned things. He took off his clothes and got on the bed between her legs. She twisted frantically but was no match for the restraints that held her.

"Relax," he told her in Spanish. "The ropes will bruise your arms and make them bleed if you continue to resist."

The sound of his voice seemed to give her more energy, and she struggled so vigorously that he was afraid she might dislocate her arms. He felt like slapping her across the face to make her stop, but he knew he might injure her if he did that.

"Stop it *puta*," he hissed, but it seemed that she couldn't even hear his words.

He put his arms around her in a bear hug holding her almost immobile and inserted his penis. He could feel her struggling with every bit of energy she had left in her body, and he could hear little grunts coming through the gag. Her efforts increased his excitement, and he ejaculated almost immediately. Her body was soaked with sweat and trembling, and she seemed to be having trouble getting enough air into her lungs. Her violent efforts had probably exhausted her. Perhaps he ought to remove the gag to allow her to breathe through her mouth as well as her nose. He didn't want her to suffocate. Not when the project was so near a successful conclusion.

He took off the gag, and she opened her mouth. A handkerchief was stuffed inside. He removed it, and she began to breathe deeply, her breasts heaving with each ragged breath.

He started getting aroused again, and in a few moments his penis was fully erect once more. He started moving again, and Helena begged softly, "*No, señor. No. Por favor, no*. Oh, blessed Mother of Jesus please help me."

He kept one hand around her waist and moved the other under her buttocks.

"I beseech you, *señor. Por favor. No."*

She wasn't struggling as hard as before. But her helplessness and the hopeless sound of her voice got him even more excited than he had been. He began kissing her face. It tasted salty from her tears. He tried to kiss her mouth, but she twisted her face from side to side resisting. That angered him, and he drew back his hand to strike her. He realized what he was about to do just in time to restrain himself.

He reached his climax again and lay on top of her. After a few minutes he wanted to roll off, but there was no place for him to lie comfortably. Helena was in the middle of the bed, and there wasn't enough room on either side of her for him because of the way her arms and legs were fastened. He thought about releasing her restraints and re-fastening them in such a way that she would be lying on her side on one side of the bed. But he knew he shouldn't do that. It would probably make *Señor* Torres unhappy.

He decided to ring the buzzer for Miguel. He figured that Miguel could help him tie Helena in a better position. He wanted to keep her all night, but he also wanted to be able to lie in a comfortable position.

He got up from the bed, but before he could press the button, Miguel came rushing into the room.

"Pardon me, *señor*," he said in a frantic voice. "You must come quickly. The one called Maria has killed the Hernandez brothers and escaped. We must find her before she gets away completely."

"What are you saying, Miguel? That's impossible."

"She killed them both. She took all the money and left. Hurry. You must help us find her."

"Don't worry. We'll find her. She can't be far away." He was already putting on his clothes.

"But *Señor* Jones. She stole their bus. She could be miles away."

Helena interrupted the men's conversation and said weakly, "You'll never find her."

Lovett said, "Miguel, you'd better do something with her and the others. We can't allow anything else to go wrong. Don't worry about Maria. I'll have her back in no time at all." He finished dressing.

"Tell *Señor* Torres not to worry. I'll return soon with the girl."

"I must go. Please forgive me," Miguel said and rushed outside.

Lovett didn't see how Maria could have killed Raul and Pedro. Maybe Miguel was just confused. But Lovett wasn't going to hang around and find out what had happened. He had been at *El Rancho Torres* long enough. In about five minutes he'd be on his way back to Texas. He wasn't going to tell anybody he was leaving. He was just going to get into a car and go.

He went outside and saw that one of the cottages was brightly lighted up. It was near the area where he kept the car that *Señor* Torres had made available for his use. He ran to the cottage and looked inside the open door. The place was full of people. They were probably Torres's employees. Two bodies were lying on the floor. One was near the door and the other closer to the middle of the room. They were Raul and Pedro. There was no question about that.

He saw Torres, went to where he was standing and laid his hand on the man's shoulder. Torres turned and said, "Yes?"

"I'm going to get her. I'll be back shortly."

"I've already sent men, but you're welcome to help."

"Thank you." He went to the car. At least, Torres wouldn't be wondering where he was for the next several hours. He'd probably be back in Texas before the man gave him another thought. Torres would certainly have his hands full for a while. Lovett didn't think he'd report the Hernandez brothers' killings. More than likely, he'd instruct his men to bury the bodies somewhere on his ranch, and nobody would ever hear of them again.

In a few minutes Lovett was on his way to Monterrey. The gas tank was almost empty when he got there so he bought enough gasoline to get him to where he was going.

He took highway 54 from Monterrey to Ciudad Miguel Alemán, and less than three hours later he was there. He left the car parked in town and walked across the bridge to Roma, Texas. He wondered if he should call Teller but decided it could wait. He didn't think he needed to be in a rush. Probably Torres had already called him.

CHAPTER VIII

Maria started the bus again. In a few moments she was on the main highway and headed toward Monterrey once more. As she rounded a curve, she saw a man and three burros blocking the road. One of the animals was lying down, and the man was beating it with a stick trying to make it stand up. The other two were standing watching. They were as motionless as statues except for their swinging tails. The man wasn't having any success. His blows didn't seem to faze the reclining burro.

For a moment Maria was panic stricken. She knew she had to stop, but she had forgotten how to do it. An instant later she remembered. She took her foot off the gas and hit the brake pedal with all her might. While she was engaged in that maneuver, she inadvertently turned the steering wheel sharply to the left. The tires screamed and the bus skidded sideways blocking both lanes before coming to a stop. Fortunately for Maria, it had been traveling at a relatively slow rate of speed. Otherwise, it would have hit the animals and probably would have turned over as well.

Maria realized that she was trembling and weak with fear. She was only about fifty feet from the man and his burros. She wanted to get the bus straightened out and back on the right side of the road, but it wouldn't move. Its engine had died when she came to the sudden stop.

She put the shift lever in park and turned the ignition key. The engine turned over, but the bus didn't start. She kept trying, but it was no use. She could hear the engine grinding away, but that was all. She turned the key with all her strength hoping that that would help. But it didn't. The engine continued to turn, but still it didn't start.

She released the key wondering if she had broken the bus when she stopped it so suddenly. What would she do if it would no longer run? She looked down the road and saw the man who was minding the burros approaching the vehicle. She turned the key again as he came closer, and he began waving his arms.

"No, *joven*. Wait. Let it rest."

She tried it again. It was no use.

The man came to the side of the vehicle and knocked on the door. She was afraid to open it, but he knocked again.

"*Joven*. Wait. Let it rest for a while."

She noticed that the stubborn burro was still lying in the road, and the other two were still standing watching it. She turned her attention back to the man. His face was dark and old and wrinkled. Surely he'd pose her no danger. She opened the door.

"What do you want, old man?" she asked him. "It's your fault that my bus is ruined and will no longer run."

"I'm sorry, *joven*. I didn't intend for my burro to lie down in the middle of the road."

"Well, why are you here bothering me? Why aren't you making your stupid burro move?"

"I came to help you. Let your battery and engine rest for a little while. Then your bus will start. But if you keep trying to start it now, the battery will die, and you'll never be able to start it again."

He climbed laboriously into the bus. "Just wait for a while, *por favor*."

"I can't wait. I have urgent business in Monterrey."

"Let me try," he told her.

She got out of the seat reluctantly, and the old man sat down. After a couple of minutes, Maria said impatiently, "Well do something. I don't have all night."

"Patience is a virtue, my little man. Be patient for just a few moments more."

He waited for another minute or so. Then, holding the gas pedal to the floor, he turned the key. The engine coughed and spluttered for a few seconds and then roared into life. The old man got up from the seat, bowed to Maria and said, "Best of luck, young man." Then, with a twinkle in his eyes, he added. "I don't know who you're trying to fool, *señorita*, but just try to talk as little as possible. If you're careful and don't talk too much, your ruse may work for a little while. But try to get somewhere where such deceit is not needed as soon as possible. Because, sooner or later, someone will see through your disguise." Without waiting for her to respond, he left the bus and went back to his burros.

The animals seemed to be relieved at his return. The one that had been lying in the road got up with no further urging, and the old man and his burros plodded off the road and into the adjoining prairie. As soon as the way in front of her was clear, Maria placed the shift lever in drive and continued her journey toward Monterrey. The gas gauge showed that the tank was almost empty. She prayed that she would get into the city before the bus ran out of gas.

She glanced at the speedometer and noticed that she was exceeding the speed limit so she released some of the pressure on the gas pedal and began slowing down. Looking in her rearview mirror she saw the flashing red lights of a police car gaining on her at a high rate of speed. Her heart almost stopped. Why hadn't she watched the speedometer more closely? Why hadn't she been more careful? She knew it would be useless to try to outrun the policeman. She tried to think of a story to tell him that would be believable but could think of nothing. Her mind was blank.

Resigned that her flight was over, she took her foot from the accelerator and began pulling to the side of the road to stop. The driver of the police vehicle seemed to pay no attention to her maneuver. The cruiser veered to the left lane and passed her, its sirens screaming. It rounded a curve in front of her and soon disappeared from view.

She stopped the bus on the shoulder ten feet or so from the highway, rested her arms on the steering wheel and began to cry softly. She was too weak to try to drive. Tears ran down her cheeks, and she began rubbing her face with the sleeve of the ragged old coat she was wearing. She looked through the windshield and had trouble seeing the road. Her vision was blurry from looking through her tears.

After about five minutes she felt well enough to drive. Her trembling had subsided somewhat, and her arms felt a bit stronger. She breathed a thank you to the blessed Virgin and once more continued her journey.

After a few miles she felt much better and began to feel that the Lord would take care of her and she would be all right. The bus crested a small hill and she could see the lights of Monterrey shining brightly ahead. She was almost there! She looked at the gas gauge again, and the needle was pointing to empty. Maybe she could get into the city before the bus ran out of gas. She had to keep driving. What else could she do?

All at once she found herself in the outskirts of town. The road narrowed. Houses lined both sides of the street only a few feet from the edge of the road. Her lane was just barely wide enough to accommodate the width of the bus. To make matters worse, vehicles of all shapes and sizes were parked haphazardly on both sides, in some places nearly blocking the roadway and making driving almost impossible.

Maria had never been to Monterrey. In fact she had never been very far from her village. Now that she had arrived, she didn't know what she was going to do. But at least, she was miles away from *El Rancho Torres*, and she knew she would think of something.

A truck stopped in front of her, blocking her way, and a man got out and walked to where a group of men were congregated on the sidewalk. Someone tried to pass Maria's bus and was met by a large truck coming from the other direction. In a moment all traffic was stopped. No one was able to move. It seemed to Maria as though a thousand angry horns were sounding.

The truck driver who had precipitated the chaos continued his conversation with the people on the sidewalk paying the pandemonium no mind. Two people got out of their blocked vehicles and went over to where the man was standing and engaged him in a heated argument. Finally, after much screaming and cursing, the truck driver strolled leisurely back to his truck and started it. The traffic jam was so bad that no one, including him, was able to move so he began blowing his horn and screaming through his rolled down window.

Gradually the traffic began to inch along once more. When Maria had enough space to move a few feet, she pressed her foot down on the accelerator. The engine coughed and sputtered and then died. She tried to start it again with vehicles all around her loudly blowing their horns. She looked at her gas gauge, and it was registering below the empty mark. She was sure that the tank was empty, and there was no use in her trying any more to start the vehicle. With no further hesitation, she pushed her hat securely onto her head, grabbed Sandra's purse and left the bus.

Maria walked quickly down the sidewalk and entered the nearest alleyway. It was strewn with litter and debris from more than a dozen overturned garbage cans. Rats scurried in every direction as she passed. She decided that it would be a good idea to get rid of the purse. If anybody saw what looked like a little ragamuffin boy carrying a purse, he'd immediately assume that the youth had stolen it and call the police. But more likely, Maria would be spotted by a group of youths who would beat her up and take the purse for themselves. When they discovered she was a girl, which would happen the moment they touched her, they would take her somewhere and have their way with her until their youthful lust was satiated. She could picture them as delighted with her naked body as kids who have found an unlocked candy store. She didn't want to risk that.

Maria saw a recessed area on one side of the alley where the garbage cans were supposed to be placed so they wouldn't impede the movement of the garbage trucks. However, the area wasn't being used. Only two or three cans were in the alcove. The others were sitting or lying lidless in the alley blocking the movement of any vehicle that may chance to enter. Garbage was scattered everywhere.

After assuring herself that she was alone, she went into the recessed area, and standing behind the filthy trash containers that were located there, she pressed herself against the fence that formed the back border to the alcove hoping she would be invisible to anyone who may happen to come into the alley.

When she was certain no one could see her, she transferred everything from the purse to her coat pocket. There were two legal documents, one of which had Sandra's name and picture on it; a good deal of Mexican money which Maria didn't take time to count; an American ten dollar bill; a compact and lipstick; and a wallet which contained several pictures in small cellophane holders and a number of plastic and paper cards. After making sure the purse was empty, she threw it into one of the garbage cans.

Maria took the envelope from her pocket that she had taken from Raul's body and opened it. It contained a thick sheaf of American one hundred dollar bills. She was afraid to take time to count them for fear somebody would chance by and see the money. Besides, there were so many that it would take her a long time to count them. She quickly closed the envelope, put it back into her pocket and continued walking.

Her destination was the bus station, but she had no idea where it was. Before she could seek directions, she had to find a restroom. She had to urinate so badly that she was afraid she was going to wet her pants. After about a hundred yards, she came to a narrow street. She saw a billiards parlor and ducked inside. Several men were standing around drinking beer, and a few were playing pool. They looked at her without much curiosity and went back to their business.

As soon as she entered, she saw a sign in the corner indicating that the restrooms were there. She almost went into the ladies' room but caught herself just in time and went into the one labeled *hombres*. Two men were standing near a sidewall urinating into a trough with water flowing into it in a constant stream from a small faucet. One was standing in such a position that she had a clear view of his penis and the amber urine splattering against the side of the trough. She averted her eyes and went into one of the stalls.

The place was filthy. She looked for toilet paper, but there was none. Only a wet newspaper and some kind of a catalogue lying in a shallow puddle on the floor. The toilet was full of excrement and hadn't been flushed. Urine and feces were on the toilet seat. It was all she could do to keep from gagging.

The two men left the urinal and went back into the pool hall without washing their hands. When Maria was satisfied that she was alone in the restroom, she came out of the cubical that she had been occupying and went into the adjacent one. It was a little cleaner but not much. It didn't have any paper at all, not even a newspaper or a catalogue. She went back into the first booth, tore out several pages from the catalogue and took them to the lavatory. The soap dispenser was broken and empty so she couldn't get any soap. The hot water faucet didn't work so she soaked four of the pages under the cold water faucet and squeezed as much water from them as she could.

She went back into the cleaner of the two booths, flushed the toilet, even though it didn't need it, and cleaned off the seat with two of the wet sheets of paper saving the other two for later. Then she covered the toilet seat as best she could with several of the dry catalogue pages, and with a sigh of resignation, she gingerly sat down.

After she was done, she felt much better. She cleaned herself with the remaining sheets of paper as well as she could hoping she would be able to do a better job when she got to the bus station. When she came out of the restroom, she decided to ask one of the men for directions to the depot. But then she remembered what the old burro tender had told her: *"I don't know who you're trying to fool, señorita, but just try to talk as little as possible. If you're careful and don't talk too much, your ruse may work for a little while. But try to get somewhere where such deceit is not needed as soon as possible. Because, sooner or later, someone will see through your disguise."*

She went outside, and the street was almost empty. It was getting very late. Probably most people were already home for the night. She saw the headlights of an approaching vehicle, and as it got closer she was able to discern that it was a bus. She decided to stop it and get aboard. Thanks to Sandra, she had enough money to pay the fare.

She got some money ready to give to the driver. The bus stopped and she stepped inside. Except for her and the driver, the vehicle was empty. She handed him a bill and he stuffed it into a box mounted on the dash to the left of the steering wheel.

"Do I get any change?"

"I don't give change. It's against company policy. If you have any complaints write a letter to the company. The next time have the correct amount available."

She knew it would be useless to argue. Besides, she was afraid her voice would give her away

"What are you doing in this part of town this time of night?" the driver demanded.

"I need to go to the bus station. Do you go near there?" she asked him softly.

"Yes," he said, "I do. In fact, I stop there to pick up passengers. But don't go there to pick pockets or steal from the customers. The police have been watching that place like a hawk."

"The police?"

"Yes. That's what I said. Why? Are they after you? Did you steal that money you just gave me?"

"No. I need to meet somebody there."

"What is the matter with your voice?" the driver demanded suspiciously.

"Nothing," she whispered. "I have a cold."

"Perhaps I shouldn't let you ride. Maybe you'll give it to me. I don't need a cold. With all my other troubles that's the last thing I need. I should make you walk. It's a very long way, and a long walk would teach you to show some manners."

Maria hesitated not knowing what to say.

"Oh, get back there and sit down. Don't bother me anymore. I have work to do and can't waste my time talking to idiots." He pulled the bus away from the curb as Maria went to find a seat.

An old lady was waiting at the next stop. She was loaded down with bags and boxes. She tried to enter the bus but was unable to get all her things through the door. Realizing she couldn't carry all the packages onto the bus at once, she laid them on the street. She studied the pile for a moment and then began picking up the parcels one at a time and working them through the door of the bus and onto its floor. Her progress was labored and slow.

The driver watched in obvious disgust. “Hurry up, old woman,” he demanded harshly. “I have a schedule to meet.”

Maria, feeling sorry for the old woman, came to her rescue. She went to the front of the bus and began moving the packages out of the way. The woman got into the bus, rummaged through her purse and handed the driver a handful of change. He threw it into his money box and said, “Hurry, *Vieja*. You’re making me late. I hope you didn’t steal any of those things. I will not allow you to carry stolen property on my bus.”

“No,” she said indignantly, “none of it is stolen.”

“Well don’t just stand there, old woman. I can’t waste my time talking to someone as dense as you.” She started back toward where Maria was sitting, and the driver drove on toward his next stop.

The woman got down on her hands and knees and began arranging her parcels into an orderly stack. Maria leaned over and helped her. Once the woman was satisfied, she sat next to Maria and looked at her with a big smile on her face.

The bus began to get more passengers as it got closer to town. At some stops, it would pick up only one person, but more often, two, three or even more people would come aboard.

“How far is it to the bus station?” Maria asked her seat mate after they had traveled what seemed to Maria to be at least four or five kilometers.

“It’s a long way. We got onto the bus near the end of the line. It’s at least three or four kilometers more. Are you meeting someone there?”

“I wanted to inquire on the price of tickets. I thought someday I would like to go somewhere, perhaps even to the United States.”

“That would be so much fun,” the woman answered. “By the way, my name is *Señora* Valdez. I should have told you earlier that you’re a very good boy to help an old woman like me.”

“Where I come from it’s only common courtesy. I don’t think I’ll ever get used to the ways of the city.”

“So you’re a country boy. I thought so. Please tell me where you’re from, and for goodness sake, what’s your name? It’s very difficult to talk to a young man who doesn’t have a name.”

Maria hadn’t come up with a name and had to think for a moment before replying. “They call me Antonio,” she finally responded.

The old lady looked at her closely, then leaned over and whispered in her ear, "I don't want the others to hear what I'm telling you, Antonio. But I don't believe Antonio is your name. In spite of the rough clothing you're wearing, I find it hard to believe that you're a boy. Still I wasn't sure until I heard your voice. It's plain to me that you're a girl and probably a very pretty one. But don't worry. Your secret is safe with me."

That *Señora* Valdez could see through her subterfuge so easily frightened her. If it was that obvious to an old woman with dim eyes, wouldn't it be even more obvious to everyone else?

She said softly in a hoarse whisper, "What am I to do?"

"I can tell you're fleeing from someone. I would guess you were molested by a perverted stepfather or uncle. Sadly such abuse occurs more frequently than we like to admit. Am I not right?"

Maria was surprised that the *señora* had mentioned an uncle. She thought of *Tío* Juan and felt a cold wave of fear and disgust wash over her.

"I want to go away somewhere, but there's no place for me to go. I was planning to catch a bus tonight."

"I don't think that would be wise. Not until you decide upon a course of action that you've carefully thought through. You come home with me. I'm all alone and have more space than I need. Stay with me for a while, and we'll come up with a plan. Besides, it's much too late to go anywhere tonight."

Maria couldn't believe what *Señora* Valdez was saying. A stranger in a large city was offering her more than anyone had ever offered her before.

"But aren't you afraid to make such a generous offer? You know nothing about me. I may be a thief or a killer. Aren't you afraid to take a stranger in?"

Señora Valdez laughed. "I doubt that you're anything as dreadful as that. I'm an old woman and credit myself with being a good judge of people's character. What I see is a young girl who has been terribly misused but couldn't even imagine doing anything bad herself."

Maria thought about the *señora's* invitation for a moment and then said, "Are you serious in your offer? Am I really welcome to come?"

"Of course, I'm serious my dear. I need someone to help me with these packages. And I'm dying of curiosity to find out your real name. But don't tell me now. I can wait until we get off of this bus."

After several more kilometers, *Señora* Valdez said, "The next stop is the bus station. We'll get off a few blocks past it."

The bus stopped to discharge passengers, and Maria saw five police cars parked in front of the bus station in a no parking area by the curb. "Look at all the officers," she said to *Señora* Valdez. "Are there always so many police cars?"

"No. Usually they park in the next block at José Martinez's restaurant where they can gossip and drink coffee and flirt with the girls. They're probably waiting to arrest somebody."

"Oh. How would they know that a criminal might be on his way there?"

"Probably somebody tipped them off. I'm sure they're too stupid and lazy to have figured it out for themselves."

Maria's stomach tightened, and a tremor passed through her body as they passed the depot. Someone must have reported her for what she had done to the Hernandez brothers at *El Rancho Torres* and for stealing the bus. Softly she thanked the blessed Virgin for uniting her with *Señora* Valdez. She had no doubt in her mind that it was the Virgin's doing.

"What is it? You look as though you just saw a ghost," the *señora* told her.

"I'm just tired. I haven't eaten for a while and am a little weak."

She didn't actually feel hungry because she had eaten at *El Rancho Torres* earlier in the afternoon, but she didn't know how else to explain her wan face and sudden weakness. After telling *Señora* Valdez that she was hungry, however, she realized that she actually was.

"I must get you home and feed you a good hot meal. Your face is as white as paper."

The *señora* reached up and pulled a cord that ran horizontally above the windows from the front to the rear of the bus. Maria heard a buzzer sound near where the driver was sitting.

"This is where we get off," *Señora* Valdez said.

Maria picked up all of the parcels but one, leaving it for the lady to carry. She let the *señora* go around her and lead her to the exit door. The older woman was already outside and Maria was stepping down the stairs to the door when the driver scolded, "This isn't your stop. You were supposed to get off at the bus station."

"I'll go back later. I must help this sweet lady with her packages," Maria told him.

"Don't try to ride with me when I come back on my return trip. You're too impertinent and won't be welcome. Now, hurry and get off my bus. I have no time to talk to fools," he responded in an angry voice.

Maria stepped down to the street, the door closed behind her and the bus drove away.

"Why is he so hateful?" Maria wanted to know.

"Who knows? We must pity people like him, but we must also do our best to avoid them. They're as dangerous as they are pathetic. They can't find happiness in their own hearts so they'll go to any length to prevent others from experiencing happiness in theirs." She paused for a moment and then continued with a sparkle in her eyes, "Now, Antonio. You must tell me your real name."

"My name is Maria Alicia Guardia," Maria told *Señora* Valdez as the bus drove away. "But please, I'm afraid to use that name. I'm in serious trouble, and I don't want anyone to know who I am. So Sandra is the name I want to be called."

"But I don't understand. A pretty young girl like you couldn't possibly be in such severe trouble as you describe. Things will be much brighter after a good night's sleep. You'll even laugh at the concerns that seem so serious tonight."

"Please. It's a long and complicated story. Can we wait until we get to your house? I'll tell you everything then."

"Certainly, we shall. And I'll honor your wishes. From now on, as far as this old lady is concerned, your name is Sandra." Maria realized that she didn't even know what her last name was supposed to be. She knew it was on some of the documents she had taken from Sandra's purse, but she hadn't taken the time to read them. She was too frightened and in too much of a hurry when she was standing in that dark alley near the place where she had abandoned the bus.

Señora Valdez led Maria down a crooked, narrow, unpaved street. There were no streetlights, and only a few houses had lights glimmering through their windows. Fortunately, the moon provided enough light for them to see where they were going. Maria wondered if the little lady had trouble traipsing down that dismal road at night when there wasn't a bright moon to light her way.

They had walked a little more than five blocks from the main road when the *señora* opened a gate in front of one of the houses and said, "We are here. This is my *casa*."

Maria followed her to the front door and waited for her to unlock it. In a moment they were inside a small living room. It was dark inside the house, much darker than outside. Leaving the door open to get as much illumination as possible from the outside, *Señora* Valdez held up her hand to grasp the string that hung from a light fixture in the middle of the living room ceiling.

It didn't take her long to find it. She was so familiar with the house that she could have found it easily even with her eyes closed. When the light came on, Maria saw a clean and tidy room. A sofa sat against one wall, and next to it was an iron end table with a glass top. A love seat was against another wall. An iron cocktail table which matched the end table sat in the center of the room. Two easy chairs and a wooden rocking chair were facing a television set which was located in one corner. The windows were covered with green curtains trimmed in white and red. Everything was fresh and bright.

Señora Valdez closed the door and said to Maria, "Come. Let's put these packages away. Then I'll fix you a hot meal. While I'm doing that, you'll take a long hot shower. I'm sorry, but I don't have a bathtub. Later, after you eat, you'll get a good night's sleep. We won't do any more talking tonight. There'll be time enough for that in the morning."

Maria felt grimy and bedraggled. She could think of nothing she wanted more than a hot shower. However, she didn't know what she would wear afterward. The only clothes she had were what she had on. She hoped *Señora* Valdez had a washing machine so she could wash them. She hated the thought of putting the dirty garments back on after she bathed.

"I hope you have a washing machine. I have no other clothes than these filthy rags I'm wearing. I do have a little money so I'll be able to buy me some things tomorrow. But for now I have only these. I must sleep in them as well as wear them during the day. So I hope I'll be able to wash them tonight before I go to bed."

"That won't be necessary. We'll throw those scraps in the trash. I have some things here that belong to my granddaughter that'll surely fit you. You and she are about the same size."

"But I couldn't do that."

"Oh yes you can. She never uses them. They're here only for a lack of a better place to be. Now come with me into the bedroom, and we'll find you something nice to sleep in. I'll fix us something to eat while you bathe and change."

They went into a tiny bedroom. It was furnished with a small bed and a night stand. The bed was covered with a brightly colored bedspread. An electric lamp was on the night stand.

"This is your room. This is where you'll sleep tonight," the *señora* told Maria.

The older woman opened a closet and said, "Here are some of the things that my Lydia left here. She's married now and doesn't come very often any more. She never bothered to take them with her, but I didn't have the heart to give them away. You're welcome to anything you can use."

Maria turned and hugged the woman tightly. "You're an angel, *señora*. You have truly saved my life. I can never thank you enough for what you're doing for me."

"*De nada*. It's nothing. I'm doing no more than you would do for me if our situations were reversed."

Maria found panties and a long nightgown, both of which were clean and fresh. She took them into the bathroom, got under the hot shower and scrubbed herself for a long time. The hot water pelting against her skin felt so good that she could have stayed under it for an hour. Finally, she got out reluctantly and dried.

She went into the kitchen where the *señora* had finished preparing their dinner and had just begun setting the table.

"Oh, you're so beautiful!" the older lady exclaimed. "What happened to the little vagabond who was here earlier?"

"Thank you. Now that I'm a girl again, I would like to help you set the table."

She started to help, but *Señora* Valdez shooed her away.

"Just relax. It's almost ready."

In a few minutes *Señora* Valdez was finished and began placing *gallena con mole,* rice, refried beans, *tamales* and corn *tortillas* on the table.

"I hope you like coffee, Sandra," she said. Being addressed by that name made her feel strange, but she knew she would have to get used to it.

"Oh, yes. I love it." Maria liked it with milk and a lot of sugar but didn't want to say so because she was afraid the *señora* didn't have either one.

Señora Valdez poured two cups of coffee. It was hot and strong and smelled wonderful.

"Sit down, Sandra. I'll get some cream and sugar from the refrigerator. I'm sure you like cream and sugar. I know I do."

As simple as the meal was, it was delicious. When they were finished, *Señora* Valdez washed the dishes and Maria dried them. Then the older woman put them away.

"It's late," Señora Valdez said when they had finished putting up the dishes and cleaning the kitchen. "It's time for bed. Sleep as long as you need to. We'll have time to get better acquainted in the morning."

Maria told the woman goodnight and went into her bedroom and went to bed. The bed was soft and comfortable and smelled like fresh lemons. In a few minutes she was asleep and didn't wake up until late the next morning.

The aroma of freshly brewed coffee woke Maria up. It took her a few moments to remember where she was. Then she felt guilty for sleeping so late. She didn't want *Señora* Valdez to think she was lazy.

She got up, quickly made the bed and went to the bathroom. After she had finished there, she went into the kitchen where the *señora* was drinking coffee and eating *pan dulce*.

"Good morning, Sandra," she said. "I hope you slept well."

"Good morning to you, *señora*. I did sleep well. Too well, I'm afraid. I'm sorry I stayed in bed so late. I don't want you to think I'm lazy."

"No. I don't think that. I'm glad you slept well. Last night I was saddened when I looked at your face. I had never seen an unhappier face on anyone, especially anyone so young. Now you look cheerful and refreshed. I hope what was troubling you last night doesn't seem so formidable now."

Maria had intended to tell the *señora* everything that had happened to her in the past several days, but now she didn't think it would be wise. She would tell her only a little bit, the part about her *tío*.

"It's still troubling me, but I'm afraid I was a bit dramatic last night. I often am when I'm tired. Ever since my father died, my *tío* has been saying things to me and trying to touch me in ways that I don't like. The other night, while I was sleeping, he got into my bed and tried to rape me. I fought him off, but now I'm afraid to go back home. He knows the mayor and the police chief and has much influence in our village. He has threatened to have me thrown in jail on fabricated charges if I return, and I think he can do it."

"Tell the police what he's doing. He's the one who'll go to jail."

"Perhaps you're right, but I don't think so. He has even made a deal with the warden of the prison. The warden wants a young girl to serve as his mistress, and my *tío* has promised him me."

"He's just making that up to frighten you."

"That could be the case, but I don't want to take the chance. I hope to go to the United States. I have a *tía* there who has invited me to visit her. I have all the necessary documents. That's why I was on my way to the bus station when I met you last night."

She felt guilty saying she planned to visit her *tía* when she had no intention of doing that. Her *tía* lived in California, and Maria was planning to go to Texas which was much closer. But she knew that the *señora* would worry if she said she was going to a place where she knew no one.

"I don't think you should rush into anything. You're welcome to stay with me as long as you wish. Now that you've told me your life's story, I think you should call me Lena. I think we know each other well enough to go by our first names."

"Lena. Are you sure you want me to?"

"Of course, Sandra. Now, what would you like to eat?"

"Please. Tell me what *you* would like to eat and I'll prepare it for you. I'm a very good cook."

"Oh, really? Let me see just how good of a cook you are. I would like *huevos rancheros y jamón*," Lena told her. "And *tortillas* heated on the *comal*. Do you think you can do that?"

"Yes. I can do that. You sit and relax, and I'll have it ready in a few minutes."

Lena's eyes danced merrily, "But that's not all. I would also like *papitas con chile*, *frijoles refritos y mas cafe*. Of course, you don't have to cook the *frijoles*. I already have some frozen in plastic containers in my freezer."

"You don't think I can do it, do you? Well just show me where you keep your food, and I'll surprise you. I'm *also* ready for a big breakfast and will fix the same thing for myself."

It didn't take Maria long to prepare the food and set it on the table. The *señora* looked at it and applauded.

"Just look at what you've done. It smells delicious. Oh, Sandra, you've truly outdone yourself."

When they finished eating, Maria washed and dried the dishes, and Lena put them into the cabinets which looked like they had been built by quality craftsmen.

"You're full of surprises, *Señora* Lena. You have a beautiful house, so modern and elegant. You even have *frijoles* in your freezer ready to be used at a moment's notice."

"Yes. I'm not the one responsible, though. My grandson did this. I would still be living as they lived one hundred years ago if it were not for him. He did this for me."

"Well, you're lucky to have such a thoughtful grandson. Does he live nearby?"

"Oh, no. His name is Raymundo. He lives in San Antonio, Texas. He's married to a woman from there and is now an American citizen, himself. He builds houses, and I think he's very rich. He did this for us when my husband was still alive. At first we resisted because we were not ready to accept the new ways. But we quickly learned to love it."

"I'm sorry to hear about your husband. How long have you been alone?"

"Almost a year. Raymundo and his wife visit me quite often. They want me to come to the United States and live with them. I don't know. Sometimes I like the idea. Sometimes I don't. I don't want to make up my mind until I'm sure."

"I think that's very wise of you. Perhaps we should go there together just to visit before you make up your mind. I'm sure we would both like it. I've read so much about it that I can't wait to see it with my own eyes."

Maria was still wearing the nightgown she had slept in. She looked at *Señora* Valdez and smiled a shy smile. "Forgive me, Lena, for getting carried away. Sometimes when I'm excited, I talk too much. If you'll excuse me, I'll get changed. I found a beautiful dress that fits me perfectly. And also some stockings and shoes."

"Yes. Go ahead. Then we'll go to town. Since you've never been to Monterrey, I'm sure you would like to do some exploring. And you may wish to do some shopping as well."

"Yes. I would like that. I'll be ready in a moment." She went into the bedroom and emerged fifteen minutes later wearing black low heeled pumps and a long blue dress that looked as though it had been custom-made for her.

Lena was waiting. They went outside. Lena locked the house behind them, and soon they were on a bus headed toward town. As they passed the bus depot, Maria looked closely to see if she could see any police cars, but there were none. Maybe the ones that had been there the night before had been watching for her, and maybe they hadn't. She would never know, but she was glad she hadn't gone inside the depot to find out.

By the time they got to town, it was after ten thirty. Lena was ready to enter a cheap little *tienda,* but Maria said, "Let's not go in here. I want to go somewhere nice."

Lena led her down the block and across the street to a large department store that looked new and expensive. "Will this one do?" the *señora* asked her.

"I think it'll do splendidly." They went inside.

Maria knew that the Mexican money she had gotten from Sandra's purse wouldn't buy very much so she went to the service desk.

"How can we help you, *señorita*?" the woman behind the counter asked her.

"Do you take American money? I was on my way to the bank to get some changed to Mexican currency when I saw your establishment and couldn't wait to come inside."

"Oh, yes, *señorita.* We are very happy to accept American money. Just bring your purchases here when you're ready to check out, and I'll give you my personal attention.

Maria went to the lingerie department and began picking out bras, panties, stockings, panty hose and slips and putting them into her shopping cart. Then she began looking at shoes.

"Remember," *Señora* Valdez told her, "I still have those clothes that you saw in my granddaughter's closet. You're welcome to anything you need."

"I know that, and I may take some of them if you're sure you want me to. But at least, I want to have brand new underwear and comfortable shoes. My feet are bruised terribly, and I need to take very good care of them. I would also like to have two pretty dresses of my very own choosing."

"I understand that, child, but are you sure you have enough money? This is a very expensive store. The merchandise is of high quality and worth the price, but still it's quite expensive."

"I'll be careful of my money," Maria promised. "Just what I have in the cart, a pair of shoes, two dresses, two blouses and a pair of casual pants for everyday use. Nothing more."

She bought a pair of pants which flattered her soft, small body and then tried on several dresses, finally finding exactly what she wanted. Then she started toward the service desk, but before she got there, she said, "Wait. I have to get a suitcase. I can't go to Texas without a suitcase."

She went to the luggage department, picked out a suitcase and put it in the cart along with the other items.

"All right." she said, "That's all." She pushed the cart to the service desk and found the lady she had talked to earlier. She paid for her purchases with three of her hundred dollar bills. When the lady offered her change, she said, "Could I please have ten dollars of that in Mexican money and the rest in American money? I'm just getting ready to go back home." She wanted the Mexican money in case she needed to make several more trips on the bus.

"Certainly, *señorita*." The woman opened a metal box which was sitting on a shelf under the counter, took out some American money and gave it to Maria.

"Thank you," Maria told her, and she and *Señora* Valdez left the store.

They were quite hungry so Maria offered to buy them lunch.

"No *hija*. If you really plan to go to America, you must be very careful with your money. Even though you plan to stay with your *tía*, you'll find it's very expensive to live there. My grandson tells me it's almost impossible to get by unless you have a good job or are rich."

"But we have to eat."

"I know, Sandra, but there's plenty food at home. We'll eat there."

They went to a bus stop, and a lady greeted *Señora* Valdez as she and Maria walked up.

"Lena. Have you heard the latest news?"

"I don't know, Rebecca. I hear much news. The latest? Who knows?"

"Terrible things have happened at *El Rancho Torres*. Terrible things, indeed." She stopped as though she was waiting for *Señora* Valdez to urge her to divulge more.

Lena didn't say anything, however, and after a short wait, Rebecca said to Maria, "Have we met, *señorita*? I don't recall seeing you before."

"No we've never met. My name is Sandra. I'm visiting *Señora* Valdez for a few days."

"Well, maybe you heard." She didn't wait for confirmation. "A gang of desperados attacked *El Rancho Torres* last night. They killed four people and stole one million *pesos*. The police think that the culprits are hiding in Monterrey."

"Well, good for them," *Señora* Valdez responded. "*Señor* Torres and his crowd are the worst crooks in Mexico. Nothing that happens to them can be worse than what they deserve."

"It's no use to talk to you. You never take anything seriously."

A bus stopped, and Rebecca, *Señora* Valdez and Maria boarded. Rebecca headed straight to two women that she evidently recognized and sat down beside them. Maria and *Señora* Valdez sat a few seats away.

"Have you heard the latest news?" Maria heard Rebecca say to the two women. "A gang of desperados raided *El Rancho Torres* last night. They killed seven people and stole ten million *pesos*. The police know who one of them is. She's a young girl from Loma Linda. They think she's hiding out in Monterrey because they found the bus she escaped in. I hope they find her soon. Young people today don't have any respect. If they put her in jail for about one hundred years, she'll learn respect there. That's what they ought to do with all the little hoodlums. Put them in jail for a hundred years."

When Maria and *Señora* Valdez got home, they had a quick lunch of chicken *tacos*, *tostadas* with lots of diced tomatoes and shredded cheese and lettuce spread on top and iced tea. As soon as they finished and cleaned up the kitchen, Maria said, "I think I'll go to the bus depot and look at their schedules. I would like to see how often the busses go to Texas and how much the tickets cost."

"You go ahead, dear. I'll wait for you here. I think I'll watch some television. Did you notice the television set? Raymundo gave it to me. I don't watch it very much, but lately I've begun to get very interested in some of the stories."

Maria changed into the pants and one of the blouses she had just purchased and put on the new walking shoes. She looked in the mirror and was pleased with her appearance.

"Lena, how do I look?"

"You look beautiful, my dear. Now please be careful."

"I will. Don't worry. I'll be back in a little while."

When she got close enough to the depot to see it clearly, there were several police cars parked in the no parking zone in front. Four or five policemen were milling about on the sidewalk in front of the station stopping some of the passersby. Maria stopped, not wanting to get any closer for fear that they would stop and question her. But she was also hesitant about turning and walking back the way she had come. She was afraid that action would certainly draw their attention and make them want to talk to her.

She was standing at a bus stop without realizing it, and while she was trying to decide what to do, a bus stopped near her and its doors opened. She quickly got inside, and the bus started moving again. Maria remembered the correct fare from the ride that she had taken earlier that morning so she deposited the proper amount and took a seat. She sat on the side of the bus that would give her a clear view of the bus station as she rode past.

As the bus drove by, she saw *Señor* Torres talking to the policeman who seemed to be in charge. Torres glanced absent mindedly at the bus as it drove by, and Maria, averting her face so he wouldn't see her through the window and recognize her, felt her body turn cold. She looked back again after she was well past the station and was relieved to see that Torres had turned his full attention back to the policeman, seemingly unaware of anything else.

"What's going on at the bus station?" she asked an old man who was sitting near her.

"They're hunting for some terrorists who have been raiding the *ranchos* near here. They've already burned several houses and killed some of the *vaqueros*. But it's stupid to look for them at a bus depot. What terrorists in their right mind would ride a bus? I'm sure that if there actually are any terrorists, they have their own cars and are far away by now."

"Does anybody know who they are?"

"No. I don't think so. Some say that they're no more than common bandits. Others think they're communists. I believe the authorities made the whole thing up and nothing really happened at all. Do you know why I believe that? Because they say that the leader is a young girl like Joan of Arc. Now who's going to believe anything that ridiculous?"

Maria didn't answer. The old man closed his eyes and leaned back in his seat, and soon he was snoring gently. Maria got off at the next stop, crossed the street and caught a bus going back toward *Señora* Valdez's house. When she passed the bus depot, *Señor* Torres was still there, and it seemed to Maria that there were even more police cars than there had been when she rode by just a few minutes earlier. As she walked down the crooked street to Lena's house, her heart was heavy with fear.

"You look downhearted, Sandra," Lena told Maria as soon as she saw her crestfallen face, "but I have news that will remove the sadness from that beautiful face and replace it with a bright smile."

"Lena, I'm so afraid—"

"Oh, I'm glad you're back so soon," Lena told her. "You'll never believe the news I received just now. My grandson, Raymundo, called while you were out. He's coming to see me next Wednesday. Yes, this coming Wednesday, the day after tomorrow. He has work to do that'll keep him here for a week. I told him I have an American friend who needs to get back to San Antonio, and he agreed to take you. So, now, you won't have to worry about riding a bus."

Maria's eyes lit up like stars. "Oh, is it really true?"

Señora Valdez wrapped her small arms around Maria, squeezing her with all her strength. "Yes *mi hija*, it's true."

"Thank you, blessed Mother of God. Thank you, blessed Jesus," Maria whispered softly as she put her arms around the old woman, returning her hug.

CHAPTER IX

"Let me show you how to work this thing," Larry Daniels told Lovett. "I like to mount it in an SUV or a van. That gives you a lot of flexibility. You can install it more or less permanently in a building if you want to, but that takes away from your flexibility. For some reason it seems like it makes it a lot easier for the cops to find, too.

"Actually, when you get right down to it, it wouldn't make sense to put it in a building, anyway. Most patients are too weak to be traveling long distances for their treatment. At least most of the ones you're going to be treating in this thing. They're usually in real bad shape by the time they get to us. Now I prefer an Explorer, like this one. That's because I like its size. It's really just exactly the right size. But any van or SUV will do. That Sienna you have there is perfect. Hell, it's probably just as good as the Explorer."

He was showing Lovett the cancer cure machine that Lovett was ready to pick up. The contraption was about eight feet long and three feet high. It was mounted in the cargo bay of Daniels' vehicle. The thing was made of yellow opaque plastic and had three round, green-tinted plastic windows on each side. It was shaped like one half of a large tube that had originally been about six feet in diameter and had been split lengthwise into two equal parts.

The bottom surface, where the patient lay during treatments, slid in and out like a drawer, making it easy to put him into the machine for his treatments and to remove him when the treatments were over. It was made of three-quarter inch plywood covered with foam rubber padding and some kind of imitation, manmade leather. There was also a pillow, for the patient's comfort, covered with the same artificial leather.

"When you're ready to start the treatments, you just pull out the bed, lay the patient on it and slide it back in. Then you plug in the machine. It'll work from the vehicle's cigarette lighter or from a regular one-ten outlet. You really always should use the one-ten. Usually you can. Just be sure to keep a long extension cord handy. We have a hundred foot one here that's part of the package. Now, watch this."

Daniels took an electrical cord that was attached to the machine and plugged it into the Explorer's cigarette lighter. "Now, look."

He turned on a switch at the end of the contraption nearer to the front of the Explorer. When he did that, the machine began humming, and purple lights illuminated its interior. The humming was very soft at first but gradually got louder and louder. Then, when the sound reached its maximum volume, it began getting softer again until it was almost inaudible. It repeated the cycle over and over, never varying its rhythm.

The same thing was happening with the lights. At first they were so dim they were difficult to see. But they gradually got brighter in perfect timing with the droning sound, reaching their brightest just as the sound reached its maximum volume and fading to their dimmest just when the sound was at its softest.

"Now, feel the bed. Go on. Crawl inside if you want to. There's nothing there that's going to hurt you."

Lovett got into the machine. The pad was vibrating.

"Go ahead. Lay down. Use the pillow."

Lovett did as Daniels told him to do. His entire body seemed to be immersed in sound, light and vibrations.

"That's all there is to it? I just plug it in?"

"Yeah. And then turn on the switch. It's not really complicated at all. But right now it's in emergency mode. It'll run your truck's battery down real fast, and you should never use it this way unless you have to. Maybe it would run a little longer if you kept the engine running. I don't know, though, because I've never tried it. Anyway, I don't even know why they designed it to work off of a battery. I guess it was more of a selling point than anything else. But it really isn't practical at all. Let me plug it into a one-ten for you."

One end of a one hundred foot cord was plugged into an outlet at the back of Daniels' house, and the other end came through the window into the SUV. Daniels plugged a short electrical cord attached to the machine into the longer one.

"Okay," he said. "All we do it flip the switch like so. Just like we did a while ago. See?" He turned on the switch, and the machine came on exactly as it had before. He let it run for a few minutes.

"That's better," Daniels said as he turned off the switch. "You can run it as long as you want to without worrying about running down your battery. Sometimes, when they're getting real desperate and know they're about to die, they like for you to run it a long time. That's fine if you don't have any more appointments right away. It makes them feel better, and the amount of extra electricity is next to nothing. You might even charge them a little more if they have any money left."

"I'm not a mechanic," Lovett said. "Can someone put it into my van?"

"Sure. That's part of the deal."

"How long will it take?"

"Can you leave your Sienna here?"

"Sure. If you can drop me off at my place."

"I can do that. We'll have it finished by noon tomorrow. We'll even deliver it when it's done."

"You know, I meant to ask you. Whatever happened to that old guy you were treating before I went to Mexico?"

"Oh, yeah. Well, he finally died. For a while it looked like I was going to have to find some way to kill him. No, I'm just kidding. I'd never do anything like that. I might just leave town and not show up at his next appointment, but I'd never kill anybody. It's not worth taking a human life, no matter how poor his health is, just to make a little more profit. And besides that, we're already taking enough risk just operating this thing. I was all set to tell the authorities that I'm a faith healer if they ever caught me. But that won't be necessary now because I'm out of this business for good."

"I don't think it would do any good to say you're a faith healer," Lovett told him. "In a business like this there's only one way to play it. Don't ever get caught. As soon as you get caught, it's over."

"You're right. That's the main reason I'm getting out. It's a real good business. But the law of averages catches up with everyone sooner or later."

"Yeah," Lovett said. "Then I'll keep it a while and sell it to somebody else. That way, everybody can stay a few steps ahead of the authorities."

"What I was getting ready to say, the old man's grand kids gave me a bonus. They kept telling me that they only wished they had found me sooner. They thanked me and gave me two thousand dollars. It's gestures like that that make this job worthwhile. It almost tempts you to accept one more patient and then one more and so on and so on until you finally get caught."

"Sammy used to warn me that as soon as you start getting complacent you're in trouble. Always quit when you're ahead. And I've found out the hard way he was right."

"Now there's one more thing I almost forgot. The patients aren't going to be happy unless you give them some kind of medication. I don't know why that is, but it's true," Daniels said.

"That's easy to understand. You never go to a doctor anymore without having to fill a prescription. Half the time, I don't think you really need it. But the doctors know you're expecting it, and of course, they're making money at the same time."

"You better believe it. Anyway, my basic mixture is honey and vinegar diluted with water. But I like to flavor it with something else. Last time, I cut up some apricots and boiled them until the water was real syrupy. Then I waited for it to get cool and strained it through a dish towel. I mixed that with the honey and vinegar solution, and it tasted pretty good. I made up some kind of a name for it, but I said the flavor came from apricot pits. I told them they still use apricot pits for treating cancer in the Scandinavian countries."

"Maybe I'll do that," Lovett told him. "If you can find something real bitter, that might work. A lot of people don't think their medicine is any good unless it tastes bad."

"I never tried that, but I'm sure it would work. The point is, you have to have something. The machine is good, but they want their medication to go with it."

"Do you happen to have any of that honey and vinegar left?"

"Yeah. There's some in my refrigerator. I'll send it over with the machine."

Lovett watched the man and woman go to the reception desk. He went and stood behind them near enough to hear what they said to the receptionist and what she told them. He could tell by the hopeless expression on their faces that they were prime candidates for his treatments.

"Good afternoon, Mrs. Calliope. And you, too, Mr. Calliope," the woman behind the desk told them. "Would you please fill out these forms?" She handed them a clipboard. The man took it, and he and his wife went to the waiting area and sat down. Lovett walked away from where he was standing, sat down, picked up a magazine and pretended to read.

The old couple completed the forms and took them back to the receptionist still clipped to the clipboard. She laid the clipboard on the counter in front of her and turned her attention to a tray of cards that she seemed to be rearranging. After a few moments, she got up, left the cubicle where she was sitting and went down the hall. Lovett went to the window and looked at the forms. He returned to his seat, took a pad of paper and a pen from his pocket and wrote down some of the information he had seen. Then he left.

He was beginning to think that getting the machine had been a mistake. He was sure he could make some money if he was able to find the right patients. But he didn't know how he was going to be able to do that. If he approached someone and they called the police, he was in real bad trouble. Like Daniels had told him, there was a lot of risk in this business.

Well, he was going to give it a try. He'd contact some cancer victims but would be very careful about what he said. Then, if he was questioned by the cops, he'd tell them there was a misunderstanding. He'd say sure he had offered help. He had felt sorry for them and just wanted to help them with their shopping, their yard work and things like that. That wasn't much of an explanation, but it was better than nothing. If he couldn't find any patients using that approach, he'd sell the machine to someone else.

He went to a movie and then to a Wendy's to eat. By the time he got back home, it was five o'clock. He decided it was time to give Mr. and Mrs. Calliope a call. He rang the number he had copied from the papers at the hospital. Mr. Calliope answered.

"My name's John Collins. I'm from the Sloan-Kettering Cancer Institute. Could I talk to you a few minutes?"

"Who did you say you are? Who gave you our name?"

"My name's John Collins. I'm calling for Dr. William Jones of the Sloan-Kettering Cancer Institute. We're conducting a study on patients with the kind of cancer your wife has. Preliminary reports look very promising. We're looking for volunteers. Do you think you would be interested?"

He heard Mrs. Calliope in the background saying, "Who is it, dear? What do they want?"

"Tell her we're conducting a study. We need people between the ages of eighteen and seventy-five who are presently being treated for cancer. One of the treatments looks very promising."

"I don't think so. She's already in a treatment program."

"Yes. Of course. That's why she was contacted. That's a prerequisite for participating in our study."

"Is there a number where I can call you back?"

"Unfortunately, not at this time. Our statisticians have selected names to ensure that we have a representative random sample. We don't want our data to be skewed or compromised in any way. I could ask Dr. William Jones to contact you. He's the physician who's in charge of the study."

"You said preliminary results are promising. What do you mean by that?"

"Well, of course, this is a double-blind study. All the data haven't yet been analyzed. But our preliminary numbers seem to indicate a remarkable rate of remission. We have to be cautious because we've not had enough time to ascertain a recurrence rate. I hear numbers like an eighty percent reduction in recurrence rates mentioned. But don't quote me, or I'll lose my job. Only doctors are allowed to give out that kind of information "

"It wouldn't interfere with her present treatments, would it?"

"No. Of course not. Absolutely not."

"Well you tell Dr. Jones to call us. We can talk to him I suppose."

"Thank you, sir. I will. You should be hearing from him in the next day or two. A week at the most."

Caleb Lovett parked in front of the house. It was made of brick and seemed to be well maintained. The shutters and trim were freshly painted. The grass was thick and green and freshly mowed. There were several pecan and oak trees in front of and at the sides of the house. A flower bed, about seven feet wide, extended from one side of the front porch to the corner of the house.

Lovett liked what he saw. As far as he could tell, the place was worth quite a bit of money. He imagined that the Calliopes either owned the house free and clear or owed very little. They could probably borrow a lot of money on it if Lovett provided them the right incentive. And that was exactly what he planned to do.

He went to the door and rang the doorbell. A man answered the door.

"Hello," the man said. "I'm Leonardo Calliope. You must be Dr. Jones."

"Yes." They shook hands. "It's a pleasure meeting you, sir. That must be your beautiful wife."

"Yes. That's my Camilla. We've been praying every day for a miracle. Maybe you're the answer to our prayers."

"We'll do our best. But we must remember that whatever happens is God's will."

Lovett went to where Camilla was sitting and sat beside her. Her face was gray and looked old. She was very thin, and her flesh seemed to hang from her bones.

"I like you, young man," she told Lovett. "Even with your education and medical degrees, you're not too proud to acknowledge the power of God."

"Of course not, Mrs. Calliope. Because the knowledge of all mankind, every human who is alive today and who has ever lived, is only a tiny invisible dot compared to the knowledge and wisdom of God. I would be nothing but a vain fool if I didn't acknowledge His power."

"You came to tell us about a study, Dr. Jones. Please tell us what it's about," Mrs. Calliope said.

"I had to see you first, before I could tell you anything. I'm glad I did. If I had done otherwise, it wouldn't have been fair to you or to the study. But I'm afraid I'll have to disappoint you. Unfortunately, you don't meet the criteria to participate."

"But why?" Leonardo Calliope asked. His voice was strained, and he was almost crying. "Why can't she participate?"

"We're not allowed to give our reasons. Too much controversy could be created. But if you'll promise not to divulge what I'm about to tell you, I owe it to you to let you know."

"We won't say a word to anybody," Mrs. Calliope told him.

"What I'm going to tell you may sound harsh and critical. But that's not its intent. I'm sure your health care providers are good people and want to help you. But we must all realize that new knowledge is being made available every day. Many doctors don't have the time or the wherewithal to keep abreast of the state of the art, either in new techniques or new technology. I'm afraid that the treatment you've been receiving, even though well intended, is not accomplishing what your doctor hoped it would."

"But he's a very good doctor," Leonardo said. "He has excellent credentials and was very highly recommended."

"I'm sure that what you're telling me is true. I strongly recommend that you continue to see him. Perhaps he'll begin using the latest weapons in this fight and turn your disease around. We must all pray for that to happen."

"Well, then, that's it? That's all that you're going to tell us?"

"I'm sorry, sir, but my hands are tied. I wish there was something else I could say. But don't be disappointed. I'm sure your doctor is doing everything he can."

"Dr. Jones. I *am* disappointed. How could I be anything else?" Mr. Calliope was openly crying. Tears were flowing down his face. "There's nothing you can do?"

"There may be something. But it would be slightly irregular. I could run a parallel test which includes only your wife. I would follow all the same protocols, give exactly the same treatments and employ identical documentation procedures. The results would be retained in a separate record and couldn't be reflected in the statistical analysis segment of the test."

"I'm not sure I understand," Camilla said.

"Basically, here's what I'm saying. You would be treated precisely as all the other test subjects. Data would be collected in the exact, same manner. But it would be held offline and not used in computing any of the statistics. Maybe I can get a waiver so it'll be sanctioned by the board. I think it'll work. Before I can make a firm commitment, I'll have to talk to some of the other physicians. We have to be sure there won't be any negative repercussions further out in the study."

"Then you think you can do it?" Mr. Calliope wanted to know.

"I think there's a very good chance. Yes. I really do."

Lovett parked his van behind the house. He went to the back door to knock, but Camilla and Leonardo Calliope already had the door open and were coming into the back yard. Camilla was so frail she could hardly walk by herself, and Leonardo walked by her side supporting her. Lovett went to her other side and put one arm around her waist, and the three of them moved slowly to the back of Lovett's van.

The men helped Camilla into the cancer cure machine. Lovett told her to lie on her back and to put the pillow under her head.

"Relax," he said. "It'll take just a moment for me to get ready."

Lovett plugged one end of his electrical cord into an outlet he had seen next to the back door of the house. The other end was already plugged into the short cord attached to the machine. Lovett went to the back of the van and said to Mrs. Calliope, "Okay, cover your eyes with the towel lying there beside you. We're about ready to start our first treatment."

She picked up a white towel lying next to the pillow and put it over her eyes. Lovett had dampened the towel slightly and sprayed it with perfume.

"Okay," he said. "The first treatment will last exactly six minutes and twenty-five seconds." He turned on the switch on the back of the machine. The purple lights came on, and the apparatus began to hum. Lovett looked at Leonardo, and the older man was staring at the machine as though he was totally spellbound.

"Mr. Calliope. Come around here. I want you to see something."

Lovett led the man around to the back of the machine.

"Look inside. But don't put your hand in there, and don't get too close. See the way it's vibrating. That's a critical part of the treatment that many physicians fail to appreciate.

That makes sure that the energy attains maximum infiltration and is evenly distributed."

"You think it's really going to help her?"

"Oh. There's no doubt about that. I can't guarantee a cure though because she's in a very late stage. If I had gotten involved three to five weeks earlier, I would have been able to make that guarantee."

"Well, listen. I want a straight answer. What are her chances?"

"You know that without these treatments, her chances would be zero. But realistically, I would say her chances are about seventy-thirty. I'm talking a seventy percent chance of long term survival. Now by long term, I'm talking five years."

"We've just got to hope, I suppose," the older man said.

"Yes. And pray."

A woman came into the back yard and walked over to where the two men were standing. Lovett wasn't too happy about the intrusion. He didn't want anybody to see what he was doing. It was too easy for them to call the authorities. If the police started investigating, the game would be over.

"Hello, Leonardo," she said. "What on earth is going on."

"Hi, Carlotta. We're giving Camilla a massage. The chemo treatments have made her weak. I thought I would surprise her with a massage. This is Mr. Jones, the masseur."

Lovett gave the woman a little wave, and she looked at him suspiciously. Then she looked back at Leonardo.

"I don't see how that thing can relax her. Those lights and that noise. It would be enough to drive a person crazy if you ask me."

"No. It's nice. I tried it myself. Now what can I do for you, Carlotta?"

"I brought over a big pan of Lasagna. It's inside on the stove. Then I came around here to see what was going on. That humming is enough to drive you crazy."

"Thanks, Carlotta. Why don't you go back inside? We'll be there in a few minutes."

"Okay," she said.

"Very pleased to meet you, ma'am," Lovett told her. She shook her head and didn't answer.

As she walked toward the gate leading out of the back yard, the timer on the machine began to buzz.

"That's the five second warning," Lovett told Mr. Calliope and went to the control switch and turned it off.

Then he came back to where Mr. Calliope was standing and said, "Thank you for keeping these treatments a secret. They'll definitely help Mrs. Calliope, and we want to continue them. Technically, though, her treatments don't fall within the scope of the study, and situations could arise that would force us to discontinue them."

"I had already planned what I would say if somebody started asking questions. She has to keep taking these treatments because you're the only hope we have."

The men went to the back of the van and helped Mrs. Calliope out. When she stood up, she had trouble maintaining her balance. They supported her while she took a few steps, and then she was able to walk by herself.

"How do you feel?" Leonardo asked her.

"Much better. Much, much better. You remember when we used to dance all night? That's how strong I feel."

"Don't overexert yourself," Lovett cautioned her. "Your strength will come back, but it'll take time."

"Would you like to come inside?" Mrs. Calliope asked him.

"No. I need to see another patient right now." Then he said to Leonardo. "I have some medication I want your wife to take. But I don't want to give it to you while your guest is here. I'll bring it by later this evening and give you dosage instructions. It's very effective. It has what we call a cocktail of some of the most powerful anti-cancer drugs known to medical science.

"It also contains an extract from apricot pits. They don't use that particular ingredient in this country very often, but they've had outstanding results with it in Norway and Denmark." He got into his van. Mr. Calliope opened the gate wide enough to let the vehicle through. As Lovett drove away, Mrs. Calliope was walking toward the back door by herself.

CHAPTER X

Andrew Calliope walked across the room and looked out the window. There wasn't a whole lot to see. There were a few cars in the parking lot just beyond the window. Off to the side, two maintenance men were applying fertilizer to the grass, and another was placing mulch around a tree. They evidently knew what they were doing because the grass was thick and dark green.

It was over. His marriage of twelve years ended. He didn't know exactly how he was supposed to feel, but he hardly felt anything at all: a touch of relief that it was over; a touch of regret that it hadn't worked. Other than those feelings, nothing. Maybe he was just numb. On the other hand, perhaps the whole mess had just dragged on so long that the actual divorce was anticlimactic.

Andy looked at the clock. It was a few minutes after six p.m. He hadn't eaten since breakfast, but he wasn't hungry. He figured that a drink was what he needed. He went into the kitchen, opened a cabinet door and took down a bottle of bourbon and a water glass. He put several ice cubes in the glass and poured in a generous amount of liquor and a little water. He went back to the window and watched the men work as he sipped his drink. Another worker had shown up. He was carrying a black vinyl trash bag and picking up litter from the parking lot. Andy was pretty impressed at how they maintained the place.

He finished his drink in a few minutes and fixed himself another. He started to carry it back to the window to evaluate the maintenance workers' progress but then decided he had done enough supervising for the afternoon. Instead, he went to the couch, picked up his remote control unit and turned on the TV. He flipped through the channels for a while and couldn't force himself to get interested in anything that he saw. He finished his second drink and decided he had better not make another one. He ought to go out somewhere and grab himself a bite to eat. If he wasn't careful, he was going to die from malnutrition and too much alcohol.

He washed his hands and face, splashed on some cologne and drove to a steak house called Blackie's. He ordered a small steak, French fries and a salad. He was tempted to get a pitcher of beer but got a Coke instead.

When he finished eating, he didn't feel like going back to his apartment and staring at the walls. He figured he might as well go someplace where he could see a few people. Some of the guys at work had told him about a place called the *Golden Horseshoe*. They said it always had a good band, and a lot of singles showed up, especially on weekends. He thought he'd check it out. Anything would be better than going back to his apartment and finishing off the bottle of booze.

He didn't have any trouble finding the *Golden Horseshoe*. It was a huge structure about four or five miles out of town and looked like a big barn. The parking lot was brightly illuminated and almost full of cars. Andy figured that he might as well go inside and see what the place was like.

It cost him eighteen dollars to get in, but that covered the first eighteen dollars of his tab so it wasn't too bad. He gave the lady selling the tickets a twenty dollar bill and she gave him two wrinkled singles.

"Set anywhere you can find room," she told him. "If you need to leave for any reason, we'll stamp your hand so you can get back in."

"Thanks," he told her and went inside to find a table.

Most of the tables were taken. He saw one with an empty chair. The other chairs were occupied by three young fellows with buzz haircuts. He figured they were probably military. He went their table and said, "Is this chair taken?"

"No," one of them responded. "Go ahead and set."

"I'm Andy," he told them.

Their names were Bill, John and Greg.

Andy sat down, and a long legged waitress with big boobs and a firm round ass came to take his order.

"Just a Coke," he told her.

"It's the same price as beer."

"That's okay. I'm trying to cut down."

The place was crowded, and everybody seemed to be in a party mood. A pretty good band was playing. A tall skinny fellow in cowboy getup was singing "By the Time I Get to Phoenix."

Three girls were sitting at a table about ten or fifteen feet away. The man who had identified himself as Greg told the other two, "They're still checking us out. Definitely interested. I'm gonna find out what's going on."

"Yeah," said John. "You do that."

Greg got up and sauntered to the girls' table. He said something to one of them, a little blonde, and she got up and went with him out onto the dance floor.

"Way to go," John said.

"Yeah. Way to go," Bill echoed. "Let's go get 'em, partner." They went to the girls' table, and in a few moments, they were dancing.

The waitress returned with Andy's Coke. He handed her a five dollar bill, and she said, "It's easier if I just keep a tab if that's okay by you. Besides, it doesn't start costing anything until it gets to eighteen dollars."

"Sure, whatever."

He wondered if it was time for him to leave Austin and go somewhere else. He had lived there all his life. Maybe it was time to start over. But on the other hand, it didn't really make any difference where he lived. Without Nancy, no place would feel like home.

He finished his Coke and ordered another. Greg, Bill and John had deserted him and were making themselves at home at the girls' table. That was okay by him. He wished them all the luck in the world.

There were a lot of women at the *Golden Horseshoe*, and Andy thought about asking one of them to dance. But it wasn't worth the trouble. It was a whole lot easier just to sit and enjoy the music. Andy remembered when he and Nancy used to go out almost every weekend. It seemed like a long time ago.

There was a cute little redhead sitting by herself near the back wall, and she kept looking in his direction. She wasn't a bit bad looking. Maybe just a tad on the heavy side, but nobody's perfect. He sure as hell wasn't. Nancy had made that clear. He looked back toward the redhead, and she smiled at him. Not too bad. Not too bad at all.

The band took a break, and somebody began playing some old Johnny Cash songs on a tape player. That gave him an opportunity to make a quick run to the restroom. When he got back to his table, he decided he didn't want any more Coke. It was too sweet and kept coming up in his throat. Maybe it would be smart to switch to plain water. Of course, that would be a waste of money because water would probably cost the same as beer.

He decided to switch to bourbon and water. He'd have only one drink and then go back to his apartment. He'd just make it a point to cut down on the booze when he was at home. Hell, he wouldn't just cut down. He'd give it up completely when he was at home. If he did that, it wouldn't hurt to have a couple of drinks when he went out. With that resolution firmly in mind, Andy felt better.

The waitress came by and said, "Are you ready for another Coke, sir?"

"How about bourbon and water, instead?" he asked her.

"Coming right up," she told him.

He decided he'd check out the redhead, just stroll over to her table and ask her to dance. He was already on his feet when four people, two men and two women, entered the door and came boisterously across the floor to where she was sitting. The women were young and appeared from where Andy was sitting to be quite pretty. Both had blonde hair and were dressed in long party dresses, one red and the other black.

The two guys were clean cut Joe College types. They had short haircuts and were wearing coats and ties. They were the only men in the place that Andy could see who were dressed like that. Most of the other patrons were in blue jeans, and their shirts, more often than not, were work shirts. Except for the two men who had just entered, nobody in the place was wearing a tie. The four newcomers sat down with the redhead and began talking and laughing loudly. It was party time at the *Golden Horseshoe.*

Andy was beginning to get a little bored. He had always loved it when he and Nancy went out. But sitting in a dance hall all alone, surrounded by strangers, wasn't the same. Perhaps he had made a mistake going there. Maybe he should just finish the drink he had ordered and go home and watch TV.

While those thoughts were running through his mind, a man and two girls came in and sat at a table about ten feet from where he was sitting. The man and one of the women were in their mid-forties. The other girl had long dark hair. She appeared to be about thirty or so, a couple of years younger than Andy. She saw him looking her way and smiled. He smiled back, but she had already turned her attention away from him and back to her companions. He decided he'd hang around for a while and see if he could get something going with her. Probably not, but what the hell. It wouldn't cost a nickel to see.

The waitress returned with his drink. He decided it would be a good idea to nurse it real slow and make it last. While he sipped the bourbon slowly, he looked at the table where Greg, Bill and John were sitting. They seemed to be doing all right. They were laughing and talking with the girls at the table as though they had known them for a thousand years.

The three newcomers had finished ordering, and the man and older woman were already on the floor dancing. The long-haired girl was drinking some kind of a frozen concoction. Two guys standing across the room were looking in her direction and talking. Andy figured one of them was encouraging the other to go to her table and ask her to dance. Old Andy wasn't about to wait to see what decision they came up with. He walked over to where she was sitting and said, "Hi, there. Would you care to dance?"

"I'd love it," she responded, and they moved onto the floor.

The girl's name Sonia, and she danced like an angel. The band was playing "Put Your Sweet Lips a Little Closer to the Phone." Sonia pressed herself closely against him, humming the tune with the band. When that song was over, she gave no indication she was ready to return to the table so they stayed on the floor and danced to several more songs.

The band took a break, and he took her back to her table and returned to his. Well, things were looking up. He had a pen and a small pad and decided he'd try to get Sonia's telephone number the next time they danced. The waitress came by, and he ordered another bourbon and water even though he still had about a quarter of his other one left.

While he was waiting for the band to return, he decided it would be a good time to make another run to the restroom. He went in, peed and washed his hands. The entire trip, from the time he left his table until he returned, took no more than three minutes. When he got back, there was a man standing by Sonia's table holding her by the hand, and she was rising to her feet. Andy figured that the two of them were getting ready to go out onto the floor and dance. But it turned out that wasn't the case. Sonia picked up her purse from the table, and she and the man walked across the floor and through the front door.

Now, that was a real kick in the butt. He should have left the damned place when he was thinking about it earlier. It was too late for that now, though. The waitress had delivered his drink. He wasn't about to leave a full glass of booze sitting on the table. He was holding the almost finished drink in his hand, and he raised it toward the waitress. "Thanks," he said.

"Sure," she replied and walked away.

He drained the amount remaining with one swallow. It was mostly water from the melted ice. He could hardly taste the liquor. Then he picked up the fresh drink, raised it to his lips and began to peruse the room once more.

There was a dark-haired girl who looked very sophisticated and classy sitting near the wall across the room from him. He had been watching her all evening but felt sure it wouldn't do any good to approach her. Several men had gone to her table, but none had been able to strike up a conversation or to get her onto the floor. Andy figured she was probably waiting for someone.

The redhead and her four companions were sitting near the back of the place. They were talking and laughing loudly and seemed to be quite drunk. The redhead looked his way, but he didn't think she was actually looking at him. Somebody in the group said something funny and they all began laughing again. The redhead didn't look his way again, at least not that he was aware of. In a little while, the five of them got up and began to dance, clapping their hands and shouting in time with the music.

When Andy had first come into the *Golden Horseshoe* earlier in the evening, it seemed that there were a lot of unattached girls in the place. But now most of them had left, and those who were still there were teamed up with somebody. As though to reinforce what he was thinking, a tall man in a suit came into the place, looked around for a moment and then went over to the sophisticated, dark-haired girl's table. She stood up when she saw him approaching and motioned to a waitress. The waitress got to her table at the same time the man did. The man took the check from the waitress, gave her some money and he and the girl left. Andy figured that was his cue to get his ass out of there and go home.

He took a couple of pretty good swallows of bourbon and set his glass down on the table. The five dancers, the two Joe College boys and the three girls, had formed a circle and were bounding rambunctiously around the floor. Nobody seemed to resent it, though. Most of the other dancers were clapping their hands and cheering the quintet's antics. The five of them came across the floor toward Andy's table like they were going to run right over him. He watched them approaching until they were so close that he realized they were too drunk and uncoordinated to change direction in time to avoid hitting him.

He jumped to his feet just as they collided with his table. It skidded across the floor for four or five feet and crashed into another table. His empty glass and the glass that was still half full were knocked several feet across the room. All six of the people involved, Andy and the five dancers, fell onto the floor in a tangled heap. The redhead was sprawled across Andy. Nobody seemed to be injured.

"I've been itching to get laid all night," she said, "but this wasn't quite what I had in mind."

They disentangled themselves, and the redhead helped Andy to his feet. Some of the customers came over to help straighten up the mess and to see if anyone was hurt.

"My name's Helen," the girl told him.

"I'm Andy."

"Andy. You've been looking me over all night. Do you like what you see?"

He was taken by surprise and didn't know how to answer.

The two men helped Andy straighten out his table while the women watched and supervised. Then all of them except Helen started back toward their table. She stayed where she was standing, watching the others leave. Then she said to Andy, "Hey, I'm sorry. I hope you're okay."

"Except for a broken back and a dislocated shoulder, I'm fine." Then he chuckled and added, "Yeah, I'm fine. I'm too tough for a little spill like that to bother me. What about you? Are you okay?"

"Yeah. Just embarrassed for making an ass of myself. Well, I guess I'd better get on back."

"Hey, no need to rush off, now that we've met. Set down, and I'll buy you whatever it is you're drinking."

"We'll see. Let me talk to those characters first." She went back to her friends' table.

A large man in a dark suit came over to where Andy was sitting. He was followed by a waitress carrying two bourbons and water which she set on the table.

The man said, "My name's George. I'm the night manager here. Are you all right?" He offered Andy his hand.

"Sure," Andy said, shaking his hand, "No blood, no foul. That's my motto."

"Well, I was thinking it might be better if I asked those folks to leave. But I wanted to talk to you first."

"No. Please don't do that. Hell, they were just having a little fun."

"Okay. Maybe not. But I think I'll go talk to them, anyway. We like for people to have fun, but we don't like for things to get out of hand."

"Everything's cool here. No kidding. I'd really appreciate it if you don't come down too hard on them."

"I hear you, man. Everything's cool here, too." He walked away.

Andy pointed to the drinks the waitress had delivered and said, "I didn't order these. Did your boss tell you to bring them?"

"No. Those people that ran you over asked me to bring them to you. They said to tell you they're sorry."

He hadn't planned to drink anymore that night unless Helen came back to his table, and he seriously doubted that she would. But what the hell, there wasn't no use in passing up a free drink. That was old Andy's motto.

He looked at the table where the people who had run into him were sitting. Big George was standing with his arms crossed in front of his chest talking to them. One of the guys saw Andy looking his way. Andy picked up one of his bourbon glasses, pointed at it and mouthed, "thank you." The fellow grinned and held up his hand making a 'V' with his index and middle finger. Andy responded by holding up the glass as though making a toast to the man and then taking a drink.

After George finished talking to Helen and the people she was with, he went to the front of the establishment and disappeared through a door behind the bar. As soon as he departed, Helen came over to Andy's table and sat down.

"Well, you're still here," Andy told her. "I thought he was getting ready to throw you out."

"No. Actually he was pretty nice. A whole lot nicer that I would've been if I were in his shoes. Just told us to get our act together, that's all."

The people that she had just left were getting up from their table, and it appeared they were getting ready to go.

Andy said, "It looks like your friends are leaving."

"Yeah, I told them to. They've been smothering me with love and affection all week. I thought I was going to suffocate. I told them to stop feeling sorry for me and to give me a chance to breathe. They didn't want to go, but I finally convinced them to scram."

"So what are you drinking?" Andy asked her.

"I was drinking frozen whiskey sours, but I've had about all I can stand. Anyway, I can't stay but a minute. I just couldn't leave without apologizing again for being such a klutz. As soon as I'm sure they're actually gone, I'm going on home myself."

"You can't just run off like that. Not after you've piqued my curiosity. Who are those characters, and why are they feeling so sorry for you?"

"Well, the two guys are my brothers and the gals are their girlfriends. I've just kicked my husband's ass out of our house because I caught him messing around with an ugly old bitch that he works with. She's old enough to be his mother, for Christ's sake. Well anyway, to make a long story short, I've not been feeling overly chipper since then, and they feel that it's their obligation to keep me cheered up."

"Okay. I'll tell you what. Why don't we order you a Coke or something, and I'll finish these drinks. Then, I'll buy you breakfast. We can go to an IHOP or somewhere. My treat. And look, I'm not trying to make a move on you or anything like that. Anyway, we'll be in separate cars."

"All right. That sounds good. But forget about the drinks. We can just leave them here."

"Oh, no. Can't do that. My motto is, never walk away from free booze."

"Well, in that case, tell you what. Let me have that." She took his half empty glass from his hand and set it on the table. Then she picked up the full glass and poured some of its contents into the other one.

"Okay. You finish that one, and I'll do this one. Then we'll split." That sounded like a good solution to Andy. He saw the waitress and motioned her over so he could settle up his tab. By the time she arrived, Andy and Helen had taken several good swallows, draining their glasses.

He didn't owe anything, but he left a tip, and he and Helen went out to the parking lot.

"Do you know someplace?" he asked her.

"Yeah. Just follow me." She led him across the lot to a white Honda Accord.

"Where are you parked?" she asked him.

He pointed to his vehicle about fifty yards away. "Right over there. That blue pickup. Just lead the way."

He trotted toward where his pickup was parked. When he got about halfway there, she caught up with him and cruised along by his side. When he got the truck started, she drove slowly away. He followed her out of the parking lot and into the adjoining street.

He stayed behind her Honda until she pulled into a *Denny's* parking lot and parked. Helen got out of her car and stood beside it. He parked, too, got out of the truck and went to join her.

"Is this all right?" she asked him.

"Sure," he said, and they went inside.

Only one section of the restaurant was open. All the others had just been cleaned and were blocked off. There were only a few people in the place. A sign said *Please Seat Yourself* so they went to a table and sat down. There were four coffee cups already on the table sitting upside in saucers and also four menus. They both picked up menus and opened them.

"I'm starving," Helen said. "How about you?"

"I could stand something."

The waitress came over with a carafe of coffee. "Would you like some coffee while you're deciding?" she asked them.

"Yes, please," Helen responded.

The woman left their table, and Helen said, "This feels kind of funny. I guess you think I'm pretty dumb."

"No. It's really no big deal. Hell, we're having breakfast. I don't see anything dumb about that."

"I know. But I've been married for a long time, and this is the first time in years that I'm with a man I don't even know. Especially in the middle of the night."

"Oh," he laughed, "I thought we *did* know each other. If you recall, we introduced ourselves over at the *Golden Horseshoe*. But since you've forgotten, my name's Andy." He thrust his hand across the table.

She laughed, too, and took his hand in her small one. "Pleased to meet you again, Andy. My name's Helen."

He ordered the big breakfast of four pancakes, three scrambled eggs, two strips of bacon, two links of sausage and a slice of ham. It came with a choice of several flavors of syrup for the pancakes and all the little packets of various kinds of fruit jelly that he wished to eat. Helen ordered waffles and sausage.

"So what about you?" Helen asked him. "Do you have a wife at home wondering where the hell you are while you're out enjoying yourself?"

"Actually, my story probably isn't a whole lot different from yours. I was married twelve years. Then, I don't really know what happened. I guess the marriage just kind of dried up like a plant that hasn't been getting enough nourishment. At some point during that twelve years, it just began to die. I didn't know it was happening until it was already over. I don't think she did, either."

The waitress brought them their food. When they were alone again, he added, "So that's my life's story. Now tell me yours."

"Well, the main thing about my life is that I'm pretty damned dumb. Sam and Charlie don't like for me to say that, but it's true. Anyway, they're my brothers. The ones you saw tonight. They tell me I'm not dumb, just naive. Whichever, I don't care. I loved that son of a bitch with all my heart, excuse the cliché. Then I walked in on them right in our bedroom. Jesus Christ, in our goddamned *bedroom*."

"Well, if they were in your bedroom, they must have wanted you to catch them. And you didn't have a clue before that?"

"No. See, I was visiting my mom. Well, something came up that she needed to do so I decided to come home a day early and surprise him. Man, I surprised him all right. Anyway, I don't want to talk about that son of a bitch anymore. How's your breakfast?"

"Well, no wonder they're so protective. I can't blame them for that."

"I guess not, but jeez. Anyway, I'm glad they went home. That's what I think I'd better do, too." She had eaten less than half her waffles.

"Yeah, I guess it's getting late. But listen, could I have your phone number? Not your address or anything like that. Just your phone number. Maybe I can call you in a day or two, and we can go out to the movies or something."

"You really want it?"

"Sure, I really want it."

"Okay. Do you have a pen? I don't have anything to write with."

Andy took out his pen and pad and handed them to her. "Be prepared. That's the Boy Scout's motto. And a damned good one. I was a Boy Scout when I was growing up. Go ahead. You write it. Sometimes I can't read my own scribbling."

She wrote down the phone number and her name. He looked at what she had written and said, "Helen Wilson."

"What's your last name?" she asked him. "Now that you know mine."

"Calliope. You know like that big thing that they play in churches."

"Thanks for being a nice guy." She got up. "I guess I'd better get home."

"I'll walk you to the car." He laid three dollars on the table and then went to the front and paid the bill. They went outside to her automobile. She opened the door and turned to face him. "It would be nice if you were to call. But don't feel obligated, okay?"

"Take care," he said. He held the door while she got inside and closed it when she was sitting comfortably. He stood there until the car started to move and waved as she drove away. She waved back and smiled.

CHAPTER XI

Caleb Lovett was feeling good. He had just acquired a new patient. Thomas Twirling was in his mid-forties, and his cancer had spread through his body. It appeared to Lovett that the man couldn't last much longer. Twirling was quite wealthy, and his wife had told Lovett that they would pay whatever it cost to get him well. When Lovett said that fifty thousand dollars would cover the first month she wrote him a check without hesitating.

He told her that the Sloan-Kettering Cancer Institute was conducting a study assessing the effectiveness of a revolutionary new approach to cancer treatment. Unfortunately, her husband couldn't be included in the study. All the participants had already been chosen using a random selection process. He assured her, however, that Mr. Twirling would get the exact same treatment as those who had been selected to participate.

"It may be too late," Lovett told her. "I wish I could have seen him sooner. Then we could have helped him. But with God's help, perhaps we'll see a miracle. Believe me, Mrs. Twirling, I've seen many."

"I ought to sue the hospital and the doctors," Mrs. Twirling said. "If you have treatments that can help him, why don't they? It really makes no sense."

"As you know," Lovett responded, "I have access to cutting-edge technology. Much of it has not yet been introduced into the medical mainstream. If our test results are as favorable as we expect them to be, then other doctors will be able upgrade their procedures."

"I'm sure that what you're telling me is true, Dr. Jones, but I suspect there's more to it than that. Sometimes I think the medical profession may not be allowing some promising cancer fighting tools to be made available. I had heard that before Tom was stricken but had always dismissed it. Now I think that perhaps it may well be true."

"Why do you say that, Mrs. Twirling? Why would they do something like that? What could they possibly gain?"

"Maybe they don't want a cure or even better treatments. I'm not talking about all doctors. I'm sure that most are honest and dedicated.

But I'm talking about the people in charge. I've been doing a great deal of research since my Tom was taken ill. I've seen a number of articles charging that many new drugs and new forms of treatment are being suppressed. They claim that the AMA won't allow a cure to be developed or made available because it would mean financial ruin to the entire medical community."

"Do you believe those articles, Mrs. Twirling?"

"I don't know. I certainly don't want to. But it's difficult not to wonder."

"Perhaps there's a grain of truth in some of those claims. But I, for one, would rejoice if cancer were obliterated this very minute. I would happily pursue another endeavor if it meant that even one less victim would have to suffer."

"I know you would," she told him. "Whatever might happen to Tom, I'll always know you did your best."

"I appreciate that, Mrs. Twirling," he said.

Andy stopped his Caterpillar and took his cell phone from the case that hung from his belt and dialed the telephone number that Helen had given him. After about ten rings, he gave up. He had been calling her every hour or so for the past three days and hadn't gotten an answer. He wondered why she didn't have an answering machine if she was going to be away so long. Well, he'd just call back later.

He should have gotten her address while he was getting her phone number. But he hadn't, and there was nothing he could do about that, now. He had most of the hill cut away and had filled in the low places making the ground almost level. By the end of the day he would be finished. They already had a new project for him to start on the next day. They planned for him to leave the rig parked where it was that night and to haul it to the new location early the next morning.

A couple of hours later he was finished, and it was still early. He had plenty of time to pick up the truck and move the dozer that night. That would probably be a smart move, too. That way he could get an early start the next morning. He shut the tractor down, grabbed his phone and rang Helen's number again. That time a man answered.

"Hello," the man said. The voice sounded like it belonged to a young man so Andy said, "Charlie?"

"No, this isn't Charlie. Who the hell are you?"

"Well, then, you must be Sam. Hi, Sam. This is Andy. Can I please talk to Helen?"

"She's not here. And I don't know any Andy."

"Wait a minute. We met at the *Golden Horseshoe*. Don't you remember?"

"The what? What's a *Golden Horseshoe*?"

"Remember. You and Charlie were there with Helen. It's a dance hall. Hell, Sam. Sure, you remember."

There was a long pause at the other end, and Andy hoped Sam wouldn't hang up the telephone.

"She's not here. She's in Houston."

"Houston? Can you give me a number where she can be reached?"

"What kind of business do you have with her, anyway?"

"Please. Just tell her I called. Just give her my number. That way she can call if she wants to. Will you do that for me?"

"You're the guy we ran over that night, aren't you?" Andy thought he detected the faint hint of a chuckle.

"Yes that's me. Will you give her my number if she calls?"

"Okay. What is it?" Andy gave him both his home number and his cell phone number.

"Did you get that?"

"Yeah, I got them." Sam read them back. "I'll try not to forget them." Then he chuckled out loud and said, "So you're the fellow that we knocked down. You know, they were going to throw us out of that place, but they said you talked them out of that."

"Hell, Sam, you were just having a little fun. There's no harm in that. That's my motto. Now, seriously, will you give her those numbers if she calls?"

"Yeah. If she calls. And don't worry. I won't forget them because I've written them down. But I can't guarantee you anything. She might not even call me, and even if she does, she might not want to talk to you." He laughed again and said, "Man, it's a wonder we didn't all break our necks" and hung up the phone without saying goodbye.

Andy climbed down from the tractor and walked around the area checking it out; it looked pretty good. There were a couple of places that could stand a bit of work, though. It would pass inspection, but it wasn't perfect. He decided he'd do a little touching up before he moved his rig. He climbed back on the dozer. An hour later he was finished.

He got into his pickup, drove back to the shop and picked up the truck he needed to move the bulldozer. About halfway back to the work site, his cell phone rang. He picked it up and said, "Calliope, here."

"Andy?" It was Helen.

"Yeah. It's me. Hi, Helen."

"Hi, Andy. I'm in Houston at my mom's. Sam tells me you were trying to call me."

"Yeah. I have been."

"Okay, listen. I'll be back Friday."

"Can I see you then?"

"I'll be at that place where I met you. You know, the *Golden Horseshoe*. I'll be there at eight o'clock."

"Okay. That'll be cool. But why don't I just pick you up at your place?"

"That might be better. Did I give you the address?"

"Nope. But let me get something to write on, and you can give it to me now. I'm gonna lay the phone down for a minute so don't go away." He had a pen in his shirt pocket, but didn't have his pad. He figured there might be a piece of paper in the glove compartment, but he couldn't reach it.

He picked up the phone and said, "Are you still there?" When she indicated she was, he continued, "Look, I'm driving this big old truck right now, and I'm going to pull over and stop. There may be something to write on in the glove compartment. So just hang on, okay?"

He pulled over to the side of the road and parked and found an old oil change receipt. The back of it was blank. He picked up the telephone, and said, "Okay. I'm ready now."

He wrote down her address, and she said, "Do you think you can find it?"

"Piece of cake. Eight o'clock then, right?"

"Eight o'clock it is."

Lovett put several daubs of petroleum jelly on Thomas Twirling's chest and affixed a bogus electrode to each spot. Copper wires ran from the electrodes to a black box inside the cancer cure machine. Then Lovett helped the man lie down on the pulled-out bed and slid it back inside.

"That diagnostic recorder will monitor his vital signs during the test," he told Mrs. Twirling. "I have the timer set for thirty-seven minutes. If you wish, you can go in the house and wait. I'll call you five minutes before the treatment's over." Lovett had changed the timing on the warning buzzer. It now sounded at five minutes before a treatment ended instead five seconds.

As Mrs. Twirling walked across the yard toward her back door, Lovett turned on his machine. The lights came on and the humming sound started. As far as Lovett was concerned, life couldn't be any better. Then he remembered what Sammy and often told him. As soon as you begin to get complacent, you're in trouble. Always quit when you're ahead.

That was good advice the first time Sammy said it, and it was just as good now. As soon as Thomas Twirling and Camilla Calliope died, it would probably make sense to get rid of the machine and get into another business. Lovett had made up his mind to do that. In a way, he hated to give it up because the apparatus was a gold mine. But on the other hand, just when you think you have it made, things have a tendency to go wrong. He didn't want to push his luck until that happened.

Before he did anything else, though, he had to get some money from the Calliopes. He already knew exactly what he was going to tell them. He hoped he hadn't waited too long already. He'd have made a move sooner if he'd known how fast Mrs. Calliope's health was going to deteriorate. As soon as he finished the treatment on Twirling, he'd go to the Calliopes' house and put his plan in motion.

He waited impatiently for the time to pass. He should have told the Twirlings that the procedure would be for twenty-seven minutes instead of thirty-seven. He forced himself to relax and be patient. He knew that ten minutes one way or the other wouldn't make a bit of difference.

Lovett went around to the back of the van so he could see inside the machine. Tom Twirling lay quietly, a peaceful expression on his face. Lovett wondered what the man was thinking. Did he really believe that the contraption he was lying in was going to help him? He probably knew better deep in his heart. But he wanted to cling to the illusion that there was something magic about the machine that could ward off the inevitable.

The five minute warning buzzer sounded. Lovett went to the back door of the house and knocked. Mrs. Twirling came to the door. Her face was white and drawn.

"Do you think it helped?" she asked.

"He's still got a few more minutes. Let's look at him then."

They walked to the van and waited for the machine to stop. Lovett pulled out the bed and disconnected the phony electrodes.

"Already?" Twirling asked. "It seemed like only a few minutes."

"No. It was thirty-seven minutes. We can't go any longer than that at the level of energy we're using. I'm going to evaluate the data from the diagnostic recorder as soon as I get back to the office. I'll also transmit it electronically back to the clinic to see if they come to the same conclusions I do. Next week we may be able to reduce the intensity and extend the time. I can't be sure, though, until we make a thorough analysis of what we collected today."

"Do you have time to come in for a cup of coffee?" Mrs. Twirling asked him.

"Unfortunately, no," he told her. "I have another appointment in just a few minutes."

Andy picked Helen up at eight o'clock. The musical, *The Music Man*, was playing live at a downtown theater, and Helen had asked Andy if he would like to see it. It sounded like a great idea to him. He had never attended a live musical or any other kind of a live stage play for that matter and thought it would be fun.

Helen had called ahead and ordered tickets. She and Andy could pick them up when they arrived at the theater. She hadn't told him he should wear a suit, but he figured he ought to. He had a dark blue one with pinstripes that he thought looked real good. He wore it with a light blue shirt and a blue and red tie. He was wearing his black dress shoes. He had looked at himself in the mirror before he left home and said to his reflection, "Andrew, you're one cool dude."

Helen was stunning. Her hair was pulled back into a French twist with soft red curls framing a face that could have been carved from ivory. She was wearing a dress with long, full sleeves that looked like it was made of crushed velvet; it almost reached the ground. When he first saw it, Andy thought it was black, but it was actually a dark blue-green. Her high heeled shoes were the same color and almost looked like they were made of the same material.

"So," Andy asked Helen, as they drove into town, "how was Houston?"

"Same old, same old. Actually, I didn't go anywhere. Just visited my mom. But I did see Harry."

"That's your husband?"

"Yeah, that's my husband. He was so damned apologetic. It was all a great big mistake. He didn't know what had gotten into him. That was the first time, and he'll never do it again. *Et cetera, et cetera, ad nauseam.*"

"What did you tell him?"

"Mostly I just listened. But I did tell him how hurt I was and how I'd never be able to trust him again. And then I cried, and that pissed me off because I didn't want him to see me cry."

"I guess the big question is: Do you still love him?"

"Yeah, I suppose that beneath all the hurt I still do. But I'm not sure I'll ever want the son of a bitch to touch me again."

Andy stopped his pickup in front of the theater and got out. He handed his keys to a parking attendant who got into his vehicle and drove it away. They went inside the lobby and found the location where the tickets were held. Helen gave the woman behind the counter her name. Andy took out his American Express card and offered it to the woman.

"They're already paid for," she said.

"Well, can't you charge it to this, instead?"

"No. I'm sorry."

Andy turned to Helen and said, "You shouldn't have done that."

"It's okay. I wanted to."

They went inside and found their seats. "I think you'll like it," she said.

"Yeah. I think so, too." They listened to the overture and waited for the curtain to go up.

When the play was over, they went to a restaurant a few blocks from the theater. Several other automobiles were entering its parking lot at the same time. As the people got out of their cars, Andy saw that they were dressed the same way he and Helen were dressed. They were probably coming from the theater, too.

They went inside and were escorted to a table. When the waiter came to ask them what they wanted to drink, Helen asked for red wine, and Andy ordered bourbon and water.

While they were looking at the menu, Helen asked him, "Well, how did you like it?"

"I enjoyed it. You know, I've been dragged to a few musicals before, and I really didn't like them all that much. Of course, they were only movies, not live stage plays. But I did enjoy this. It's amazing how talented some people are."

"I liked it, too. I've seen the movie several times, but that's just not the same."

The waiter came by, and they ordered. Neither was very hungry so they both chose the cheese and broccoli soup and salad. When the waiter left, Helen said, "Andy, I was thinking all through the play. Harry wants me to give him another chance, and I'm not sure what I should do. I know I don't want him in the house. I told him that. And the way I feel right now, I don't think I ever will."

Andy waited to see if she was going to continue, but she didn't say anything else. After a few moments, he asked her, "So, what are you going to do?" He wasn't really in the mood for discussing old Harry. He had been hoping that after they finished eating he could take her to his place or maybe go to hers. But there probably wasn't much of a chance of that happening as long as she was all upset and worried about Harry.

"I don't know. He understands why I don't want him to move back in, and he won't argue with that. He just wants me to promise I'll wait at least a year before I file for a divorce. He thinks that'll give him time to gain back my trust."

"Well, what do *you* think? Are you in a great big rush to divorce him? Would it hurt to wait a year?"

The waiter brought their soup and salad plates and a huge bowl of salad which he set it in the middle of the table.

"Is everything all right?" he asked them.

"We would like more wine and bourbon," Andy said, "and a couple of big glasses of ice water."

"Coming right up, sir."

When they were alone again, Helen said, "No, it's not that. But if I'm going to go through with it, I don't want it to drag on forever. I want to get it over with and get on with my life. I have a girl friend who's been separated for seventeen years. I doubt that she even knows where he is. But she won't let go. I don't want to be like that."

"Well, then. How about six months? Or four? Set a firm time frame you both agree on. No, wait. He doesn't have to agree. Don't give him that option. Just set a firm time frame that he understands. Tell him you'll give him that much time, and then you'll decide what to do. It'll be up to him to clean up his act in the meantime and to convince you that he's cleaned it up. Otherwise, you start the proceedings."

"Would that be fair to Harry? Me laying down ultimatums? Maybe your first suggestion was better. Set a date that we both agree on."

"If you want to be fair, that's fine. He was certainly being fair to you when you caught him in bed with another woman. And besides, Helen, can't you see? If you let him make the decision, you'll be just like your girl friend. Seventeen years from now, you'll still be married and still be trying to figure out what you're going to do."

She leaned across the table and touched his hand. "Thank you for listening. I promise I won't say another word about you know who tonight. Now I think we'd better eat this soup before it gets cold."

When they got to her house, he walked her to the door. While she was retrieving her keys from her purse, she said, "Thanks Andy. I enjoyed the play. And I really want to thank you for being such a good listener." That sounded to Andy like she wasn't going to invite him in.

"It *was* fun, wasn't it?" Andy said. "I hope you make the right decision about you know who. Just remember what Ricky Nelson said. 'You can't please everyone so you've got to please yourself.'"

She opened the door and then turned toward him, standing almost against him. "You can call me again if you want to."

He took her into his arms and kissed her. She moved against him, returning his kiss. Her mouth was warm and sweet, but then she pulled away. "I think I'd better go inside." Then she stepped back toward him and touched his face. "Please don't feel bad that I'm not asking you in. I'm a little confused right now, and it's going to take me a while to get my head straightened out."

"That's okay."

She stood watching him, not moving. He knew she was waiting for him to try to change her mind. He started to do that but decided not to. He'd just call her back in a day or so and find out what she had decided to do about Harry.

"Remember what I said. You can call me if you want to. But don't feel like you have to." She turned away again, and that time she entered the house and closed the door behind her. He went back to his pickup and got inside.

Hell, the night was still young. Andy figured it was a way too early to go home. He pulled the truck onto the road and headed for the *Golden Horseshoe*. When he got to the door, the woman who sold tickets told him that the place was closed. Jesus, he hadn't realized it was that late. But it wasn't really that big of a deal. He'd haul ass back to his pickup and drive into town. He knew a few places there that stayed open all night.

He was turning around to leave when three girls came out the door. They were laughing, and all seemed to be trying to talk at the same time. Andy recognized one of them. She was Sonia, the long haired girl he had danced with the last time he was there. She recognized him at the same time.

"Hello," she told him. "I'm afraid they won't let you in. The *Golden Horseshoe* is closed."

"That's right," one of the others said. "The *Golden Horseshoe* is closed. We know it's closed. They got real huffy when we wanted to stay a few teensy weensy little minutes more."

"I remember your name," Sonia told him. "It's Andy. So what you plan to do now, Andy, since you can't get into the *Golden Horseshoe*?"

"You think you're pretty smart, don't you? Well, I remember your name, too, Sonia. And guess what. I don't care if the *Golden Horseshoe* is closed. There are at least a thousand other places around Austin that are open."

"Yeah. Like where?"

"Well, I'm going to one. You girls want to follow me?"

"Man, it must be a swanky place." Then she said to the girls, "This is Andy. How about that cool suit?"

"Hi girls. If you want to follow me, you're welcome."

"I've got to get on home. Jerry'll be really pissed off if I'm much later. He probably already is," one of the girls said.

"Yeah. Me, too," the other one told them.

"I'm with Betty," Sonia told Andy. "I guess we can't go tonight. But call me. Maybe some other time."

"Okay, fine. But hell, we could go in my pickup. I can take you home."

"No. I'd really better go on home. But give me a call sometime."

Andy took a pen and pad from his coat pocket and handed it to her. She took it, wrote down her telephone number and handed it back. Then she and the other two girls started toward their cars. After a couple of steps, Sonia turned back and said. "Call me Andy. No kidding, I want you to call me." Then she caught up with the other girls, and he could hear them giggling and talking as they headed for their cars.

When he got to his pickup, he had already changed his mind. There wasn't any use in driving into town just to get drunk. He'd go home, have a few drinks and go to bed. Then in a couple of days he just might give Sonia a call and find out if she was really interested or just playing games.

When he got home, he mixed himself a strong drink, a water glass of bourbon over ice. He didn't see any use in diluting it with water. As the ice cubes melted, they would provide all the water he needed. He carried the bourbon into the living room and turned on the television. *The Music Man* was playing. He wondered if that was some kind of a sign. He started to flip through the channels and see if he could find anything else. Then he decided, what the hell, he might as well watch it again.

He finished his drink and went to the kitchen to fix another. When he got back to the living room, he had lost track of what was going on in the movie. He started surfing the channels and came across an old movie with Randolph Scott and Carry Grant. He watched it for a while but couldn't figure out what was going on. It looked like Carry Grant was getting ready to marry somebody because he thought his wife was dead. It turned out, though, that she wasn't dead at all. She had been in a shipwreck and had been stranded on an island with Randolph Scott for the past seven years. It wasn't all that interesting as far as old Andy was concerned so he flipped to another channel.

He had a few more drinks but didn't know how many; he had already lost count. He looked at the clock, and it was four thirty. He reckoned it was about time to go to bed. He went to the bathroom and peed and brushed his teeth. Then he took off his pants and shirt, dropped them onto the floor and went to bed. He wondered what old Helen was doing about now. He should have talked her into letting him come into her house. She would have let him, too. He was quite sure of that. But it was too late to worry about it now. It was spilt milk or water over the dam or something like that.

The liquor was coming up in his throat mixed with a taste of bitter acid. He didn't feel like getting up but knew he had to take something or he wouldn't be able to get to sleep at all. He got up and went to the kitchen. After a few minutes rummaging around in a cabinet, he located a large bottle of Tums and some Alka Seltzer. He shook out a handful of Tums and ate them. Then he put two Alka Seltzer tablets into a glass, ran in a little water from the faucet and watched the tablets fizz. When they were fully dissolved, he drank the liquid down and went to bed again.

Lovett drove his van behind the Calliopes' house and plugged in his machine. The back door opened, and Leonardo Calliope was standing there. Calliope looked old and tired. He was skinnier than before, and his clothes hung loosely on his bony frame. His eyes seemed to have sunken deeper into his wrinkled face.

"How's Mrs. Calliope feeling?" Lovett asked him.

"She's very weak," Leonardo told him. "I think the treatments she's been getting down at the hospital have been doing more harm than good. She was real strong the other evening after you gave her that last treatment and all the next day. But now it seems like she's going downhill."

Lovett stepped inside the house and went into Camilla's room where she was lying on the bed. He took her wrist in his hand pretending to take her pulse while he looked at his watch.

"Let's go outside for a minute and let her rest." Lovett told Calliope.

He led the older man out of the bedroom and through the back door. As soon as they were outside, he said, "She has a very weak pulse, sir. Is she still taking her regular treatments?"

"Yes, sir. I thought you told us it would be all right."

"Yes, Mr. Calliope. It's certainly all right. I'm glad you continued. I was worried that you may have become disillusioned and stopped."

"No. But I'm ready to. I don't think they're helping her at all. I've been wondering, Dr. Jones. Do you think it would help if you saw her more often? And maybe made the treatments last a little longer?"

"I wish I could, but unfortunately something has come up. My superiors at the clinic have forbidden me to continue with my offline procedures. They've told me that I must devote my entire efforts to the sanctioned project."

"What does that mean?" Leonardo Calliope asked fearfully. "I'm not sure what you mean."

"It's not going to pose as much of a hardship on you as it is on some of the others."

"What do you mean, hardship? What are you trying to tell me, Dr. Jones?"

"I can no longer treat any patients who aren't officially in the study. But fortunately for you and Mrs. Calliope, you still have your regular doctor. Some of my patients have no one at all."

There was a small table and four chairs on the patio close to where Lovett and Leonardo were standing. The older man pulled one of the chairs away from the table and sat down. Lovett sat on another chair. Calliope had a stricken expression on his face; his eyes were staring at nothing. A tear ran down one cheek, and he brushed it away with his sleeve.

"Then you can't treat her anymore? What'll we do, Dr. Jones? She's been looking forward to this treatment. What can I tell her?" Leonardo was sobbing.

"I told my superiors I've made commitments. I told them it won't interfere with the study. They wouldn't listen."

"What'll we do? Without your help, she'll die," Calliope said softly.

"I wanted to resign. I wanted to walk away. If I had enough money to continue these treatments, that's what I'd do. I would walk away from that clinic and help people like your beautiful wife and my other patients who'll be affected."

Leonardo got up and walked across the yard to the back fence. He put his hands on the top railing and stood there for several minutes. Lovett remained where he was sitting, watching the old man. Finally, Leonardo came back to the table and sat down again. Lovett didn't speak. He was waiting to see what Mr. Calliope was going to say.

"How much money would you need to continue the treatments?" Calliope finally asked him.

"I don't know. They're very expensive."

"Listen," the old man said. "I've been thinking ever since you brought me the news. I'm not a rich man, but I could raise a little money. Not nearly enough, I'm sure. I don't want you to quit your job. But could you do this?" His voice was pleading.

"Maybe you could take some vacation time to visit her," Calliope continued. "Or some sick time. Or come on weekends. I can borrow maybe sixty or seventy thousand dollars. I know that's not much, but please. For Camilla's sake." His voice was pleading.

"I don't want to take your money," Lovett told him. "And besides, I can't hide what I'm doing from my superiors. I've been documenting Mrs. Calliope's case just as I promised you I would. I'm required to give them all my documentation."

"Stop documenting it. Tell them you're not treating her anymore. I swear I won't tell anybody. Please, Dr. Jones. You're our only hope."

Lovett stood up. "Let me see what I can come up with." He started walking toward his van, and Calliope got up to follow him.

"Wait there a minute," Lovett told him. "I need to check something." He walked to the rear of the van and got out a tool box that was sitting on the floor by the side of the machine. He opened the box, took out several tools, went around to the front door and got inside the van. Then he leaned over the back of the seat and began working on some gauges attached to the machine. He was in that position for about ten minutes. All the time, Mr. Calliope was looking his way with troubled eyes.

Finally Lovett got out of the van, walked around it and put the tools back into the tool box. Then he went back to where Leonardo Calliope was sitting.

"All right, Mr. Calliope. We can go ahead and give your wife a treatment. You must promise you won't tell anybody. If the clinic finds out, they'll revoke my medical license. I'm not worried about that, though. I can always find something. But it'll also jeopardize the study, and I *am* worried about that."

"Are you sure we should?" Calliope wanted to know.

"I disconnected the patient count meter. She won't be tabulated, so they won't know I've treated an extra patient. If they want to fire me, that's all right. Your wife's health is much more important than my medical license." Calliope sat where he was without moving. He looked at Lovett with an expression of uncertainty on his face.

"Come on," Lovett said. "Let's go inside and get Mrs. Calliope."

Calliope stood up and led Lovett into the house. Camilla had gotten out of bed and was sitting on a couch. The two men helped her outside to the van. They put her in the machine, and Lovett turned it on. Then he and Calliope returned to the patio where they had been sitting earlier.

"They have a tamper detecting mechanism on the patient count meter. I believe I was able to bypass it without being detected. But there are internal devices that can't be circumvented so easily."

"What does that mean? Can Camilla continue her treatments?"

"Well, she could if we had them in a funded program. Unfortunately, we don't. I wish I could reach into my own pockets for the money, but I can't. Until the clinic acquires additional federal grants, I'm afraid we're at a dead end."

"Then sixty or seventy thousand isn't enough?" Calliope wanted to know.

"We could make it work. There are always nonessential procedures that can be eliminated. But that's not the point. I don't want to use your money."

"But it would be enough?"

"Yes, sir, it would. Let's try this. See if you can come up with sixty-five thousand. I'll contact our comptroller at the same time and see if we can reimburse you after the fact."

"When do you need it?"

"I'll be back the same time next week. Do you think you could have it then?"

"Yes, sir. I will. How do you want it made out?"

"The check? Just make it out to William Jones. That'll be fine."

Lovett got up and walked to his van. He looked at Camilla and hoped she would last until he got his hands on the money. He wouldn't wait around after that. He wouldn't tell the Calliopes or the Twirlings goodbye. He'd just go.

He was thinking about going back home to San Antonio. He had been away too long and really missed the place. Maybe he could get in touch with Sammy. It seemed like his old buddy had fallen off the face of the earth. He had been trying to get in touch with Sammy ever since he had gone to haul the dope for his friend. Lovett sure hoped nothing bad had happened to Sammy. Maybe he'd just drop in from out of the blue. It sure would be nice to see him again.

Lovett had discovered he wouldn't have any trouble getting rid of the cancer cure machine when he was ready to sell it. Daniels had called him two days before and told him he was planning to go to Phoenix and was interested in getting into the cancer curing business there. He was looking for a machine to take with him. Lovett had informed Daniels that he might be willing to sell the machine back and would let him know within a month. Daniels had agreed to wait that long before trying to find another one.

When Mrs. Calliope's treatment was over, Lovett and Calliope helped her back into the house. She seemed to be a bit stronger than she was before the treatment. As Lovett started to leave, she told him, "I feel so much better, now. I think I'm going to make Leonardo take me out dancing."

"You'll be the prettiest one there," Lovett assured her.

Calliope walked to the door with Lovett.

"Don't worry," Calliope said as Lovett left. "You be here next week. I'll have your money ready."

"Thank you," Lovett told him. "I wish there were some other way. I'll talk to our comptroller, but I can't promise anything."

"I know that," Leonardo responded. "I know you'll do your best."

The telephone woke Andy from a sound sleep. He didn't know how long it had been ringing. He looked at the clock. It was twelve fifteen. The night stand was next to his bed, and he was able to pick up the telephone without getting up.

"Hello," he said. His voice sounded hoarse. He cleared his throat.

"Hello," he said again.

"Andy?" It was Helen.

"Oh, hi, Helen. Yeah, this is Andy. Sorry, I had a frog in my throat there for a minute."

"I don't know why I'm calling. Anyway, I want to thank you for last night. After you left, I was sorry I didn't invite you in."

"Thank *you.* It's probably better that you didn't. Not until you get your feelings straightened out about old Harry."

"I guess that's what I'm calling you about. He showed up a little bit after I got home. He wants me to take him back."

"What did you say?"

"Well, you know. We've been married a long time, Andy. Do you think it would be foolish of me to take him back? He promised he'd never do it again."

"Nobody can make that decision except you. But while you're thinking about it, don't forget how he treated you. Don't take him back just to be nice. And remember, you're talking about your future, the rest of your life."

"Thank you, Andy. You're a real good friend. I'm glad you didn't come in, though, because that would have really complicated things. I think I'm going to let him come back on a trial basis, but I thought I would call you and let you know what I've decided. I wanted to be fair to you by telling you."

"Thanks, Helen. I really hope everything works out."

"I guess I shouldn't say this but I will anyway. I'm not sorry you kissed me. I really enjoyed that. I'll always have that memory. Even if I can never tell anybody, I'll always have it in my heart."

"Thanks, Helen. And listen, if he doesn't treat you right, don't put up with it. You're a beautiful woman, and there are a thousand men out there who would love to have the opportunity to take care of you."

"Bye, Andy. He's changed. I know he has. Maybe I'll call you sometime and let you know how we're doing."

"You do that, Helen. I really want you to."

He had a headache but not a very bad one. It wasn't from the booze. He was fairly sure of that. Of course, he had drunk quite a bit but not really all that much. He could remember lots of times when he had drunk a whole lot more. He was probably just hungry. He decided he'd take a quick shower and go out somewhere and grab a bite to eat.

But first he needed some aspirin. He went to the kitchen and took four, washing them down with a big gulp of water. Then he went to the bathroom and took a long hot shower. He didn't shave, but he splashed a generous portion of aftershave lotion on his face, anyway. He looked into the mirror, and the reflection looking back at him looked pretty good. There was some puffiness under his eyes, but that would go away as soon as he had a little more time to wake up. His eyes had a bit of red in them, but you couldn't really say they were bloodshot.

A lot of places were still serving breakfast. In fact some of them served it all day. But Andy felt like eating lunch. After all, it was almost two o'clock. He knew where a Red Lobster was and decided to go there. He wasn't all that crazy about sea food, but he did like their chicken fingers. Nobody made as good of chicken fingers as the Red Lobster.

He had to wait twenty minutes before the hostess led him to his booth. As soon as he sat down, he had to go to the bathroom to pee. When he got back, his mouth was parched and dry, and he felt dehydrated. When the waitress came by to take his order, he asked for a large glass of ice water and a bourbon and water. He was only going to drink one, though. If he was going to begin tapering off, he might as well start right then.

The chicken fingers and fries were delicious. By the time he had taken a couple of bites, he was already feeling a lot better. When the waitress came to his booth again, he was tempted to order another drink, but decided that he wouldn't. He had already made up his mind that one was all he was he was going to have, and he wasn't about to change his mind now.

He wasn't sure what he was going to do with the rest of the day. Maybe his best bet was to pick up a newspaper somewhere and go back home and read it and watch TV. Then he could go out later that night. Saturday night was always the best time to go out so he wasn't about to waste this one.

He'd try one of the places downtown that he hadn't been to in quite a while. There sure wasn't any use in calling Helen. She would be all lovey-dovey with Harry. At least for the next few weeks she would. He didn't want to call Sonia, either. He'd wait a few days before he did that. If he called her this soon, she would think he was too goddamned eager.

On the way home, he stopped by a 7-Eleven and picked up a newspaper. He wondered what Nancy was doing. They used to enjoy the weekends when they were still together. They would usually eat a late breakfast and then might catch a movie or maybe just drive around. Whatever she was doing, he hoped she was happy.

When he got home, he was very thirsty. A big glass of tomato juice poured over ice would sure hit the spot. He didn't have any, though, and had to settle for a glass of ice water. He should've gotten some tomato juice while he was picking up the paper. He made a mental note to get some the next time he went out.

He drank so much water that it hurt his stomach, and he could hear it sloshing around inside, but he was still thirsty. Evidently his body wasn't absorbing it the way it was supposed to. He probably needed some sports drink like Gatorade. From the commercials he had seen, it quenched your thirst a lot better than plain water did when you were as thirsty as he was feeling.

He knew if he added just a dash of bourbon that would help. But he wouldn't do that because he'd already had enough booze. Of course, when he went out later that night, he might have one or two. But no more until then.

He grabbed his television remote control and sat in his recliner. There probably wasn't goddamned thing worth watching on TV, but he turned the set on anyway. Saturday's a bad day for watching television. In fact, Saturday's a bad day for staying home, period, especially if you're by yourself. Of course, if you're with somebody you care for it's okay.

They were showing reruns of some soccer game from South America. He couldn't understand how anybody could watch that game. There was a hell of a lot of running around and kicking the ball, but it didn't make any sense at all to Andy. Maybe if he understood the rules, it would be more interesting. But he doubted that. He couldn't see how anything could make it interesting.

He flipped through the channels until he came to a program that looked like a vampire show. The vampire had a girl cornered and was evidently trying to catch her so he could drink her blood. He had already claimed at least one other victim because his face was smeared with blood and little drops of it were dripping to the floor. The girl was so skimpily dressed that almost everything she had was exposed. Even where she was covered, nothing was really hidden because the material clung to her like a second skin and was almost transparent. Andy couldn't blame the vampire for wanting to get his hands on that.

He decided he'd watch it for a while to see how the girl got out of her predicament. Some young guy accompanied by an old priest would probably show up at the last minute to save her. Then, even though this part wouldn't be shown, but would be left to your imagination, as soon as they thanked the old priest and got by themselves, she would reward her handsome rescuer with her ample endowments. He wished Helen or Sonia was there to reward him the same way.

He dozed off and was awakened by the telephone for the second time that day. He picked it up and said, "Hello."

"Hi, Andy. This is Tony. I'm afraid I have some bad news. Mom's very weak. The doctors don't expect her to make it through the night. I think you'd better get here as soon as you can."

"How's Dad?"

"Not too good."

"Thanks, Tony. I'm on my way." He hung up the phone.

There was only one person that he had to get in touch with before he left. That was Robert, his boss. He picked up the telephone again and dialed Robert's number.

"Robert," he said, "my mom's real sick. They don't know how much longer she's going to last. I'm leaving right now and will probably be gone for a week."

"Sure, Andy. Sorry to hear it. Take your time. What's the situation at the work site?"

"I finished it up yesterday and moved the rig over to the next job."

"Okay. That's no priority. It'll wait. Take all the time you want. And give me a call as soon as you get more news about your mom."

"Thanks, Robert. That I will." He hung up the telephone and started gathering up the things he'd take with him. He packed the suit he'd worn the night before. He hoped he wouldn't need it but knew he probably would.

Lovett parked his van in front of Larry Daniels' house. He was glad that Daniels was taking the cancer cure machine off his hands. Lovett had made more money with it than he had ever made in any other business, but he had never felt comfortable. He was always afraid the cops were just getting ready to pounce. Well, now it was almost over. In a few more minutes he'd drive away from Daniels' house and wouldn't have to worry anymore.

He was glad Daniels was taking the machine out of the state. Leonardo Calliope and Mrs. Twirling would both be running to the cops pretty soon. Sooner or later it would dawn on them that they were victims of a scam. The police would be looking all over the state for the machine, and Lovett was glad it would be somewhere else.

Even if they found it, they couldn't tie it to him. He had made it a point to wear surgical gloves every time he was around it so he had never left his fingerprints on it. Besides that, the authorities would be hunting for a Dr. William Jones. He'd discarded that identity and was now plain old Caleb Lovett.

He didn't think that anyone who had seen him as Dr. Jones would recognize him at a casual glance. He'd shaved off his moustache and was beginning to grow his hair longer. Instead of a suit or a coat and tie, he wore blue jeans and an open necked shirt.

Daniels opened the door as Lovett got out of the vehicle and stood on the front steps waiting. When Lovett was halfway to the porch, a couple of men came out the front door and stood behind Daniels. Lovett recognized them as the men who had transferred the machine from Daniels' Explorer to Lovett's van. He was glad they were there. They would have the machine moved back into the Explorer in short order, and he'd be on his way.

"Hi, Cal," Daniels greeted him.

"Hi Larry." Lovett came on up to where Daniels was waiting, and they shook hands.

"You know, I sort of missed that machine," Daniels said.

"Well, I made some pretty good money, but I want to quit while I'm ahead. If some of the relatives start complaining, they'll search this state with a fine-tooth comb hunting for that thing."

"I know that," Daniels answered. "That's why we're leaving in just a few minutes. As soon as we get it back in my Explorer, we're on our way to Phoenix."

"You ought to do real well. There's a lot of old people there with good retirement incomes, and the place is booming."

"I think we'll do all right," Daniels said.

CHAPTER XII

Andy knocked at the door of his parents' house, but nobody answered his knock. He knocked again. Still nobody answered. He tried the door, and it was unlocked so he went inside.

"Hello," he called out to anybody that might be there. But nobody responded. He set his suitcase on the floor of the entryway and hung his suit in the closet. Then he went into the living room and yelled, "Anybody home?" Apparently nobody was, but he went into each of the bedrooms just to be sure.

Everybody was probably at the hospital. He found a telephone directory in the living room on the telephone stand and opened the yellow pages to Hospitals. There was only one. He dialed its number, and the operator verified that his mother was a patient.

"Can you connect me with her room?" he asked the woman.

"Oh, no. She's in the ICU."

"Can you tell me how to get there?"

"Yes, sir. Do you have a pen and paper?"

"Yes. Just a minute." There were two pens and a tablet pad on the telephone stand. He opened the tablet to a blank page and picked up a pen.

"Okay, ma'am. I'm ready."

He wrote down the directions she gave him, got in his pickup and headed toward town. It didn't take him long to find the hospital. He parked his truck and went inside and to the reception desk. A lady there told him his mom was in the ICU and how to get there.

"You'll have to wait in the waiting room, sir. No one's allowed in the ICU except authorized medical personnel."

When he found the ICU waiting room, he saw Tony and their father. Leonardo Calliope was sitting on a sofa looking tired and small. Tony was sitting on the arm of the sofa drinking a soda. Tony saw Andy enter and came to greet him. They shook hands and hugged and then went to where their father was sitting. The older man didn't bother to get up.

Andy sat by him and said, "Hi, Pop. It's good to see you."

"She's not going to make it, son. Did Tony tell you that?"

"He told me she was feeling bad." He started to say she would be okay, but decided against it. He could tell by looking at his father's face that he had already accepted what was coming.

"No. She's not going to make it. And it's my fault."

"It's not anybody's fault, Pop," Tony told him. "Certainly not yours."

"I would give anything if I could turn back the clock. I've prayed to God every day to take me instead of her. But He won't do that. He's punishing me for what I've done to her."

Andy sat by his father wishing he could say something that would ease the old man's pain. But he knew that no words were adequate at a time like that. "Pop. She knows how much you love her. We all do." His father's shoulders were shaking, and Andy knew that the old man was silently crying. A doctor came from the ICU, spotted the three of them and came over.

"Mr. Calliope," he said to their father. "You may come in for a few minutes." Leonardo stood up and followed the doctor into the room.

"They told me no one was allowed in to see her," Andy said.

"Yeah. I know. But that doesn't make sense," Tony told him.

In a little while the doctor came back out and told Andy and Tony they could go in.

"She's very weak so try not to tire her," he said.

When they got inside, their mother was lying on the bed. It was adjusted so she was almost sitting up. She looked almost transparent and seemed to have hardly any substance.

"Boys," she smiled stretching her frail arms toward them.

"Mama," they said, each grasping one of her fragile hands.

"I love you both. I just have a little while so I wanted to tell you goodbye. Don't be sad or angry. We must accept God's will."

"You're going to be okay, Mama," Andy said.

"No. I'm leaving now. But I have a gift for each of you. Would you get them, Leonardo?"

Their father went to a night stand, picked up two Bibles and handed one to Andy and the other to Tony.

"They contain the Word of God. Please read them." She smiled a wan smile. "You do as your mother says. I may even quiz you on them when we meet again."

A doctor and two nurses entered the room. One of the nurses was pushing a stand loaded down with medical paraphernalia.

"You'll have to leave for a few minutes," the doctor said. "But please wait right outside."

About ten minutes later, the doctor and nurses emerged. "I'm sorry," the doctor said. "We did everything we could."

"She's gone?" the old man asked softly.

"Yes, I'm sorry. But she didn't suffer, Mr. Calliope. She just drifted off to sleep."

"Can I go back in?"

"Of course. Come on in. All of you."

The doctor led them into the room where Camilla was lying. Then he left them with her. Their mother appeared to Andy to be in a peaceful sleep. Leonardo took her hand and knelt by the side of the bed.

"I love you, my darling," he told her.

Tony went to the bed and touched her face. He stood there for a moment and then went back to the waiting room. Andy leaned over and kissed her and then waited by where his father was kneeling.

"We'll take you home when you're ready, Pop," he told his father.

"Go outside with your brother. I want to be alone with her for a while. There are some things I need to tell her. I won't be long."

Andy went back into the waiting room where Tony was sitting on a couch.

"Pop says he'll be out in a few minutes. He wants to be alone with her for a little while."

"Yeah. He feels guilty. He keeps blaming himself. But if it's anyone's fault, it's that son of a bitch that conned them into using his goddamned cancer cure machine."

That was a new one on Andy. He hadn't heard anything about such a machine and didn't know what Tony was talking about.

"What do you mean? What cancer cure machine?"

"I'm not exactly sure. They were real secretive about it. From what I was able to gather, someone contacted them and said he had a machine that would cure mom's cancer. Said they were conducting some kind of a clinical test."

"So Pop let them use the goddamned thing on Mom?"

"Yeah. That's what I think happened. But I doubt that it did any harm. I think she still saw her real doctor."

Their father came out of the room. It was obvious he had been crying, but he was trying not to let it show.

"Okay, boys. Let's go. I'm sure you both need to get some rest."

They told one of the nurses they were leaving and went outside.

Andy followed Tony to his car, a red Taurus. Tony and their father got inside.

"Where are you parked?" Tony asked him.

"Not too far."

"Jump in. I'll take you."

Tony dropped Andy off at his pickup and waited for him to get it started. Andy followed them to their dad's house, and they went inside.

"What would you like to eat," Andy asked his father. "I'm going to order some pizza or something."

"Whatever you want. But first let me make a few calls. I didn't tell our friends how sick she really was. I hoped she would make it. I have to let some of them know what's happened. They'll be very angry that I didn't tell them sooner." He picked up the phone and made a short call.

"That was Carlotta Delvecchio. She told me not to make any more calls, just to get some rest. She'll take care of everything. Let her do it. I don't feel like arguing with her."

In less than thirty minutes, the house was overflowing with people. Everyone was gathered around Mr. Calliope extending their condolences. As soon as they discovered there was nothing in the house to eat, some of the people began making telephone calls ordering food, and others got in their cars and went to get some. In an hour, the house was full of every kind of food imaginable.

"This'll have to do for today," Mrs. Delvecchio told Andy and Tony. But tomorrow we'll have real food. I'll prepare some myself, and I'm sure that many other of your father's friends will do the same." Then she added in a scolding voice, "Why didn't somebody tell me how sick she was? Nobody was told a thing, and then this. That poor, poor man."

"I know," Tony told her. "Our father's a proud man. Sometimes too proud for his own good, I'm afraid. He didn't tell us, either. I happened to come into town yesterday to see how they were doing, and that's when I found out."

"Well, if you ask me, it was that so-called cancer expert that was to blame. If he had stayed out of the picture, Camilla would still be spry and happy. I tried to tell your father, I tried to tell them both, but they wouldn't listen. And I wasn't the only one. They wouldn't listen to anybody."

"What so-called cancer expert, Mrs. Delvecchio?" Andy asked her.

"Well, he called himself Dr. Jones. That was enough right there to make *me* suspicious. If you don't want anybody to know your real name, what do you call yourself? Jones, that's what. Well, he had this contraption that he hauled around in his van. He'd park around behind the house, and they would put your poor mom inside that so-called cancer machine. When he turned it on, it made all kind of humming noises, and the lights inside it would get bright, and then they would get dim and almost go out. They kept going bright, dim, bright, dim, always at the same rhythm. And all the time, that confounded machine kept humming like the dickens. But the humming noise wouldn't stay at the same pitch. It would get louder and higher as the lights got brighter, and then it would get softer and lower as the lights got dimmer. I was afraid it was going to electrocute her."

"Are you sure, Mrs. Delvecchio? How often did they do that?"

"Of course, I'm sure. I came right out and watched the first three times because Camilla asked me to. But then Dr. Jones wouldn't allow me to come any more. He said it would interfere with his concentration. But of course, that thing didn't help her. She just got worse and worse because she wasn't seeing her real doctor anymore. Then one day Dr. Jones didn't show up. At first your father didn't know why. But finally he realized he wasn't coming because he'd already drained your parents dry."

A knot formed in Andy's stomach as he listened. He wondered if what she was telling him was true. His parents had always been so logical and rational that he found it hard to accept that they could be duped by a con man. At the same time, he knew that it's virtually impossible to turn away from any possibility of hope, no matter how remote, when faced with cancer. He also knew that there were people unscrupulous enough to take advantage of that.

"What do you mean? How had he drained them dry?"

"Maybe I shouldn't be telling you this. Maybe it's none of my business. But I think it *is* my business because your mother and I were friends. They mortgaged this house to the hilt to get the money to pay him. Your mother refused to sign at first, but your father made her. I really don't know how the poor man's going to be able to make the payments. But of course, that's *not* any of my business."

"You're sure what you're telling me?"

"Yes, Andy, I'm sure. But your father doesn't know I know. He and that so-called doctor pretended that Jones was only giving her massage therapy. Well, your mother told me different. She claimed he was some kind of a fancy cancer expert. I've never spoken a word of this before because she swore me to secrecy. It's been a burden for me to keep it to myself. But now that she's gone, I think I'm released from that vow. At least I feel it's okay to tell you and Tony even if I don't tell anyone else." She paused for a moment, and then added, "Please excuse me. I've got to help arrange the table. Now, be sure to take care of your father. He'll be lost without her." She walked away, and Andy went to find Tony.

When he located Tony, Andy told him what Mrs. Delvecchio had said.

"Let's see if we can find out how much of it's true," Tony suggested. "If some son of a bitch bilked them out of their money, that's bad enough. But if he contributed to Mom's death, he ought to be rotting in jail. Let me do a little snooping. I'll see if I can find out anything about this mysterious Dr. Jones."

"And then?"

"Well, that depends on what I find out."

"Tell me what I can do, Tony. I want to help."

"Here's what I suggest. Let me do a little checking first. I know a lot of people around here who would be willing to help me. In fact, I think I'll talk to Mom's doctor and Dad's banker right away. They should certainly be able to tell us something."

"Well, brother, I've got to be getting back. I promised my boss I'd be back to work Monday. But if you think it'll do any good, I'll stay here and help," Andy told Tony.

"No. You go on back. I'll keep you up to speed. I've got to be getting back home myself."

"I've been thinking. What if Dad has mortgaged the house like Mrs. Delvecchio said? He may have to sell it and move in with one of us."

"Yeah. I know. That's something we'll have to find out. And I plan to know before I go back to San Antonio."

Tony had talked to his mother's physician, Dr. Jonas Goldberg, and had found out that shortly before her death, their mother had stopped coming in to see him. Goldberg's nurse had called her several times trying to find out why she had canceled her appointments. Goldberg had even called her twice himself, urging her to come. But she told him she didn't need his treatments anymore.

Goldberg told Tony that one evening he drove out to their parents' house and knocked on the door. Mr. Calliope answered his knock but didn't invite him in. Their father told Goldberg that he and their mother had found another doctor. When Goldberg asked him who it was, Mr. Calliope wouldn't tell him. The doctor asked if he could come into the house and talk to Mrs. Calliope, but their father would not allow it. He said they had already made up their minds and didn't want Goldberg interfering.

Goldberg checked with some of his colleagues to see if he could find out who was treating Mrs. Calliope but was unable to get that information. He was worried about her, but there was nothing he could do. Then, just a week ago, Mr. Calliope brought her into his office without an appointment. She was so weak she couldn't stand up by herself, and Mr. Calliope was practically carrying her. Goldberg's receptionist called an ambulance which took Mrs. Calliope to the hospital. There was nothing anyone could do to save her.

"So, that's what I got from Dr. Goldberg," Tony said. "I asked him if he'd heard about any con men who may have been in the area claiming they could cure Mom. He said it was certainly a possibility because things like that do happen. But there was no evidence to indicate it had happened in this case. Frankly, he said, he was at a loss. He couldn't come up with any logical reason to explain why their mother and father had acted as irrationally as they had."

"Well, keep me informed, little brother," Andy told him.

"Don't worry," Tony responded. "I will."

"Listen, Andy, I'm sorry about your mom. If you need more time, you know, to help your dad or anything like that, it'll be okay," Robert said.

"There's nothing real urgent?"

"Just the same old stuff. And I'm serious. It might do you good."

"Okay, I'll tell you what. I wouldn't mind taking a few days off."

"Take all the time you need, Andy. Just keep in touch."

"Will do, Robert." Andy left the office and drove home.

When he got there, he had a message from Tony on his machine. Tony said he had gone back to San Antonio and had taken their father with him. He asked Andy to give him a call.

Andy picked up the telephone and called his brother.

"I got your message," he said when Tony answered.

"I can't talk much right now," Tony said. "Pop mortgaged the house to the limit. He almost cried when he told me. I talked him into putting it on the market and coming to San Antonio with me. There wasn't really any other choice."

"You'll be okay?"

"Yeah. But I'm not worried about me. I'm worried about Pop."

"Do you think it'll sell?"

"Yeah. But he may still owe money. He'll probably get less than what he owes. But he's got it priced low enough so that it ought to sell right away and get him out from under the payments."

"I don't know what to say. I'll keep in touch. I'm taking off from work for a couple of days and won't be home. I'll call you as soon as I get back."

They talked a little while longer before saying goodbye. Andy felt so helpless about what had happened to his father that he couldn't keep a lump from rising in his throat or stop the tears from filling eyes. If he ever got his hands on that goddamned Dr. Jones, he'd kill the son of a bitch.

The weather was hot, even for Texas, and there wasn't a hint of a breeze. Andy climbed into his pickup and headed out of town. Heat waves washed across the road making the whole area in front of him look like a lake. No one except Dutch Heflin knew where he was going. He hadn't told anyone else.

Heflin owned a large ranch about fifty miles from town. There was a small canyon in the middle of the place that nobody except the old timers knew about, and that was Andy's destination. The pastures leading up to its edge were flat grassland giving no clue that the canyon was there. Local folklore had it that when the Indians in that area used to hunt buffalo they were never short of meat. They would simply drive as many of the unsuspecting animals as they needed over the canyon's hidden rim.

Many years later, after the buffalo were gone and the surrounding area became a ranch, it wasn't unusual for a cow to wander up to the chasm's edge and fall over. But that didn't happen anymore because the place was fenced with barbed wire.

A crude road, hardly more than a trail, led from the grassy pastureland of the ranch into the mouth of the canyon. But even though the road was never maintained and was seldom used, it was smooth enough that almost any vehicle could navigate it without a problem.

The inside of the canyon seemed like a different world from the surrounding countryside. A stream flowed from the base of the almost perpendicular cliff at the canyon's head into a rather large pool in the middle of its floor. The stream ended there, presumably rejoining the underground water table.

The pool was about one hundred feet across at its widest point and probably twice that long. It was difficult to determine how deep it was by looking at it. The little lake was clear, but because of the way shadows fell across its surface, even on the brightest days, it was impossible to see through the water. Some of the shade came from the canyon's rim, but the pool was also bordered by trees which were much greener and lusher than those in the pasture.

Even when the sun was straight overhead, it was impossible to see into the pool's depths. The water reflected back the sun's brilliance along with the sky and any clouds that were floating there. The pond was teeming with fish. Heflin had stocked it years before and normally didn't allow anyone to fish there. He was making an exception in Andy's case.

"Catch as many as you want," he told Andy. "And shoot a few rabbits and squirrels. It'll be good for you to get away for a while."

Most of the canyon's floor was flat sandstone. There were only scattered patches of skimpy grass. But, somehow, hardy blackberry and dewberry bushes and small trees were all about. There was one area, about a quarter of an acre in size, which bordered on the pond, where the sandstone was covered with a deep layer of rich soil. The grass grew green and thick there. It seemed that the cattle hadn't managed to find it, or if they had, they hadn't taken advantage of their discovery. Andy was planning to set up his tent in a shady spot in that grassy area right next to the pool.

He arrived at his destination at about six o'clock in the afternoon. The hottest time of the day had already passed, but it was still hot. He drove his pickup into the canyon's mouth and parked on a flat sandstone surface just a few yards from his proposed campsite. He got out of his vehicle and noticed that the temperature inside the canyon was pleasantly cool. A gentle breeze stirred the leaves and pushed little waves across the grass.

Andy unloaded his pickup and immediately began to make the site livable. His tent was pretty big, but it didn't take him long to set it up. He probably wouldn't even use it if the weather stayed nice. After finishing that task, he got a folding chair and table from his truck and set them by the side of the tent. He had a small shovel but decided not to take it out of the truck. He could always find it if he needed it.

He put a gasoline lantern on the table and checked it to make sure it worked properly. He laid his flashlight on the table next to the lantern. As far as Andy was concerned, you never went anywhere without a flashlight. He took his little portable gasoline stove inside the tent. He'd probably take it out in the morning to make coffee and heat his meals. Finally, he put his CD player and CD's on the table.

Satisfied that his tent was securely anchored and his lantern would provide him with sufficient light, he hung a hammock between two trees. He threw two blankets into it so he could cover himself if the nights were too cold. That was where he planned to sleep unless it rained.

He wasn't going to be at the canyon any more than three or four days so he didn't need a lot of food. He had enough corn chips and potato chips for the entire duration of his planned stay and had made sliced ham sandwiches, complete with mustard, lettuce and tomatoes, and a thermos of coffee for the first evening meal.

For subsequent meals, however, he needed to have food that wouldn't spoil. He had selected four cans of pork and beans, four cans of beef stew, a large loaf of whole wheat bread, two boxes of Ritz crackers, a half dozen apples, five Milky Way candy bars and about a pound of coffee which he carried in a plastic bag. He also had a roll of paper towels, a plastic plate, a metal bowl, a fork, a steak knife, a plastic cup and a pot for brewing the coffee. As far as food was concerned, Andy was sufficiently outfitted for his stay.

But food was a minor priority. What he needed for the next several days was plenty of bourbon and pot, and he had enough of both. The marijuana, in fact, was already rolled into cigarettes which were in a plastic sandwich bag. He wasn't worried about anyone seeing him. Nobody would be able to find this place even if he was looking for it. That was the main reason he had chosen it.

He was hungry and thought it would be a good idea to eat something before he set up his fishing lines and had a drink. Before he started his meal, he put a CD into his CD player and turned it on. Then he poured himself a cup of coffee, unwrapped his sandwich, opened a package of potato chips and began to eat. When he finished, he put the trash into a plastic bag. He wanted the area to be as neat and clean when he left it as it had been when he arrived.

After he finished eating and stowing his trash, he began putting his fishing poles in place. That task took about twenty minutes. Now he was ready for a drink so he took a cup to the pool and filled it about half full of water. He went back to the tent and finished filling the cup with bourbon. He returned to the pool once more and checked his fishing lines.

He had only one fish, and it was too small to keep so he threw it back. He decided he'd check his lines from time to time until he went to bed. Anything he caught after that would just have to wait for him until morning. He planned to relax, have a few drinks and maybe smoke a couple of joints. The next day he'd go out and do a little shooting.

He slowly walked around his campsite sipping his drink and listening to the music. While he was doing that, he sauntered over to the pickup to see if he had forgotten to take out anything. Lying on the seat on the passenger side was the Bible his mother had given him just minutes before she died. He took it from the pickup and went back to the table.

Andy didn't know much about the Bible. His mother used to read it every day. She probably knew most of it by heart. Andy went to church from time to time but not very often. His mother had always told him that the Bible contained all the truth in the world. Andy couldn't argue with that. He had heard a lot of other people say the same thing. He held the book in front of his eyes, stared at it thoughtfully and laid it down. Then he lit a joint, picked the Bible up again and opened it.

He decided he'd read for a while. First, though, he needed to refresh his drink. He went to the pond and got a little water in his cup, brought it to the table and poured in some bourbon. He took a large drink and savored its taste for a while before swallowing it. He set the cup on the table and picked up his marijuana cigarette. He took a long drag bringing the smoke deeply into his lungs, slowly exhaled it through his mouth and nose and opened the Bible.

He wasn't well schooled in the Scriptures and didn't know what he was going to find inside, but that didn't matter. When his mother used to be troubled, she would close her eyes, open the Bible and place her finger on one of the pages. The verse where her finger rested would give her all the guidance she needed. She explained to Andy that God directed her search. He guided her hand to the correct page and pointed her finger to the right verse. Andy wondered if that same approach would work for him. He had seen it work for her many times. Of course, she had more faith than he did. That probably counted for something.

He took another sip of his drink and noticed that the cup was getting low again. He started to go to the pool to add more water but decided not to. Instead, he just finished his joint and refilled the cup with bourbon. He decided he'd get more water when he fixed his next drink.

Andy closed his eyes, just as his mother used to do, and opened the Bible. He placed his finger on the page, but before he began reading, he took another swallow of the bourbon.

The words on the page told an incredible story. Jesus' disciples were in a boat, and a terrible storm blew in. Jesus was on the shore watching them. When He noticed they were in trouble, he walked across the water and stood on its surface near the boat. That terrified the disciples; they thought Jesus was a ghost. But when Peter, one of the apostles, expressed his fear, Jesus invited Peter to walk with Him. Peter, keeping his eyes on Jesus, began walking across the rough waves. But then he took his eyes away from the Lord and immediately sank into the sea.

It was beginning to get dusky so Andy lit the lantern. He picked up his cup to take another drink, but it was empty. He went to the pond to get more water. When he got to the water's edge, he stood and gazed at its calm surface. He realized that if he had enough faith, he could walk across the pond to the other side. He knew, though, that he could never have the kind of faith that would allow him to do that. Peter had managed to walk only a short distance, even with Jesus at his side, before he lost his faith and began to sink into the sea. And none of the other disciples had even dared to attempt what Peter had accomplished.

Andy dipped his cup into the water filling it about half full, walked slowly back to the table and filled the cup the rest of the way up with his bourbon. Before tasting it, he went inside the tent and got another reefer from the bag where they were stored. He went outside and sat at the table. Then he lit the cigarette and took a deep drag. It calmed his nerves and relaxed him.

He decided he'd read another passage from the Bible. He wasn't sure he had sufficiently understood the one he had just read to get any help from it. He had learned something new, though. He had heard the story about Jesus walking on water about a thousand times, but he had never known that Peter had done the same thing. Maybe the Scriptures were telling him that we all have the power to do amazing things if we only have faith.

He opened the Bible again and began to read the verse where his finger pointed. The bourbon and marijuana had affected his vision and everything looked blurry. The words on the page were fuzzy and almost impossible for him to make out. By concentrating with all of his effort, he was able to get the gist of the story he was reading.

Jesus told Peter that he'd deny knowing Him three times before the cock crowed the next morning. Peter didn't think that he would and assured Jesus that he'd never deny Him.

Shortly thereafter, Jesus was in some kind of terrible trouble. Andy supposed that it was when they were about to nail Him to the cross. Anyway, someone named Caiaphas was questioning Him. When Peter realized how much danger Jesus was in, he decided he'd better go somewhere and hide so he wouldn't get into the same kind of a mess. A servant girl saw Peter, recognized him and asked him if he was one of Jesus' men.

Peter was afraid to admit he knew Jesus so he lied and said the girl was wrong. Another servant disputed Peter. He said he recognized Peter and Peter was definitely one of Jesus' men. Again Peter denied he knew Jesus. A third person said Peter had come from Nazareth with Jesus. For a third time, Peter said that it wasn't true. As soon as Peter made the third denial, a cock crowed in the distance, and Peter ran away and began to cry. He realized he had done exactly what Jesus had said he would do.

Andy closed the Bible and took another deep draw on his reefer and a big swallow of his booze. He wondered if he had opened the Bible to the right place. The stories he had read were interesting, but he couldn't see how they'd given him any guidance. Maybe he would read some more the next day after he did some shooting. Right now he was getting sleepy, but it was too early to go to bed. He decided he'd walk about and do a little exploring.

He finished his marijuana cigarette, drank the rest of his liquor, got slowly to his feet and began walking toward the head of the canyon. He had gone about fifty yards when he decided he had to pee. He went to a large tree and urinated against it. While zipping up his fly, he realized he was thirsty. Not for booze but for plain water. He returned to the table and got his cup and filled it with water from the pond.

He resumed his exploration, taking frequent little sips from the cup as he walked. He saw a thick dewberry bush loaded with berries and stopped to pick some. They were large and bursting with juice. Nothing tasted better than fresh dewberries. When he and Tony were kids, they were always going out to pick a couple of gallons of dewberries so their mom could bake dewberry pies.

He wondered how Tony was doing. He hadn't seen him since the funeral. That had been a week ago. He really had to give his little brother a call. Probably, he should've brought his cell phone with him. He'd thought about bringing it but had decided against it. If he was going to get away, he couldn't do it holding a phone against his ear. In the morning he'd find a pay phone and make a quick call to Tony. That wouldn't take but a few minutes, but he'd feel a lot better afterward. Then he'd come back to the canyon.

He walked toward the cliff at the head of the canyon where the stream which fed the pool began. He wanted to see what kind of an opening the water flowed from. But the sun had disappeared behind the canyon's rim, and it had gotten quite dark. He'd left his flashlight back on the table by the tent so he decided any further exploration would have to wait until the next morning after he called his brother.

He went back to the table and sat down. The first CD was finished, and another one was playing. If he was going to do any more reading that night, he had better begin. He opened the Bible again and began to read once more. The passage he had selected told about the battle between David and Goliath. Andy's eyes were bleary, and he had trouble focusing them, but finally he was able to finish the story.

He especially liked the part where David killed the giant with his slingshot. When David took Goliath's sword and cut off the giant's head, Andy closed the Bible and muttered under his breath, "That's exactly what I was looking for. I'll find that son of a bitch and kill his ass as sure as David killed that giant." Satisfied with that decision, he decided it was time to get some sleep.

He had planned to leave everything where it was but changed his mind. It would probably be better to put the bourbon inside the tent with the pot. He put the chair right inside the door, set the whiskey on it and put the marijuana cigarettes next to the whisky. He placed his cup next to the bourbon. Then he picked up his pistol and flashlight, extinguished the lantern and began walking toward the hammock

Andy was ready to crash. It was barely light enough for him to move around, and the skies were getting darker. There was an almost full moon, but he couldn't see it. In the past hour, black clouds had blown in and blotted out the sky. He turned the flashlight on as he walked to the hammock. The weight of the gun in his other hand gave him a sense of security. He thought about checking his fishing lines but didn't feel like it. That could wait until the morning.

He probably wouldn't need his gun, but he always felt better when he had it with him. There wasn't anybody that would screw around with old Andy while he had it. At least nobody in his right mind. When he got to the hammock he wrapped himself in the blankets like a cocoon, and in a few minutes he was fast asleep.

Andy didn't know how long he had been sleeping when something woke him up. He opened his eyes, and it was almost as bright as day. The clouds were gone, and the near-full moon lighted up the canyon. He looked at his watch; it was twelve-twenty. He figured he had gone to bed at about ten.

He heard a noise by the tent, and when he looked in that direction he saw a man sitting on a chair drinking coffee. He had used Andy's coffee pot to brew it in. In fact, the pot was still sitting on his Coleman stove. The fellow was sitting on Andy's chair just like he owned it. He must have taken it out of the tent because Andy distinctly remembered he had put it inside before he went to bed.

Andy was startled at the sight of the fellow just sitting staring at him like a big-assed bird, but he wasn't scared. The dumb son of a bitch that had invaded his campsite was the one that had better be scared. He found his pistol, gripped its handle firmly, untangled himself from the blankets and got out of the hammock. Pointing the gun directly at the intruder, Andy walked toward him. The stranger didn't seem to be the least bit perturbed. He took a sip of coffee as he watched Andy approach.

"What the fuck you doing here?" Andy demanded when he was a few feet from where his unwelcome visitor was sitting. "Don't you know it's not polite to sneak into somebody's camp in the middle of the night? It's also dangerous as hell."

"I mean you no harm, Andrew. I come as a friend. I've traveled a long way to talk to you."

"How do you know my name? How did you find me?"

"You asked for my help. I've always known your name."

The stranger set Andy's cup on the table and stood up. He looked like a goddamned hippy. He was tall, about six foot four, but he was as skinny as a scarecrow and couldn't weigh over a hundred and fifty pounds. His hair was wavy, a light reddish brown; it was parted in the middle and hung just below his shoulders. He had a moustache and beard, both of which were neatly trimmed and the color of his hair. He had large eyes. Even in the bright moonlight it was impossible to discern their color, but Andy got the impression that they were hazel.

The strangest thing about the man was the way he was dressed. He was wearing a white linen shirt with large sleeves that hung to his wrists and loose fitting pants of the same color and fabric. Over those articles of clothing, he had on a long, white, loose fitting robe that was made of some kind of material that looked like cheesecloth. It, too, had long sleeves, and it hung to within an inch of the ground. It completely covered his shirt and pants, but it was almost transparent, and Andy could easily see them through it.

Andy had seen pictures of Jesus, and the man looked almost exactly like some of those pictures. Only Jesus wasn't so tall and skinny. Otherwise, the similarity was uncanny. He knew that people could do funny things with their appearance if they wanted to. He had seen a lot of Elvis impersonators that looked almost exactly like Elvis because of the way they dressed and wore their hair and sideburns. Some were fat, and some were skinny. Some were tall and others were short. Hell, some were even black or Mexican or Asian. But you still knew who they were impersonating.

That was evidently what this fellow was doing. Only he was trying to look like Jesus instead of Elvis. People probably told him all the time how much he looked like Jesus. Apparently, he wanted old Andy to do the same thing. Well, Andy wasn't going to comment at all on his appearance. If that was what the man was waiting for, he was going to have a long wait.

"I didn't ask for anybody's help, and I didn't tell anybody my name." Andy kept his gun trained on the man as he spoke. "But I *am* telling you this. I don't want to talk to anybody, and I don't want anybody snooping around where I'm trying to have a little privacy. Now, I recommend you get out of my goddamned camp before I blow your ass away and throw you in the lake."

The man sat back down. "Why don't you join me, Andrew? We'll talk a few minutes, and then I'll leave. You came to this spot seeking answers. I've come to give you those answers."

"I don't know what you want, mister," Andy responded. "Go ahead and talk, but don't take all night. Anything to get you out of here." He had already decided to pack up and leave as soon as he ran the man off. He was afraid to go back to sleep. The crazy son of a bitch would likely just sneak back and cut Andy's goddamned throat while he was sleeping.

"Just don't try any funny moves," Andy continued. "And give me my coffee cup. If I'm going to listen to you talk all night, I need something to drink while I'm listening."

"This is my cup. Yours is inside the tent." Andy started to dispute him, but on closer inspection, he discovered that the cup the man was holding wasn't his after all.

"I'll be back in a minute," Andy said. He went to the hammock and got the flashlight. Then he came back to the tent.

Andy turned on the flashlight and backed through the tent's door keeping his pistol pointed at his visitor as he retreated. His cup was on the grass inside, about where the chair had been sitting. He picked it up and put it under his left arm so he could hold the flashlight in his left hand and continue holding the pistol in his right hand. When he got outside, the stranger hadn't moved.

"I'll be right back," Andy said. He laid the flashlight on the table, carried the cup to the pool and got some water. When he got back to the tent, he set the cup on the ground, went inside and got his liquor bottle. He went back outside and poured some liquor into the cup. Then he set the bottle on the ground and picked up the cup. All that time he continued holding the pistol in his right hand.

He wasn't about to offer his visitor a drink. Not until he knew what the fellow was doing there. Besides, he was pissed off and about to tell the man that. Here he was standing up, and his uninvited guest was sitting in the only chair. If that wasn't audacity, Andy didn't know what was. Andy was ready to tell the man he had brought the chair for his own use, but before he could do that, his visitor stood up.

"Why don't you use the chair, Andrew. I'm just as comfortable sitting on the ground." The intruder walked a few steps away to a small tree and sat down and leaned against its trunk.

Andy sat in the chair. He was still holding the gun, and that was beginning to make him feel a little foolish. But what are you supposed to do when some long-haired hippie comes strolling into your camp in the middle of the night? Especially when you're a thousand miles from nowhere?

Generally, you would think if somebody stumbles across your camp it might be pure coincidence. But if he knows your name and starts talking to you like he's your long lost cousin, you can bet your ass there's no coincidence about it at all. That son of a bitch has something up his sleeve and has tracked you down on purpose.

"Okay," Andy told him, "we've been talking all night, and we've not even been introduced. You know my name, but I don't have any idea who you are."

"You already know, Andrew. You've already figured it out."

"Before we go any further, I'd like to get two things off my chest. First of all, stop calling me Andrew every time you open your mouth. I know what my name is without you saying it every ten seconds. And second, don't think that I'm drunk enough or stoned enough to fall for that phony Jesus get up you're wearing. You might pull it on a lot of people, but it sure as hell isn't gonna work on old Andy."

"Fair enough, my friend. As I told you before, you know who I am. So you may call me what you wish. I'll leave that up to you."

"Hell, I know at least a million names. But I don't know what yours is."

"Why don't you pick one?"

Andy took a long drink. He'd come up with a name, all right. But it wasn't going to be Jesus, and it wasn't going to be Christ.

"Okay, buddy. How does Jesse sound? Or Christian?" He hadn't intended to say Christian. It had just slipped out. "No, forget about Christian. I don't know what religion you are. Hell, you might be a Muslim for all I know. I'll just call you Jesse since you've made it pretty clear you're not gonna tell me what your real name is, anyway."

"That's fine. It's close enough."

"Okay, Jesse. Would you like something to drink? I mean I have some bourbon whiskey if you'd like some. I'm sure I could find a glass or cup or something in the truck."

"No, thank you. I've come to give you some advice. I'll be here for only a few minutes more. First of all, I want you to know that your mother is at peace. She was a good woman and will spend the rest of eternity in peace. Next, listen to your brother, and you'll learn the hiding place of the one you're seeking. But remember the commandment: Thou shalt not kill."

Andy interrupted, "Look, I'm trying to find the son of a bitch that killed my mother. You tell me I must not kill. Why didn't you tell that to David when he knocked Goliath on his butt with a slingshot and cut off his head? I can't guarantee what I'll do if I ever get my hands on that son of a bitch."

"Just remember the commandment. Finally, you'll meet a young girl who'll be very dear to your brother. She'll tell you an incredible story, but it'll be true. Listen to her and believe. After hearing her, you'll become angry, but however angry you become, don't forget the commandment."

When the man finished talking, both men continued to sit. Andy wasn't sure whether the fellow was finished. After a few minutes, he said, "Is that all?"

"No. There's one more thing. You should take all of those marijuana cigarettes and throw them into the lake. Or better yet, bury them. They won't do anything for you except get you into trouble. I know you're using them because of your divorce and your mother's death. But they're of no help whatsoever. It wouldn't hurt to cut down on the alcohol, either. Deep in your heart, you know that, and you also know she wouldn't approve. *Now*, I'm done unless you have any questions."

"Thanks for the lecture. You're probably right about the pot. Maybe I *will* throw it away. Now, how are you so sure my brother will find this guy? We don't even know his real name."

"Your brother will have that information."

"Why can't you tell me now? Wouldn't that be a lot easier?"

"Perhaps. But I've told you what you need to know. The rest is up to you."

"Well, Jesse. I'll tell you why you're talking in riddles. It's because you don't know anything. You're not telling me a thing but bullshit."

"You'll see."

Jesse crossed his arms. When he did that, his sleeves fell away from his wrists exposing them to Andy's view. Andy could see that they were badly scarred.

The sight unnerved him. He had seen pictures of Jesus on the cross with nails driven through His hands. But later he had been told that they had actually been driven through His wrists. If they had been in His hands, they couldn't have supported his weight.

"Are those scars real?"

"You know they are."

The man got up and began walking away.

"Is that all? Are you leaving?"

"Yes. That's all." He walked toward the mouth of the canyon and behind a stand of trees that was no more than twenty yards away. Andy waited for him to emerge on the other side of the trees and into the road, but he didn't reappear. After a few minutes, Andy decided that the fellow wasn't leaving after all. He was probably going to hide in the woods until Andy went to sleep and then come back and rob or murder him.

As far as Andy was concerned, that wasn't about to happen. He got into his pickup and drove to the trees where the man had disappeared. There wasn't a trace of the fellow. He maneuvered the truck so that its lights shone into the woods, but he could see nothing. Then, with his headlights still illuminating the area, he walked into it and searched every square inch of ground. Old Jesse had vanished.

Andy got into the pickup and drove out of the canyon and followed the access road for about a mile. There were no vehicle lights ahead of him. He turned the truck around and drove back to camp. There was still a lot of night left, but he didn't feel like going back to bed. He'd go back to the campsite, pack up everything and leave.

In the few minutes it had taken him to search for Jesse, the clouds had blown back in and covered the moon and stars. It was so dark he couldn't move around without using his flashlight. He knew he would have trouble packing up his gear in the darkness, so he decided to leave the area and return in the morning. He didn't feel comfortable spending the rest of the night there.

He wasn't too worried about leaving all his things. They would be safe unless Jesse came back and stole them. Andy figured that probably wasn't going to happen. Not if Jesse was who Andy thought he might be. Nobody else would be able to find Andy's campsite in a thousand years.

There was one thing he was going to do, though, before he left. He was going to get rid of the damned pot. He got his flashlight and the sandwich bag that contained the cigarettes and walked over to the lake. He unrolled one of the reefers and let the marijuana fall into the water.

As he watched it floating on the surface, he changed his mind. He went to the pickup, got his shovel and dug a hole about a foot deep. He put the cigarettes into the hole and covered them up. Maybe Jesse was happy now. At least Andy hoped so.

He decided not to tell anyone about his adventure. They would think that he was making the story up or had gone completely nuts. In the back of his mind he thought he knew who his visitor was. He was absolutely certain the man was real, not a figment of his imagination. He remembered the story about doubting Thomas and smiled.

CHAPTER XIII

Maria no longer went by the name of Maria. She now called herself Sandra Garcia, the name on the birth certificate and driver's license of the real Sandra Garcia whom she had known so briefly. Now that she was in San Antonio, she could hardly believe how fortunate she was. Raymundo knew a woman named Mrs. Molina who owned a small *tienda*. She was a widow living on a social security pension her husband had left her. However, it appeared she was going to be forced to sell the store unless she could find someone dependable to help her.

"I'm sure you need a job," Raymundo told her. "I can introduce you to Mrs. Molina. She needs somebody to work full time. She has two young men helping now, but both of them are going to college and can work only part time. Would you like to talk to her?"

"Of course, I need to work. But how can I? I don't speak any English at all." She had told Raymundo that even though she had been born in the United States, she could speak no English. Her father and mother were Mexicans. She had been born in California while they were there working in the fields. But now that her parents were dead, she wanted to go to the United States to start a new life.

"You'll be able to get by. Very few of the customers know any English, either. Anyway, I'm sure you'll learn it quickly. It'll not seem so difficult after you've been here a while."

It turned out that not only did Mrs. Molina have a job for Maria, she also had an apartment over the store that Maria could use as long as she worked there. Maria fell in love with the apartment as soon as she saw it.

"I would love to work for you if you think I can do it," she told the older woman.

"I'll be with you every day until you feel you're able to manage by yourself. It'll not take you long. It's not very complicated, and you appear to be a very bright girl."

Mrs. Molina had been right in that assessment. In just a few days, Maria had no trouble running the store.

Maria finished eating breakfast and washed and put away the dishes. She inspected her apartment and was satisfied with its appearance. The bathroom and kitchen were spotless. The freshly vacuumed carpet looked brand new. It was an hour before she had to go to work so she picked up her English textbook and sat down on the couch. She opened the book and tried to study. The words were meaningless. They seemed to run together and make no sense at all. She wondered if she would ever learn. After ten minutes, she closed the book and went down to the store. There were no customers that she could see.

Samuel Perez, one of the college students who helped part time, greeted her as she came inside.

"Good morning," he said in English. "My, but don't we look ravishing this morning?"

She didn't understand anything except "good morning," but she smiled and said, also in English, "Good morning, Sam. So do you."

He applauded and said, "You'll be an *Americana* in no time. We'll just bleach your hair and get you some blue contacts, and nobody will know the difference."

She still didn't know what he was saying. She smiled again and said, "Thank you. If you want to leave a little early, that'll be okay."

"Thanks. See you later." In a moment he was gone.

Mrs. Rodriguez, one of the first customers Maria had met, came into the *tienda*.

"Good morning, Sandra," she said as she entered.

"Good morning, Mrs. Rodriguez. You're looking well today."

"Thank you, Sandra." Mrs. Rodriguez pushed her shopping cart down one of the aisles and soon disappeared from view.

In about ten minutes she returned; her cart was about half-full.

"Could you please help me, Sandra? I can't find any *hojas*. And I need some real *masa*. Not the *masa harina* that you have in the back. It doesn't work as well for what I want to do."

"Yes, Mrs. Rodriguez. We have them both."

She showed the woman where the items were and then went back behind the counter to wait on a little girl who was buying a bar of candy. The child paid her, smiled shyly, and skipped happily from the store.

In a few minutes, Mrs. Rodriguez came to the counter to check out. She was about fifty years old. Her hair was almost black, except for a few streaks of gray, and was pulled back in a bun. Her large round eyes were the color of a Hershey bar, so dark that it was difficult to discern the pupils. She was wearing a white sleeveless blouse and a pale green skirt that fell a few inches below her knees. Her bare legs were smooth and brown.

"Did you find everything you need?"

"Yes, I did. You were very helpful. I notice you speak very good Spanish. Not many young people speak it correctly anymore."

"Do you speak English?" Maria asked her.

The woman just shrugged her shoulders and replied, "No. Maybe a little bit. My husband knows it better because sometimes he has to use it in his work."

"What about your children?"

"Oh, yes. They speak it all the time. And my grandchildren can't speak Spanish at all." She sighed. "Once we forget our language, we lose our culture, and that makes me sad. But after all, they're American citizens regardless of the color of their skin, and if they're to succeed, I suppose they must adopt the way of the Anglos."

Maria didn't have any trouble working in the *tienda*. Most of the people who came in spoke Spanish. But she knew that Mrs. Rodriguez was right. If she was going to stay in her new country, she would have to learn the language.

At a few minutes before four-thirty, Fidencio Salinas entered the store to relieve her. "Has it been busy?" he asked.

"A little bit. Not very." She grabbed her purse and headed for the door.

"How are your classes?" he called to her departing back.

"Awful. I don't think I'll ever learn."

"Don't worry. You will. Look at me. You're a whole lot smarter than I am."

"Of course, I am," she responded. "But you grew up here, and that gives you an advantage."

"You don't have to be so quick to agree," he said, but she was already gone.

She walked to the high school two blocks down the street where she was studying English. She had been taking it for three weeks and was beginning to get discouraged. It seemed she would never learn. Mrs. Fernandez, her instructor, had been surprised that she knew no English at all.

"How were you able to grow up in this country without learning at least some English?" the woman had asked her.

"I didn't grow up here," she replied. "My parents were Mexican citizens, and we lived in a little house in Mexico. I'm an American because I was born here. Every year we came to the United States to pick fruit, but we never associated with any Americans. When the fruit picking season was over, we went back home to our village."

Although what she said wasn't true, it was the best story she could come up with to explain why, as an American, she wasn't able to speak the language. She hoped the blessed Mother would forgive her for her little deception.

"So now you've decided you want to live here?"

"Yes. My parents have both passed away. I have nothing left in Mexico. So I've decided to make my future here."

"Well, don't be discouraged, Sandra. It's very hard to learn a new language, but you'll be all right. Perhaps you'll meet someone here who speaks both languages, someone who can help you." Maria was sure Mrs. Fernandez was right, but she knew no one. And then she realized that maybe she did know someone after all. Perhaps Fidencio would help her.

"Perhaps I will. I hope so. It's so difficult."

Antonio Calliope, a young man two or three years older than Maria, entered the school building at the same time she did, and they walked to the classroom door together. He was the most gorgeous thing she had ever seen. He wasn't a student. He was working evenings as a volunteer teaching mathematics to adults. Maria wasn't sure what kind of work he did during the day. Whatever it was, his bosses probably liked him because they allowed him to take off one afternoon each week and come in to Mrs. Fernandez's class to help her.

Sometimes he sat up in front of the class with Mrs. Fernandez. Mostly, though, he sat with the students only two seats away from Maria, and every time she looked at him her heart began acting crazy, and she could feel her face grow warm.

He was tall and slim with wavy brown hair and gray eyes. As they waited for Mrs. Fernandez to arrive, the other six students joined them. At four forty-five, Mrs. Fernandez arrived and opened the door, and everyone entered and took their seats. Antonio sat with the students.

"Good afternoon, ladies and gentlemen," Mrs. Fernandez greeted the students in English as soon as they were seated.

"Good afternoon, Mrs. Fernandez," they replied in unison.

"Very good." She approached one of the students and said to him, "Carlos. Can you please tell the class what kind of work you do?"

"Yes. I work for a landscaping company. I make the ground beautiful."

"How do you make the ground beautiful?"

"I plant grass and flowers and trees. I make the ground level or sometimes smooth slopes."

"Very good, Carlos."

She left Carlos and approached Maria. "Sandra," she said, "can you tell us what kind of work you do?"

"I work in a store. I sell groceries."

"What are some of the items you sell?"

"I don't know items. What are items?"

"Items are things," she said, still speaking English

"Oh, *cosas*. I sell bread and meat and milk. I sell soap, too. Sometimes, some people buy much beer, *cerveza*."

Some of the students laughed.

"Very good, Sandra. I suppose many of your customers like beer."

"I like to drink a cold beer sometimes when I finish work on a very hot day," Carlos said.

"I do too," Antonio told him. "We'll have to find out where Sandra's store is located."

The class was over at seven forty-five. As Maria walked back toward the store, Antonio caught up with her.

"Do you mind if I walk with you?" he said in English. She thought she understood him but wasn't sure.

"What did you say?" she asked in Spanish.

"May I walk with you?" he asked, also in Spanish. Then he changed to English. "Please, let's try to talk in English. We'll use Spanish only when it's impossible to do otherwise."

She shrugged her shoulders. "I'll try English. I don't know many words."

"Okay. Are you going home, now?"

"Yes." Then in Spanish, "I have to fix something to eat."

"No. Tell me in English."

"I don't know."

"Okay," he said in Spanish. "Let's go out somewhere to eat. I know a lot of good places. You can practice your English while we're eating. I think you can learn much more that way than you can in class."

"Thank you. But I have plenty to eat at home."

"Look. Why are we walking? Let me take you in my car."

"It's not far. Only two blocks."

"All right. I'll walk with you." She didn't protest.

When they got to the store, Maria told him, "This is where I live."

"This is the *tienda* where you work."

"Yes. I know. I have an apartment above it. The owner is kind enough to let me live there." After a pause, she added, "How did you know that this is where I work? When we were in class, you told Carlos that I would have to show you so you could buy some beer."

"Because I know everything. I'm a very smart person."

"Thank you for walking me home, Antonio." She opened the door and went inside. Mrs. Molina was behind the counter, and Fidencio was getting ready to leave.

"Did you learn a lot of English tonight?" Fidencio asked her.

"Sure," she said in English. "I'm almost an expert. Soon, I'll talk nothing else." She wished that were true. But she was beginning to think she would never learn. She thought about what Antonio had told her, and of course, he was right. She could learn much more by practicing with him than she could learn in class. Then why had she turned him down? She knew the answer to that question. She was afraid of what it might lead to. She was afraid of how her heart beat when she looked at him. How she trembled and felt weak when he was near.

She had planned to go to her apartment, quickly fix herself a meal and then spend some time studying her English. Suddenly that idea wasn't very appealing. She knew she would stare at the pages for the rest of the night and learn nothing. She should have taken Antonio up on his offer.

What was it that had made her so certain that going to eat with him would lead to anything? He probably didn't like her. And even if he did, she could certainly control her emotions and not make a fool of herself. Maybe it wasn't too late for her to change her mind. If she hurried, she might be able to catch him before he got back to the schoolhouse where his car was parked.

"Excuse me," she said to Fidencio and Mrs. Molina. "I forgot something."

She went back outside and ran toward the school. When she got there, she saw a car's lights come on. Then it began moving slowly across the parking lot toward the exit. She didn't know whether or not it belonged to Antonio. She didn't know what his car looked like, but that didn't deter her. She ran toward the exit hoping she would get there in time for the driver to see her.

The automobile was traveling slowly so she had no trouble making it in time. It stopped, and Maria went to the window. It wasn't Antonio in the car. It was Mrs. Fernandez.

"Why, Sandra. What's the matter?"

Maria was embarrassed and didn't know what to say.

"Nothing. I was just looking for somebody."

"Antonio? So you took my advice?"

Maria was flustered. "What advice?"

"To find someone to practice with. Well you're in luck. I just saw Antonio getting into his car. He'll be here in just a minute."

At that moment, Maria heard a car's engine start and saw its lights turn on.

"I'll see you tomorrow," Mrs. Fernandez said. "And I'm sure your English will be much improved."

Maria watched her drive away and waited for Antonio.

Lovett had been trying to get in touch with Sammy Norton for more than two weeks and hadn't had any luck. When he called the phone he got a message that it was disconnected. He guessed he'd just have to wait until Sammy got in touch with him.

He wanted to tell Sammy he was moving to San Antonio, but it looked like he wasn't going to be able to do that. Lovett wasn't too worried, though. If Sammy wanted to find him, he would. Lovett figured that even if he moved to Timbuktu, Sammy would find some way to get in touch if he wanted to.

Lovett wasn't sure what he was going to do in San Antonio, and he didn't really care. He had enough money to last for a while and wasn't going to worry. He might even take a vacation somewhere or just rent a nice place and relax for a few weeks.

He decided he'd wait until he was situated and then try again to get a hold of Sammy. If he found his friend, they would work out something together. Otherwise, Lovett would come up with some kind of a project by himself.

He didn't need his van anymore. He thought about trading it in on a Lexus but changed his mind. He might as well wait until he had something going in San Antonio before he started shopping for a new automobile.

Lovett didn't have much furniture, but he did have some pretty good things he wanted to take to San Antonio with him. He thought he might drive down and find an apartment and then come back to Austin, rent a U-haul truck and do the moving himself. Then he decided against doing that. He'd hire somebody to move his things for him. It wouldn't be all that expensive, and besides, he had plenty of money.

The rent on his apartment wasn't due for two weeks. That would give him enough time to drive down to San Antonio, find an apartment and come back and get his things moved. He figured he might as well leave first thing the next morning. Tonight, though, he was going to celebrate. He had just gotten rid of his cancer cure machine, and as far as he was concerned, that was sufficient cause for celebration.

He was going out off and on with a girl named Janette, but she was out of town for the week. She worked for a software development company somewhere on Highway 183 and was away from home a lot of the time. Most of her trips were to California, but she traveled all over the United States and occasionally to Europe. She had invited him to go to California with her, but he hadn't been able to go. He had wanted to be sure he got the money from Calliope and Mrs. Twirling and sold the cancer cure machine to Daniels.

Lovett wasn't sure how much fun the trip would've been, anyway. Lately, he and Janette hadn't been getting along very well. She didn't know exactly what kind of work he did and was always questioning him trying to find out. Several times she had urged him to apply for a job at the company where she worked. He'd have to start as a trainee, but the job had a lot of potential. The company offered after-work training courses and would also pay for any college courses that the employees took as long as the courses were job-related.

When Lovett told her he wasn't interested, she had insisted. It was a great opportunity, she said, that may not come along again. He told her he was happy just the way things were. When she persisted, he told her he'd promise not to try to run her life if she'd promise not to run his. That had hurt her feelings, but at least, it had shut her up for a while.

Lovett hadn't called her for a few days, and then she had called him and invited him to go with her on the trip. He figured that was her way of apologizing and trying to patch things up. He told her he wished he could go, but unfortunately, he had other commitments that prevented it. He wasn't going anywhere until he had his hands on Calliope's and Mrs. Twirling's checks.

He decided he'd eat a nice dinner and have a few drinks. There were several places he was familiar with that had music and dancing. There were usually plenty of singles at most of the places, and he thought he might even be able to pick up something. He'd just go out and relax and see what developed.

He took a shower and started to shave. Just as he spread the lather on his face, the telephone rang. He went into the bedroom and picked it up.

"Hello," he said.

"Cal?" said a woman's voice on the other end.

"Yeah. This is Cal."

"This is May," the voice answered. "Remember me?"

"Of course, I remember you. Where in hell are you?"

"I'm in Houston. I'm trying to locate Sammy Norton. Do you happen to have his number?"

"No. I wish I did. I've been trying to find that old horse thief, myself. So what are you doing in Houston?"

"Well, actually I'm leaving. You don't know how I can get in touch with Sammy?"

"No. I'm sorry. I sure don't."

"Well darn! Listen, I know it would be imposing, but if I flew into Austin, do you think you could put me up for a few days?"

"Where's April? Sure, I can. I'm getting ready to move to San Antonio, but I can put you both up."

"She's not with me. Listen. I'm at Hobby Field. If I can get on a flight to Austin, could you pick me up?"

"Sure. What time?"

"I don't know. I'm going to check right now. Don't go anywhere. I'll call you right back." She hung up the telephone.

He wondered what that was all about. Maybe she was with Sammy, and they were trying to surprise him. Hell, she was probably calling from Sammy's cell phone, and they would be knocking on his door any minute.

He went back into the bathroom, finished shaving and splashed his face liberally with aftershave lotion. Then he got dressed. If old Sammy and the twins were planning to surprise him, they ought to be there any time.

Lovett was hungry but decided not to go anywhere. He'd hang around and wait for May's call. Probably she and Sammy, and April, too, for that matter, were pulling a fast one on him. He hoped so because it would be fun to see them again. On the other hand, May might really be by herself and calling from Houston. He'd just wait and see. He didn't think he'd starve to death while he waited.

The telephone rang again.

"Hello. Cal Lovett here."

"Cal. It's me again. I'll be at the airport at seven thirty. Are you sure you can pick me up?"

"I'll be there. What airline?"

She told him the airline and flight number.

"Okay," he said. "And don't eat anything. We can go somewhere when you get in."

Caleb Lovett woke up feeling like shit. There was a naked girl lying beside him and he was naked, too. His head was pounding like somebody was beating on it with a hammer. He threw the covers back and sat up. That movement woke the girl, and she asked plaintively, "Where you going, Cal?"

When she said that, everything came back to him.

"Christ, May, I've got to pee. And I've got to find some aspirins." He staggered across the floor and went into the bathroom and turned on the light. After he finished urinating, he opened the medicine cabinet and took out a bottle of aspirin. He shook out five into his hand and tossed them into his mouth. He picked up a plastic glass from the lavatory counter, filled it with water and drank it, washing the tablets down. Then he came back into the bedroom and pulled back the drapes letting in some light.

"Come on back to bed, honey. It's still the middle of the night," May told him.

He looked at a clock on the dresser, and it was eight forty-five. She was right. It was way too early to get up. He went to the bed and got back under the covers.

She turned toward him wrapping her arms around him and snuggling close pushing her tits firmly against his chest. "I think I could get used to this," she said.

At the same time, he put his arms around her, and holding her rear end with both hands, he pulled her even closer.

"Me, too. You never finished your story last night. Now, why are you back? Didn't you like Houston?"

"Why? Are you sorry I'm here?"

"No. I'm just being polite. You started to tell me about it last night and never got around to finishing."

"Well, that's your fault. You were too busy messing around to listen."

"I guess you've got me there. So, now that you're back, do you have any plans?"

"Well, there was supposed to be something for April and me. But it fell through because April took off to Las Vegas with this guy. They wanted me to go with them. He has a friend or something there they really wanted me to meet. But I don't like the guy April went with so I doubt if I would like his friend any better. Anyway, I decided to come here instead. I really hoped Sammy would be here."

"Yeah. Me, too."

"Anyway, I called the place where they wanted April and me to work. They told me they needed us both, or it was no deal. It was supposed to be a twin act, so they wouldn't hire me without her. As far as I know, they're still looking for a set of twins. Anyway, today I'm supposed to interview for this job downtown teaching aerobics. Pretty dull, but I suppose it'll pay the bills. What about you?"

"Nothing right now. I was curing people of cancer. It got pretty hairy, and I sold the machine. Now, I'm ready to do something else."

"Well, that was mean. I'm glad you stopped. You just build up those poor people's hope, and then their whole world comes crashing down around them."

"Maybe so, but the doctors do the same thing," Lovett told her. "And they can't cure them any more than we can."

"I'm glad you stopped, anyway."

"To tell you the truth, I was planning to go to San Antonio today and look for an apartment."

"I bet I know what you're going to do right now, though. I feel your big old thing beginning to wake up." She reached down and grasped his penis which had begun to swell. At the touch of her hand, it became rigid.

"Is that all you know how to do?" he asked her.

"Why? You don't like it?" she laughed.

"I guess it'll do for starters." She turned onto her back, and in a moment he was on top of her.

She wrapped her legs around his waist when he was deep inside and said, "Okay, mister smart ass, I don't hear you complaining now."

"Shut up and fuck," he said and covered her mouth with his. She began kissing him and probing his mouth with her tongue while she moved her body against his. In a few minutes, she twisted her face away and began breathing deeply through her open mouth.

"Go, go, go," she panted. And then, "I'm coming. Oh, Jesus, I'm coming."

He ejaculated at the same time. They lay unmoving for a while and then rolled onto their sides facing each other, taking care to remain joined together as they did so.

"Umm," she said. "That was good."

"How good?"

"Well, not perfect, mister smart ass. But okay."

"You want to go again?"

"In your dreams, superman." She snuggled closer and kissed him. "I'm sorry I had to turn my face away, but I needed oxygen. Jesus you're good. Don't move. Let's just stay here like this for a while." He lay, holding her. He had almost drifted off to sleep when she began kissing him again and stroking his back and butt. He lay still, not responding, pretending to be asleep. But that tactic didn't dissuade her. She laid her leg over his and continued caressing and kissing him. His penis which was still inside, began getting hard again. He started turning her onto her back, trying to stay coupled as he did so, but she resisted his efforts.

"Let's stay like this. I like it side by side like this."

When they were finished, they lay facing each other for a while, and then May said, "God, I'm sleepy. I think I'll get some sleep." She turned her back toward him and said, "Hold me."

He held her, one of his hands on a breast and his penis against her behind. In a few minutes they were both asleep.

They woke up at eleven thirty and got up and showered.

"What time is your interview?" he asked her.

"Oh, yeah. The interview. I had just about forgotten about that."

"Well, let's go out and find something to eat. You know you don't have to go to that old interview. You could go to San Antonio with me."

"I don't know."

"Okay. Let's go out and eat, anyhow."

When they got back to his apartment, he said, "I'm going to leave in a little while. You're welcome to come with me, or you can use my apartment while I'm gone. But I'm kinda far out in the boonies, and you would be pretty well stranded without a car."

"The aerobics place has an apartment right over the studio. I'm supposed to live there. It goes with the job. So I guess I'll stay there," she said.

"But what if you don't get the job? What then?"

"Oh, no. They've already promised it to me. I was just going to talk to them to see if I wanted to take it. It's mine, and the apartment, too, if I want them."

"I'll tell you what. Why don't you call them and tell them you were delayed for a couple of days? Then come on to San Antonio with me. I'm coming back day after tomorrow, anyway. You can talk to them, then."

She thought it over for a few minutes and then said. "Would you mind taking me over there? It's called the Lifeline Aerobics Center, and it's right downtown. Let me talk to them and see what they say. If it's all right with them, I'll ride down with you. Would that make you too late?"

"No. Not at all. Anything that works for you works for me."

Lovett sat in the lounge waiting for May to complete her interview. When she came out to join him, he said, "Well?"

"I think I'm going to take it. I promised them I would start tomorrow."

"Then, that means you're not going to San Antonio with me?"

"No. I don't think so. I'd better check out my apartment and get ready for tomorrow. You won't be too angry at me, will you? Especially if I promise you a real fun party when you get back?"

"It would be nice if you could come, but that's okay. I'll stop by on my way back just to let you know I'm here."

"I'll be waiting," she said. They kissed, and he got into his van and headed for San Antonio.

He decided he'd get a real luxurious apartment. In the back of his mind, he hoped to talk May into coming down and staying with him for a while. She wouldn't have any trouble finding a job in San Antonio if she wanted to. There were as many aerobics places there as there were in Austin.

He had enough money so he wouldn't have to worry about the apartment's cost. He didn't have enough to last forever, of course, but that didn't bother him. He was going to take off a month or so and relax. Then he'd have a new business going in no time at all.

He found an apartment that was exactly what he wanted. He was sure May would like it, too. When he got back into Austin, he stopped by the Lifeline Aerobics Center and went inside. A young woman was sitting behind the reception desk.

"May I help you, sir?" she asked him.

"Yes. I was just wondering if May's in. You know, the new girl that just started."

"She didn't take the job. She went somewhere. Oh yeah. I think it was Las Vegas."

"Are you sure?" Lovett asked her.

"Yeah. I think so. Wait just a minute." She picked up the telephone, and in a few seconds, another woman came out to join her."

"This gentleman is looking for May. You know, the girl that talked to us a couple of days ago. Do you remember where she said she was going?"

"Yes, sir," she said, addressing Lovett. "She decided she didn't want the job after all. She went to Las Vegas. She has a twin there you know."

"Thank you," Lovett said. He went back outside, got into his van and drove to his old apartment.

The first week he was in San Antonio, Lovett spent every night in a different bar. He'd go home when the place closed and sleep until noon. Then he'd get up and go somewhere to eat. After that he'd go to a shopping mall and walk around for a while and maybe catch a movie. It didn't take very long until that routine began to get monotonous.

He wished May hadn't run off to Las Vegas. It sort of pissed him off the way she had just gone without saying a word. Even though he was a little disappointed, he wasn't overly surprised. It had been pretty obvious that she was a flake the first time he saw her.

He had thought about taking Janette to San Antonio with him but had changed his mind. She had turned into a real pain in the ass and was making it clear she wanted to get married. As far as Lovett was concerned, she could marry somebody else. He sure wasn't about to be tied down. If he ever did decide to settle down, it would be with someone like May. When she wrapped her legs around him it didn't make much difference whether she was flaky or not.

He decided he might as well find some kind of a legitimate job. If Sammy ever got in touch with him, they could run some kind of a scam. But in the meantime he wanted to do something where he could use his real name.

Lovett had just got out of bed and the time was eleven fifteen. He figured he'd forget about the mall and the movie. He shaved and showered and went to a Waffle House for breakfast. Then he picked up a newspaper and returned to his apartment.

He had no idea what kind of a job he was looking for. He couldn't think of anything he was qualified to do. He had found out he wasn't cut out to sit behind a desk all day when he was working for Walter Carver punching useless numbers into a computer.

He started laughing when he remembered the last time he had seen old Walter and Vicki. He wondered if they'd ever recovered.

Lovett knew he'd be able to find something. It would be nice if it paid a decent wage, but it didn't have to. It would give him something to fill his day. But more importantly, it would explain where his money came from in case the IRS ever started snooping around and asking questions.

He opened the classified advertising pages to the employment section and began to scan the ads. Under the Administration heading he saw a job for Department Assistant. He began to read the ad and couldn't understand what it meant: Proficiency with PCs including an intermediate to advanced knowledge of Microsoft Word and Excel are required, and intermediate knowledge of Power Point is preferred—

He stopped reading at that point and began turning the pages looking for something else. He might as well forget about anything in Administration.

There were jobs for accountants, architects and attorneys. He flipped through a few more pages and saw a lot of jobs for drivers. All kinds of drivers: Auto parts delivery, concrete truck drivers, limousine drivers, dump truck drivers, and lots more. There were jobs for editors and graphic designers. Lovett didn't see a thing he was remotely interested in or qualified to do.

He was about to throw the paper aside and watch TV for a while when he saw an ad that looked interesting. Young man to train for management position in upscale pawnshop. Good hours. Good pay. Good benefits.

Lovett got a pen and some paper and called the phone number shown in the ad.

"Hello. *Gold And More*," a man's voice answered. "Mr. Gold speaking."

"I just saw your ad. I think I'm exactly the right man for the job."

"Okay, young man. What's your name?"

"Lovett. Cal Lovett."

"Well come on by. I'd like to take a look at you. Do you have a pencil and something to write on?"

"Yes, sir. I sure do." The man gave him the address, and Lovett wrote it down.

"Do you think you can find it?"

"Yes, sir. I have a map here. If I have any trouble, I'll call you back. But if it's on the map, I'll find it."

Tony and Maria were dancing in the middle of a tiny dance floor in a tavern overlooking the San Antonio River. He had told her he liked for his friends to call him Tony. She was glad. She liked Tony better than Antonio because it sounded so American. They talked almost exclusively in English, now. Once in a while, he'd have to use Spanish to make her understand, but not very often. She still found it difficult to converse at the store or in her English class, but she was getting quite proficient in the language when she was with him.

When the song was over, they returned to their table. As soon as they were seated, he picked up his frozen margarita, held the glass in front of him and said, "To the most beautiful *and* the smartest girl in the world."

She picked hers up and clinked it against his. "Thank you, kind sir. You've already said that three times tonight, but I'm not complaining. Without your help, I never would have learned anything."

She had just finished Mrs. Fernandez's beginning English course and had made an A on the final test. In a week, she was scheduled to begin a more advanced class. Each day the students would be required to stand in front of the class and present a current event. The final test would be to write and give a ten minute speech. She would be allowed to use only four three-by-five cards for notes.

"It's really scary," she told Tony, "but I think I can do it."

"I know you can. Now, let me ask you a question. What happened to that shy little girl I met such a short time ago?"

"I'm the one who should be asking questions. I know nothing about you."

"Oh? I suppose I'll tell you my life's story someday. But right now let's celebrate."

"Let me switch to Spanish for just a moment," she said in Spanish, "because I can express what I'm trying to tell you much better in my native language. Yes. I do want to celebrate, and that's what I'm doing. Did you know that before I met you, I had never tasted a margarita? One time, when I was young and foolish, I did taste a frozen daiquiri but only one. And here I'm drinking margaritas like water. But while we celebrate, I would like for you to tell me something about yourself, mister mystery man."

"So, beautiful Sandra," he said, his eyes silently laughing. "I'm the one who led you astray and turned you into the wicked girl you are today. Well, I won't say I'm sorry. I love wicked women much more than innocent little girls."

Her heart almost stopped when he said "love," but she tried to keep her expression from changing.

"Okay. You don't have to answer. I'm sometimes too curious for my own good."

"So, you're curious? Did you know, beautiful Sandra, that curiosity killed a cat? But let me assure you that there's nothing mysterious about me at all. I'm nothing but a humble accountant. I own a very small company. There are five of us in all."

"And you're the boss?"

"Of course, I'm the boss."

"I wondered how you could come to the school every week. Now I know."

"Now that I'm no longer a mystery man are you disappointed?"

"Not at all. I think that accounting is a very exciting profession. Right up there with skydiving and motorcycle racing."

"Oh, much more exciting than either of those." They both laughed.

The band was playing a mambo, and several couples were on the floor. Maria jumped up and grabbed his hand. "Did we come here to talk or dance?"

"Now, that's what I wanted to hear, beautiful Sandra. That's what I wanted to hear."

Joseph Gold put on his coat and hat. He started for the door but then returned to where Lovett was standing. "I think you have the hang of it, son," he said. "But if you have any problems, call me. The most important thing you've got to remember is to always get the customer information. If he doesn't have a valid identification card such as a driver's license or military ID, we don't do business with him, you understand?"

Lovett understood, all right. If he had heard the old man's lecture once, he had heard it a thousand times.

"Yes, sir. I'll make sure. And I'll tag the item with an identification number and put the information in the computer."

"Good boy. Now we never can slip up on that. If the police ever come by to check our inventory, we have to have one hundred percent accountability for every item we have in the shop."

Yes, sir," Lovett said. "I'll be very careful. You can count on that."

Once more Gold started toward the door. Then he turned and said, "Remember, Cal. Call me if you have any questions at all. It's always better to be safe than sorry."

"Yes, sir, Mr. Gold. I'll call you if I have any questions."

"Good boy," Mr. Gold said. He opened the door and left the shop. Lovett was glad to see him go. For a while he had wondered if the old fart was ever going to leave.

Lovett waited until Mr. Gold's car left the parking lot, and then he made a telephone call. A man answered the phone and said, "Bob Snow here."

"Bob. This is Cal Lovett. Come on in. The old man just left, and I'm ready to talk business."

"Give me ten minutes," the man said and hung up the telephone.

Lovett was sorry he was using his real name. Otherwise, he'd be able to mark down everything in the shop while Gold was away, dispose of it quickly and walk away with the money. It was too late for that now. He should have thought about it earlier.

The plan he and Snow had come up with wasn't too bad, though. Snow had a gang of teenagers breaking into houses on the other side of San Antonio and in surrounding towns as far away as Austin, Laredo and Corpus Christi. They would bring all the gold they could find into the *Gold And More* pawnshop, and Lovett would take it off their hands. He'd give the items identification numbers and enter a bogus name and address for each one. Lovett would get a twenty percent kickback in cash.

After a while, Snow and another man came into the *Gold And More* pawnshop. Snow was carrying a large briefcase. He went to the window Lovett was standing behind and laid the briefcase on the counter between them. The other man stood by the door waiting.

"I've got some stuff here I thought you might be interested in," Snow told Lovett. He opened the briefcase and dumped its contents onto the counter.

"Can you handle that?" Snow asked.

Lovett looked at the mound of gold jewelry and whistled. "I don't know. Yeah, I think so. There's a hell of a lot of gold there." There were bracelets, necklaces and earrings in the stack. One of the charm bracelets was loaded with heavy gold charms.

"You better believe it," Snow responded. "Can you handle it?"

"Yeah. But not all at once. It would look too suspicious. Let's spread it out over a week or so."

"Shit. I thought you said you could handle it."

"I can. But let's kind of build up to it. It'll look a whole lot better if we build up to it gradually. I don't usually handle that much gold in a month."

Snow shrugged his shoulders. He picked up part of the pile and put it back into his briefcase.

"What about that?" he asked indicating the remaining items. "Can you take care of that today?"

"Yeah. That won't be any problem."

Lovett studied the jewelry for a while and then weighed it. "I can give you four thousand," he said.

"Bullshit. It's worth six."

Lovett said, "Forty-five is all that I can go."

"Okay. Make it five thousand. You take a thousand and give me four."

"All right. That'll work for now. We'll see how the stuff moves. I might be able to give you a little more or a little less the next time depending on how fast we can get rid of the stuff. But the check will have to be for five. We'll have to cash it and get my thousand from it."

"That's fair enough," Snow said. "You've got to keep the books straight."

"Now," Lovett said, "I need to get an address and signature on these papers. I can't do it myself. It's too risky."

"Okay." Snow turned toward his companion who was still standing by the door. "Hey, Randy. Come on over here a minute."

The man came to the window where Snow and Lovett were standing.

"Hi," Lovett said. "My name's Cal." He extended his hand. Randy ignored it.

"Print the name and address here," Snow told Randy showing him where to put the required information. "And then sign here." Snow made a check mark on the line where he wanted Randy to sign his name.

Randy took a three by five card from his pocket, laid it on the counter top and copied a name and address from it onto the paper Lovett had asked Snow to sign. The name he wrote was Robert L. Snow. Then he signed the same name on the signature line.

"How do you want the check made out?"

"Just make it out to Robert L. Snow. But don't be surprised if I have another name the next time you see me."

"Hell," Lovett laughed. "I'll be surprised if you don't."

He wrote out a check for five thousand dollars. "I suppose I could hang up my OUT TO LUNCH sign and go with you to get it cashed."

"What's the matter? You don't trust me?"

"Of course, I trust you. You need me as much as I need you."

"Hey, man. I was kidding." Then Snow told Randy. "Give the man a thousand dollars." Randy took a roll of bills from his pocket, peeled off ten one hundred dollar bills and handed them to Lovett.

"Thank you, Lovett told him."

"See you in a couple of days," Snow said, and he and Randy left the shop.

The telephone rang, and Lovett picked it up. "Hello," he said.

A man said, "Cal. Is that you?" The voice sounded familiar, but Lovett couldn't quite figure out who it was.

"Maybe. Who's calling?"

"It's me. Daniels."

"Oh. Larry. You're not trying to peddle your machine, are you?"

"No. I plan to keep it for a while longer."

"So, what's up, Larry?"

"Art Teller's been trying to get in touch with you. He'd like for you to give him a call."

"How did you find me?"

"I knew you were in San Antonio so I didn't have a whole lot of trouble. I didn't want to give Teller too much information, though, because I knew you liked to go by the name of Jones when you deal with him. I did tell him you were in San Antonio, though."

"I've got no problem with that. So what's old Art up to? I hope he's not complaining about that Mickey Mouse Mexican job."

"I don't think so. I think he has another one he'd like for you to do. Anyway, he wants you to give him a call."

"I don't see any problem with talking to the man," Lovett said. Daniels gave him a telephone number.

"He said he'll be waiting for your call."

"Thanks, Larry. It was good talking to you. Glad you're making money. And thanks for not telling him my name or giving him my number."

"No problem, Cal. And, yeah. I'm doing okay." Lovett hung up the phone and went to a pay telephone to call the number Larry had given him.

"What's up, Art?' he said when Teller answered the phone. "They're not complaining about that Mexican job, are they?"

Arthur chuckled. "Man, they really fucked that one up, didn't they? No, a lot of people got mad as hell over that fiasco, but nobody's complaining about you. In fact, they would like for you to come down again."

"I don't think so, Art. They ran that goddamned show like a bunch of idiots. It's a wonder somebody didn't come in and shut the whole operation down. I was glad to get out of that place in one piece."

"Listen, Bill. I'm going to be in San Antonio all next week. Let me just drop by and talk to you. They've got it organized a hell of a lot better now. Don't say no until I've had a chance to talk to you."

"Well, I'm going to be real blunt. Would they make it worth my while? I don't want to risk getting my ass shot off and not have anything to show for it."

"The money won't be any problem, Bill. That's something you won't have to worry about. I can guarantee you that." Lovett figured he might as well listen to what Teller had to say. He certainly didn't have a thing to lose.

"There's just one problem. I'm trying to keep a low profile so I'm not giving out my telephone number to anybody. Daniels has it, and a few others, but nobody else. So I'll need a way to keep in touch. Maybe you could give me a cell number so I can call you."

Daniels chuckled. "I can certainly understand that." He gave Lovett his number. "I'll be in town about one o'clock Monday, maybe a little after. Give me a call at that number."

"Thanks for thinking of me, Art. Maybe we can work something out."

"I think we can," Teller said as he hung up the telephone.

CHAPTER XIV

Lovett parked his van and went into the *Gold And More* pawnshop. A policeman was talking to Mr. Gold. Lovett felt like going back out to his van and driving away, but he knew he couldn't do that. Instead, he walked nonchalantly over to where the two of them were talking.

"Hi," he said. "What's going on?"

"Mr. Lovett?" the policeman asked.

"Yes, sir. I'm Cal Lovett. Can I help you?"

"That jewelry you took in day before yesterday was stolen property," Mr. Gold said. "How could you let that happen?"

"Mr. Gold. Please. Let me talk to Mr. Lovett," the policeman said.

"They've already cashed the check you gave them," Gold said.

"What's stolen? What check? What are you talking about?" Lovett said, turning his face from Mr. Gold to the policeman and back again as he asked his questions.

"Please, Mr. Gold," the policeman said. He picked up a pouch that was lying on the counter, opened it and emptied out its contents. It was the jewelry Snow had brought in two days before.

"Do you recognize this?" the policeman asked.

Of course, he recognized it, but he didn't tell the policeman that. He picked up one of the items and said, "Let me see. Yes. A man and a woman came in with these. They're very good pieces. I wrote him a check, but I think it was reasonable."

"Why didn't you call me?" Mr. Gold demanded. "You should have known they were stolen. Who else would bring in that much jewelry except a thief?"

"Do you think you would recognize him, Mr. Lovett?" the policeman wanted to know. "Do you think you could identify him if you saw his picture?"

"Hell, I can show you who it was. I have his name and address right in the log."

"We've already checked them out, and they're false."

"I don't understand," Lovett said. "Look. He showed me his driver's license and completed all of the required paperwork. What was I supposed to do?"

"Could you come down to the office and look at some pictures?" the policeman asked.

"You mean right now? Sure, if it's all right with Mr. Gold."

"It's all right with him," the policeman said.

Lovett followed the policeman to his car. The man held the door open for Lovett, and he got inside.

"I'm Sergeant Johnson," the policeman told him.

They parked in front of a police station, and Lovett followed Johnson inside and to a room that looked like a conference room.

"Wait here," Johnson told him. He left the room and returned shortly followed by a young policewoman.

"This is officer Roan," Johnson told him. The woman looked at him without smiling. She turned on a large TV set, and Snow's picture appeared on the screen.

"Does this look like the man that brought in the jewelry?"

"I don't know. I don't think so. I didn't really pay that much attention."

"Well, I think that's the man. And I think you recognize him," Johnson said.

"I don't remember. I wish I had paid more attention."

"Do you know it's a violation of the law to make a false statement to a police officer?"

"No, sir. I didn't. But I'm not surprised. Is that all?"

"We have a few more pictures we'd like you to look at."

Officer Roan pressed a button on the remote control unit she was holding. A picture of the man that Snow had called Randy appeared on the screen.

"What about him? Does his face look familiar?"

"I really don't think so."

They showed him several more pictures. He told them he wasn't sure whether or not any of them was the man who had come into the shop. He didn't think so, though.

Officer Roan then showed him several women. He told Sergeant Johnson that he didn't recognize any of them.

"Okay," Sergeant Johnson told him. "I'll take you back to the shop."

While they were riding back to the *Gold And More*, Johnson said, "I think you're lying to us, Mr. Lovett, and I think I know why. I think you and Green are in it together."

That assertion frightened Lovett, but it also puzzled him. "Who's Green? The man that brought me the stuff was named Snow."

"So now you remember him?"

"Sure, I remember him. That's the name I wrote in the logbook. I just don't remember what he looks like. Maybe if I saw him in person, I could give you more information."

"Well, Snow is just one of the names he uses. We think his real name is Green." Johnson drove into the parking lot and parked in front of the pawnshop.

"I suggest you try real hard to remember, Mr. Lovett. If we find out you're lying or involved with Green, you'll be in a lot more trouble than you realize." Lovett got out of the car and went into the *Gold And More* pawnshop.

"I don't want you in here anymore, you little bastard," Joseph Gold thundered at him. "You're fired."

Lovett was frightened and angry. The goddamned cops had treated him like shit. He wasn't about to take the same kind of bullshit from Gold. He was ready to take out his frustrations on the little old man. He walked toward Gold with his fists clenched. His body was trembling with rage. He'd teach the son of a bitch how to keep his mouth shut.

"Don't you start on me you miserable little Jew bastard. Don't you start on me or I'll break your fucking neck and tear this goddamned place apart." Then he realized what he was about to do and stopped and took a deep breath.

"Don't look so goddamned scared you pathetic little asshole. I'm out of here. I'm going to Mexico to rip off a bunch of dumb Mexicans. I can make more money there in a week than I can make in this pitiful place in a year."

Lovett stormed out the door. He almost ran over a woman who was standing with her back to the door talking to a television camera.

She turned and thrust a microphone into Lovett's face. His first impulse was to grab it from her hand and throw it across the parking lot. He quickly realized that if she was filming for a television news program, such a reaction on his part would be exactly what she wanted. He smiled and said, "Yes, ma'am. Can I help you?"

"You can if you're Mr. Lovett."

"Yes. I'm Cal Lovett. How can I help you?"

"I'm Jennifer Stone from Channel Seven news. Are you an employee of the *Gold And More* pawnshop."

"No, ma'am. Not anymore."

"But you were an employee?"

"Yes, ma'am. But not anymore."

"Were you fired, Mr. Lovett?"

"No ma'am. I resigned."

"Mr. Lovett. Is it true that the *Gold And More* pawnshop accepts stolen goods in violation of state statutes?"

"Absolutely not."

"Did you knowingly accept stolen goods?"

"That's absolutely ridiculous."

"Then, Mr. Lovett, are you denying that this shop fences stolen property?"

"Of course, I deny it. Now if you'll excuse me, I have things I need to do."

"Do you know someone named Barry Green? Are you accepting stolen property from him? Are you getting kickbacks?"

"I'm sorry ma'am. I don't know what you're talking about. Now, please. I have to go."

"Are you going to get in touch with Mr. Green?" she asked him.

He had already begun walking toward his van. He could hear Jennifer Stone calling his name, but he didn't bother to look back.

As soon as Lovett was out of the parking lot, he picked up his cell phone and dialed Snow's number. When Snow answered, Lovett said, "Hey Bob. Cal here."

"Yeah, Cal. What in hell's going on?"

"The cops have been all over my ass all day."

"Yeah. I know. I drove by and saw the sons of bitches. What in hell's going on?"

"They had me at the police station looking at pictures. They showed me your picture. And Randy's, too. They wanted me to identify you."

"What did you tell them?"

"Hell, Bob. You know what I told them. I told them I'd never seen you in my life. They didn't believe me and told me so. Anyway, I just wanted to warn you. They know you brought in the stuff, and they're looking all over hell for you."

"Thanks, Cal."

"I quit the goddamned job. And listen. I'm getting my ass out of town for a while. I think you ought to do the same. No kidding. They had your picture and they know it's you. Only they called you Green instead of Snow."

"Thanks for calling, Cal." Snow hung up the telephone.

Maria was afraid. She was going with Tony to his house. That wasn't what frightened her, though. His father, Leonardo Calliope, lived with Tony, and Maria was nervous about meeting him. Tony's mother had recently died of cancer, and Tony had talked his father into putting his house for sale and moving to San Antonio.

When they went inside the house, Tony introduced Maria to his father.

"She's a looker," Mr. Calliope told Tony. "Is there anything you'd like to tell your old father? Any announcements you'd like to make?"

Maria blushed, and Tony said, "We're friends. We met at school."

"Do you like my son?" Leonardo asked.

"He's very nice," she said.

"See there. She likes you."

"I was very sorry to hear about your wife, sir," Maria said.

"Thank you, Sandra. You don't have to all me sir. Why don't you call me Leonardo?"

"Are you sure? I can call you Mr. Calliope if you wish."

"Leonardo is fine. Or Pop. The boys call me Pop. Why don't you just call me that?"

"Pop. Okay. If that's not too disrespectful."

"Don't let that one get away, Tony." Leonardo motioned to the couch. "Have a seat. I'll fix some coffee." He went to a cabinet and took down a can of coffee. Maria got up and went to where he was standing.

"Let me do that, please," she said. She took the can from Leonardo's hands, went to the coffee pot and began to measure out the coffee into the brewer. Leonardo went back to the couch and sat down.

The television was on, and Leonardo said, "Where's the remote control? I don't think we need that." The news was on, and a woman reporter was talking to a man standing outside a pawnshop.

"The coffee's almost ready," Maria told them. "Do you want me to bring it in there?"

The man on the TV screen said, "That's absolutely ridiculous."

"Then, Mr. Lovett, are you denying that this shop fences stolen property?"

"Of course, I deny it—"

Leonardo had found the remote control unit and turned the TV set to another channel.

Maria rushed into the room; her face was white. "Wait," she said in Spanish. "Please turn it back to the other program."

Leonardo didn't know what she was saying. Tony took the remote from his father's hand and turned the set back to the channel they had just been watching.

"That's he. That's Mr. Jones," Maria said in Spanish.

"What is it, Sandra?" Tony said.

"That's the one I told you about. The one who tried to sell me." She was still speaking in Spanish.

"Does she know him?" Leonardo asked Tony. Then he said, "Well I'll be a son of a bitch. That's Dr. Jones. That's the man with the cancer cure machine."

"Are you sure?" Tony asked. "You told me he had a moustache."

"Yes. He did. That's why I didn't recognize him right away. He must have shaved it off."

"He wore a moustache in Mexico, too, but that's he," Maria said. "Now we've got to report him to the authorities."

"I doubt if that will do any good. I'm going to call my brother. We'll figure out what to do with the son of a bitch."

Andy was drinking a cup of coffee when he involuntarily began thinking about old Jesse. He still couldn't figure out what the fellow had been doing wandering about the countryside in the middle of the night. Andy hoped he didn't keep doing it. He'd wake somebody up some night and get himself shot.

Jesse had told Andy that some girl Tony knew would identify the cancer cure quack. That statement was scary in a way because Andy couldn't figure out how the man had possessed enough information even to hazard a prediction. How could some girl who had never met Andy or Tony or their parents be of any help in locating the phony doctor? The answer was she couldn't.

Andy would normally dismiss a story such as Jesse's as nothing more than the babbling of an addled mind. But he couldn't bring himself to do that. Although he couldn't fully admit it to himself, Andy half suspected that Jesse might be exactly who he seemed to be.

The telephone rang interrupting his reverie, and Andy picked it up.

"Hello," he said.

"Hi, Andy." It was Tony.

"Yeah. Hi, Tony."

"Hey, brother, I'm about to tell you something you won't believe."

"Don't say anything else. Let me guess. A young girl that you know identified that quack that was treating Mom when she died," Andy said.

"Jesus. How did you know that? Who told you?"

"Let's just say it was a lucky shot in the dark and leave it at that. Have the cops picked him up?"

"No. That's the problem. I'm not sure we have enough proof to go to the cops. I don't want to do anything that'll scare him away."

"We've got a bad connection here, brother."

"It's a little complicated. He's here in San Antonio. You were right about the girl. I still don't believe you knew that."

"Okay, why don't you start from the beginning?"

"Like I said before, it's complicated. Pop's identified him, too. It's him all right."

"I'm totally confused. Pop identified him, too? How?"

"It's a long story. But I'll try."

"No, wait. Listen, I'll be there. I just started a new project, but that's okay. Somebody else will have to do it."

He clearly remembered the exact words Jesse had told him: *"Just remember the commandment. Finally, you'll meet a young girl who'll be very dear to your brother. She'll tell you an incredible story, but it'll be true. Listen to her and believe. After hearing her, you'll become angry, but however angry you become, don't forget the commandment."*

Andy had been to his brother's place before so he didn't bother to call when he got into San Antonio. He drove to the house and knocked on the door. His father opened it.

"Come on in," Leonardo said.

"Hello, Pop. It's good to see you." They embraced. The old man felt small and bony in his arms.

"Tony isn't here right now, but he said to call him the minute you got in. His number's there by the telephone." Andy dialed the number.

"I'll be right there," Tony said. "Have you eaten anything?"

"Just a bite. When you get here, I'll take you and Pop out somewhere to eat."

When Tony arrived, he had a beautiful girl with him. She was probably the girl Jesse had referred to. Tony introduced her as Sandra.

"Let me take everybody out to eat," Andy said.

"Save your money, brother. I'll treat."

"Let me fix something," Maria said. "I'm a very good cook."

"There's not a hell of a lot in the house," Tony said.

"Let's go to the grocery store," Maria suggested. "Your brother and father can visit while we're shopping."

When she and Tony returned from the store, Maria shooed the men from the kitchen. In an hour and a half, she called them to the table. She had prepared baked chicken breasts with barbecue sauce, baked potatoes, French bread toasted under the broiler with butter and garlic, and green beans. She had butter and sour cream for the potatoes.

"There's tea or Cokes, whichever you prefer," she said, "and for dessert I have German Chocolate cake. I didn't bake it, though. We got it from the frozen food department of the grocery store."

After they finished the meal, she served everyone coffee and cake.

"I thought coffee would go better with the dessert," she said.

"You better grab her," Leonardo told Tony.

Andy wondered if Tony had any kind of a plan. Maybe their best bet was to go to the cops. They had seen Jones on television and knew where he worked. Maybe Leonardo should just tell the authorities his story and let them take it from there. It would be up to them to obtain enough evidence to convict him. Perhaps there were other cancer patients who had been defrauded by the phony Dr. Jones who would come forward.

"What do you have up your sleeve?" he asked Tony.

"I don't want to see him walk. And I'm afraid that's what'll happen if we report him to the cops. He'll never go to trial. There's not enough evidence to convict him."

"You don't think they would believe me?" Leonardo asked.

"I don't think your testimony alone would be enough, Pop. We'd have to find other people he conned. That might be real difficult to do because our wily Dr. Jones is probably real good at covering his tracks," Tony said.

"Well, then. Do you have any suggestions?" Andy wondered.

"Yes, I do," Tony said. "I'm just not sure we could pull it off. He was in Mexico kidnapping girls and selling them. They sold them to rich oil sheiks and whorehouses. Sandra even saw them kill one because she tried to escape. I'll tell you what I want to do. I want to take our good doctor to Mexico and turn him over to the relatives of the girls he kidnapped."

Maria said, "I'm tired of deceiving you. I want to tell you a story. I've all ready told part of it to Tony but not all. Now, I want to tell all of you why I had to leave Mexico. My name isn't Sandra, it's Maria. If you have time, I would like to tell you why I had to change my name. I would also like to tell you about Mr. Jones. They killed the real Sandra, and I had to take her identity to escape with my life. "

"We have time," Leonardo told her.

Maria told them the story. She told about being kidnapped by her *Tío* Juan and Andres Gonzalez; about the Hernandez brothers, Raul and Pedro; about Sandra's death and how she had to steal Sandra's purse and money to escape; about killing Raul and Pedro and stealing their money; about how some of the other girls were raped; how she was fortunate because the men hadn't been allowed to rape her. The man who was buying her was rich and powerful and had been promised a virgin. When she was finished, she said softly, "Blessed Virgin. Please forgive me." The men were quiet; Maria was crying.

Andy parked his truck near the *Gold And More* pawnshop. It was twenty minutes until nine. He had called the place that morning and found out it closed at nine. He got out of the truck, went to a front window and looked inside. There was no one there except an elderly man sitting behind a counter shielded by what looked like bullet-proof glass. Andy went inside and up to the glass shield.

"Hello," the man said. "Can I help you?"

"My name's Andy Calliope. Is Mr. Lovett around?" That was the name the television reporter had used. Andy wondered if that was the fellow's real name. Maybe yes; maybe no. It was hard to say. The man probably had a million scams and a different name for every scam.

"No. He doesn't work here anymore. Are you a friend of his?"

"No, sir. I'm not. I have reason to believe he's a criminal."

The man looked at him suspiciously. "Are you a cop? I've already seen enough cops to last me a lifetime."

Andy saw a name plate on the counter in front of him that said Mr. Gold.

"No I'm not a policeman. Are you Mr. Gold?"

"Yes. That's me. I don't want to talk to anybody. Please leave me alone."

"Yes, sir. I will. Can you tell me where he went?"

"I had to let him go. He was trying to use my shop to conduct an illegal business. When I told him he could no longer work here, he got very angry. I thought he was going to strike me. But then he just laughed and called me a bad name."

"If I can find him, I can make sure he goes to jail. Do you have any idea where he may have gone?"

"I know where he is, all right. At least I know where he said he was going. He's in Mexico. He told me he was going to Mexico to rip off some dumb Mexicans. I don't like to use language like that, but that's what he said."

"To Mexico, huh? Did he say anything else?"

"No. Just that I was lucky he didn't break my neck and wreck my shop for firing him. He said he could make more money in one week in Mexico than he could make in a year working for me."

"But he didn't say where in Mexico?"

"No. He didn't. When he left, I was very relieved to see him go. My knees were shaking so badly I had to sit down. He really frightened me, Mr.— I'm sorry, young man. I'm afraid I've forgotten your name."

"Calliope, sir. And thank you." Andy left the shop and went to his pickup.

Andy, Tony and Maria drove into Loma Linda in Tony's red Taurus. It was a dusty little village with unpaved streets. Most of the automobiles they saw bouncing over the roads looked like they were falling apart. A few cars were parked by the side of the road. Several had flat tires, one didn't have any wheels and two were sitting on broken concrete blocks.

Several skinny dogs walked listlessly about like they were looking for something to eat. Little dirty faced *muchachos* played in the streets in front of some of the houses. A man walked slowly down the road holding a huge bunch of balloons. Another man rode a bicycle down the street. A basket loaded with various types of candies was mounted on the back of his bicycle.

"*Dulces*. Get your *dulces* here," the man on the bicycle repeated over and over in a sing-song voice.

"That's my house," Maria told the men, pointing toward one of the houses. "The one my *Tío* Juan stole from me. And the house over there belongs to *Señora* Lopez. People say she's a *bruja,* but actually she's an angel."

"Does she know where you are?" Tony asked her.

"I'm sure she thinks I'm dead."

"Let's surprise her," Andy said.

Tony parked his car in front of Se*ñ*ora Lopez's house, and they all got out.

"We'll follow you," Andy told Maria. She led them up the sidewalk and knocked on the front door. A woman opened it, stared at Maria for a moment as though she were seeing a ghost and then threw her arms around her.

"*Mi hija*!" she said. "*Mi hija.* I didn't think I would ever see you again. Come inside. All of you. Come inside." They entered her house.

"*Señora* Lopez. These gentlemen are my friends. They're brothers. Andrew and Antonio Calliope. But they like Andy and Tony better."

"What happened, Maria? Juan Guardia said you had run away with a rich *gringo*. I knew he was lying, but I didn't know how to find out the truth."

"I didn't run away. My *Tío* Juan and Andres Gonzalez kidnapped me and tried to sell me. The holy Virgin heard my prayers and delivered me from their hands."

She told the old woman about being taken to *El Rancho Torres* with several girls to be sold. She told about Sandra's death and her own escape. She didn't tell *Señora* Lopez about the death of the Hernandez brothers.

"We've come to put an end to their activities," Tony said.

"I'm afraid that's impossible. They're too powerful. They hold the government officials in the palms of their hands. *Señor* Torres decides who'll hold office and who will not. I think it would be much safer for all of you to go back home before any one knows you're here."

"I've never heard of your running away from a fight," Maria retorted.

"I relish a good fight. But I'm cunning and strong. You're but a young girl, and your friends don't know the ways of this country."

"We don't plan to do anything by ourselves. We want to get help from people who have been hurt by *Señor* Torres and his lapdog politicians. People whose sisters or wives have been taken away and raped and sent to far away countries," Tony said.

"They're too frightened. I would love to do something if I knew how. But it's too dangerous for you and your brother. You would stand out like two black sheep amidst many innocent white lambs."

"Where are Maria's *Tío* Juan and Andres Gonzalez?" Andy asked.

"They're both gone. I'm not sure where they went. They just disappeared. I've been told they're in hiding. I've been told they've left Mexico. I've been told they're in prison. I've been told they're dead. Which of those stories is true? Who knows? I only know that our village is better off without them."

"Then no one is living in my house?" Maria asked her.

"It's no longer your house. The government has requisitioned it. It now belongs to them."

"But now that she's here, won't they return it to her?" Andy asked.

"No. She can't stay here. She's wanted for murder, thievery and a dozen other crimes. The wardens of several prisons have already thrown dice to see who can have her when she's captured. The filthy little man who won her has offered a two hundred and fifty thousand *peso* reward for anyone providing information that leads to her apprehension. Please Maria. For your safety you must leave at once."

"*Señora* Lopez is right," Andy said. "You take her back home, Tony. I'll stay here."

Then he said to *Señora* Lopez, "*Señora*. If I come back here, to your house, later, can you help me? You said you like a good fight. Well, I do, too. I think between us we can put these criminals out of business."

They decided Tony would take Maria back to San Antonio. They considered taking her to the airport in Monterrey and letting her fly back to Texas. But that was too risky because there was a slight chance the airport was under surveillance. Maria had sufficient identification showing she was Sandra Garcia, but they were still afraid. The authorities could have someone with them who actually knew Maria. After all, there were two hundred and fifty thousand *pesos* at stake.

Tony and Maria took Andy into Monterrey where Andy rented a car. When he drove away from the rental agency, Tony and Maria headed for Texas. The brothers had agreed that Tony would return as soon as he could. In the meantime, Andy would begin working on the first phase of their plan. He drove back to *Señora* Lopez's house, and she had already started making telephone calls.

"It'll work like a chain letter," she told him. "I'll call everyone I know who may be able and willing to help us. Then they'll call everyone they know. Before long, everyone in Mexico will be contacted. I will know when that point has been reached when I make a call and hear myself answer."

Within the next few days, a meeting would be held in a dilapidated old barn about fifty miles from Loma Linda. Pepe Lopez, *Señora* Lopez's son, would come in from Vera Cruz to conduct the meeting. *Señora* Lopez suggested it would be better if someone from Mexico did the talking. "They don't trust *Americanos* and wouldn't listen to you or your brother," she said.

"I would like to see the place where the meeting will be held," Andy said. "I would also like to see *El Rancho Torres*. Do you know anyone who could take me? Someone we can trust?"

"I've already contacted someone. He's on his way now. He'll be here soon. I have fresh coffee and plenty of sweet bread. You can have some while you wait."

She poured him some coffee and heated some pastries on a *comal* and put three of them on the table in front of him.

"Felipe will be here in a few minutes," she said. She went back to the telephone and continued making calls.

In thirty minutes or so, a large man knocked on the door, and *Señora* Lopez ushered him inside. He was well over six feet tall and looked like he weighed at least two hundred and sixty pounds. His face was dark and pockmarked. His eyes were almost black. A pink scar ran across his right cheek from his scalp to the corner of his mouth. His hair was jet black and combed straight back. He had applied enough oil to it to make sure it stayed in place. *Señora* Lopez introduced him to Andy. His name was Felipe Navarro.

"I understand you're here to punish some of our people," Felipe said in English. "What business is it of yours what happens here? Don't you have enough crime in your own country to keep you occupied?"

"The criminal we want to punish is an American. He caused my mother's death. That's the main reason *I* want to punish him. But he also came to your country and kidnapped your young girls and sold them to rich men from far away countries. I've been told a young girl was killed trying to escape from him right here at *El Rancho Torres*."

"Come outside with me," Felipe said. "I want to show you something." He told *Señora* Lopez that they were leaving and led Andy through the door. Andy followed the big man wondering if he should be frightened.

An old Ford truck was parked outside. Felipe went to the driver's door and got inside. Andy climbed into the passenger seat. Felipe started the truck, and they drove away.

"Where are we going?" Andy asked him.

"You'll see."

They pulled onto the main road. The truck lumbered along at forty-five miles per hour. The roadway was full of potholes, and Felipe didn't try to avoid them. It seemed like he didn't even notice them. Every time the truck hit one it jarred Andy's body. Once he had just opened his mouth to say something when the truck hit a particularly deep one. The impact traveled from the truck's seat up Andy's spine and snapped his jaw shut. He felt like it almost shattered his teeth.

"Are you doing that on purpose?" Andy shouted. "Jesus Christ. See if you can miss at least one before we get to wherever it is we're going."

Felipe slowed down the truck and laughed. "I thought you were one tough *gringo*. But you're as soft and delicate as a girl."

"Of course, I'm soft and delicate. I expect to be the brains of this operation. But why don't you stop this truck and back it up about a hundred yards?"

"What are you talking about?"

"You missed that hole back there. Maybe if you try again, you can hit it and knock your goddamned wheels off."

"You know what, Andy? I think you like to joke."

They drove on in silence. Felipe was driving more slowly than before and was doing a pretty good job of avoiding the potholes. Andy suspected he had been hitting them on purpose before just to see Andy's reaction.

After thirty minutes or so, Felipe slowed the truck and turned into a rutted road winding through the scrubby trees. The road ended at a crude lean-to. Felipe stopped the truck and got out. Andy also got out and went around to where Felipe was standing. Felipe unzipped his pants, took out his penis and began peeing.

When he finished, he said, "Nobody lives here. The goatherds use it sometimes. I don't know why. It doesn't give them much protection. I would prefer to sleep outside."

Andy didn't respond. He stood waiting to see what Felipe was going to show him. Felipe went to the rear of the lean-to and stopped. He stood gazing into the pasture as though he was looking for something. Then he started walking through the stunted little trees with Andy following him.

After about fifty yards, Felipe stopped by a mound of dirt. He didn't have to say anything. Andy knew it was a grave. It couldn't be anything else. He wondered who was in the grave and why Felipe had led him to it.

"Do you know what this is?" Felipe said, kicking at the dirt.

"It looks like a grave."

"That's what it is. You might call it two graves. Or one grave with two bodies in it."

"What are we doing here?"

"*Señora* Lopez said you were asking about Juan Guardia and Andres Gonzalez. This is where they are."

"Who put them there?" Andy asked.

"Many were involved. I wasn't there, but I know what happened. Many have told me the story, and all of them say the same thing."

Guardia had sent Gonzalez out to pick up four young girls to take to *El Rancho Torres*. Gonzalez got careless and kidnapped the daughter of a prominent official by mistake. He took her to Guardia's house and raped her before he delivered her to the ranch.

Torres had invited several important politicians to his ranch to sample the girls' charms before the buyers came to claim them. He and some of the other men recognized the official's daughter and were aghast. Torres called the girl's father and told him his daughter had been abducted, but that Torres and his men had caught the kidnapper. He said he wouldn't turn the man over to the police. Instead, he'd hold him for the official. When the man came to pick up his daughter, he brought a mini army of his thugs to pick up Gonzalez.

The men rounded up a number of other toughs to help them take care of Gonzalez. When they began working him over, he implicated Juan Guardia. That didn't do him any good. The mob wreaked its justice on both of them. First they tied them to poles and castrated them. Next, they cut off their penises, crammed them into their mouths and taped their mouths shut. After that, they doused them with gasoline and burned them to death. Finally, they cut off their heads, arms and legs and buried the bodies in the grave that Felipe and Andy were standing by.

"I just wanted to show you the kind of justice your friend will receive if he's caught. There'll be no trial. It won't matter whether he's innocent or guilty. The justice represented by this mound of dirt is all the justice he'll receive."

Andy was feeling nauseated. He wondered if Dr. Jones deserved the kind of treatment that had been meted out to Guardia and Gonzalez. Maybe he ought to tell *Señora* Lopez to stop what she was doing before it was too late.

"Do you think I should talk to *Señora* Lopez? Should we stop doing what we're planning to do while there's still time?"

"I don't know what we should do. The punishment will be well beyond cruel and unusual. But I'm afraid it's too late to think about that now. The wheels are already turning, and they can't be stopped."

Lovett turned off the highway and drove toward the main gate to *El Rancho Torres*. Arthur Teller had promised him that everything would be better organized this time. It sure as hell better be. Lovett had made it clear that the moment anything looked the least bit suspicious, he was going to drive away from the ranch without looking back.

He stopped his rental car by the gate and went to the speaker mounted on one of the posts. As soon as he pressed the button a voice said, "Hello, Mr. Jones. Come on in." As he walked back to his car, the gate began to swing open. He drove through it and toward the main house.

When he got to the gate in front of the house it was already open. He drove through and parked. Miguel was waiting for him. He got out of his car and shook Miguel's hand.

"Welcome to *El Rancho Torres*," Miguel said. "We are happy to see you again."

"I'm glad to be here. Do you know when the customers will arrive?"

"Yes," Miguel said. "They'll be here within the next few days. In the meantime you may make yourself at home. You'll have every convenience at your disposal. We will make sure that this is an experience you'll never forget."

Andy rented a motel room and waited for Tony to get back from Texas. He showed *Señora* Lopez where the motel was located so she could direct Tony to it when he returned.

Tony wasn't gone long. He dropped Maria off and was back the next day. *Señora* Lopez accompanied Tony to the motel where Andy was staying. The *señora* and Tony followed Andy to the car rental company where Andy turned in his rental car. Then the brothers took the *señora* back to her house.

They went to *Señora* Lopez's house every day to see how the project was progressing. "We'll be ready soon," she assured them.

It turned out she was right in her assessment. Exactly one week after Andy and Tony had first come to Mexico, she told them the meeting would be held the following evening.

The next afternoon, Tony, Andy and *Señora* Lopez drove out to the meeting place. It was an old barn about sixty feet long and thirty feet wide. It was about seventy miles from Loma Linda in the direction of *El Rancho Torres* and five miles from the main road. There used to be a farmhouse nearby, but now it was nothing but a small pile of rubble. Everything even remotely usable had long since been carried away.

The barn was about ready to fall down, too. It was made of rotten boards and mud blocks and was partially covered with rusty sheet metal. Much of the metal had been pulled off and taken away exposing the mud to the elements, and most of it had eroded away.

The place didn't have a roof. It had caved in many years before. Almost all of it had been removed or had rotted away. Andy was glad the barn's roof was missing. He'd have been afraid to go into the building, otherwise.

Señora Lopez had asked everyone to be there by seven o'clock. It was now eight fifteen, and people were still straggling in. Andy estimated that about fifty men were there. So far, the only woman was *Señora* Lopez.

The men had come in a varied assortment of mostly miserable looking vehicles. They were milling around drinking liquor and beer and smoking cigarettes. There was a lot of loud laughing and joking going on, and everyone seemed to be in a festive mood. Quite frequently, someone would amble away from the rest of the crowd, turn his back to afford a semblance of modesty and urinate.

A truck with high sideboards drove up and parked. It was at least forty years old. All its paint was gone, and the cab was beginning to rust away. Twelve men climbed down from the truck's bed and mingled with the crowd that was already there.

Señora Lopez walked to one end of the barn carrying a brass cowbell. She rang it, and the men turned toward her to hear what she was going to say.

"Gentlemen," she said loud voice, "it's time for the meeting to begin. I'm *Señora* Lopez. I would like to introduce my son, Pepe."

"It's said that you're a *bruja*," somebody shouted.

"I'll *bruja* your ass if you don't be quiet and listen." The crowd broke into cheers and applause.

"I hope you've had a course in crowd control," Tony whispered to his brother. "You might have your hands full with this bunch."

"No problem, bro. I took Crowd Control 101. These characters are like putty in my hands."

Pepe held a bullhorn to his lips with his right hand. "Gentlemen," he said. "I'm glad you're here. Rich men from across the oceans have desecrated our country. They have stolen our virgins and taken them to their heathen lands. They have thumbed their noses at our laws. They have spit in the faces of our people—"

"Not too bad," Tony said.

Pepe continued to talk for several minutes, but then the listeners began to shout. It was impossible to understand what they were saying, because everyone was yelling at the same time.

Pepe held up his left hand, palm forward, toward the crowd. "Please, gentlemen," he said into the bullhorn.

"Where are these people?" Andy heard someone shout above the roar of the crowd.

"They're at *El Rancho Torres*. But we must decide on the action we'll take. That's why we're here tonight."

As soon as the men heard *El Rancho Torres*, they stopped listening to what Pepe was saying and bolted for their vehicles. In minutes, a ragtag caravan was heading toward the ranch.

"How would you like to see that bunch coming to get you?" Tony said.

"You think we ought to follow them or go home?" Andy wondered.

"Hell. We've come this far. Let's do it."

They followed the motley parade down the road. It was about midnight when they arrived at the ranch. It was identified by a gate with a huge sign arched over it that said *EL RANCHO TORRES*. The gate was locked denying entry to the ranch. Several men climbed down from the lead truck and began examining the gate. After several minutes of discussion, they began shouting and motioning for the vehicles behind them to back up and give them room to maneuver and reposition their truck. Nobody paid them any attention.

Finally, after more talking and explaining, they were able to persuade the people behind them to back up a few feet. With at least ten men directing him, the driver of the truck was able to turn his vehicle around so it was facing the road with its back aimed in the direction of the gate.

The driver eased the truck forward until it was bumper to bumper with another truck and could move no further. Then he put the vehicle into reverse, pressed the accelerator to the floor and engaged the clutch. The truck lurched backwards and rammed into the gate. The vehicle hadn't had enough distance to gain much speed so the gate held.

Men began getting out of some of the other vehicles and came to the gate to discuss strategy. After ten minutes of loud arguing, they had devised a plan. The drivers went back to their vehicles and moved them out of the way. The driver of the truck that had slammed into the gate drove about one hundred feet forward. Then he put the truck into reverse and came roaring back again. The vehicle crashed through the gate without slowing down. The other vehicles rolled through, as well.

After about a half mile, they came to the main house. It was a large pink mansion made of granite blocks. It was protected by a ten foot high fence constructed of stone and steel. A locked gate barred their entrance. Once again, the men climbed down from the vehicles and began to converse.

"*Mira*," one of the men said. "Get out of my way. I can knock the gate down with my dump truck."

He pointed toward his truck. It was huge and had a massive bumper that shielded the entire front of the vehicle. The bumper was made of heavy steel pipes welded across the front making the truck a virtual battering ram. It looked like it had been specifically designed for the job at hand. The driver went back toward his truck, and the other drivers moved their vehicles out of the way.

The driver revved his engine and came roaring toward the gate. The truck smashed into it at a high rate of speed. The impact knocked the gate loose from the hinges and sent it skidding down the road almost to the front door of the *hacienda*. The truck stopped, and the driver got out. He joined the rest of the mob who were already charging into the house.

A tall, slim man dressed in a tuxedo came rushing outside as though to see what was going on. Six or seven men grabbed him and began beating him. One of them went inside the house, picked up a chair and came back outside and began pounding the man with it. A heavyset fellow with a pockmarked face came running through the door firing a pistol. Two men fell before some of the others tackled him to the porch. One of the men wrenched the gun from his hand and shot him in the face.

People were running through the house exploring every room. There were naked girls in two of the bedrooms lying on their backs, legs and arms outspread, secured to the beds. Both had duct tape across their mouths. A naked man was raping one of the girls. In the other room, a man had just finished and was putting on his clothes.

Several men grabbed the two men and dragged them outside. About twenty people came running over to join the fun. Eight men grabbed one of the naked fellows and held him helpless on his back. A man opened a pocket knife, got a good grip on the prone man's scrotum and expertly cut off the end.

The victim screamed in pain and terror; everyone else laughed. The man with the knife worked one of the fellow's testicles through the opening he had made and cut the testicle out. A moment later, he did the same to the other one. Then he went to where they were holding the other man and castrated him. The men who had participated left the two victims bleeding on the ground and went into the house. A man carrying a pistol came over to where they lay, shot both of them in their abdomens and went into the house.

"Where are the rest of the *vaqueros*?" someone shouted.

"They ran like rabbits," a man answered. "They're hiding in the pastures with the cows."

"Let's go get them."

"You go if you wish to. I want to stay here and see what I can find." Nobody seemed interested in hunting for the employees who had run away.

The girls had been released and were getting dressed. *Señora* Lopez stood watching them. She saw Andy and called him over.

"Pepe and I will take the girls to my house," she told him. "You and your brother had better leave. If the police arrive, you'll be in serious trouble."

"So will you. So will everybody."

"But we're Mexicans. You're not. I know what I'm saying, Andy, and I beg you to go. Even our own people could turn on you."

Then she told the girls, "Come with me, girls. I'll take you to my house. Tomorrow we'll locate your families."

"We must get our things," one of the girls said. "They're in the cottage."

"Come with me. I'll take you there," *Señora* Lopez said.

Andy followed them outside where Pepe was waiting in a minivan.

"It's only a little way. We can walk," one of the girls said.

The six girls began walking down a lane. *Señora* Lopez went with them; Pepe followed in the van. Andy went back inside to see if he could locate Tony.

As *Señora* Lopez and the girls walked away, two women came rushing into the house.

"What's happening here?" one of them asked. She was small and dark and her eyes were almost as black as coal.

"Who are you?" someone asked her.

"I'm *Señora* Salguero. This is *Señora* Salazar."

"What are you doing here?"

"I'm here to check on the girls. There are nine more at the cottages."

The man with the pistol said, "The girls are okay. We'll take care of them at the cottages."

"But we want to help," *Señora* Salazar told him.

"We've killed all of the men, old woman. Now, get out of here before we kill you, too."

He waved his gun menacingly. "Get out. Both of you." The women turned and fled through the front door.

The mob was tearing the house apart. They were taking everything outside and loading it into their vehicles: mattresses, beds, dressers, chairs, sofas, tables. Everything in the house. Two men were lugging a table top to their truck. Another was carrying its legs to his vehicle. Eight men had ripped out a bathtub and were dragging it across the front yard. People were taking out the windows and tearing off the doors. Others were running across the grass carrying armloads of clothing and bedding.

Andy went outside. Five bodies were sprawled in front of the house. One of them had been shot by one of the men from the ranch. He had also shot another one, but that one had still been alive when some of his friends loaded him into a truck and drove away. The other four had been killed by the mob. He studied the faces of those four. One of the castrated ones looked like Mr. Lovett, A.K.A. Dr. Jones. Andy saw Tony and called him over.

"I think this is our friend. What do you think?" Andy said.

"I think you're right," Tony responded. "But you know what else I think? I think we'd better be getting our asses out of here before the goddamned Mexican army invades this place. But somebody needs to get the girls back to *Señora* Lopez's place. Let's see if she needs us."

"I just saw her and Pepe. They already have the girls."

"I understand that there were more at some cottages."

"Yeah. They found them. I think they found them all."

The crowd was going back and forth from the house to the vehicles stripping the place bare.

"They won't have any use for half of that stuff," Andy said.

"Probably not."

Some men came outside and began dragging the bodies into the house.

"I suppose that means that they're gonna torch the place," Andy said.

"I suppose it does. After they've taken everything they can carry away."

"I think we'd better get out of here," Andy said.

"I second that motion, brother." With no further delay, they got into Tony's car and headed for Texas.

CHAPTER XV

Maria waited for Fidencio Salinas to come into the store. It was four-forty, and he was already ten minutes late. She wanted to go to upstairs to her apartment to study her English for a while. At seven o'clock, Tony was coming by to pick her up. That would give her an hour and a half to study before she started getting ready.

She had finished Mrs. Fernandez's English course. Mrs. Fernandez was impressed at how well Maria had done. Maria was disappointed, though. It seemed to her that she had learned hardly anything all. Of course, she could speak some English. But she couldn't speak it nearly as well as she had hoped to.

Mrs. Fernandez had told her that a more advanced class was beginning in two weeks.

"You should take it," the woman said. "But more importantly, you should try to use your English more. Perhaps you should go to work where you're forced to speak English."

"But I don't think I could," she protested.

"Well, try to associate more with people who speak English. That's the best way to learn it."

"I know," she said.

Fidencio came into the store. "I'm sorry," he said. "My mother is not well, and I had to do some things for her before I could come in."

"That's okay," Maria told him. She went outside and climbed the stairs to her apartment.

She wished she could go back home. She felt so alone. Everything was so different here. If only she were in Mexico, she could speak in her own language. She wouldn't have to be struggling to learn a new one. She wondered if she would ever feel at home in this strange land.

Tío Juan was dead. Andres Gonzalez was dead. Mr. Jones was dead. So were the Hernandez brothers. Yet Maria wasn't free. She couldn't go back home. She was a wanted criminal in her own country, and that made her sad.

She loved Mexico. She had thought about taking a new name and going back. Perhaps she could start over somewhere else, somewhere far away from Loma Linda. But she knew such thoughts were nothing more than foolish daydreams. She didn't dare take such a risk. She cringed at the thought of some dirty old warden getting his hands on her. That would almost certainly happen if she went back.

She wished she knew how Tony felt about her. If only he loved her the way she loved him, she wouldn't want to go back. She would want nothing but to be with him. Yet it seemed that he thought of her only as a friend.

Several times she had almost told him how she felt, but she'd always lost her nerve at the last minute. She was afraid such a confession might drive him away. And it was much better to have him only as a friend than not to have him at all.

Maria went upstairs, turned on the TV and put a DVD into the DVD player. Then she sat down in front of the TV set.

"Good morning," a young man said to a policeman. "I have been in Chicago for only two weeks. Would you please tell me how to get to the library?" Then the screen went blank, and the words were displayed in English on the screen.

"Good morning," Maria said. "I have been in Chicago for only two weeks. Would you please tell me how to get to the library?"

At six o'clock, she turned off the television and began getting ready to go out. She and Tony hadn't made any plans so she didn't know where they were going. Probably to a movie. Or maybe to a dance. It didn't really make any difference to her as long as they were together.

Tony knocked on her door at a quarter of seven.

"So, Mr. Calliope. Where are we going tonight?"

"Someplace special," he told her. "There's something very important I would like to ask you.

Andy parked his pickup in the *Golden Horseshoe* parking lot and went to the front door. He didn't really feel like going in but didn't know what else to do. He certainly didn't want to spend the night drinking booze at home and watching TV. He paid the eighteen dollar cover charge and went inside. The place was fairly crowded, but he saw an empty table near the back of the room.

In a few minutes a waitress came by, and he ordered bourbon and water. While he was waiting for it to be delivered, he checked out the room. He saw a couple of familiar-looking guys and realized they were Sam and Charlie, Helen's brothers. They were with the same girls they'd been with when Helen was there. One of the men saw him and waved. He waved back. He thought maybe he should go to their table and say hello but decided not to.

The waitress delivered his drink, and he sat and sipped it. He wondered if he was a whole lot better off sitting in a nightclub getting drunk than he'd be sitting home watching TV and getting drunk there. At least here he had a lot of company. If he was home he'd be all by himself.

But actually that wasn't a true assessment of the situation. He didn't have a lot of company here, when you really thought about it. He was surrounded by a bunch of people who didn't mean a thing to him. In a way he was just as alone here as he'd be sitting in his living room.

Well, he'd hang out for a while and see what developed. If he didn't have any luck, he'd go back home and watch TV and go to bed at a reasonable hour. He wondered what Helen was doing. It would be interesting to know how she and old Harry were getting along. He felt like asking her brothers, but decided that would be foolish.

He scrutinized the room some more and saw Sonia, the long haired girl he had danced with when he was here before. She had given him her phone number and asked him to call her sometime. He figured it might be a good idea to see if he could get something going with her. At least he could give it a try. He ought to go to her table and see if she still remembered him.

He started to get up and someone touched him on the shoulder. It was one of the women with Sam and Charlie.

"Hi," she said. You probably don't remember me. I'm Mona, a friend of Helen's."

He finished rising and turned to face her. "Sure, I remember you. The last time I was here you and your friends tried to kill me."

She laughed. "Well not really. But it probably seemed that way to you."

"Nah. I'm just kidding. How *is* Helen, anyway? And while I'm at it, how's old Harry?"

"Actually, that's why I came over. Tell me to shut up and mind my own business any time you want to, but would it be okay if I told you something? Something that's absolutely none of my business?"

"Sure. That's the kind of stuff I love to hear."

"I told Sam and Charlie I was coming over, and they didn't think it was a good idea. But here I am. I don't know how many times you saw Helen, but that doesn't really matter. I *do* know she liked you. She's mentioned you several times. I've told her to give you a call, but she's too stubborn. She said you'd think she's dumb."

"What about old Harry? The last time I talked to Helen, everything was hunky-dory."

"She kicked Harry out. They're through. Now, like I said it's none of my business. I don't even know your status. You may be engaged or married for all I know. I saw you sitting here by yourself, and it seemed like some kind of an omen. So I'm sticking my neck a way out. I have her telephone number here that I'd like to give you. I don't know how she'd react if you *did* give her a call. 'Cause she doesn't have a clue I'm doing this."

She handed him a card with a phone number written on the back. He took it from her hand and said, "Thanks."

She said, "Thank *you*. I gotta get back to the table." She stood up and walked away.

Andy's drink had almost turned to water. He sipped it, wondering what he ought to do. The waitress came by, and he ordered another drink. He checked his watch, and it was only eight fifteen. Still way early. Was it was too late to give Helen a call? Maybe, but he didn't think so. If he was going to call her at all, now was as good a time as any.

He opened his cell phone and called the number Mona had given him. Helen answered after a couple of rings.

"Hello," she said. "Andy, is that you?"

"Yeah. How you doing?'

"I'm great. I didn't expect to be hearing from you."

"I like to surprise people. I saw Sam and Charlie just now, and decided to give you a call. Just to see how you and Harry are doing."

"You talked to them, didn't you?"

"I said hello. But I did talk to Mona." Helen didn't say anything for a long time. Andy said, "Are you still there?"

" Mona didn't have any business telling you anything."

"She knows that. But she did, and I'm glad. If you're gonna get pissed off at someone, get pissed off at me, not her. She cares a lot for you or she wouldn't have told me what she did."

There was another long pause, and then she said, "Exactly what did she tell you?"

"Hey. It's early. Would you come meet me at the *Golden Horseshoe*, or could I pick you up?"

"I don't particularly care for that place. I only went there 'cause my brothers dragged me. And I'm not about to go back as long as they are there."

"Hmm," Andy said. "Are you hungry?"

"Thanks for calling, Andy, but it's pretty late."

"Wait. Can I ask you something?"

"Sure. Ask away."

"Remember that IHOP where we ate breakfast the night old Harry came back from Houston?"

"Yes. I remember it. Why?"

"I'm hungry. I'm gonna go there and grab a bite to eat. Would you meet me there?"

She laughed. "Andy, Andy, Andy. You're so persistent. But it's late."

"Please."

"You really going there?"

"Yep. I really am."

Okay. Meet me in the waiting area by the front door. I'll be there as soon as I can. Don't start without me."

"Geez, I sure am hungry, but I suppose I could wait."

He told the waitress he was leaving, left a tip on the table and went outside.

Maria's heart was happy because she was going to marry the man she loved. At the same time, she was sad because she knew hardly anyone in her new country. It would be so wonderful if only she could get married in Loma Linda. If she could do that, everyone she knew would come to her wedding. Of course, most of them had moved far away from her village. But that wouldn't make any difference. If they knew she was getting married, they would come. It would make no difference how far they had to travel. Even if they had to journey from the most remote corners of Mexico, she was sure they would come.

Maria knew, though, that she could never go back. Not even for an occasion as joyous as her wedding. She knew the fate that awaited her if she did.

She thought about calling some of her friends in Mexico and letting them in on the good news. But she didn't think it would be a good idea.

It would be better if everybody in Loma Linda forgot about her. That would make it more likely that someday she might be able to return, at least for a visit.

There was somebody in America she should call. She ought to call her *Tía* Carla. A wave of guilt rushed over her for not having called her before. She still had the card Carla had given her the last time they were together. It was a miracle she hadn't lost it.

She went to the telephone and called the number on the card. Her *Tía* Carla answered. Maria recognized the voice immediately.

"Hello, *Tía*," she said in Spanish.

"Maria. Is that you?" Carla answered, also in Spanish.

"Yes, *Tía*." Maria's voice broke with happiness. "It is I. I'm sorry I waited so long to call you."

"Where are you, *hija*? Are you okay?"

"Yes. I'm fine. I'm in Texas. I'm going to get married to a wonderful man."

"Oh, Maria! When?"

"We haven't yet set the date."

"Where are you in Texas? I'll fly there immediately. I'm sure Bill will want to come, too. There are so many things I need to tell you."

"*Tía* Carla. I'm sorry I didn't call you before. So many terrible things have happened."

"But you're all right now?"

"Yes, but I'm afraid. Everything's too wonderful to continue. I keep waiting for something to go wrong."

"I can't believe I'm actually talking to you. Everybody thinks you're dead."

"I'm alive. But there were times when death was very close."

"Don't go anywhere," *Tía* Carla told her. "We'll be there as soon as we can catch a flight.

Five people sat at a table in *Señor* Montemayor's office. They were *Señor* Montemayor, Father José, *Señora* Lopez and Andy and Tony Calliope. A heavyset woman slowly entered the room carrying five cups. She painstakingly placed one in front of each of the people sitting at the table and then left the room.

"Thank you, *Señora* Velasquez," *Señor* Montemayor told her as she left the office.

Then, directing his question to *Señora* Lopez and the Calliope brothers, *Señor* Montemayor said, "Are you certain you're not mistaken? Are you sure it's Maria Alicia Guardia that you've seen?"

"We're certain," *Señora* Lopez said.

"We were told she was kidnapped and taken to *El Rancho Torres*," Father José told her. "Some say from there she was taken to another country. Others tell us she was murdered."

"She *was* kidnapped," *Señora* Lopez responded. "And she *was* taken to *El Rancho Torres*. But she wasn't taken to another country, and she wasn't murdered although another young girl was. The blessed Virgin allowed Maria to escape. Not only have I seen her with these old eyes of mine, I've also touched her to make sure she's not a ghost."

Señora Velasquez returned to the office carrying a carafe of coffee, a pitcher of cream and a container of sugar on a tray. She carefully set the tray on the table and shuffled slowly out of the room once more.

Andy said, "May I?" and picked up the carafe and beginning filling the cups.

"Why didn't she accompany you?" Father José asked.

"She's afraid," *Señora* Lopez said, addressing both the priest and *Señor* Montemayor. "She fears she'll be put in jail and one of the fat old wardens will take her to use for his pleasure. That's what she has been told will happen to her. You both know her fears aren't exaggerated. Such is often the fate of beautiful young girls who are accused of breaking the law."

"Sadly, what you're saying is true," *Señor* Montemayor said.

"It makes no difference whether they're guilty or not," the *señora* continued. *Pesos* are placed in the right hands, and a foul old warden has a new toy."

Señora Velasquez shuffled slowly back into the room with a tray piled high with various kinds of *pan dulce*. She placed the tray on the table and left the room once more.

"There are evil men in our beautiful country," *Señora* Lopez said. "They kidnap helpless young girls; girls who are poor or orphans; girls who have no one to protect them. They sell these girls to rich men from foreign countries. They're whisked out of Mexico without leaving a trace. The ones who can't be sold to the foreigners are sold to brothels in our own border cities."

Señora Lopez paused, and Tony said, "Maria gave up her name and fled from her country because she was afraid. She was afraid of the things that *Señora* Lopez was just talking about. But recently she was told she has no reason to be afraid anymore, that she can return in safety, that she's no longer considered a criminal in the country she loves. The three of us, *Señora* Lopez, my brother and I, are here today to find out if what Maria was told is true."

"It's true," Father José said. "*Señor* Montemayor was given special investigatory powers by the president. He graciously invited me to help him, and I accepted his invitation. We were assigned an elite team of federal officers to help us in our investigation."

"Several people are already in prison as a result of our probe," *Señor* Montemayor said. "And many more are awaiting trial."

"Everyone in Loma Linda misses Maria," Father José said. "We all cried when we heard she was gone. Especially the little children."

There was a knock on the door, and *Señora* Velasquez came into the room without waiting to be invited.

"*Señor* Montemayor," she said. "Chief Flores is here. He wishes to see you."

"Chief Flores? Certainly. Send him in."

Señora Velasquez stepped back outside. In a moment a man who appeared to be in his mid-forties entered the room. He was dressed in a policeman's uniform and was holding his hat in his hand. He was slim, over six feet tall and had large brown eyes and dark curly hair. He was accompanied by Carla Davenport.

Everyone at the table stood up. *Señor* Montemayor went to greet the newcomers. He shook hands with the policeman and took Carla's hand in his. "It's good to see you *Señora* Carla," he said. "Forgive me if I don't recall your married name."

"Carla Davenport," she said. "It's good to see you, *Señor* Montemayor." She stood on her tiptoes and kissed him on the cheek. Then she said to Father José, "It's good to see you, Father."

"Let me introduce you to the others," *Señor* Montemayor said.

Carla laughed. "I already know these characters," she said. She embraced *Señora* Lopez.

"How are you, *Señora*?" Carla asked her.

Señor Montemayor introduced Chief Flores to Andy and Tony. "Call me Jaime," Flores told them.

"Chief Flores. This is certainly a pleasure. What can we do for you?" *Señor* Montemayor asked.

"*Prima* Carla asked me to come," he responded.

"Please everybody, sit down," *Señor* Montemayor said.

When everybody was seated, Carla said, "For a long time I've been very sad, and I wasn't alone in my grief. Everyone in Loma Linda was sad. We thought we had lost Maria forever. Last week I got a wonderful surprise. Maria called me to tell me that she's alive and well. But her heart was troubled. She feared she would never be able to see her beloved country again."

Carla told how she had explained to Maria that she was no longer in danger. Even after Carla's assurances, Maria was still afraid. Maria had seen many terrible things, and her heart was still filled with fear.

Carla told Maria that the criminals had been removed from their positions of power. The new police chief was none other than Carla's cousin, Jaime Flores.

"My *primo* is here tonight to convince Maria she's no longer in danger," Carla said.

"Where is this Maria I've heard so much about?" Flores asked. "If she would come here, I'm sure I could convince her she's in no danger, whatsoever."

"I think we're convinced," Tony said. "Maria and I are engaged to be married. We hope to be married here."

"That's wonderful news," Father José said. "Congratulations." He rose to his feet. Tony stood up, too, and grasped the priest's extended hand.

Señor Montemayor walked around the table and stood near Tony. When Tony and Father José completed their handshake, the *señor* grabbed Tony's hand.

"Congratulations, my boy. When is this happy event to occur?"

"Soon." He turned to face the priest. "We hope it will be in your church, sir, and that you'll perform the ceremony."

"Of course, I will. I would be honored."

"If you gentlemen have a few more minutes, we'll bring Maria here. She's very close by," Tony informed the group.

"She's here in Loma Linda?" *Señor* Montemayor asked.

"Yes. But we had to be sure she would be safe before she could show herself. We'll return with her shortly."

"We'll wait for you," *Señor* Montemayor said.

Tony, Andy and *Señora* Lopez left the room.

"Do you think it's safe?" Andy asked as soon as they were outside.

"I'm sure of it," *Señora* Lopez said. "Both Father José and *Señor* Montemayor are honorable men. I've known Jaime since he was born. Nobody could be more decent and honorable than he."

Maria, Tony, *Señora* Lopez, Father José and *Señor* Montemayor were in *Señor* Montemayor's office. Andy wasn't there. He had gone back to work at his job in Texas.

"Tony tells me you young people plan to get married," Montemayor said to Maria. "Ah, to be young again."

"Yes, *señor*, we do."

"We want to be sure everything's in order. That we'll have no nasty surprises," Tony said.

Montemayor laughed. "Everything certainly is in order, Tony. We can assure you there'll be no surprises. Now, I understand Maria wants to give us the papers she used to escape from *El Rancho Torres*. That pleases me. It pleases all of us. As soon as those documents get into the proper hands, we'll start an official investigation into Sandra Garcia's death and the events surrounding it. The American authorities are eager to see them as well."

Maria was glad to be giving Montemayor the documents that had saved her life. She was tired of pretending she was Sandra Garcia. It wasn't fair to Sandra, and it wasn't fair to her. She took an envelope from her purse and handed it to *Señor* Montemayor. "These are the things that were in Sandra's purse. The magic documents that allowed me to escape. I couldn't have survived without them. But now I don't need them anymore."

Montemayor took the envelope from her hand. "Thank you, Maria," he said. "I'll give them to the proper authorities here in Mexico. They, in turn, will contact their counterparts in the United States. I can assure you there'll be a full and thorough investigation. A proper inquiry wouldn't be possible without them."

"I hope the authorities will be able to proceed. I'm certain that Sandra has relatives and friends who have been wondering what happened to her. They've probably been waiting all this time for her to call," Maria said.

"I'm sure you're right, Maria. But all her relatives and friends will be found. They'll be given the sad news. They will also be told that the ones responsible have been severely punished," *Señor* Montemayor responded.

"Is Maria safe now that she no longer has the papers?" Tony said. "Is there a chance she could be arrested and taken away?"

"She's safe. Don't worry about that," Montemayor said. "We'll have deputies guarding her for as long as she's here."

There was a knock at the door. "Come in," Montemayor said. The door opened, and *Señor* Pablo Soto, the real estate agent who had put Maria's house on the market, entered carrying a briefcase.

"Ah, S*eñor* Soto," Montmayor said. He got up, walked over to Soto and shook his hand. "I'm glad you were able to be here so promptly."

"*De nada*. I'm grateful you set the events in motion that allowed me to come."

Soto went to where Maria was sitting. She gave him her hand. "Ah, Maria," he said. I'm pleased to see you again. Your loveliness lights up the room."

"Thank you, *Señor* Soto," she said.

"Now, now, now," he said. "Remember. My name is Pablo."

"Is everything in order, Pablo?" Montemayor said. "Did you have any trouble?"

"No, *señor*. I didn't. Perhaps you would like to make the presentation?"

"That's very considerate of you, *Señor* Soto. I would be honored to make the presentation." No one in the room except Montemayor and Soto seemed to know what the two men's discussion was about.

Soto set his briefcase on the table, opened it and extracted a large manila envelope. Montemayor took the envelope from Soto's hand.
"Thank you. You may sit down if you wish," Montemayor said.

"Thank *you*," Soto said, and sat down.

Montemayor stood up. "I'm sure that all of you are wondering what this is about," he said to everyone. "So let me assuage your curiosity. When Maria was taken from our village, she had placed her house on the market. *Señor* Soto was her real estate agent. When Maria disappeared, several mistakes were made. As a result of those mistakes, Maria's house was appropriated by the state. Now that additional information has come to light, it has been ascertained that the acquisition of her property was in error. Consequently, the government has agreed to pay Maria for the property. I'm holding here a check made out in her name. It's for the full amount the house was listed for minus commissions and certain other legitimate expenses."

He took the check from the envelope and held it up so everyone could see it.

Maria gasped. “Is it true? Is it really true?”

“Yes, Maria. It’s true.” Montemayor took the check and envelope to Maria and handed them to her.

“Thank you,” Maria said. “I never dreamed this was going to happen. What’ll I do with all this money?”

She looked at the check, put it into the envelope and handed the envelope to Tony.

“Please hold this for me,” she told him. “I’m so overwhelmed I’m afraid I may lose it.”

There are documents in that envelope that you’ll have to sign. *Señor* Soto will show you what they are,” Montemayor told her.

Soto said, “It’ll take only a minute. If you’ll come with me, please.” He stood up and retrieved the envelope Tony was holding. Then he led Maria to a table in the corner of the room.

“Is it all right if Tony comes with us?” Maria asked. “I would like for him to see what I’m signing.”

“Certainly,” Soto said. Tony went to where Maria and Soto were sitting and joined them.

When Maria had signed the necessary documents, Father José said, “My church will be ready for the ceremony. But remember, you must have a civil wedding first. The civil ceremony will unite you in the eyes of the government. My ceremony will unite you in the eyes of God and His Church.”

Maria was pleased that she and Tony would be able to marry in Loma Linda. But she was sad that only a few of her friends would be able to attend. It would be impossible to locate and notify all the people she would like to have present. The wedding was only two weeks away.

Señora Lopez noticed the somber expression on Maria’s face and asked her, “What is it, Maria? You seem sad.”

“I always dreamed of a large wedding with all my friends and relatives there. But that’s not to be. My closest relatives are dead. And most of my friends are scattered throughout Mexico. They won’t even know I’m getting married. Many of them think I’m dead.”

“Perhaps you should postpone your wedding,” Father José said. “Perhaps you should delay it six months or a year. That would give you the opportunity to plan for a wonderful ceremony. It would give you time to contact your friends, to tell them you're alive and happy and to invite them to your wedding."

"No. I've thought about that. I plan to go back to the United States as soon as possible. I can't do that until Tony and I are married."

Señor Montemayor handed Maria the envelope that contained Sandra's papers. "You may keep these until you come back for the wedding. You can give them to me then."

"No. You keep them please, and give them to the proper officials. It'll be all right. It was just a silly dream, anyway."

Señora Lopez said, "I know what'll work. I'll start making calls."

"You mean like we did before?" Tony asked her.

"Exactly," *Señora* Lopez said.

"I'm not sure what you're saying," *Señor* Montemayor said.

"Neither am I," Father José told the *señora.*

"Don't worry," she responded. "I understand, and Tony understands. Half the people in Mexico will be at Maria's wedding."

Maria, Tony and *Señora* Lopez left *Señor* Montemayor's office and went to *Señora* Lopez's house.

"We'll locate your friends, Maria. We'll tell them about your wedding. Perhaps a few of them will be able to come, perhaps many. Now I need some names." She gave Maria a pencil and a tablet. "Give me the names of as many of your friends as you can remember. I'll take it from there. Also any telephone numbers would be helpful."

Maria wrote down the names of several of her friends and two or three telephone numbers and handed the tablet to *Señora* Lopez. The *señora* took it and went to her telephone. In a few moments, she had her son, Pepe, on the line.

"Pepe," she said. "Maria Alicia Guardia is here. We must contact all her friends. I have several names for you."

After she read Pepe the names, she said to Maria and Tony, "He'll call all the people he can get a telephone number for. Then each of them will start calling. Some will use the Internet. It should be only a matter of time before everybody in Mexico knows Maria is getting married."

"Thank you, *señora,*" Maria told her. "I hope Pepe is able to locate at least some of the people on that tablet."

"Don't worry, Maria. What I said before is true. Very soon everybody in Mexico will know you're getting married."

"Is there any place in Loma Linda where we can eat?" Tony asked the women. "I would like to treat you ladies."

"No. There are some places, but none of them serve anything that's edible," *Señora* Lopez said.

"We can get something at *Señor* Montemayor's market. I'll fix us a delicious meal," Maria said.

"That won't be necessary," *Señora* Lopez told them. "I have plenty of food here."

"You've done too much for us already," Tony said. Then he said to Maria, "You'd better go with me. Otherwise I might get lost. Besides, I don't have a clue what to buy."

When Maria and Tony returned from the market, *Señora* Lopez was on the telephone. She hung it up just as they came inside.

"That's the third call I've received advising me of Maria's wedding," she told them. One was from Oaxaca, one was from San Luis Potosí and this last one was from Hermosillo. I assure the both of you that by this time tomorrow, everyone in Mexico will know about your wedding."

The weather was perfect. A cool breeze moved lazily across the prairie stirring the lonely blades of grass and the leaves on the stunted trees. A few snow-white clouds floated in a brilliant sky. A dozen camper trailers were parked in and around Loma Linda. Most were old and shabby. Only two or three looked modern or reasonably well-maintained. Scores of tents had been set up throughout the area. It seemed as though a thousand people had come to Loma Linda to attend Maria and Tony's wedding.

Many of the visitors were busy preparing food. Some used grills of various sizes they had brought from home. Others made do with such items as five-gallon cans, or anything else they could scrape up, and used scraps of wood or other flammable debris as fuel. Some built bonfires on the ground and cooked their food over them.

Many people held signs; others had posted them in front of their tents or campers. There were numerous slogans such as *Tony and Maria; We Love You, Maria; God Bless You, Maria;* and *Maria, Maria, Maria.*

Maria's wedding was almost ready to begin. The church wasn't nearly large enough to accommodate the throng that had come to Loma Linda to attend and to get a glimpse of Maria. Father José had decided to hold the ceremony outside. Everything necessary had been put in place by the townspeople under the supervision of members of Father José's Church.

Señora Montemayor had asked Maria if *Señor* Montemayor could give her away. Maria was pleased they would ask. She had told both of them it would be an honor. In just a few minutes, the *señor* would escort her to the altar where Father José and Tony were waiting.

She and Tony had been married in a civil ceremony earlier in the day and were already husband and wife under the laws of her country. But as far as Maria was concerned, that didn't count. They wouldn't be truly married until Father José performed the ceremony that would unite them in the eyes of God.

At two o'clock, all activity ceased. A crowd began gathering in front of the altar waiting for the wedding to begin. The visitors were drinking beer, tequila and other alcoholic beverages and seemed to be in a hearty mood. All day long, people had marched up the road to *Señora* Lopez's house to greet Maria and offer her their best wishes. Maria knew many of them. Others were complete strangers. Her eyes were brimming with tears of happiness.

"You're very popular," *Señora* Lopez told her.

"Isn't it wonderful?" Maria responded.

"They're ready. *Señor* Montemayor is waiting outside and Father José is ready to began," *Señora* Lopez said.

"I'm ready, too." She went outside where *Señor* Montemayor was waiting. He took her arm. As they walked toward the altar the crowd began to shout, "*Viva* Maria. *Viva* Maria. We love you. We love you. We love you."

Maria could see Tony waiting for her. She smiled in his direction. Then she waved to the crowd. Her heart was overflowing with happiness and love.

Leonardo Calliope hugged Maria. "Welcome to the family," he told her. "If I were twenty years younger, I would've married you myself."

"It's not too late," she laughed. "We can still run away together. You say the word, and I'll forget about Tony."

"I just might take you up on that. Where are we going to run to?"

"Anywhere. Fiji, Samoa, Timbuktu. Who cares where?"

The old man laughed. "It's tempting," he said. Then he said to Tony, "Congratulations, son. I told you she was right for you the first time I saw her."

"I remember, Pop."

"Both of my sons have found beautiful women," the old man said. "And we are all here together. I think a celebration is in order. We'll go out to a nice Italian restaurant and celebrate."

"There's no need for that," Maria said. "Helen and I can fix a meal better than any old restaurant. Right, Helen?"

"Sure, we can. Andy and I'll go to the store and get everything we need," Helen said. She and Andy had been going together since the night he had called her from the *Golden Horseshoe* and talked her into meeting him for a late snack.

"We don't need anything," Maria told her. "We're completely stocked. I've become a bona-fide Italian since I married Tony."

The women went into the kitchen leaving the three men alone to drink wine and talk.

In a little while, Maria and Helen called the men into the kitchen. When everyone was seated and served, Leonardo said, "I have a story I would like to tell you."

He paused a moment and then continued. "There's a canyon Camilla and I used to visit years ago. Even after the boys got older, we went there quite often. It's a peaceful place, a wonderful place for a picnic. An old rancher named Dutch Heflin owns it. Hardly a day passes that I don't think about it. So here's my story. I think it's true. But it's so strange that perhaps I dreamed part of it. Maybe I dreamed the entire thing."

Many years ago, before either Andy or Tony was born, Leonardo and Camilla took Camilla's mother to Heflin's canyon. Her name was Minerva. Her husband, Camilla's father, had died a year earlier, and Minerva was living with Leonardo and Camilla. Minerva was suffering from breast cancer, and her doctor had given up all hope. He could do nothing for her except give her medication to keep her comfortable and ease her pain. Minerva had made Leonardo and Camilla take her because she wanted to see the canyon once more before she died.

It was a beautiful day. The three of them, Camilla, her mother and Leonardo, drove out to the canyon. They brought along a picnic lunch, folding chairs and a small folding table. There were no clouds to shield them from the sun so Leonardo put the chairs, table and picnic basket under a tree near the little lake in the middle of the canyon's floor. A nice breeze was blowing, and it was very comfortable in the shade. They enjoyed their meal and laughed and talked.

Minerva had brought along her Bible. She never went anywhere without it. After they finished eating, she asked Leonardo and Camilla to go and enjoy the canyon. She wanted to be alone for a while to rest and read her Bible. They didn't want to leave her by herself, but she was insistent so they strolled about exploring the lovely place.

At about four o'clock, Camilla and Leonardo decided it was time to go home. They didn't want Minerva to get too tired. They were surprised when they got back; she wasn't tired at all. She felt stronger than she had felt in years.

"Did you see that nice young man?" she asked them. "The one who came by to chat with me for a while?" They hadn't seen anybody.

"What nice young man?" Camilla said.

"I'm not sure," Minerva responded. "I won't tell you any more unless you promise not to laugh."

Camilla said, "Of course, we won't, Mom."

"You, too," she said to Leonardo. "You have to promise, too."

"Of course, I won't laugh," he said.

"I think it was Jesus. But I'm not sure. I asked Him, but He just smiled. He said that in my heart I knew who he was."

Minerva said she had talked with Him and was no longer troubled. A few weeks later she died.

"That's a sad story," Maria said. "But it's also nice. Do you think she really saw Jesus?"

"I don't know," Leonardo said. "Of course, I didn't believe it at the time."

Andy remembered his experience at the canyon and felt a strange chill flow through his body.

"What about now?" he asked his father. "Do you believe it now?"

"You be the judge. The story isn't over yet. Remember just before you boys went to Mexico when I told you I was going on a senior citizens' tour? Well, that wasn't quite true. I was feeling a bit depressed, but I didn't want anyone to know it. I was still feeling like your mother's death was my fault. I borrowed Tony's sleeping bag without telling him and put it in the car. I knew he wouldn't miss it. You didn't, either, did you, Tony?"

"Nope. I sure didn't, Pop."

"Well, I drove out to Heflin's Canyon. I thought I might feel closer to God out there. I'm not a very religious man, but when I got there, I did a lot of praying. I don't want to go into what I prayed about because that's between me and God. Anyway, after a while, I felt a whole lot better. I almost decided to go back home. I thought it might be kind of silly for an old man like me to be sleeping on the hard ground when I had a nice comfortable bed at home. But something made me want to spend the night there.

"About two o'clock in the morning, something woke me up. I saw a man sitting on the ground leaning against a tree. Now, here's what's strange about this whole story. I wasn't afraid or even startled.

"I got out of my sleeping bag and went to tell him hello. He stood up when he saw me coming. Now you've all seen pictures of Jesus. That's exactly who he looked like. The white robe, the beard, the eyes. He even had scars on his wrists.

"He said, 'Hello, Leonardo. I've been expecting you.'

"'Who are you?' I asked him.

"'You know who I am,' he said.

"'How can I know that?' I asked him. I almost believed I *did* know but was afraid to say that out loud.

"'Minerva told you about me when I visited her at this exact location many years ago. Yes, Leonardo. You know who I am. But you may call me by any name you want,' he told me."

Everyone was listening to Leonardo's story. They had forgotten to eat. The food was getting cold.

"We didn't talk very long. Five minutes. Ten at the most. He told me things that comforted me." Leonardo paused. "Well, that's the story I wanted to tell you. I don't know whether it means anything or not. But since then, I feel better. I know Camilla is all right. I've come to accept my loss. I don't have the guilt in my heart that was weighing it down before."

"I think you really saw Him," Helen said.

"Maybe. Maybe not. Perhaps it was just a dream."

The old man took a bite of food and a sip of wine. "You're certainly right," he told Maria. "No restaurant could begin to match what you and Helen have done."

"Hear, hear," Andy said. "Hear, hear," Tony echoed. The three men held up their glasses in a salute to the women.

"You're sure the food hasn't gotten too cold?" Helen said. "We can get you fresh plates."

"No. It's fine," Leonardo said.

"Did you ever come up with a name for your visitor?" Andy asked his father.

"Yes I did. Jesse just popped into my mind, and I called him that. He didn't seem to mind. He just smiled and said Jesse seemed to be a popular name. I never have figured out what he meant by that."

Leonardo sat on the sofa in Tony's living room trying to read a magazine. He was having trouble concentrating. He was thinking about his house. Nobody had made an offer, and he was beginning to feel discouraged. He had hoped he'd be able to sell it right away and pay off the loan he had taken out for Camilla's treatments. Then, perhaps, he could rent a room or a small apartment and not have to stay with Tony and Maria.

He knew he'd always be welcome there. But now that the two young people were married, they should have the house to themselves. Besides, he didn't feel comfortable depending on them to take care of him. He was still young enough and healthy enough to live by himself.

He had called Mrs. Delvecchio earlier that morning to hear the latest news and to find out how his friends were getting along. Everyone was doing fine. Mrs. Delvecchio told him Roger Martin, the man who owned the Chevrolet dealership, needed someone to drive a parts delivery pickup.

Their conversation had made Leonardo feel homesick. It would be nice if he could take the delivery job and move back home. But his only income was a small company pension and social security. Even with Martin's job, he wouldn't make enough money to move back into his house and pay off the loan.

Leonardo hadn't worked since coming to live with Tony. He did a little maintenance around the house and helped with the chores. Two nights a week, he did some volunteer work at a hospital. But he was beginning to feel useless. He felt he needed to find more to keep busy. It wasn't good for him to sit home day after day watching TV and reading.

He decided it was about time for him to go to work. He supposed if they needed a parts delivery driver in his small town, he could certainly find a job in San Antonio. It would be good for him to keep active, and he could use the extra money to pay toward his loan.

Maria noticed that Leonardo seemed to be in a pensive mood. She commented to Tony, "Your father has looked distracted all day. Do you think he's all right?"

"I'll talk to him. I think he's okay physically. He's still taking Mom's death real hard."

They went to the sofa where Leonardo was sitting and sat down beside him.

"What you reading, Pop?" Tony asked him.

"I don't know. I wasn't really reading. I was just sitting here daydreaming."

"Do you feel okay?" Maria asked him.

"I was thinking about my house. It's strange nobody's made me an offer for it."

"Don't worry, Pop," Tony said. "Somebody will."

"It would be nice if I could pay off the loan and move back. I was talking to Carlotta Delvecchio this morning. There's a job opening at the Chevrolet place. I thought about calling Roger Martin and telling him I would take it. He's the owner. But of course, I can't. Anyway, that's what I was thinking about."

"Pop," Maria said. "You know you're welcome here. You'll always be welcome here."

"I know that, Maria. But it would be nice if I had my own place, and you and Tony were by yourselves."

"How is everybody back home?" Tony asked.

"Everybody's fine. Nothing's changed. Some of them miss me or at least say they do."

"Of course, they miss you," Maria told him. She stood up. "Please excuse me," she said. "I'll be right back." She went into the bedroom. In a couple of minutes she came back to the door and caught Tony's attention.

"Tony," she said, "would you please come in here for a minute?"

Tony excused himself and went into the bedroom. Maria was holding a brown envelope. She handed it to Tony.

"Open it," she told him.

He opened it. It was stuffed full of one hundred dollar bills. He looked at them for a long moment and then looked at her.

"Hmm," he said. "Do you have any more of these laying around?"

"No. That's the only one."

"How much is here?"

"I don't know. I haven't counted it. That's the money I took when I ran away from *El Rancho Torres*."

"Well," Tony said.

"Tony. Let's take it and the money from my *casa* and pay off your father's house with it. It may not be enough, but it'll help."

"You never mentioned this," Tony said.

"I told you I had taken some money."

"Yes," Tony said. "I remember that. I thought it was just a few dollars. I didn't realize it was so much."

Tony looked into the living room, and Leonardo was reading his magazine.

"Let's see how much it is," Tony said. They counted it. There was twenty-four thousand, seven hundred dollars.

"That's a strange number," Tony said.

Maria remembered that she had taken out three hundred dollars when she first arrived in Monterrey and went shopping with *Señora* Valdez.

"I used three hundred dollars in Monterrey," she said. "There must have been twenty-five thousand, originally."

"I think Pop owes around sixty-five thousand. This'll help, but I doubt that it'll be enough."

"We have nineteen thousand from my house. That makes almost forty-four. That would leave a bit more than twenty-one."

"But Honey. That's your money. I don't want to touch it."

"Well, I do. And besides, it's not mine. It's ours. Let's go talk to Leonardo.

"Don't you want to think about it? If you still feel the same way tomorrow, we can talk to him then."

"Tony, please. Let's talk to him right now." She had a determined expression on her face.

"All right. Sweetheart, did I ever tell you how much I love you?"

"Probably. But tell me again. I never get tired of hearing that."

"I love you."

"Again."

"I love you, silly." He kissed her.

"I like that," she said.

They went back into the living room where Leonardo was sitting.

"Pop," Tony told him, "you know you're welcome to stay here forever. We don't even have to tell you that."

"It's okay, Tony. I guess I was just feeling a little down a while ago."

"Maria and I have something we would like to tell you."

After they finished talking, Leonardo said, "I can't take your money, Maria."

"Your money was stolen. I managed to get some of it back. Please, Pop. We want you to have it," Maria said.

"Call that Chevrolet guy," Andy said. "See if the job's still open."

"Are you sure?"

"Hurry up," Andy told him, "before somebody else gets it."

Leonardo sat as though he was undecided. Finally he said to Maria, "Do you want to think about this? If you still want to do it tomorrow, I'll call Roger then."

"Please call," Maria said. "We'll feel the same way tomorrow and a thousand years from now." She picked up the telephone handset and handed it to Leonardo. He took it from her hand and dialed.

"Martin Chevrolet," a woman's voice answered.

"My name's Leonardo Calliope. Could I please talk to Mr. Roger Martin?"

After a few minutes, Leonardo said, "Roger. This is Leonardo Calliope. Do you still need someone to deliver parts?"

www.ingramcontent.com/pod-product-compliance
Lightning Source LLC
LaVergne TN
LVHW020537100826
845148LV00010B/1500
* 9 7 8 0 9 7 0 8 8 3 3 1 5 *